Praise for *New York Times* bestselling author
Lindsay McKenna

"McKenna provides heartbreakingly tender romantic development that will move readers to tears. Her military background lends authenticity to this outstanding tale, and readers will fall in love with the upstanding hero and his fierce determination to save the woman he loves."
—*Publishers Weekly* on *Never Surrender*

"Talented Lindsay McKenna delivers excitement and romance in equal measure."
—*RT Book Reviews* on *Protecting His Own*

"Lindsay McKenna will have you flying with the daring and deadly women pilots who risk their lives… Buckle in for the ride of your life."
—*Writers Unlimited* on *Heart of Stone*

Praise for *USA TODAY* bestselling author
Merline Lovelace

"Merline Lovelace rocks! Like Nora Roberts, she delivers top-rate suspense with great characters, rich atmosphere and a crackling plot!"
—*New York Times* bestselling author Mary Jo Putney

"Lovelace's many fans have come to expect her signature strong, brave, resourceful heroines and she doesn't disappoint."
—*Booklist*

"Ms. Lovelace wins our hearts with a tender love story featuring a fine hero who will make every woman's heart beat faster."
—*RT Book Reviews* on *Wrong Bride, Right Groom*

NEW YORK TIMES BESTSELLING AUTHOR

LINDSAY McKENNA

USA TODAY BESTSELLING AUTHOR

MERLINE LOVELACE

THE COUGAR
&
TEXAS MISSION

Previously published as *The Cougar* and *Texas...Now and Forever*

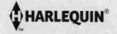

ISBN-13: 978-1-335-00692-9

The Cougar & Texas Mission

Copyright © 2019 by Harlequin Books S.A.

First published as The Cougar
by Harlequin Books in 1998 and
Texas...Now and Forever by Harlequin Books
in 2003.

Recycling programs
for this product may
not exist in your area.

The publisher acknowledges the copyright holders
of the individual works as follows:

The Cougar
Copyright © 1998 by Lindsay McKenna

Texas...Now and Forever
Copyright © 2003 by Harlequin Books S.A.

Special thanks and acknowledgment are given to
Merline Lovelace for her contribution to the Lone Star
Country Club series.

HARLEQUIN®
™ www.Harlequin.com

Printed in U.S.A.

CONTENTS

Lindsay McKenna is proud to have served her country in the US Navy as an aerographer's mate third class—also known as a weather forecaster. She was a pioneer in the military romance subgenre and loves to combine heart-pounding action with soulful and poignant romance. True to her military roots, she is the originator of the long-running and reader-favorite Morgan's Mercenaries series. She does extensive hands-on research, including flying in aircraft such as a P3-B Orion sub-hunter and a B-52 bomber. She was the first romance writer to sign her books in the Pentagon bookstore. Visit her online at lindsaymckenna.com.

Visit the Author Profile page
at Harlequin.com for more titles.

THE COUGAR

Lindsay McKenna

To my cyberfriends: Melissa Weaver, Carla Rowan,
Maria Theresa Bohle and Carol B. Willis

Chapter 1

"This wasn't a very good idea, Rachel Donovan." The words rang out briefly in the interior of the brand-new car that Rachel was driving. Huge, fat snowflakes were falling faster and faster. It was early December. Why shouldn't it be snowing in Oak Creek Canyon, which lay just south of Flagstaff, near Sedona? Her fingers tightened around the steering wheel. Tiredness pulled at her. A nine-hour flight from London, and then another six hours to get to Denver, Colorado, was taking its toll on her. As a homeopathic practitioner, she was no stranger to the effects of sleep deprivation.

Rubbing her watering eyes, she decided that the Rachel of her youth, some thirty years ago, was at play this morning. Normally, she wasn't this spontaneous, but in her haste to see her sisters as soon as possible, she'd changed her travel plans. Instead of flying into

Phoenix, renting a car and driving up to Sedona, she'd flown into Denver and taken a commuter flight to Flagstaff, which was only an hour away from her home, the Donovan Ranch.

Home... The word made her heart expand with warm feelings. Yes, she was coming home—for good. Her older sister, Kate, had asked Rachel and their younger sister, Jessica, to come home and help save the ranch, which was teetering on the edge of bankruptcy. A fierce kind of sweetness welled up through Rachel. She couldn't wait to be living on the ranch with her sisters once again.

Glancing at her watch, she saw it was 7:00 a.m. She knew at this time of year the highways were often icy in the world famous canyon. There was a foot of snow on the ground already—and it was coming down at an even faster rate as she drove carefully down the twisting, two-lane asphalt highway. On one side the canyon walls towered thousands of feet above her. On the other lay a five-hundred-foot-plus drop-off into Oak Creek, which flowed at the bottom of the canyon.

How many times had she driven 89A from Sedona to Flag? Rachel had lost count. Her eyes watered again from fatigue and she took a swipe at them with the back of her hand. Kate and Jessica were expecting her home at noon. If she got down the canyon in one piece, she would be home at 9:00 a.m. and would surprise them. A smile tugged at the corners of her full mouth. Oh, how she longed to see her sisters! She'd missed them so very much after leaving to work in England as a homeopath.

The best news was that Kate was going to marry her high school sweetheart, Sam McGuire. And Jessica had found the love of her life, Dan Black, a horse wrangler who worked at the ranch. Both were going to be married seven days from now, and Rachel was going to be their maid of honor. Yes, things were finally looking up for those two. The good Lord knew, Kate and Jessica deserved to be happy. Their childhood with their alcoholic father, Kelly Donovan, had been a disaster. As each daughter turned eighteen, she had fled from the ranch. Kate had become a rebel, working for environmental causes. Jessica had moved to Canada to pursue her love of flower essences. And Rachel—well, she'd fled the farthest away—to England.

Rachel felt the car slide. Instantly, she lifted her foot off the accelerator. She was only going thirty miles an hour, but black ice was a well-known problem here in this part of Arizona. It killed a lot of people and she didn't want to be the next victim. As she drove down the narrow, steep, road, dark green Douglas firs surrounded her. Ordinarily, Rachel would be enthralled with the beauty and majesty of the landscape—this remarkable canyon reminded her of a miniature Grand Canyon in many respects. But she scarcely noticed now. In half an hour, she would be home.

Her hands tightened on the wheel as she spotted a yellow, diamond-shaped sign that read 15 mph. A sharp hairpin curve was coming up. She knew this curve well. She glanced once again at the jagged, unforgiving face of a yellow-and-white limestone cliff soaring thousands of feet above her and disappearing into the heavily falling snow. Gently she tested her brakes on the invisible, dangerous black ice. The only thing between her and the cliff that plunged into the canyon was a guardrail.

Suddenly, Rachel gasped. Was she seeing things?

Without thinking, she slammed on the brakes. Directly in front of her, looming out of nowhere, was a huge black-and-gold cat. Her eyes widened enormously and a cry tore from her lips as the car swung drunkenly. The tires screeched as she tried to correct the skid. Impossible! Everything started to whirl around her. Out of the corner of her eye, she saw the black-and-gold cat, as large as a cougar, jump out of the way. Slamming violently against the cliff face, Rachel screamed. The steering wheel slipped out of her hands. A split second later, she watched in horror as the guardrail roared up at her.

The next moment there was a grinding impact. Throwing up her hands to protect her face, she felt the car become airborne. Everything seemed to suddenly move into slow motion. The car was twisting around in midair. She heard the glass crack as her head smashed against the side window. The snow, the dark shapes of the fir trees, all rushed at her. The nose of the car spiraled down—down into the jagged limestone wall well below the guardrail. Oh, no! She was going to die!

A thousand thoughts jammed through her mind in those milliseconds. What had been up on that highway? It wasn't a cougar. What *was* it? Had she hallucinated? Rachel knew better than to slam on brakes on black ice! How stupid could she be! But if she hadn't hit the brakes, she'd have struck that jaguar. Had there been a jaguar at all? Was it possible? She had to be seeing things! Now she was going to die!

Everything went black in front of Rachel. The last thing she recalled was the motion of her car as it arched down like a shot fired from a cannon, before hitting the side of the cliff. The last sound she heard was her own scream of absolute terror ringing through the air.

* * *

Warm liquid was flowing across Rachel's parted lips. She heard voices that seemed very far away. As she slowly became conscious, the voices grew stronger— and closer. Forcing open her eyes, she at first saw only white. Groggily, she looked closer and realized it was snow on part of the windshield. The other half of the windshield was torn away, the white flakes lazily drifting into the passenger's side of the car.

The accident came back to her as the pain in her head and left foot throbbed in unison. Suddenly she realized she was sitting at an angle, the car twisted around the trunk of a huge Douglas fir.

Again she heard a voice. A man's voice. It was closer this time. Blinking slowly, Rachel lifted her right arm. At least *it* worked. The seat belt bit deeply into her shoulder and neck. The airbag, deflated now, had stopped her from being thrown through the windshield. A branch must have gouged out the right half of the windshield. If anyone had been sitting there, they'd be dead.

It was cold with the wind and snow blowing into the car. Shivering, Rachel closed her eyes. The image of the jaguar standing in the middle of that icy, snow-covered highway came back to her. How stupid could she have been? She knew not to slam on brakes like that. Where had the jaguar come from? Jaguars didn't exist in Arizona! Her head pounded as she tried to make sense of everything. She was in trouble. Serious trouble.

Again, a man's voice, deep and commanding, drifted into her semiconscious state. Help. She needed medical help. If only she could get to her homeopathic kit in the back seat. Arnica was what she needed for tissue trauma. Her head throbbed. She was sure she'd have a goose egg. Arnica would reduce the swelling and the pain.

The snowflakes were falling more thickly and at a faster rate now. How long had she been unconscious? Looking at her watch, Rachel groaned. It was 8:00 a.m. She'd been down here an hour? She had to get out! Rachel tried to move, but her seat belt was tightly constricting. She hung at a slight angle toward the passenger side of the car. Struggling weakly, she tried to find the seat belt latch, but her fingers were cold and numb.

"Hey! Are you all right?"

Rachel slowly lifted her head. Her vision was blurred for a moment, and when it cleared she noticed her side window was gone, smashed out, she guessed, in the crash. A man—a very tall, lean man with dark, short hair and intense blue eyes, wearing a navy blue jacket and pants—anchored himself against the car. He was looking at her, assessing her sharply. Rachel saw the patch on his jacket: EMT. And then she saw another patch: Sedona Fire Department.

"No…no… I'm not all right," she whispered, giving up on trying to find the seat belt latch.

"Okay…just hold on. Help's here. My name is Jim. We're from the Sedona Fire Department. We got a 911 call that an auto had flipped off the highway. Hold on while I get my buddies down here."

Rachel sank back, feeling relief. This man… Jim… radiated confidence. Somehow she knew she'd be okay with him. She watched through half-closed eyes as he lifted the radio to his strong-looking mouth and talked to someone far above them. The snow was thickening. The gray morning light accentuated his oval face, his strong nose and that mouth. He looked Indian. Rachel briefly wondered what kind. With his high cheekbones and dark hair, he could be Navajo, Hopi or from one of many other tribal nations.

Something about him made her feel safe. That was good. Rachel knew that he could get her out of this mess. She watched as he snapped the radio onto his belt and returned his full attention to her, trying to hide his worry.

"Helluva way to see Arizona," he joked. "The car is wrapped around this big Douglas fir here, so it and you aren't going anywhere. My buddies are bringing down a stretcher and some auto-extrication equipment. My job is to take care of you." He smiled a little as he reached in the window. "What's your name?"

"Rachel…" she whispered.

"Rachel, I'm going to do a quick exam of you. Do you hurt anywhere?"

She closed her eyes as he touched her shoulder. "Yes…my head and my foot. I—I think I've got a bump on my head."

His touch was immediately soothing to her, though he wore latex gloves. But then, so did she when she had to examine a patient. With AIDS, HIV and hepatitis B all being transmissible via blood and fluids, medical people had to protect themselves accordingly. As he moved his hands gently across her head, she could feel him searching for injury. Something in her relaxed completely beneath his ministrations. She felt his warm, moist breath, his face inches from hers as he carefully examined her scalp.

"Beautiful hair," he murmured, "but you're right— you've got a nice goose egg on the left side of your head."

One corner of her mouth turned up as she lay against the car seat. "If that's all, I'm lucky. I hate going to hospitals."

Chuckling, Jim eased a white gauze dressing against her hair and then quickly placed a bandage around her head. "Yeah, well, you'll be going to Cottonwood Hospital anyway. If nothing more than to make sure you're okay."

Groaning, Rachel barely opened her eyes. She saw that he'd unzipped his jacket and it hung open, revealing a gold bar over the left top pocket of his dark blue shirt that read J. Cunningham. *Cunningham.* Frowning, she looked up at him as he moved his hands in a gentle motion down her neck, searching for more trauma.

"Cunningham's your last name?" she asked, her voice sounding faint even to her.

"Yeah, Jim Cunningham." He glanced down at her. She was pasty, her forest green eyes dull looking. Jim knew she was in shock. He quickly pressed his fingertips against her collarbone, noticing her pale pink angora sweater and dark gray wool slacks. Under any other circumstance, she would turn a man's head. "Why?" he teased, "has my reputation preceded me?" He quickly felt her arms for broken bones or signs of bleeding. There were some minor cuts due to flying glass from the windshield, but otherwise, so far, so good. He tried not to show his worry.

"Of the Bar C?" she asked softly, shutting her eyes as he leaned over her and pressed firmly on her rib cage to see if she had any broken ribs. How close he was! Yet his presence was utterly comforting to Rachel.

"Yes…how did you know?" Jim eased his hands down over her hips, applying gentle pressure. If she had any hip or pelvic injuries, they would show up now. He watched her expression closely. Her eyes were closed, her thick, dark lashes standing out against her pale skin. She'd had a nosebleed, but it had ceased. Her lips parted, but she didn't answer his question. Looking down and pushing aside the deflated airbag, he saw that her left foot was caught in the wreckage. *Damn.* That wasn't a good sign. His mind whirled with possibilities. He needed to get a cuff around her upper arm and check her blood pressure. What if her foot was mangled? What if an artery was severed? She could be losing a lot of blood. She could die on them.

He had to keep her talking. Easing out of the car window, he reached into his bright orange EMT bag. Looking up, he saw his partner, Larry, coming down, along with four other firefighters bringing the stretcher and ropes as well as auto-extrication equipment.

"Well," Jim prodded, as he pushed up her sleeve and slipped the blood-pressure cuff around her upper left arm, "am I a wanted desperado?"

Rachel needed his stabilizing touch and absorbed it hungrily. Consciousness kept escaping her. For some reason she would slip away, only to be brought back by his deep, teasing voice. "Uh, no...."

"You sound like you know me. Do you?" He quickly put the stethoscope to her arm and pumped up the cuff. His gaze was focused on the needle, watching it closely as he bled off the air.

Rachel rallied. Opened her eyes slightly, she saw the worry in Jim's face. The intensity in his expression shook her. "You don't remember me, do you?" she said, trying to tease back. Her voice sounded very faraway. What was going on? Why wasn't she able to remain coherent?

Damn! Jim kept his expression neutral. Her blood pressure wasn't good. Either she had a serious head injury or she was bleeding somewhere. He left the cuff on her arm and removed the stethoscope from his ears. She lay against the seat, her eyes closed, her body limp. Her breathing was slowly becoming weaker and weaker. His medical training told him she was losing a lot of blood. Where? It *had* to be that foot that was jammed in the wreckage.

He *had* to keep her talking. "I'm sorry," he apologized, "I don't remember you. I wish I did, though." And that was the truth. She was a beautiful woman. *Stunning* was a word Jim would use with her. Her dark brown hair was thick and long, like a dark cape across her proud shoulders.

"Listen, I'm going to try and get this door open." Jim made a signal to Larry to hurry even faster down the slippery incline. Studying the jagged cliff, Jim realized that if the car hadn't wrapped itself around this fir tree, it would have plunged another three hundred feet. More than likely, Rachel would be dead.

Larry hurried forward. He was a big man, over six feet tall, and built like a proverbial bull.

"Yeah, Cougar, what are the stats?" He dropped his bag and moved gingerly up to Jim.

Scowling, Jim lowered his voice so no one but his partner would hear. "She's dumping on us. I think she's hemorrhaging from her left foot, which is trapped beneath the dash of the car. Help me get this door open. I need to get a cuff on her upper leg. It'll have to act like a tourniquet. Then those extrication guys can get in here and cut that metal away so we can get her foot free to examine it."

"Right, pard."

Rachel heard another male voice, but it was Jim's voice she clung to. Her vision was growing dim. What was wrong with her? She heard the door protest and creak loudly as it was pulled opened in a series of hard, jerking motions. In moments, she heard Jim's voice very close to her ear. Forcing open her eyes, she saw that he was kneeling on the side of the car where the door was now open. She felt his hand moving down her left leg, below her knee.

"Can you feel that?" he demanded.

"Feel what?" Rachel asked.

"Or this?"

"No...nothing. I feel nothing, Jim."

Jim threw Larry a sharp look. "Hand me your blood-pressure cuff. We're going to apply a tourniquet." In the gray light of the canyon, with snowflakes twirling lazily around them, Jim saw that her left foot and ankle had been twisted and trapped in the metal upon impact. With Larry's help, he affixed the cuff around her slim calf and then inflated it enough to halt the blood flow in that extremity.

Four other firefighters arrived on scene. Larry put a warm, protective blanket across Rachel. He then got into the back seat and held her head straight while Jim carefully placed a stabilizing cervical collar around her neck, in case she had an undetected spinal injury. He was worried. She kept slipping in and out of consciousness.

As he settled into the passenger seat beside her, and the firefighters worked to remove the metal that trapped her leg, Jim tried to draw her out of her semiconscious state.

"Rachel," he called, "it's Jim. Can you hear me?"

She barely moved her lips. "Yes…"

He told her what the firefighters were going to do, and that there would be a lot of noise and not to get upset by it. All the while, he kept his hand on hers. She responded valiantly to his touch, to his voice, but Jim saw Larry shake his head doubtfully as he continued to gently hold her head and neck.

"You said you heard of me," Jim teased. He watched her lashes move upward to reveal her incredible eyes. Her pupils were wide and dilated, black with a crescent of green around them. "Well? Am I on a wanted poster somewhere?" he asked with a smile.

Jim's smile went straight to Rachel's heart. It was boyish, teasing, and yet he was so male that it made her heart beat a little harder in her chest. She tried to smile back and realized it was a poor attempt. "No… not a wanted poster. I remember you from high school. I'm Rachel Donovan. You know the Donovan Ranch?"

Stunned, Jim stared. "Rachel Donovan?" His head whirled with shock. That was right! He recalled Jessica Donovan telling him over a month ago that Rachel, the middle daughter, was moving home from England to live at the ranch.

"That's me," Rachel joked softly. She forced her eyes open a little more and held his gaze. "You used to pull my braids in junior high, but I don't think you remember that, do you?"

Jim forced a grin he didn't feel at all. "I do now." And he did. Little Rachel Donovan had been such a thin stick of a girl in junior high. She had worn her long, dark brown flowing mane of hair in braids back then, like her mother, Odula, an Eastern Cherokee medicine woman. Rachel was the spitting image of her. Jim recalled the crush he'd had on little Rachel Donovan. She'd always run from him. The only way he'd get her attention was to sneak up, tweak one of her braids and then run away himself. It was his way of saying he liked her, for at that age, Jim had been too shy to tell her. Besides, there were other problems that prevented him from openly showing his affection for her.

"You were always teasing me, Jim Cunningham," Rachel said weakly. Her mouth was dry and she was thirsty. The noise of machinery filled the car. If it hadn't been for Jim's steadying hand on her shoulder, the sound would have scared her witless.

"Hey, Cougar, we're gonna have to take the rest of this windshield out. Gotta pull the steering wheel up and away from her."

Jim nodded to Captain Cord Ramsey of the extrication team. "Okay." He rose up on his knees and took a second blanket into his hands.

"Rachel," he said as he leaned directly over her, "I'm going to place a blanket over us. The firefighters have to pull the rest of the window out. There's going to be glass everywhere, but the blanket will protect you."

Everything went dark before Rachel's eyes. Jim Cunningham had literally placed his body like a wall between her and the firefighters who were working feverishly to free her. She felt the heat of his body as he pulled the blanket over their heads. How close he was! She was overwhelmed by the care he showed toward her. It was wonderful.

When he spoke, his voice was barely an inch from her ear.

"Okay, they're going to pull that windshield any moment now. You'll hear some noise and feel the car move a bit. It's nothing to be concerned about."

"You're wonderful at what you do," Rachel whispered weakly. "You really make a person feel safe… that everything's going to be okay even if it isn't…."

Worried, Jim said, "Rachel, do you know what blood type you are?"

"AB positive."

His heart sank. He struggled to keep the disappointment out of his voice. "That's a rare blood type."

She smiled a little. "Like me, I guess."

He chuckled. "I have AB positive blood, too. How about that? Two rare birds, eh?"

Rachel heard the windshield crack. There was one brief, sharp movement. As Jim eased back and removed the blanket, she looked up at him. His face was hard and expressionless until he looked down to make sure she was all right. Then his features became very readable. She saw concern banked in his eyes.

"Listen, Jim, in the back seat there's a kit. A homeopathic kit. It's important you get to it. There's a remedy in there. It's called Arnica Montana. I know I'm bleeding. It will help stop it. Can you get it for me? Pour some pellets into my mouth?"

He frowned and looked in the back seat. There was a black physician's bag there on the seat next to Larry. "You a doctor?"

"No, a homeopath."

"I've vaguely heard about it. An alternative medicine, right?" He reached over the back seat and brought the leather case up front, resting it against his thigh as he opened it. He found a small plastic box inside along with a lot of other medical equipment. "This box?" he asked, holding it up for her to look at.

"Yes…that's the one. I'll need two pills."

Opening it, Jim located the bottle marked Arnica. He unscrewed the cap and put a couple of white pellets into her mouth.

"Thanks…." Rachel said. The sweetness of the small pellets tasted good to her. "It will help stop the shock and the bleeding."

Jim put the bag aside. Worriedly, he took another blood-pressure reading. She was no longer dumping as before. He suspected the tourniquet on her lower leg had halted most of the bleeding, and that was good news.

"Did I hear someone call you Cougar?"

Distracted because the extrication team was finally prying the metal away from her foot, Jim nodded. "Yeah, that's my nickname."

"H-how did you get it?" Rachel felt the power of the homeopathic remedy begin to work on her immediately. "Listen, this remedy I took will probably make me look like I'm unconscious, but I'm not. It's just working to stabilize me, so don't panic, okay?"

Jim nodded and placed himself in front of Rachel to protect her again as the extrication equipment began to remove the metal from around her foot. "Okay, sweetheart, I won't panic." He watched her lashes drift down as he shielded her with his body. Her color was no longer as pasty, and that was promising. Still, her blood pressure was low. Too low.

Looking up at Larry, Jim said, "As soon as we get her out of here, have Ramsey call the hospital and see if they've got AB positive blood standing by. We're going to need it."

"Right."

Rachel savored Jim's nearness. She heard the screech of metal as it was being torn away to release her foot. She hoped her injury wasn't bad. She had a wedding to attend in a week. Her foot couldn't be broken!

"What's the frown for?" Jim asked. Her face was inches from his. He saw the soft upturn of the corners of her mouth. What a lovely mouth Rachel had. The spindly shadow of a girl he'd known was now a mature swan of indescribable beauty.

"Oh…the weddings—Katie and Jessica. I'm supposed to be their maid of honor. My foot… I'm worried about my foot. What if I broke it?"

"We'll know in just a little while," he soothed. Instinctively, he placed his hand on her left shoulder. The last of the metal was torn away.

"Cougar?"

"Yeah?" Jim twisted his head toward Captain Ramsey.

"She's all yours. Better come and take a look."

Rachel felt Jim leave her side. Larry's hands remained firm against her head and neck, however.

Cunningham climbed carefully around the car. The temperature was dropping, and the wind was picking up. Blizzard conditions were developing fast. Jim noted the captain's wrinkled brow as he made his way to the driver's side. Getting down on his hands and knees, squinting in the poor light, he got his first look at Rachel's foot.

He'd been right about loss of blood. He saw where an artery on the top of her foot had been sliced open.

Quickly examining it, he placed a dressing there. Turning, he looked up at the captain.

"Get the hospital on the horn right away. We're definitely going to need a blood transfusion for her. AB positive." Rachel had lost a lot of blood, there was no doubt. If he hadn't put that blood-pressure cuff on her lower leg when he did, she would have bled to death right in front of him. Shaken, Jim eased to his feet.

"Okay, let's get her out of the car and onto a spine board." When he looked up to check on Rachel, he saw that she had lost consciousness again. So many memories flooded back through Jim in those moments. Good ones. Painful ones. Ones of yearning. Of unrequited love that was never fulfilled. Little Rachel Donovan. He'd had a crush on her all through school.

As Jim quickly positioned the spine board beneath Rachel with the help of the firefighters, he suddenly felt hope for the first time in a long time. Maybe, just maybe, life was giving him a second chance with Rachel. And then he laughed at himself. The hundred-year-old feud between the Cunninghams and Donovans was famous in this part of the country. Still he wondered if Rachel had ever had any feelings for him?

Right now, Jim couldn't even think about the past. His concern was for Rachel's loss of blood and her shock. The clock on the car had stopped at 7:00 a.m. That was when the accident had probably occurred. And it had taken them an hour to get here. Whether he wanted to admit it or not, her life hung in a precarious balance right now.

"Hey," Ramsey said, getting off the radio, "bad news, Cougar."

"What?" Jim eased Rachel onto the spine board and made her as comfortable as possible.

"No AB positive blood at Cottonwood."

Damn! "Try Flagstaff."

Ramsey shook his head. "None anywhere."

Placing another blanket across Rachel, Jim glanced up at his partner. "You tell Cottonwood to stand by for a blood transfusion, then," he told the captain. "I've got AB positive blood. She needs at *least* a pint or we aren't going to be able to save her."

"Roger," Ramsey grunted, and got on the radio again to the hospital.

Chapter 2

The first thing Rachel was aware of was a hand gently caressing her hair. It was a nurturing touch, almost tender as it brushed across her crown. Unfamiliar noises leaked into her groggy consciousness, along with the smell of antiseptic. Where was she? Her head ached. Whoever was caressing her hair soothed the pain with each touch. Voices. There were so many unfamiliar voices all around her. Struggling to open her eyes, she heard a man's voice, very low and nearby.

"It's okay, Rachel. You're safe and you're going to be okay. Don't try so hard. Just lay back and take it easy. You've been through a lot."

Who was that? The voice was oddly familiar, and yet it wasn't. The touch of his hand on her head was magical. Rachel tried to focus on the gentle caress. Each time he followed the curve of her skull, the pain went away, only to return when he lifted his hand. Who was this man who had such a powerful touch? Rachel was no stranger to hands-on healing. Her mother, Odula, used to lay her hands on each of them when they were sick with fever or chills. And amazingly, each time, their aches and pains had disappeared.

The antiseptic smell awakened her even more—the smell of a hospital. She knew the scent well, having tended many patients at the homeopathic hospital in London. Her mind was fuzzy, so she continued to focus on the man's hand and his nearness. She felt his other hand resting on her upper arm, as if to give her an anchor in the whirling world of gold-and-white light beneath her lids.

Gathering all her strength, Rachel forced her lashes to lift. At first all she saw was a dark green curtain in front of her. And then she heard a low chuckle to her right, where the man was standing—the one who caressed her as if she were a very beloved, cherished woman. His warm touch was undeniable. Her heart opened of its own accord and Rachel felt a rush of feelings she thought had died a long time ago. Confused by the sights and sounds, she looked up, up at the man who stood protectively at her side.

Jim's mouth pulled slightly. "Welcome back to the real world, Rachel." He saw her cloudy, forest green eyes rest on him. There was confusion in their depths. Nudging a few strands of long, dark brown hair away from her cheek, he said in a low, soothing tone, "You're at the Flagstaff Hospital. We brought you here about an hour ago. You had a wreck up on 89A coming out of Flag earlier this morning. Do you remember?"

Rachel was mesmerized by him, by his low tone,

which seemed to penetrate every cell of her being like a lover's caress. He had stilled his hand, resting it against her hair. His smile was kind. She liked the tenderness burning in his eyes as he regarded her. Who was he? His face looked familiar, and yet no name would come. Her mouth felt gummy. Her foot ached. She looked to the left, at her surroundings.

"You're in ER, the emergency room, in a cubical," Jim told her. "The doc just got done looking at you. He just stitched up your foot where you severed a small artery. You took a pint of whole blood, and he said the bump on your head is going to hurt like hell, but it's not a concussion."

Bits and pieces of memory kept striking her. The jaguar. The jaguar standing in the middle of that ice-covered highway. Rachel frowned and closed her eyes.

"The cat…it was in the middle of the road," she began, her voice scratchy. "I slammed on the brakes. I didn't want to hit it…. The last thing I remember is spinning out of control."

Jim tightened his hand slightly on her upper arm. He could see she was struggling to remember. "A cat? You mean a cougar?"

Everything was jumbled up. Rachel closed her eyes. She felt terribly weak—far weaker than she wanted to feel. "My kit…where is it?"

Jim saw a dull flush of color starting to come back to her very pale cheeks. The blood transfusion had halted her shock. He'd made sure she was covered with extra blankets and he'd remained with her in ER throughout the time, not wanting her to wake up alone and confused.

"Kit?"

"Yes…" She moved her lips, the words sticking in her dry mouth. "My homeopathic kit…in my car. I need it…."

He raised his brows. "Oh…your black bag. Yeah, I brought it in with me. Hold on, I'll be right back."

Rachel almost cried when he left her side. The strong, caring warmth of his hand on her arm was very stabilizing. The noise in ER was like a drum inside her head. She heard the plaintive cry of a baby, someone else was groaning in pain—familiar sounds to her as a homeopath. She wished she could get up, go dispense a remedy to each of them to ease their pain and discomfort. She wasn't in England any longer, though; she was in the U.S. Suddenly she felt disoriented.

Her ears picked up the sound of a curtain being drawn aside. She opened her eyes. He was back, with her black leather physician's bag.

"Got it," he said with a smile, placing the bag close to her blanketed leg.

As he opened it, Rachel tried to think clearly. "Who are you? I feel like I know you…but I'm not remembering names too well right now."

His mouth curved in a grin as he opened the bag. "Jim Cunningham. I'm the EMT who worked with you out at the accident scene." He pulled out the white, plastic box and held it where she could see it.

"Oh…"

Chuckling, he said, "Man, have I made a good impression on you. Here you are, the prettiest woman I've seen in a long time, and you forget my name."

His teasing warmth fell across her. Rachel tried to smile, but the pain in her head wouldn't let her. There was no denying that Jim Cunningham was a very good-looking man. He was tall, around six foot two, and lean, like a lithe cougar with a kind of boneless grace that told her he was in superb physical condition. The dark blue, long-sleeved shirt and matching pants he wore couldn't hide his athletic build. The silver badge on his left pocket, the gold nameplate above it and all the patches on the shoulders of his shirt gave him a decided air of authority.

Wrinkling her nose a little, she croaked, "Don't take it personally. I'm feeling like I have cotton stuffed between my ears." She lifted her hand and found it shaky.

"Just tell me which one you want," he said gently. "You're pretty weak yet. In another couple of hours you'll feel a lot better than you do right now."

Alarmed at her weakness, Rachel whispered, "Get me the Arnica."

"Ah, the same one you used out at the accident site. Okay." He hunted around. There were fifty black-capped, amber bottles arranged by alphabetical order in the small case. Finding Arnica, he uncapped it.

"Now what?"

"My mouth. Drop a couple of pellets in it."

Jim carefully put two pellets on her tongue. "Okay, you're set." He capped the amber bottle. "What is this stuff, anyway? The ER doc wanted to know if it had side effects or if it would cause any problems with prescription drugs."

The pellets were sugary sweet. Rachel closed her eyes. She knew the magic of homeopathy. In a few minutes, her headache would be gone. And in a few more after that, she'd start feeling more human again.

"That's okay," Jim murmured as he replaced the vial into the case, "you don't have to answer the questions right now." He glanced up. "I called your family. I talked to Kate." He put the box back into Rachel's bag and set it on a chair nearby. "They're all waiting out in the visitors' lounge. Hold on, I'll get them for you."

Rachel watched through half-closed eyes as Jim opened the green curtain and disappeared. She liked him. A lot. What wasn't there to like? she asked herself. He was warm, nurturing, charming—not to mention terribly handsome. He had matured since she'd known him in school. He'd been a tall, gangly, shy kid with acne on his face. She remembered he was half-Apache and half-Anglo and that they'd always had that common bond—being half-Indian.

So many memories of her past—of growing up here in Sedona, of the pain of her father's alcoholism and her mother's endless suffering with the situation—flooded back through her. They weren't pleasant memories. And many of them she wanted to forget.

Jim Cunningham… In school she'd avoided him like the plague because Old Man Cunningham and her father had huge adjoining ranches. The two men had fought endlessly over the land, the often-broken fence line and the problems that occurred when each other's cattle wandered onto the other's property. They'd hated one another. Rachel had learned to avoid the three Cunningham boys as a result.

Funny how a hit on the head pried loose some very old memories. A crooked smile pulled at Rachel's mouth. And who had saved her? None other than one of the Cunninghams. What kind of karma did she have? She almost laughed, and realized the pain in her head was lessening quickly; her thoughts were rapidly clearing. Thanks to homeopathy. And Jim Cunningham.

"Rachel!"

She opened her eyes in time to see Jessica come flying through the curtains. Her younger sister's eyes were huge, her face stricken with anxiety. Reaching out with her right hand, Rachel gave her a weak smile.

"Hi, Jess. I'm okay…really, I am…."

Then Rachel saw Kate, much taller and dressed in Levi's and a plaid wool coat, come through the curtains. Her serious features were set with worry, too.

Jessica gripped Rachel's hand. "Oh, Rachel! Jim called us, bless him! He didn't have to do that. He told us everything. You could have died out there!" She gave a sob, then quickly wiped the tears from her eyes. Leaning down, she kissed Rachel's cheek in welcome.

Kate smiled brokenly. "Helluva welcome to Sedona, isn't it?"

Grinning weakly, Rachel felt Kate's work-worn hand fall over hers. "Yes, I guess it is."

Kate frowned. "I thought you were flying into Phoenix, renting a car and driving up from there?"

Making a frustrated sound, Rachel said, "I was going to surprise you two. I got an earlier flight out of Denver directly into Flag. I was going to be at the ranch hours earlier that way." She gave Kate a long, warm look. "I really wanted to get home."

"Yeah," Kate whispered, suddenly choked up as she gripped her sister's fingers, "I guess you did."

Sniffing, Jessica wiped her eyes. "Are you okay, Rachel? What did the doctor say?"

Rachel saw the curtains part. It was Jim Cunningham. Her heart skipped a beat. She saw how drawn his face was and his eyes seemed darker than she recalled.

He came and stood at the foot of the gurney where she was lying.

"Dr. Forbush said she had eight stitches in her foot for a torn artery, and a bump on the head," he told them. He held Rachel's gaze. She seemed far more alert now, and that was good. When he'd stepped into the cubicle, he'd noticed that her cheeks were flushed. Pointing to her left foot, he said, "She lost a pint of blood out there at the wreck. She got that replaced and the doc is releasing her to your care." And then he smiled teasingly down at Rachel. "That is, unless you want to spend a night here in the hospital for observation?"

Rachel grimaced. "Not on your life," she muttered defiantly. "I work in them, I don't stay in them."

Chuckling, Jim nodded. He looked at the three Donovan sisters. "I gotta get going, but the head nurse, Sue Young, will take care of getting you out of this place." He studied Rachel's face and felt a stirring in his heart. "Stay out of trouble, you hear?"

"Wait!" Rachel said, her voice cracking. She saw surprise written on his features when he turned to tell her again. "Wait," she pleaded. "I want to thank you…." Then she smiled when she saw deviltry in his eyes as he stood there, considering her plea.

"You serious about that?"

"Sure."

"Good. Then when you get well, have lunch with me?"

Stunned, Rachel leaned back onto the bed. She saw Jessica's face blossom in a huge smile. And Kate frowned. Rachel knew what her older sister was thinking. He was a Cunningham, their enemy for as long as any of them could recall.

"Well…"

Jim raised his hand, realizing he'd overstepped his bounds. "Hey, I was just teasing. I'll see you around. Take care of yourself...."

"I'll be right back," Kate murmured to her sisters, and she quickly followed after him.

Jim was headed toward the small office in the back of ER where EMTs filled out their accident report forms when he heard Kate Donovan's husky voice.

"Jim?"

Turning, he saw her moving in his direction. Stepping out of the ER traffic, he waited for her. The serious look on her face put him on guard. She was the oldest of the three Donovan daughters and the owner of a ranch, which was teetering precariously on the edge of bankruptcy. He knew she had worked hard since assuming the responsibilities of the ranch after Kelly died in an auto accident earlier in the year. Because of that, Jim also knew she had more reason to hate a Cunningham than any of the sisters. Inwardly, he tried to steel himself against anything she had to say. His father, unfortunately, had launched a lawsuit against Kate's ranch right now. There was nothing Jim could do about it, even though he'd tried to talk his father into dropping the stupid suit. Driven by the forty-year vendetta against Kelly Donovan, he'd refused to. It made no difference to him that the daughters were coming home to try and save their family ranch. The old man couldn't have cared less.

With such bad blood running between the two families, Jim was trying to mend fences where he could. His two older brothers weren't helping things, however. They derived just as much joy and pleasure out of hurting people, especially the Donovans, as their old man. Jim was considered the black sheep of the family, probably because he was the only Cunningham who wasn't into bad blood or revenge. No, he'd come home to try and fix things. And in the months since he'd been home, Jim had found himself living in hell. He found his escape when he was on duty for the fire department. But the rest of the time he was a cowboy on the family ranch, helping to hold it together and run it. Ordinarily, he'd loved the life of a rancher, but not anymore. These days his father was even more embittered toward the Donovans, and now he had Bo and Chet on his side to wage a continued war against them.

As Kate Donovan approached him, Jim understood how she felt toward him. It wasn't anything personal; it was just ancient history that was still alive and injuring all parties concerned. Even him. The darkness in her eyes, the serious set of her mouth, put him on guard. He studied her as she halted a few feet away from him, jamming her hands into the deep pockets of the plaid wool jacket she wore.

"I want to thank you," Kate rasped, the words coming out strained.

Reeling, Jim couldn't believe his ears. He'd expected to catch hell from Kate for suggesting lunch with Rachel. He knew she had a lot of her father in her and could be mule headed, holding grudges for a long time, too.

"You didn't have to call us," Kate continued. "You could have left that to a nurse here in ER, I know." Then she looked up at him. "I found out from the nurse before I went in to see Rachel that you saved her life—literally."

Shrugging shyly, Jim said, "I did what I could, Kate.

I'd do it for anyone." He didn't want her to think that he'd done something special for Rachel that he wouldn't do for others. In his business as an EMT, his job was to try and save lives.

"Damn, this is hard," Kate muttered, scowling and looking down at her booted feet. Lifting her head, she pinned him with a dark look. "I understand you just gave her a pint of your blood. Is that true?"

He nodded. "Rachel's blood type is a rare one." Looking around the busy hospital area, he continued, "This is a backwoods hospital, Kate. They can't always have every rare blood type on hand. Especially in the middle of Arizona, out in the wilds." He tried to ease her hard expression with his teasing reply.

Kate wasn't deterred in the least. "And your partner, Larry, who I just talked to out at the ambulance, said you'd stopped Rachel from losing even more blood by putting a tourniquet on her leg?"

"I put a blood-pressure cuff around Rachel's lower leg to try and stop most of the bleeding, yes." Inwardly, Jim remained on guard. He never knew if Kate Donovan was going to pat him on the head or rip out his jugular. Usually it was the latter. He saw her expression go from anger to confusion and then frustration, and he almost expected her to curse him out for volunteering his own blood to help save Rachel's life. After all, it was Cunningham blood—the blood of her arch enemy. The enemy that her father had fought against all his life.

Kate pulled her hand out of her pocket and suddenly thrust it toward him. "Then," she quavered, suddenly emotional, "I owe you a debt I can't begin to pay back."

Staring at her proffered hand, Jim realized what it took for Kate to do that. He gripped her hand warmly.

The tears in her eyes touched him deeply. "I'm glad it was me. I'm glad I was there, Kate. No regrets, okay?"

She shook his hand firmly and then released it. "Okay," she rasped nervously, clearing her throat. "I just wanted you to know that I know what really happened."

He gave her a slight smile. "And there's nothing to pay back here. You understand?" He wanted both families to release the revenge, the aggressive acts against one another. Kelly Donovan was dead, though Jim's father was still alive and still stirring up trouble against their closest neighbors. Kate was struggling to keep the ranch afloat, and Jim admired her more than he could ever say. But if he told her that she wouldn't believe him, because he was a Cunningham—bad blood.

Nodding, she wiped her eyes free of tears. "You sure know how to balance ledgers, don't you?"

Scrutinizing her closely, Jim said quietly, "I assume you're talking about the ledger between our two families?"

"Yes." She stared up at him. "I can't figure you out—yet."

"There's nothing to figure out, Kate."

"Yes," she growled, "there is."

His mouth curved ruefully. "I came home like you did—to try and fix things."

"Then why does your old man have that damned lawsuit against us?"

Kate's frustration paralleled his own. Opening his hands, Jim rasped, "I'm trying to get him to drop the suit, Kate. It has no merit. It's just that same old revenge crap from long ago, that's all."

She glared at him. "We are hitting rock bottom financially and you and everyone else knows it. Rachel came home to try and make money to help us pay the bills to keep our ranch afloat. If I have to hire a lawyer and pay all the court costs, that's just one more monetary hemorrhage. Can't *you* do anything to make him stop it?"

"I'm doing what I can."

She looked away, her mouth set. "It's not enough."

Wearily, Jim nodded. "Kate, I want peace between our families. Not bloodshed or lawsuits. My father has diabetes and often refuses to take his meds, so he exhibits some bizarre behavior."

"Like this stupid lawsuit?"

"Exactly." Glancing around, Jim pulled Kate into the office, which was vacant at the moment. Shutting the door, he leaned against it as he held her stormy gaze. "Let's bury the hatchet between us, okay? I did not come home to start another round of battles with you or anyone else at the Donovan Ranch."

"You left home right after high school," Kate said in a low voice. "So why did you come back now?"

"I never approved of my father's tactics against you or your family. Yes, I left when I was eighteen. I became a hotshot firefighter with the forest service. I didn't want to be a part of how my father was acting or behaving. I didn't approve of it then and I don't now. I'm doing what I can, Kate. But I've got a father who rants and raves, who's out of his head half the time. Then he stirs up my two brothers, who believe he's a tin god and would do anything he told them to do. They don't stop to think about the consequences of their actions."

Kate wrapped her arms against her body and stared at him, the silence thickening. "Since you've come back, things have gotten worse, not better."

Releasing a sigh, Jim rested against the edge of the desk. "Do you know what happens when a diabetic doesn't watch his diet or doesn't take his meds?" he asked in a calm tone.

"No," she muttered defensively. "Are you going to blame your old man's lawsuit and everything else on the fact that he's sick and won't take the drugs he's supposed to take?"

"In part, yes," Jim said. "I'm trying to get my brothers to work with me, not against me, on my father taking his medication daily. I'm trying to get our cook to make meals that balance my father's blood sugar and not spike it up so he has to be peeled off the ceiling every night when I get home."

Kate nodded. "If you think I feel sorry for you, I don't."

"I'm not telling you this to get your sympathy, Kate," he said slowly. "I'm trying to communicate with you and tell you what's going on. The more you understand, the less, I hope, you'll get angry about it."

"Your father is sick, all right," Kate rattled. "He hasn't changed one iota from when I was a kid growing up."

"I'm trying to change that, but it takes time." Jim held her defiant gaze. "If I can keep channels of communication open between us, maybe I can put out some brushfires before they explode into a wildfire. I'd like to be able to talk with you at times if I can."

Snorting, Kate let her arms fall to her sides. "You just saved Rachel's life. Your blood is in her body. I might be pigheaded, Cunningham, but I'm not stupid. I owe you for her life. If all you want in return is a little chat every once in a while, then I can deal with that."

Frustration curdled Jim's innards. He'd actually

given one and a half pints of blood and he was feeling light-headed, on top of being stressed out from the rescue. But he held on to his deteriorating emotions. "I told you, Kate—no one owes me for helping to save Rachel's life."

"I just wonder what your father is going to say. This ought to make his day. Not only did you save a Donovan's neck, you gave her your blood, too. Frankly," Kate muttered, moving to the door and opening it, "I don't envy you at all when you go home tonight. You're going to have to scrape that bitter old man of yours off the ceiling but good this time."

Jim nodded. "Yeah, he'll probably think I've thrown in with the enemy." He said it in jest, but he could tell as Kate's knuckles whitened around the doorknob, she had taken the comment the wrong way.

"Bad blood," she rasped. "And it always will be."

Suddenly he felt exhausted. "I hope Rachel doesn't take it that way even if you do." There was nothing he could do to change Kate's mind about his last name, Cunningham. As her deceased father had, she chose to associate all the wrongdoings of the past with each individual Cunningham, whether involved in it or not. And in Jim's case, he was as much the victim here as were the Donovan sisters. He'd never condoned or supported what his father had done to Kelly Donovan over the years, or how he'd tried to destroy the Donovan Ranch and then buy it up himself. But Kate didn't see it—or him—as separate from those acts of his father. She never would, Jim thought tiredly.

"Rachel's a big girl," Kate muttered defiantly. "I'm not going to brainwash her one way or another about you Cunninghams."

"Right now, Rachel needs peace and quiet," Jim answered. "She was in pretty deep shock out there. If you could give her two or three days of rest without all this agitation, it would help her a lot."

Kate nodded. "I'll make sure she gets the rest."

The office turned silent after Kate Donovan left. Sighing, Jim rubbed his brow. What a helluva morning! His thoughts moved back to Rachel. Old feelings he'd believed had died a long time ago stirred in his chest. She was so beautiful. He wondered if she had Kate's bitterness toward the Cunninghams. Jim cared more about that than he wanted to admit.

First things first. Because he'd given more than a pint of blood, he'd been taken off duty by the fire chief, and another EMT had been called in to replace him on the duty roster. Well, he'd fill out the accident report on Rachel and then go home. As he sat down at the desk and pulled out the pertinent form, Jim wondered if news of this event would precede him home. He hoped not— right now, he was too exhausted to deal with his father's ire. What he felt was a soul tiredness, though, more than just physical tiredness. He'd been home almost a year now, and as Kate had said, not much had changed.

Pen in hand, the report staring up at him, Jim tried to order his thoughts, but all he could see was Rachel's pale face and those glorious, dark green eyes of hers. What kind of woman had she grown into after she'd left Sedona? He'd heard she'd moved to England and spent most of her adult life there. Jim understood her desire to escape from Kelly Donovan's drunken, abusive behavior, just as he'd taken flight from his own father and his erratic, emotional moods. Jim's fingers tightened around the pen. Dammit, he was drawn to

Rachel—right or wrong. And in Kate Donovan's eyes, he was dead wrong in desiring Rachel.

With a shake of his head, he began to fill out the form. Why the hell had he asked Rachel out to lunch? The invitation had been as much a surprise to him as it had been to the Donovan women. Kate was the one who'd reacted the most to it. Jessica was too embroiled in worry for Rachel to even hear his teasing rejoinder. And Rachel? Well, he'd seen surprise in her green eyes, and then something else.... His heart stirred again—this time with good, warm feelings. He wondered at the fleeting look in Rachel's eyes when he'd made his sudden invitation.

Would she consider going to lunch with him? Was he crazy enough to hold on to that thought? With a snort, Jim forced his attention back to his paperwork. Right now, what he had to look forward to was going back to the Bar C and hoping his father hadn't heard what had happened. If he had, Jim knew there would be a blisteringly high price to pay on his hide tonight.

Chapter 3

"I heard you gave blood to one of those Donovan bitches."

Jim's hand tightened on the door as he stepped into the Cunningham ranch house. Frank Cunningham's gravelly voice landed like a hot branding iron on him, causing anger to surge through Jim. Slowly shutting the door, he saw his father in his wheelchair sitting next to the flagstone fireplace. The old man was glaring at him from beneath those bushy white eyebrows, his gray eyes flat and hard. Demanding.

Jim told himself that he was a grown man, that his gut shouldn't be clenching as it was now. He was over thirty years old, yet he was having a little boy's reaction to a raging father. Girding himself internally, Jim forced himself to switch to his EMT mode. Shrugging out of his heavy jacket, he placed it on a hook beside the door.

"Looks like news travels fast," he said as lightly as

possible. Judging from the wild look in his father's eyes, he guessed he hadn't taken diabetes medication.

"Bad news always does, dammit!" Frank punched a finger at Jim as he sauntered between the leather couch and chair. "What are you doing, boy? Ruining our good name? How could you?"

Halting in front of him, Jim placed his hands on his hips. He was tired and drained. Ordinarily, giving blood didn't knock him down like this. It was different knowing who the accident victim was, though. He was still reeling from the fact that it was little Rachel Donovan, the girl he'd had a mad crush on so long ago.

"Have you taken your pill for your sugar problem?" Jim asked quietly.

Cursing richly, Frank Cunningham snarled, "You answer my questions, boy! Who the *hell* do you think you are, giving blood to—"

"You call her a bitch one more time and it will be the last time," Jim rasped, locking gazes with his angry father. "Rachel doesn't deserve that from you or anyone. She could have died out there early this morning."

Gripping the arms of his wheelchair with swollen, arthritic fingers, Frank glared at him. "You don't threaten me, boy."

The word *boy* grated on Jim's sensitized nerves. He reminded himself one more time that he'd come home to try and pull his family together. To try and stop all the hatred, the anger and fighting that the Cunninghams were known for across two counties. Maybe he'd been a little too idealistic. After all, no one had even invited him back. It was one thing to be called home. It was quite another to wonder every day whether he'd have a home to come back to. Frank Cunningham had thrown

him out when he was eighteen and Jim had never returned, except for Christmas. Even then, the holidays
became a battleground of sniping and snarling, of deal-
ing with the manipulations of his two brothers.

"Look, Father," Jim began in a strained tone, "I'm
a little out of sorts right now. I need to lie down for a
while and rest. Did you take your medicine this morning at breakfast? Did Louisa give it to you?"

Snorting, Frank glared at the open fireplace, where
a fire crackled and snapped. "Yes, she gave it to me,"
he muttered irritably.

A tired smile tugged at the corners of Jim's mouth.
"Did you take it?"

"No!"

In some ways, at seventy-five, Frank was a pale ghost
of his former self. Jim recalled growing up with a strap-
ping, six-foot-five cowboy who was tougher than the
drought they were presently enduring. Frank had made
this ranch what it was: the largest and most prosperous
in the state of Arizona. Jim was proud of his heritage,
and like his father, he loved being a cowboy, sitting on
a good horse, working ceaselessly during calving season and struggling through all the other demanding
jobs of ranching life.

Pulling himself out of his reverie, Jim walked out
to the kitchen. There on the table were two tiny blue
tablets, one for diabetes and one for high blood pressure. He picked them up and got a glass of water. He
knew his father's mood was based directly on his blood
sugar level. If it was too high, he was an irritable son
of a bitch. If it was too low, he would go into insulin
shock, keel over unconscious and fall out of his wheelchair. Jim had lost track of how many times he'd had to

pull his father out of insulin shock. He could never get it through Frank's head that he might die from it. His father didn't seem to care. Frank's desire to live, Jim realized, had left when their mother died.

Jim walked back out into the living room. It was a huge, expansive room with a cathedral ceiling and the stuffed heads of elk, deer, peccary and cougar on the cedar walls. The aged hardwood floor gleamed a burnished gold color. A large Navajo rug of red, black and gray lay in the center of the room, which was filled with several dark leather couches and chairs set around a rectangular office table.

"Here, Dad, take it now," Jim urged gently.

"Damn stuff."

"I know."

"I *hate* taking pills! Don't like leaning on anything or anyone! That's all these are—crutches," he said, glaring down at the blue pill in his large, callused palm.

Jim patiently handed him the glass of water. Neither of his brothers would ensure that Frank took his medicine. If they even saw the pills on the kitchen table, they ignored them. Jim had once heard Bo say that it would be just that much sooner that the ranch would be given to him.

As he stood there watching his father take the second pill, Jim felt his heart wrench. Frank was so thin now. His flesh, once darkly tanned and hard as saddle leather, was washed out and almost translucent looking. Jim could see the large, prominent veins in his father's crippled hands, which shook as he handed the glass back to him.

"Thanks. Now hit the hay. You look like hell, son."

Jim smiled a little. Such gruff warmth from his father

was a rare gift and he absorbed it greedily. There were moments when Frank was human and compassionate. Not many, but Jim lived for them. "Okay, Dad. If you need anything, just come and get me."

Rubbing his hand through his thick silver hair, Frank grunted. "I got work to do in the office. I'll be fine."

"Okay...."

Jim was sitting on his bed and had pushed off his black boots when he heard someone coming down the hardwood hall. By the sound of the heavy footsteps, he knew it was Bo. Looking up, he saw his tall, lean brother standing in the doorway. By the state of his muddied Levi's and snow-dampened sheepskin coat, Bo had been out working. Taking off his black Stetson hat, he scowled at Jim.

"What's this I hear about you giving blood to one of those Donovan girls? Is that true? I was over at the hay and feed store and that was all they were talkin' about."

With a shake of his head, Jim stretched out on top of his double bed, which was covered with a brightly colored, Pendleton wool blanket. Placing his hands behind his head, he looked up at the ceiling.

"Gossip travels faster than anything else on earth," he commented.

Bo stepped inside the room. His dark brows drew down. "It's true, then?"

"Yeah, so what if it is?"

Settling the hat back on his head, Bo glared down at him. "Don'tcha think your goody two-shoes routine is a little out of control?"

Smarting at Bo's drawled criticisms, Jim sat up. "I

know you wish I'd crawl back under a rock and disappear from this ranch, Bo, but it isn't going to happen."

Bo's full lips curved into a cutting smile. "Comin' home to save all sinners is a little presumptuous, don't you think?"

Tiredness washed across Jim, but he held on to his deteriorating patience. "Someone needs to save this place."

"So you gave blood to Rachel Donovan. Isn't that a neat trick. You think by doing that, you'll stop the war between us?"

Anger lapped at him. "Bo, get the hell out of here. I'm beat. If you want to talk about this later, we'll do it then."

Chuckling indulgently, Bo reached for the doorknob. "Okay, little bro. I'll see you later."

Once the door shut, Jim sighed and lay back down. Closing his eyes, he let his arm fall across his face. The image of Rachel Donovan hovered beneath his eyelids. Instantly, he felt warmth flow through his tense body, washing away his irritation with his father, his anger toward his younger brother. She had the most incredible dark green eyes he'd ever seen. Jim recalled being mesmerized by them as a young, painfully shy boy in junior high. He'd wanted to stare into them and see how many gold flecks he could find among the deep, forest green depths.

Rachel had been awkward and skinny then. Now she was tall, elegant looking and incredibly beautiful. The prettiest, he felt, of the three sisters. She had Odula's face—high cheekbones, golden skin, dark brown hair that hung thick and heavy around her shoulders. Finely arched brows and large, compassionate eyes. Her nose was fine and thin; her mouth—the most delectable part of her—was full and expressive. Jim found himself wondering what it would be like to kiss that mouth.

At that thought, he removed his arm and opened his eyes. What the hell was he doing? His father would have a stroke if he suspected Jim liked Rachel Donovan. Frank Cunningham would blow his top, as usual, and spout vehemently, "That's like marrying the plague!" or something like that. Donovan blood, as far as Frank was concerned, was contaminated filth of the worst kind. Jim knew that to admit his interest in Rachel would do nothing but create the worst kind of stress in this household. His older brothers would ride roughshod over him, too. He was sure Frank would disown him—again—as he had when Jim was eighteen.

Jim closed his eyes once more and felt the tension in his body. Why the hell had he come home? Was Bo right? Was he out to "save" everyone? Right now, he was trying to juggle his part-time job as an EMT and work full time at the ranch as a cowboy. Jim didn't want his father's money, though Bo had accused him of coming home because their father was slowly dying from diabetes. Bo thought Jim was hoping to be written back into the will. When Jim had left home, Frank had told him that the entire ranch would be given to Bo and Chet.

Hell, Jim couldn't care less about who was in the will or who got what. That didn't matter to him. What did matter was family. His family. Ever since his mother had died, the males in the family had become lost and the cohesiveness destroyed. His mother, a full-blooded Apache, had been the strong, guiding central core of their family. The backbiting, the manipulation and power games that Bo and Chet played with their father wouldn't exist, Jim felt, if she were still alive. No, ever since his mother's death when he was six years old, the family unit had begun to rot—from the inside out.

Jim felt the tension bleeding out of him as he dwelled on his family's history. He felt the grief over losing her mother at such a young, vulnerable age. She had been a big woman, built like a squash, her black, flashing eyes, her copper skin and her playful smile so much a part of her. She'd brought joy and laughter to the ranch. When she died, so had the happiness. No one had laughed much after that. His father had changed drastically. In the year following his mother's death, Jim saw what loving and losing a person did to a man. Frank had turned to alcohol and his rages became known county wide. He'd gotten into bar fights. Lawsuits. He'd fought with Kelly Donovan on almost a daily basis. Frank Cunningham had gone berserk over his wife's passing. Maybe that's why Jim was gun-shy of committing to a relationship. Or maybe Rachel Donovan had stolen his heart at such a young age that he wanted no one but her—whether he could ever have her or not.

All Jim could do back then, was try to hold the rest of his suffering, grieving family together. He hadn't had time for his own grief and loss as he'd tried to help Bo and Chet. Even though he was the youngest, he was always the responsible one. The family burden had shifted to Jim whenever their father would disappear for days at a time. Frank would eventually return, unshaven and dirty, with the reek of alcohol on his breath. The weight of the world had been thrust upon Jim at a young age. Then, at eighteen, right after high school graduation, Jim had decided he had to escape. And he did—but the price had been high.

Slowly, ever so slowly, Rachel's face formed before his closed eyes again. Jim felt all his stress dissolve before the vision. She had such a peaceful look about her. Even out there at the accident site, she hadn't panicked. He admired her courage under the circumstances.

Suddenly, anger rose within him. Dammit, he *wanted* to see her again. How could he? If Frank knew, he'd hit the ceiling in a rage. Yet Jim refused to live his life knowing what his father's knee-jerk reaction would be. Still, it was hell having to come back to the ranch and take a gutfull of Frank's verbal attacks. But if Jim moved to his own place in Sedona, which was what he wanted to do, who would make sure his father took his meds?

Feeling trapped, he turned on his side. He felt the fingers of sleep encroaching on his worry and his desires. The last thing he saw as he drifted off was Rachel trying to smile gamely up at him in the ER when she regained consciousness. He recalled how thick and silky her hair had felt when he'd touched it. And he'd seen how his touch had affected her. In those moments, he'd felt so clean and hopeful again—two things he hadn't felt in a long, long time. Somehow, some way, he was going to find a way to see her again. He *had* to.

Rachel absorbed the warmth of the goose-down quilt lying over her. She was in her old bed, in the room she'd had as a child. She was back at the Donovan Ranch. Gloomy midafternoon light filtered through the flowery curtains at the window. Outside, snowflakes were falling slowly, like butterflies. The winter storm of this morning had passed on through.

Her foot ached a little, so she struggled to sit up. On

the bedstand was her homeopathic kit. Opening it, she found the Arnica and took another dose.

"You awake?"

Rachel heard Jessica's hopeful voice at her door before her younger sister smiled tentatively and entered the room. Jessica's gold hair was in two braids and the oversize, plaid flannel shirt she wore highlighted her flushed cheeks.

"Come on in," Rachel whispered.

Pushing a few strands of hair off her face, Jessica sat down at the bottom of the bed and faced Rachel. "I thought you might be awake."

"I slept long and hard," Rachel assured her as she placed the kit back on the bed table. She put a couple of pillows behind her and then pushed the quilt down to her waist. The flannel nightgown she wore was covering enough in the cool room. There was no central heating in the huge, main ranch house. Only the fireplace in the living room provided heat throughout the winter. Rachel didn't mind the coolness, though.

Jessica nodded and surveyed her. "How's your foot?"

"Okay. I just took another round of Arnica."

"What does that do for it?"

Rachel smiled, enjoying her sister's company. Jessica was so open, idealistic and trusting. Nothing like Kate, who distrusted everyone, always questioning their motives. "It reduces the swelling of the soft tissue. The pain will go away in about five minutes."

"Good." Jessica rubbed her hands down her Levi's. "I was just out checking on my girls—my orchids. The temperature is staying just fine out there in the greenhouse. This is the first big snow we've had and I was a little worried about them."

Rachel nodded. "Where's Kate?"

"Oh, she and Sam and Dan are out driving the fence line. Earlier today, she got a call from Bo Cunningham who said that some of our cattle were on their property—again."

Groaning, Rachel said, "Life doesn't change at all, does it, Jess?"

Giggling, Jessica shook her head. "No, it doesn't seem to, does it? Don't you feel like you're a teenager again? We had the same problems with the Cunninghams then as we do now." She sighed and opened her hands. "I wish they wouldn't be so nasty toward us. Frank Cunningham hates us."

"He hates everything," Rachel murmured.

"So how did Jim turn out to be so nice?"

"I don't know." Rachel picked absently at the bed-cover. "He *is* nice, Jess. You should have seen him out there with me, at the accident. I was in bad shape. He was so gentle and soothing. I had such faith in him. I knew I'd be okay."

"He's been home almost a year now, and he's trying to mend a lot of fences."

"Are you saying he was nice to me because of the feud between our families?"

Jessica shook her head. "No, Jim is a nice guy. Somehow, he didn't get Frank's nasty genes like the other two boys did." She laughed. "I think he has his mother's, instead."

Rachel smiled. "I know one thing. I owe Jim my life."

"You owe him more than that," Jessica said primly as she tucked her hands in her lap. "Did he tell you he gave a pint of *his* blood to you?"

"What?" Rachel's eyes grew wide.

"Yeah, the blood transfusion. You lost a lot from the cut across your foot," she said, pointing to Rachel's foot beneath the cover. "I found out about it from the head nurse in ER when we came in to see how you were. Jim had called us from hospital and told us what had happened. Well," she murmured, "he was selective in what he told us. He really downplayed his part in saving you. He's so humble that way, you know? Anyway, I was asking the nurse what all had been done for you, because we don't have medical insurance and I knew Kate would be worrying about the bill. I figured I'd do some investigating for her and get the info so she wouldn't have to do it later." Clasping her hands together, she continued, "You have a rare type of blood. They didn't have any on hand at the hospital, nor did they have any in Cottonwood. So I guess Jim volunteered his on the spot. He has the same blood type as you do." She smiled gently. "Wasn't that sweet of him? I mean, talk about a symbolic thing happening between our two families."

Rachel sat there, digesting her sister's explanation. Jim's blood was circulating in her body. It felt right. And good. "I—see...." Moistening her lips, she searched Jessica's small, open face. She loved her fiercely for her compassion and understanding. "How do you feel about that?"

"Oh, I think it's wonderful!"

"And Kate?" Tension nagged at Rachel's stomach over the thought of her older sister's reaction. Kate held grudges like their father did.

Jessica gazed up at the ceiling and then at her. "Well, you know Kate. She wasn't exactly happy about it, but like she said, you're alive and that's what counts."

"I'm glad she took the high road on this," Rachel murmured, chuckling.

Jessica nodded. "We owe Jim so much. Kate knows that and so do I. I think he's wonderful. He's trying so hard to patch things up between the two families."

"That's a tall order," Rachel said. She reached for the water pitcher on the bed stand. Pouring herself a glassful, she sipped it.

"I have faith in him," Jessica said simply. "His integrity, his morals and values are like sunshine compared to the darkness of the Cunningham ranch in general. I believe he can change his father and two brothers."

"You're being overidealistic," Rachel cautioned.

"Maybe," she said. Reaching out, she ran her hand along Rachel's blanketed shin. "We're all wondering *what* made you skid off 89A. You know that road like the back of your hand. And you're used to driving in snow and ice."

Setting the glass on the bed table, Rachel frowned. "You're probably going to think I'm crazy."

Laughing, Jessica sat up. "Me? The metaphysical brat of the three of us? Nooo, I don't think so, Rachel." Leaning forward, her eyes animated, she whispered, "So tell me what happened!"

Groaning, Rachel muttered, "I saw a jaguar standing in the middle of 89A as I rounded that last hairpin curve."

Jessica's eyes widened enormously. "A jaguar? You saw a jaguar?"

Rachel grimaced. "I told you you'd think I was crazy."

Leaping up from the bed, her sister whispered, "Oh, gosh! This is *really* important, Rachel." Typical of Jessica, when she got excited she had to move around. She quickly rounded the bed, her hands flying in the air. "It was a jaguar? You're positive?"

"I know what I saw," Rachel said a bit defensively. "I know I was tired and I had jet lag, but I've never hallucinated in my life. No, it *was* a jaguar. Not a cougar, because I've seen the cougars that live all around us up here. It was a jaguar, with a black-and-gold coat and had huge yellow eyes. It was looking right at me. I was never so startled, Jess. I slammed on the brakes. I know I shouldn't have—but I did. If I hadn't, I'd have hit that cat."

"Oh, gosh, this is *wonderful!*" Jessica cried. She clapped her hands together, coming to a sudden halt at the end of Rachel's bed.

"Really? What's so wonderful about it? If this story ever gets out, I'll be the laughingstock of Sedona. There're no jaguars in Arizona."

Excitedly, Jessica whispered, "My friend Moyra, who is from Peru, lived near me for two years up in Canada. She helped me get my flower essence business going, and tended my orchid girls with me. What a mysterious woman she was! She was very metaphysical, very spiritual. Over the two years I knew her, she told me that she was a member of a very ancient order called the Jaguar Clan. She told me that she took her training in the jungles of Peru with some very, very old teachers who possessed jaguar medicine."

Rachel opened her mouth to reply, but Jessica gripped her hand, her words tumbling out in a torrent. "No, no, just listen to me, okay? Don't interrupt. Moyra told me that members of the Jaguar Clan came from around the world. They didn't have to be born in South

America to belong. I guess it has something to do with one's genes. Anyway, I saw some very strange things with Moyra over the two years she was with me."

"Strange?"

"Well," she said, "Moyra could read minds. She could also use mental telepathy. There were so many times I'd start to ask her a question and she'd answer before I got it out of my mouth! Or…" Jessica paused, her expression less animated "…when Carl, my ex-husband, was stalking me and trying to find out where I was hiding, Moyra told me that she'd guard me and make sure he never got to me. I remember four different times when she warned me he was close and protected me from being found by him."

"You mean," Rachel murmured, "she *sensed* his presence?"

"Something like that, but it was more, much more. She had these heightened senses. And—" Jessica held her gaze "—I saw her do it one day."

"Do what?"

Jessica sighed and held up her right hand. "I *swear* I'm telling you the truth on this, Rachel. I was taking a walk in the woods, like I always did in the afternoon when I was done watering my girls in the greenhouse. It was a warm summer day and I wanted to go stick my feet in the creek about half a mile from where we lived. As I approached the creek, I froze. You won't believe this, but one minute I saw Moyra standing in the middle of the creek and in the next I saw a jaguar! Well, I just stood there in shock, my mouth dropping open. Then suddenly the jaguar turned back into Moyra. She turned around and looked right at me. I blinked. Gosh,

I thought I was going crazy or something. I thought I was seeing things."

Jessica patted her sister's hand and released it. "There were two other times that I saw Moyra change into a jaguar. I don't think she meant for me to see it—it just happened."

"A woman who turns into a jaguar?" Rachel demanded.

"I know, I know," Jessica said. "It sounds crazy, but listen to this!" She sat down on the edge of the bed and faced Rachel. "I got up enough courage to ask Moyra about what I'd seen. She didn't say much, but she said that because she was a member of this clan, her spirit guide was a male jaguar. Every clan member has one. And that this spirit guide is her teacher, her protector, and she could send it out to help others or protect others if necessary." Excitedly, Jessica whispered, "Rachel, the last thing Moyra told me before I drove down here to live was that if I ever needed help, she would be there!"

Stymied, Rachel said, "That jaguar I saw was Moyra—or Moyra's spirit guardian?" Rachel had no trouble believing in spirit guardians, because Odula, their mother, had taught them from a very early age that all people had such guides from the invisible realms. They were protectors, teachers and helpers if the person allowed them to be.

"It must have been one or the other!" Jessica exclaimed in awe.

"Because," Kate Donovan said, walking through the door and taking off her damp wool coat, "about half a mile down 89A from where you crashed, there was a fuel-oil tanker that collided with a pickup truck." She halted and smiled down at Jessica, placing her coat on a chair. "What you don't know, Rachel, is that five minutes after you spun out on that corner, that pickup truck slid into that tanker carrying fuel oil. There was an explosion, and everyone died."

Stunned, Rachel looked at Jessica. "And if I hadn't spun out on that corner..."

Kate brought the chair over and sat down near her bed. "Yep, *you* would have been killed in that explosion, too."

"My God," Rachel whispered. She frowned.

Jessica gave them both a wide-eyed look. "Then that jaguar showing up saved your life. It really did!"

Kate combed her fingers through her long, dark hair, which was mussed from wearing a cowboy hat all day. "I heard you two talking as I came down the hall. So you think it was your friend's jaguar that showed up?"

Jessica nodded. "I have no question about it. Even now, about once a month, I have this dream that's not a dream, about Moyra. She comes and visits me. We talk over what's happening in our lives. Stuff like that. She's down at a place called the Village of the Clouds, and she said she's in training. She didn't say for what. She's very mysterious about that."

"So, your friend comes in the dream state and visits with you?" Rachel asked. Odula had placed great weight and importance on dreaming, especially lucid dreaming, which was a technique embraced wholeheartedly by the Eastern Cherokee people.

"Yes," Jessica said in awe. "Wow...isn't that something?" She looked up at Kate. "How did you find this out?"

"At the ER desk as I was signing Rachel out. Once they had you extricated from your rental car," Kate told

Rachel, "Jim's ambulance had to drive up to Flagstaff to get you ER care because of that mess down on 89A. There was no way they could get through to the Cottonwood Hospital. There were fire trucks all over the place putting out the fire from that wreck."

Rachel studied her two sisters. Kate looked drawn and tired in her pink flannel shirt, Levi's and cowboy boots. She worked herself to the bone for this ranch. "Once upon a time, jaguars lived in the Southwest," Rachel told them.

"Yeah," Kate muttered, "until the good ol' white man killed them all off. I hear, though, they're coming back. There're jaguars living just over the border in Mexico. It wouldn't surprise me if they've already reached here." She rubbed her face. "And this Rim country where we live is ideal habitat for them." She smiled a little. "Maybe what you saw wasn't from the spirit world, after all. Maybe it was a live one. The first jaguar back in the States?"

"Oh," Jessica said with a sigh, "that would be neat, too!"

They all laughed. Rachel reached out and gripped Kate's work-worn hand. "It's so good to be home. It feels like old times, doesn't it? The three of us in one or the other's bedroom, chatting and laughing?"

"Yeah," Kate whispered, suddenly emotional as she gripped Rachel's hand. "It's nice to have you both here. Welcome home, sis."

Home. The word sent a tide of undeniable warmth through Rachel. She saw tears in Jessica's eyes and felt them in her own.

"If it wasn't for Jim Cunningham," Rachel quavered, "I wouldn't be here at all. We owe him a lot."

Kate nodded grimly. "Yes, we do."

"Tomorrow I want to see him and thank him personally," Rachel told them. "Jessica, can you find out if he's going to be at the fire department in Sedona?"

"Sure, no problem." She eased off the bed and wiped the tears from her eyes. "He's the sweetest guy."

Kate snorted. "He's a Cunningham. What's the old saying? A tiger can't change his stripes?"

Rachel grinned at her older sister's sour reaction. "Who knows, Kate? Jim may not be a tiger at all. He may be a jaguar in disguise."

"You know his nickname and his Apache name are both Cougar," Jessica said excitedly.

"Close enough for me," Rachel said with a smile.

Chapter 4

"Hey, Cunningham, you got a visitor!"

Jim lifted his head as his name was shouted through the cavernous area where the fire trucks and ambulance sat waiting for another call. The bay doors were open and bright winter sunlight poured inside the ambulance where Jim sat, repacking some of the shelves with necessary items.

Who could it be? Probably one of his brothers wanting to borrow some money from him as usual. With a grunt he eased out of the ambulance and swung around the corner.

His eyes widened and he came to an abrupt halt. Rachel Donovan! Swallowing his surprise, he stood watching as she slowly walked toward him. Noontime sunlight cascaded down, burnishing her long dark hair with hints of red and gold. She wore conservative, light gray woolen slacks and a camel-colored overcoat.

Struck by her beauty, her quiet presence as she met and held his gaze, he watched her lips lift into a smile. Heat sheeted through him as he stood there. Like a greedy beggar, he absorbed her warm gaze. Her green eyes sparkled with such life that he felt his breath momentarily hitch. This wasn't the woman he'd met at the car accident. Not in the least. Amazed that she seemed perfectly fine three days after nearly losing her life, Jim managed a shy grin of welcome.

"Hey, you look pretty good," he exclaimed, meeting her halfway across the bay.

Rachel felt heat sting her cheeks. She was blushing again! Her old childhood response always seemed to show up at the most embarrassing times. She studied the man before her; he was dressed in his usual dark blue pants and shirt, the patches for the fire department adorning the sleeves. When he offered his hand to her, she was struck by the symbolic gesture. A Donovan and a Cunningham meeting not in anger, but in friendship. As far as she knew it was a first, and Rachel welcomed it.

As she slid her hand into his big square one she felt the calluses and strength of it. Yet she could feel by his grip that he was carefully monitoring that strength. But what Rachel noticed most of all was the incredible warmth and joy in his eyes. It stunned her. He was a Cunningham, she, a Donovan. Nearly a century-old feud stood between them, and a lot of bad blood.

"I should hope I look better," Rachel replied with a low, husky laugh. "I'm not a homeopath for nothing."

Jim forced himself to release Rachel's long, thin fingers. She had the hands of a doctor, a surgeon, maybe. There was such a fluid grace about her as she moved.

Suddenly he remembered that she could have bled to death the other day if they hadn't arrived on scene to help her when they had, and he was shaken deeply once again.

"I'm just finishing up my shift." He glanced at his watch. "I have to do some repacking in the ambulance. Come on back and keep me company?"

She touched her cheek, knowing the heat in it was obvious. "I didn't want to bother you—"

"You're not a bother, believe me," he confided sincerely as he slid his hand beneath her elbow and guided her between the gargantuan fire trucks to the boxy ambulance that sat at the rear.

As Rachel allowed him to guide her, she saw a number of men and women firefighters, most of them watching television in the room off the main hangar. Yet she hardly noticed them. So many emotions were flowing through her as Jim cupped her elbow. What she recalled of him from junior high was a painfully shy teenager who couldn't look anyone directly in the eye. Of course, she understood that; she hadn't exactly been the homecoming queen type herself. Two shadows thrown together by life circumstance, Rachel thought, musing about their recent meeting.

Once they reached the back of the ambulance, Jim urged her to climb in. "You can sit in the hot seat," he joked, and pointed to the right of the gurney, where the next patient would lie.

Rachel carefully climbed in. She sat down and looked around. "Is this the one I was in?"

Jim smiled a little and opened up a box of rolled bandages. He counted out six and then stepped up into the ambulance. "Yes, it was," he said, sliding the plastic door on one of the shelves to one side to arrange the bandages. "We call her Ginger."

"I like that. You named your truck."

"Actually, my partner, Larry, named her." Jim made a motion toward the front of the ambulance. "All the fire trucks are ladies and they all have names, too." He studied Rachel as he crouched by one of the panels. "You look like your accident never happened. How are you feeling?"

With a slight laugh, she said, "Well, let's put it this way—my two sisters, Kate and Jessica, are getting married this Saturday out at the ranch. I'm their maid of honor. I could *not* stay sick." She pointed to her foot, which sported a white dressing across the top. "I had to get well fast or they'd have disowned me for not showing up for their weddings."

"You look terrific," Jim murmured. "Like nothing ever happened."

She waved her hands and laughed. "*That* was thanks to you and homeopathy. When I got back to the ranch, I had Jessica bathe the wound with tincture of Calendula three times a day." She patted her injured foot. "It really speeded up the healing."

"And that stuff you took? What did you call it? Arnica? What did it do for you?"

She was pleased he remembered the remedy. "Arnica reduces the swelling and trauma to injured soft tissue."

He slid the last door shut, his inventory completed. "That's a remedy we could sure use a lot of around here. We scrape so many people up off the highway that it would really help."

Rachel watched as he climbed out of the ambulance. There was no wasted motion about Jim Cunningham.

He was lithe, like the cougar he was named after. And she liked the sense of steadiness and calmness that emanated from him like a beacon. His Apache blood was obvious in the color of his skin, his dark, cut hair and high cheekbones. What she liked most were his wide, intelligent eyes and his mouth, which was usually crooked in a partial smile. Jim was such an opposite to the warring Cunningham clan he'd been born into. He was like his mother, who had been known for her calm, quiet demeanor. Rachel knew little more about her, except that she'd been always full of laughter, with a twinkle in her eye.

"We're done here," Jim said genially, holding out his hand to her. He told himself he was enjoying Rachel too much. He wondered if she was married, but he didn't see a wedding ring on her left hand as he took it into his own. She stepped carefully out of the ambulance to the concrete floor beside him. "And I'm done with my shift." He glanced at his watch. "Noon, exactly." And then he took a huge risk. "If I recall, up at the Flag hospital I offered you lunch. I know a great little establishment called the Muse Restaurant. Best mocha lattes in town. How about it?" His heart pumped hard once, underscoring just how badly he wanted Rachel to say yes.

Jim saw her forest green eyes sparkle with gold as he asked her the question. Did that mean yes or no? He hoped it meant yes and found himself holding his breath, waiting for her answer. As he studied her up-turned face, he felt her undeniable warmth and compassion. There was a gentleness around her, a Zenlike quality that reminded him of a quiet pool of water— serene yet very deep and mysterious.

"Actually," Rachel said with a laugh, "I came here

to invite *you* to lunch. It was to be a surprise. A way of thanking you for saving my neck."

A powerful sensation moved through Jim, catching him off guard. It was a delicious feeling.

"That's a great idea," he murmured, meaning it. "But I asked first, so you're my guest for lunch. Come on, we'll take my truck. It's parked just outside. I'll bring you back here afterward."

Rachel couldn't resist smiling. He looked boyish as the seriousness in his face, the wrinkle in his brow disappeared in that magical moment. Happiness filled her, making her feel as if she were walking on air. Once again Jim cupped his hand on her elbow to guide her out of the station. She liked the fact that he matched his stride to hers. Normally she was a fast walker, but the injury to her foot had slowed her down.

Jim's truck was a white Dodge Ram with a shiny chrome bumper. It was a big, powerful truck, and there was plenty of Arizona—red mud which stuck to everything—on the lower half of it, probably from driving down the three-mile dirt road to the Cunningham ranch. He opened the door for her and she carefully climbed in.

Rachel was impressed with how clean and neat the interior was, unlike many men's pickups. As she hooked the seat belt, she imagined the orderliness came from him working in the medical field and understanding the necessity of cleanliness. She watched as Jim climbed in, his face wonderfully free of tension. He ran his fingers through his short, dark hair and then strapped himself in.

"Have you thought about the repercussions of being seen out in public with me?" he drawled as he slipped the key into the ignition. The pickup purred to life, the engine making a deep growling sound.

Wrinkling her nose, Rachel said, "You mean the gossip that will spread because a Cunningham and a Donovan broke bread together?"

Grinning, he nodded and eased the truck out of the parking spot next to the redbrick building. "Exactly."

"I was over at Fay Seward's, the saddle maker's, yesterday, and she was telling me all kinds of gossip she'd heard about us."

Moving out into the traffic, slow moving because of the recent snow, Jim chuckled. "I'll bet."

Rachel looked out the window. The temperature was in the low thirties, the sky bright blue and filled with nonstop sunlight. She put her dark glasses on and simply enjoyed being near Jim as he drove from the tourist area of Sedona into what was known as West Sedona. "I really missed this place," she whispered.

The crimson rocks of Sedona created some of the most spectacular scenery he'd ever seen. Red sandstone and white limestone alike were capped with a foot of new, sparkling snow from the storm several days before. With the dark green mantle of forest across the top of the Rim, which rose abruptly to tower several thousand feet above Sedona, this was a place for an artist and photographer, he mused.

Glancing over at her, he asked, "Why did you stay away so long?"

Shrugging, Rachel met his inquiring gaze. "Isn't it obvious? Or is it only to me?"

Gripping the steering wheel a little more tightly, he became serious. "We both left when we were kids. Probably for similar reasons. I went into the forest service and became a firefighter. Where did you go? I heard you moved overseas?"

Pain moved through Rachel. She saw an equal amount in Jim's eyes. It surprised her in one way, because the men she had known never allowed much emotion to show. "I moved to England," she said.

"And Jessica went to Canada and Kate became a tumbleweed here in the States."

"Yes."

Jim could feel her vulnerability over the issue. "Sorry, I didn't mean to get so personal." He had no right, but Rachel just seemed to allow him to be himself, and it was much too easy to become intimate with her. Maybe it was because she was in the medical field; she had a doctor's compassion, but more so.

With a wave of her hand, she murmured, "No harm done. I knew when I moved home to try and help save our ranch that there were a lot of buried wounds that needed to be aired and cleaned out and dressed."

"I like your analogy. Yeah, we all have old wounds, don't we?" He pulled into a shopping center with a huge fountain that had been shut off for the winter. Pointing up the walk, he said, "The Muse—a literary café. All the writers and would-be writers come here and hang out. Since you're so intelligent, I thought you might enjoy being with your own kind."

Smiling, Rachel released the seat belt. "How did you know I'm writing a book?"

Jim opened his door. "Are you?"

With a laugh, she said, "Yes, I am." Before she could open her own door, Jim was there to do it. He offered his hand and she willingly took it because the distance to the ground was great and she had no desire to put extra stress on the stitches still in her foot.

"Thank you," she said huskily. How close he was! How very male he was. Rachel found herself wanting to sway those few inches and lean against his tall, strong frame. Jim's shoulders were broad, proudly thrown back. His bearing was dignified and filled with incredible self-confidence.

Unwilling to release her, Jim guided Rachel up the wet concrete steps. "So what are you writing on?" The slight breeze lifted strands of her dark hair from her shoulders, reminding him how thick and silky it was. His fingers itched to thread through those strands once again.

"A book on homeopathy and first aid. I'm almost finished. I already have a publisher for it, here in the States. It will be simultaneously published by an English firm, too."

He opened the door to the restaurant for her. "How about that? I know a famous person."

With a shake of her head, Rachel entered the warm restaurant, which smelled of baking bread. Inhaling the delicious scent, she waited for Jim to catch up with her. "Mmm, homemade bread. Doesn't it smell wonderful?"

He nodded. "Jamie and his partner, Adrian, make everything fresh here on the premises. No canned anything." He guided her around the corner to a table near the window. Each table, covered in white linen, was decorated with fresh, colorful flowers in a vase. The music was soft and New Age. In each corner stood towering green plants. Jim liked the place because it was alive with plants and flowers.

Rachel relinquished her coat to Jim. He placed it

on one of several hooks in the corner. The place was packed with noontime clientele. In winter and spring, Sedona was busy with tourists from around the world who wanted to escape harsh winters at home. The snow-fall earlier in the week was rare. Sedona got snow per-haps two to four times each winter. And usually, within a day or two, it had melted and been replaced with forty-degree weather in the daytime, thirty-degree tempera-tures at night.

Sitting down, Jim recognized some of the locals. He saw them watching with undisguised interest. The looks on their face said it all: a Cunningham and Donovan sitting together—peacefully—what a miracle! Frown-ing, Jim picked up the menu and then looked over at Rachel, who was studying hers.

"They've got great food here. Anything you pick will be good."

Rachel tried to pay attention to the menu. She liked the fact that Jim sat at her elbow and not across from her. It was so easy to like him, to want to get to know him better. She had a million questions to ask him, but knew she had to remain circumspect.

After ordering their lunch, and having steaming bowls of fragrant mocha latte placed in front of them, Rachel began to relax. The atmosphere of the Muse was low-key. Even though there wasn't an empty table, the noise level was low, and she appreciated that. Setting the huge bowl of latte down after taking a sip, she pressed the pink linen napkin briefly to her lips. Settling the napkin back in her lap, she met and held Jim's warm, interested gaze. He wasn't model handsome. His face had lines in it, marks of character from the thirty-some years of his life. His thick, dark brows moved up a bit in inquiry as she studied him.

"I know what you're thinking," he teased. "I'll bet you're remembering this acne-covered teenager from junior high school, aren't you?"

She folded her hands in front of her. "No, not really. I do remember you being terribly shy, though."

"So were you," he said, sipping his own latte. Jim liked the flush that suddenly covered her cheeks. There was such painfully obvious vulnerability to Rachel. How had she been able to keep it? Life usually had a way of knocking the stuffing out of most people, and everyone he knew hid behind a protective mask or wall as a result. Rachel didn't, he sensed. Maybe that was a testament to her obvious confidence.

"I was a wallflower," Rachel conceded with a nervous laugh. "Although I did attend several clubs after school."

"Drama and photography, if my memory serves me."

Her brows rose. "That's right! Boy, what a memory *you* have." She was flabbergasted that Jim would remember such a thing. If he remembered that, what else did he recall? And why would he retain such insignificant details of her life, anyway? Her heart beat a little harder for a moment.

With a shy shrug, Jim sipped more of his latte. "If the truth be told, I had a terrible crush on you back then. But you didn't know it. I was too shy to say anything, much less look you in the eyes." He chuckled over the memory.

Gawking, Rachel tried to recover. "A crush? On me?"

"Ridiculous, huh?"

She saw the pain in his eyes and realized he was

waiting for her to make fun of him for such an admittance. Rachel would never do that to anyone. Especially Jim.

"No!" she whispered, touched. "I didn't know...."

"Are you sorry you didn't know?" Damn, why had he asked that? His stomach clenched. Why was it so important that Rachel like him as much as he had always liked her? His hands tightened momentarily around his bowl of latte.

"Never mind," he said, trying to tease her, "you don't have to answer that on the grounds it may incriminate you—or embarrass me."

Rachel felt his tension and saw the worry in his eyes. A scene flashed inside her head; of a little boy cowering, as if waiting to get struck. Sliding her fingers around her warm bowl of latte, she said, "I wish I had known, Jim. That's a beautiful compliment. Thank you."

Unable to look at her, he nervously took a couple of sips of his own. Wiping his mouth with the napkin, he muttered, "The past is the past."

Rachel smiled gently. "Our past follows us like a good friend. I'm sure you know that by now." Looking around, she saw several people staring openly at them with undisguised interest. "Like right now," she mused, "I see several locals watching us like bugs under a microscope." She met and held his gaze. Her lips curved in a grin. "Tell me our pasts aren't present!"

Glancing around, Jim realized Rachel was right. "Well, by tonight your name will be tarnished but good."

"What? Because I'm having lunch with the man who saved my life? I'd say that I'm in the best company in the world, with no apology. Wouldn't you?"

He felt heat in his neck and then in his face. Jim

couldn't recall the last time he'd blushed. Rachel's gently spoken words echoed through him like a bell being rung on a very clear day. It was as if she'd reached out and touched him. Her ability to share her feelings openly was affecting him deeply. Taking in a deep breath, he held her warm green gaze, which suddenly glimmered with tears. Tears! The soft parting of her lips was his undoing. Embarrassed, he reached into his back pocket and produced a clean handkerchief.

"Here," he said gruffly, and placed it in her hand.

Dabbing her eyes, Rachel sniffed. "Don't belittle what you did for me, Jim. I sure won't." She handed it back to him. He could barely meet her eyes, obviously embarrassed by her show of tears and gratitude. "You and I are in the same business in one way," she continued. "We work with sick and injured people. The only difference is your EMT work is immediate, mine is more long-term and certainly not as dramatic."

He refolded the handkerchief and stuffed it back into his rear pocket. "I'm not trying to make little of what we did out there for you, Rachel. It wasn't just me that saved your life. My partner, Larry, and four other firefighters were all working as a team to save you."

"Yes, but it was your experience that made you put that blood-pressure cuff on my leg, inflate it and stop the hemorrhaging from my foot."

He couldn't deny that. "Anyone would have figured that out."

"Maybe," Rachel hedged as she saw him begin to withdraw from her. Why wouldn't Jim take due credit for saving her life? The man had great humility. He never said "I," but rather "we" or "the team," and she found that a remarkable trait rarely seen in males.

Lowering her voice, she added, "And I understand from talking to Kate and Jessica, that you gave me a pint of your blood to stabilize me. Is that so?"

Trying to steel himself against whatever she felt about having his blood in her body, Jim lifted his head. When he met and held her tender gaze, something old and hurting broke loose in his heart. He recalled that look before. Rachel probably had forgotten the incident, but he never had. He had just been coming out of the main doors to go home for the day when he saw that a dog had been hit by a car out in front of the high school. Rachel had flown down the steps of the building, crying out in alarm as the dog was hurled several feet onto the lawn.

Falling to her knees, she had held the injured animal. Jim had joined her, along with a few other concerned students. Even then, Rachel had been a healer. She had torn off a piece of her skirt and pressed it against the dog's wounded shoulder to stop the bleeding. Jim had dropped his books and gone to help her. The dog had had a broken leg as well.

Jim remembered sinking to his knees directly opposite her and asking what he could do to help. The look Rachel was giving him now was the same one he'd seen on her face then. There was such clear compassion, pain and love in her eyes that he recalled freezing momentarily because the energy of it had knocked the breath out of him. Rachel had worn her heart on her sleeve back then, just as she did now. She made no excuses for how she felt and was bravely willing to share her vulnerability.

Shaken, he rasped, "Yeah, I was the only one around with your blood type." He opened his hands and looked at them. "I don't know how you feel about that, but I caught hell from my old man and my brothers about it." He glanced up at her. "But I'm not sorry I did it, Rachel."

Without thinking, Rachel slid her hand into his. Hers was slightly damp, while his was dry and strong and nurturing. She saw surprise come to his eyes and felt him tense for a moment, then relax.

As his fingers closed over Rachel's, Jim knew tongues would wag for sure now about them holding hands. But hell, nothing had ever felt so right to him. Ever.

"I'm grateful for what you did, Jim," Rachel quavered. "I wouldn't be sitting here now if you hadn't been there to help. I don't know how to repay you. I really don't. If there's a way—"

His fingers tightened around hers. "I'm going hiking in a couple of weeks, near Boynton Canyon. Come with me?" The words flew out of his mouth. What the hell was he doing? Jim couldn't help himself, nor did he want to. He saw Rachel's eyes grow tender and her fingers tightened around his.

"Yes, I'd love to do that."

"Even though," he muttered, "we'll be the gossip of Sedona?"

She laughed a little breathlessly. "If I cared, really cared about that, I wouldn't be sitting here with you right now, would I?"

A load shifted off his shoulders. Rachel was free in a way that Kate Donovan was not, and the discovery was powerful and galvanizing. Jim very reluctantly released her hand. "Okay, two weeks. I'm free on Saturday. I'll pack us a winter picnic lunch to boot."

"Fair enough," Rachel murmured, thrilled over the

prospect of the hike. "But I have one more favor to ask of you first, Jim."

"Name it and it's yours," he promised thickly.

Rachel placed her elbows on the table and lowered her voice. "It's a big favor, Jim, and you don't have to do it if it's asking too much of you."

Scowling, he saw the sudden worry and seriousness on her face. "What is it?"

Moistening her lips, Rachel picked up her purse from the floor and opened it. Taking out a thick, white envelope, she handed it to him. "Read it, please."

Mystified, Jim eased the envelope open. It was a wedding invitation—to Kate and Jessica's double wedding, which would be held on Saturday. He could feel the tension in Rachel. His head spun with questions and few answers. Putting the envelope aside, he held her steady gaze.

"You're serious about this…invitation?"

"Very."

"Look," he began uneasily, holding up his hands, "Kate isn't real comfortable with me being around. I understand why and—"

"Kate was the one who suggested it."

Jim stared at her. "What?"

Rachel looked down at the tablecloth for a moment. "Jim," she began unsteadily, her voice strained, "I've heard why you came back here, back to Sedona. You want to try and straighten out a lot of family troubles between yourself, your father and two brothers. Kate didn't trust you at first because of the past, the feud between our families…actually, between our fathers, not us for the most part." She looked up and held his dark, shadowed gaze. "Kate doesn't trust a whole lot of peo-

ple. Her life experiences make her a little more paranoid
than me or Jessica, but that's okay, too. Yesterday she
brought this invitation to me and told me to give it to
you. She said that because you'd saved my life, she and
Jessica wanted you there. That this was a celebration of
life—and love—and that you deserved to be with us."

He saw the earnestness in Rachel's eyes. "How do
you feel about it? Having the enemy in your midst?"

"You were never my enemy, Jim. None of you were.
Kelly had his battles with your father. Not with me, not
with my sisters. Your brothers are another thing. They
aren't invited." Her voice grew husky. "I *want* you to
be there. I like Kate's changing attitude toward you. It's
a start in healing this wound that festers among us. I
know you'll probably feel uncomfortable, but by showing up, it's a start, even if only symbolically, don't you
think? A positive one?"

In that moment, Jim wished they were anywhere but
out in a public place. The tears in Rachel's eyes made
them shine and sparkle like dark emeralds. He wanted
to whisper her name, slide his hands through that thick
mass of hair, angle her head just a little and kiss her
until she melted into his being, into his heart. Despite
her background, Rachel was so fresh, so alive, so brave
about being herself and sharing her feelings, that it allowed him the same privilege within himself.

He wanted to take her hand and hold it, but he
couldn't. He saw the locals watching them like proverbial hawks now. Jim didn't wish gossip upon Rachel or
any of the Donovan sisters. God knew, they had suffered enough of it through the years.

One corner of his mouth tugged upward. "I'll be
there," he promised her huskily.

Chapter 5

"Where you goin' all duded up?" Bo Cunningham drawled as he leaned languidly against the open door to Jim's bedroom.

Jim glanced over at his brother. Bo was tall and lean, much like their father. His dark good looks had always brought him a lot of attention from women. In high school, Bo had been keenly competitive with Jim. Whatever Jim undertook, Bo did too. The rivalry hadn't stopped and there was always tension, like a razor, between them.

"Going to a wedding," he said.

He knotted his tie and snugged it into place against his throat. In all his years of traveling around the U.S. as a Hotshot, he'd never had much call for wearing a suit. But after having lunch with Rachel, he'd gone to Flagstaff and bought one. Jim had known that when his two brothers saw him in a suit, they'd be sure to make

fun of him. Uniform of the day around the Bar C was
jeans, a long-sleeved shirt and a cowboy hat. He would
wear his dark brown Stetson to the wedding, however.
The color of his hat would nearly match the raw umber
tone of his suit. A new white shirt and dark green tie
completed his ensemble.

Bo's full lips curled a little. "I usually know of most
weddin's takin' place around here. Only one I know of
today is the Donovan sisters."

Inwardly, Jim tried to steel himself against the inevitable. "That's the one," he murmured, picking up
his brush and moving it one last time across his short,
dark hair. It was nearly 1:00 p.m. and the wedding was
scheduled for 2:00. He had to hurry.

"You workin' at bein' a traitor to this family?"

Bo's chilling question made him freeze. Slowly
turning, he saw that his brother was no longer leaning
against his bedroom door, but standing tensely. The
stormy look on his face was what Jim expected.

Picking up his hat, Jim stepped toward him. "Save
your garbage for somebody who believes it, Bo." Then
he moved past him and down the hall. Since Jim had
come home, Bo had acted like a little bantam rooster,
crowing and strutting because their father was planning on leaving Bo and Chet the ranch—and not Jim.
Frank Cunningham had disowned his youngest son the
day he'd left home years before. As Jim walked into the
main living area, he realized he'd never regretted that
decision. What he did regret was Bo trying at every turn
to get their father to throw him off the property now.

As Jim settled his hat on his head, he saw his father positioned near the heavy cedar door that he had
to walk through to get to his pickup. The look on his

father's face wasn't pleasant, and Jim realized that Bo, an inveterate gossip, had already told him everything.

"Where you goin', son?"

Jim halted in front of his father's wheelchair. As he studied his father's eyes, he realized the old man was angry and upset, but not out of control. He must have remembered his meds today. For that, Jim breathed an inner sigh of relief.

"I'm going to a wedding," he said quietly. "Kate and Jessica Donovan are getting married. It's a double wedding."

His father's brows dipped ominously. "Who invited you?"

"Kate did." Jim felt his gut twist. He could see his father's rage begin to mount, from the flash of light in his bloodshot eyes to the way he set his mouth into that thin, hard line.

"You could've turned down the invitation."

"I didn't want to." Jim felt his adrenaline start to pump. He couldn't help feeling threatened and scared—sort of like the little boy who used to cower in front of his larger-than-life father. When Frank Cunningham went around shouting and yelling, his booming voice sounded like thunder itself. Jim knew that by coming back to the ranch he would go through a lot of the conditioned patterns he had when he was a child and that he had to work through and dissolve them. He was a man now, not a little boy. He struggled to remain mature in his reactions with his father and not melt into a quivering mass of fear like he had when he was young.

"You had a choice," Frank growled.

"Yes." Jim sighed. "I did."

"You're doin' this on purpose. Bo said you were."

Jim looked to his right. He saw Bo amble slowly out of the hallway, a gleeful look in his eyes. His brother *wanted* this confrontation. Bo took every opportunity to make things tense between Jim and his father in hopes that Jim would be banned forever from the ranch and their lives. Jim knew Bo was worried that Frank would change his will and give Jim his share of the ranch. The joke was Jim would never take it. Not on the terms that Frank would extract from him. No, he wouldn't play those dark family games anymore. Girding himself against his father's well-known temper, Jim looked down into his angry eyes.

"What I do, Father, is my business. I'm not going to this wedding to hurt you in any way. But if that's what they want you to believe, and you want to believe it, then I can't change your mind."

"They're *Donovans!*" Frank roared as he gripped the arms of his wheelchair, his knuckles turning white. His breathing became harsh and swift. "Damn you, Jim! You just don't get it, do you, boy? They're our enemies!"

Jim's eyes narrowed. "No, they're not our enemies! You and I have had this argument before. I'm not going to have it again. They're decent people. I'm not treating them any differently than I'd treat you or a stranger on the street."

"Damn you to hell," Frank snarled, suddenly leaning back and glaring up at him. "If I wasn't imprisoned in this damned chair, I'd take a strap to you! I'd stop you from going over there!"

"Come on, Pa," Bo coaxed, sauntering over and patting him sympathetically on the shoulder. "Jim's a turncoat. He's showin' his true colors, that's all. Come on, lemme take you to town. We'll go over to the bar and have a drink of whiskey and drown our troubles together over this."

Glaring at Bo, Jim snapped, "He's diabetic! You know he can't drink liquor."

Bo grinned smugly. "You're forcing him to drink. It's not my fault."

Breathing hard, Jim looked down at his father, a pleading expression in his eyes. Before Frank became diabetic, he'd been a hard drinker. Jim was sure he was an alcoholic, but he never said so. Now Jim centered his anger on Bo. His brother knew a drink would make his father's blood sugar leap off the scale, that it could damage him in many ways and potentially shorten his life. Jim knew that Bo hated his father, but he never showed it, never confronted him on anything. Instead, Bo used passive-aggressive ways of getting what he wanted. This wasn't the first time his brother had poured Frank a drink or two. And Bo didn't really care what it did to his father's health. His only interest was getting control of the ranch once Frank died.

Even his father knew alcohol wasn't good for his condition. But Jim wasn't about to launch into the reasons why he shouldn't drink. Placing his hand on the doorknob, he rasped, "You're grown men. You're responsible for whatever you decide to do."

The wedding was taking place at the main ranch house. The sky was sunny and the sky a deep, almost startling blue. As Jim drove up and parked his pickup on the graveled driveway, he counted more than thirty other vehicles. Glancing at his watch, he saw that it was 2:10 p.m. He was late, dammit. With his stomach still in knots from his confrontation with his father, he gathered up the wedding gifts and hurried to the porch of the ranch house. There were garlands of evergreen with pine cones, scattered with silver, red and gold glitter, framing the door, showing Jim that the place had been decorated with a woman's touch.

Gently opening the door, he saw Jessica and Kate standing with their respective mates near the huge red-pink-and-white flagstone fireplace. Rachel was there, too. Reverend Thomas O'Malley was presiding and sonorously reading from his text. Walking as quietly as he could, Jim felt the stares of a number of people in the gathered group as he placed the wrapped gifts on a table at the back of the huge room.

Taking off his hat, he remained at the rear of the crowd that had formed a U around the two beautiful brides and their obviously nervous grooms. Looking up, he saw similar pine boughs and cones hung across each of the thick timbers that supported the ceiling of the main room. The place was light and pretty compared to the darkness of his father's home. Light and dark. Jim shut his eyes for a moment and tried to get a hold on his tangled, jumbled emotions.

When he opened his eyes, he moved a few feet to the left to get a better look at the wedding party. His heart opened up fiercely as he felt the draw of Rachel's natural beauty.

Both brides wore white. Kate had on a long, traditional wedding gown of what looked to Jim like satin, and a gossamer veil on her hair. Tiny pearl buttons decorated each of her wrists and the scoop neck of her dress. Kate had never looked prettier, with her face flushed, her eyes sparkling, her entire attention focused on Sam McGuire, who stood tall and dark at her side.

In their expressions, Jim could see their love for one another, and it eased some of his own internal pain.

Jessica wore a tailored white wool suit, decorated with a corsage of several orchids. In her hair was a ringlet of orchids woven with greenery, making her look like a fairy. Jim smiled a little. Jessica had always reminded him of some ethereal being, someone not quite of this earth, but made more from the stuff of heaven. He eyed Dan Black, dressed in a dark blue suit and tie, standing close beside his wife-to-be. Jim noticed the fierce love in Black's eyes for Jessica. And he saw tears running down Jessica's cheeks as she began to repeat her vows to Dan.

The incredible love between the two couples soothed whatever demons were left in him. Jim listened to Kate's voice quaver as she spoke the words to Sam. McGuire, whose face usually was rock hard and expressionless, was surprisingly readable. The look of tenderness, of open, adoring love for Kate, was there to be seen by everyone at the gathering. Jim's heart ached. He wished he would someday feel that way about a woman. And then his gaze settled on Rachel.

The ache in his heart softened, then went away as he hungrily gazed at her. He felt like a thief, stealing glances at a woman he had no right to even look at twice. How she looked today was a far cry from how she'd looked out at the accident site. She was radiant in a pale pink, long-sleeved dress that brushed her thin ankles. A circlet of orchids similar to Jessica's rested in her dark, thick hair, which had been arranged in a pretty French braid, and she carried a small bouquet of orchids and greenery in her hands. She wore no make-up, which Jim applauded. Rachel didn't need any, he thought, struck once again by her exquisite beauty.

Her lips were softly parted. Tears shone in two paths across her high cheekbones as the men now began to speak their vows to Kate and Jessica. Everything about Rachel was soft and vulnerable, Jim realized. She didn't try to hide behind a wall like Kate did. She was open, like Jessica. But even more so, in a way Jim couldn't yet define. And then something electric and magical happened. Rachel, as if sensing his presence, his gaze burning upon her, lifted her head a little and turned to look toward him. Their eyes met.

In that split second, Jim felt as if a lightning bolt had slammed through him. Rachel's forest green eyes were velvet, and glistening with tears. He saw the sweet curve of her full lips move upward in silent welcome. Suddenly awkward, Jim felt heat crawling up his neck and into his face. Barely nodding in her direction, he tried to return her smile. He saw relief in her face, too. Relief that he'd come? Was it personal or symbolic of the fragile union being forged between their families? he wondered. Jim wished that it was personal. He felt shaken inside as Rachel returned her attention to her sisters, but he felt good, too.

The dark mass of knots in his belly miraculously dissolved beneath Rachel's one, welcoming look. There was such a cleanness to her and he found himself wanting her in every possible way. Yet as soon as that desire was born, a sharp stab of fear followed. She was a Donovan. He was a Cunningham. Did he dare follow his heart? If he did, Jim knew that the hell in his life would quadruple accordingly. His father would be outraged. Bo would use it as another lever to get him to look unworthy to Frank. Jim had come home to try and change the poisonous condition of their heritage. What was more important—trying to change his family or wanting to know Rachel much, much better?

There was a whoop and holler when both grooms kissed their brides, and the party was in full swing shortly after. Jim recognized everyone at the festive gathering. He joined in the camaraderie, the joy around him palpable. The next order of business was tossing the bridal bouquets. Jim saw Rachel stand at the rear of the excited group, of about thirty women, and noticed she wasn't really trying to jockey for a position to possibly catch one of those beautiful orchid bouquets. Why not?

Both Kate and Jessica threw their bouquets at the same time. There were shrieks, shouts and a sudden rush forward as all the women except Rachel tried to catch them. Ruby Forester, a waitress in her early forties who worked at the Muse Restaurant, caught Jessica's. Kate's bouquet was caught by Lannie Young, who worked at the hardware store in Cottonwood. Both women beamed in triumph and held up their bouquets.

Remaining at the rear of the crowd, Jim saw two wedding cakes being rolled out of the kitchen and into the center of the huge living room. From time to time he saw Rachel look up, as if searching for him in the crowd of nearly sixty people. She was kept busy up front as the cakes were cut, and then sparkling, nonalcoholic grape juice was passed around in champagne glasses.

After the toast, someone went over to the grand piano in the corner, and began to play a happy tune. The crowd parted so that a dance floor was spontaneously created. A number of people urged Kate and Sam out on the floor, and Jim saw Jessica drag Dan out there, too. Jim felt sorry for the new husbands, who obviously weren't first-rate dancers. But that didn't matter. The infectious joy of the moment filled all of them and soon both brides and grooms were dancing and whirling on the hardwood oak floor, which gleamed beneath them.

Finishing off the last of his grape juice, Jim saw a number of people with camcorders filming the event. Kate and Jessica would have a wonderful memento of one of the happiest days of their lives. He felt good about that. It was time the Donovans had a little luck, a little happiness.

After the song was finished, everyone broke into applause. The room rang with laugher, clapping and shouts of joy. The woman at the piano began another song and soon the dance floor was crowded with other well-wishers. Yes, this was turning into quite a party. Jim grinned and shook a number of people's hands, saying hello to them as he slowly made his way toward the kitchen. He wanted to find Rachel now that her duties as the maid of honor were pretty much over.

The kitchen was a beehive of activity, he discovered as he placed his used glass near the sink. At least seven women were bustling around placing hors d'oeuvres on platters, preparing them to be taken out to serve to the happy crowd in the living room. He spotted Rachel in the thick of things. Through the babble he heard her low, husky voice giving out directions. Her cheeks were flushed a bright pink and she had rolled up the sleeves on her dress to her elbows. The circlet of orchids looked fetching in her hair. The small pearl earrings in her ears, and the single-strand pearl necklace around her throat made her even prettier in his eyes, if that were possible.

Finally, the women paraded out, carrying huge silver platters piled high with all types of food—from meat to fruit to vegetables with dip. Jim stepped to one side and allowed the group to troop by. Suddenly it was quiet in the kitchen. He looked up to see Rachel leaning against the counter, giving him an amused look.

He grinned a little and moved toward her. The pink dress had a mandarin collar and showed off her long, graceful neck to advantage. The dress itself had an empire waistline and made her look deliciously desirable.

"I got here a little late," he said. "I'm sorry."

Pushing a strand of dark hair off her brow, Rachel felt her heart pick up in beat. How handsome and dangerous Jim looked in his new suit. "I'm just glad you came," she whispered, noting the genuine apology in his eyes.

"I am, too." He forced himself not to reach out and touch her—or kiss her. Right now, Rachel looked so damned inviting that he had to fight himself. "Doesn't look like your foot is bothering you at all."

"No, complete recovery, thanks to you and a little homeopathic magic." She felt giddy. Like a teenager. Rachel tried to warn herself that she shouldn't feel like this toward any man again. The last time she'd felt even close to this kind of feeling for a man, things hadn't ended well between them. Trying to put those memories aside, Rachel lifted her hands and said, "You clean up pretty good, too, I see."

Shyly, Jim touched the lapel of his suit. "Yeah, first suit I've had since... I don't remember when."

"Well," Rachel said huskily, "you look very handsome in it."

Her compliment warmed him as if she had kissed him. Jim found himself wanting to kiss her, to capture that perfect mouth of hers that looked like orchid petals, and feel her melt hotly beneath his exploration. He looked deep into her forest green eyes and saw gold flecks of happiness in them. "I hope by coming in late I didn't upset anything or anyone?"

She eased away from the counter and wiped her hands on a dish towel, suddenly nervous because he was so close to her. Did Jim realize the power he had over her? She didn't think so. He seemed shy and awkward around her, nothing like the charge medic she'd seen at her accident. No, that man had been confident and gentle with her, knowing exactly what to do and when. Here, he seemed tentative and unsure. Rachel laughed at herself as she fluttered nervously around the kitchen, realizing she felt the same way.

"I have to get back out there," she said a little breathlessly. "I need to separate the gifts. They'll be opening them next."

"Need some help?"

Hesitating in the doorway, Rachel laughed a little. "Well, sure.... Come on."

Jim and Rachel took up positions behind the linen-draped tables as the music and dancing continued unabated. He felt better doing something. Occasionally, their hands would touch as they closed over the same brightly wrapped gift, and she would jerk hers away as if burned. Jim didn't know how to interpret her reaction. He was, after all, a dreaded Cunningham. And more than once he'd seen a small knot of people talking, quizzically studying him and then talking some more. Gossip was the lifeblood of any small town, and Sedona was no exception. He sighed. Word of a Cunningham attending the Donovan weddings was sure to be the chief topic at the local barbershop come Monday morning.

Worse, he would have to face his father and brothers

tonight at the dinner table. His stomach clenched. Trying to push all that aside, he concentrated on the good feelings Rachel brought up in him. Being the maid of honor, she had to make sure everything ran smoothly. It was her responsibility to see that Kate and Jessica's wedding went off without a hitch. And it looked like everything was going wonderfully. The hors d'oeuvres were placed on another group of tables near the fireplace, where flames were snapping and crackling. Paper plates, pink napkins and plenty of coffee, soda and sparkling grape juice would keep the guests well fed in the hours to come.

It was nearly 5:00 p.m. by the time the crowd began to dissipate little by little. Jim didn't want to go home. He had taken off his coat, rolled up his shirtsleeves and was helping wash dishes out in the kitchen, along with several women. Someone had to do the cleanup. Kate and Sam had gone to Flagstaff an hour earlier, planning to stay at a friend's cabin up in the pine country. Jessica and Dan had retired to their house on the Donovan spread, not wanting to leave the ranch.

Jim had his hands in soapy water when Rachel reappeared. He grinned at her as she came through the doorway. She'd changed from her pink dress into a pair of dark tan wool slacks, a long-sleeved white blouse and a bright, colorful vest of purple, pink and red. Her hair was still up in the French braid, but the circlet of orchids had disappeared. The pearl choker and earrings were gone, too.

She smiled at him as she came up and took over drying dishes from one of the older women. "I can see the look on your face, Mr. Cunningham."

"Oh?" he teased, placing another platter beneath the warm, running water to rinse it off.

"The look on your face says, 'Gosh, you changed out of that pretty dress for these togs.'"

"You're a pretty good mind reader." And she was. Jim wondered if his expression was really that revealing. Or was it Rachel's finely honed observation skills that helped her see through him? Either way, it was disconcerting.

"Thank you," she said lightly, taking the platter from him. Their fingers touched. A soft warmth flowed up her hand, making her heart beat a little harder.

"I'm sorry I didn't get to dance with you," Rachel said in a low voice. There were several other women in the kitchen and she didn't want them to overhear.

Jim had asked her to dance earlier, but she had reluctantly chosen kitchen duties over his invitation. He'd tried not to take her refusal personally—but he had. The Cunningham-Donovan feud still stood between them. He understood that Rachel didn't want to be seen in the arms of her vaunted enemy at such a public function.

"That's okay. You were busy." Jim scrubbed a particularly dirty skillet intently. Just the fact that Rachel was next to him and they were working together like a team made his heart sing.

"I wished I hadn't been," Rachel said, meaning it. She saw surprise flare in his eyes and then, just as quickly, he suppressed his reaction.

"You know how town gossip is," Jim began, rinsing off the iron skillet. "You just got home and you don't need gossip about being caught in the arms of a Cunningham haunting your every step." He handed her the skillet and met her grave gaze.

Pursing her lips, Rachel closed her fingers over his as she took the skillet. She felt a fierce longing build in her. She saw the bleakness in Jim's eyes, and heard the past overwhelming the present feelings between them. She wanted to touch him, and found herself inventing small ways of doing just that. The light in his eyes changed as her fingertips brushed his. For an instant, she saw raw, hungry desire in his eyes. Or had she? It had happened so fast, Rachel wondered if she was making it up.

"That had nothing to do with it, Jim," she said, briskly drying the skillet. "Kate told me you'd come home to try and mend some family problems. She told me how much you've done to try and make that happen. I find it admirable." Grimacing, she set the skillet aside and watched him begin to scrub a huge platter. "I really admire you." And she did.

Jim lifted his chin and glanced across his shoulder at her. There was pleasure in his eyes. Shrugging her shoulders, Rachel said, "I don't know if you'll be successful or not. You have three men who want to keep the vendetta alive between us. And I'm *sure*," she continued huskily, holding his gaze, "that you caught hell today for coming over here."

Chuckling a little, Jim nodded and began to rinse the platter beneath the faucet. "Just a little. But I don't regret it, Rachel. Not one bit."

She stood there assessing the amount of discomfort she heard in his voice. She was a trained homeopath, taught to pay attention to voice tone, facial expressions and body language, and sense on many levels what was really being felt over what was being verbally said. Jim was obviously trying to make light of a situation that, in her gut, she knew was a huge roadblock for him.

"Did your father get upset?"

Obviously uncomfortable, Jim handed her the rinsed platter. "A little," he hedged.

"Probably a lot. Has Bo changed since I saw him in school? He used to be real good at manipulating people and situations to his own advantage."

Jim pulled the plug and let the soapy water run out of the sink. "He hasn't changed much," he admitted, sadness in his voice.

"And Chet? Is he still a six-year-old boy in a man's body? And still behaving like one?"

Grinning, Jim nodded. "You're pretty good at pegging people."

Drying the platter, Rachel said, "It comes from being a homeopath for so many years. We're trained to observe, watch and listen on many levels simultaneously."

Jim rinsed off his soapy hands and took the towel she handed him. "Thanks. Well, I'm impressed." He saw her brows lower in thought. "So, what's your prescription for my family, Doctor?"

She smiled a little and put the platter on the table behind them. The other women had left, their duties done, and she and Jim were alone—at last. Rachel leaned against the counter, with no more than a few feet separating them. "When you have three people who want a poisonous situation to continue, who don't want to change, mature or break certain habit patterns, I'd say you're in over your head."

Unable to argue, he hung the cloth up on a nail on the side of the cabinet next to the sink. Slowly rolling his sleeves down, Jim studied her. "I won't disagree with your assessment."

Her heart ached for him. In that moment, Rachel

saw a vulnerable little boy with too much responsibility heaped upon his shoulders at too young an age. His mother had died when he was six, as she recalled, leaving three little boys robbed of her nurturing love. Frank Cunningham had lost it after his wife died. Rachel remembered that story. He'd gone on a drinking binge that lasted a week, until he finally got into a fight at a local bar and they threw him in the county jail to cool down. In the meantime, Bo, Chet and Jim had had to run the ranch without their grief-stricken father. Three very young boys had been saddled with traumatic responsibilities well beyond their years or understanding. Rachel felt her heart breaking for all of them.

"Hey," she whispered, "everyone's leaving. I'd love to have some help moving the furniture back into place in the living room. It's going to quiet down now. Do you have time to help me or do you have to go somewhere?"

Jim felt his heart pound hard at the warmth in her voice, the need in her eyes—for his company. Her invitation was genuine. A hunger flowed through him. He ached to kiss Rachel. To steal the goodness of her for himself. Right now he felt impoverished, overwhelmed by the situation with his family, and he knew that by staying, he was only going to make things worse for himself when he did go home. His father expected him for dinner at 6:00 p.m. It was 5:30 now.

As Jim stood there, he felt Rachel's soft hand, so tentative, on his arm. Lifting his head, he held her compassionate gaze. "Yeah, I can stick around to help you. Let me make a phone call first."

Smiling softly, Rachel said, "Good."

Chapter 6

Jim enjoyed the quiet of the evening with Rachel. The fire was warm and cast dancing yellow light out into the living room, where they sat on the sofa together, coffee in hand. It had taken them several hours to get everything back in order and in place. Rachel had fixed them some sandwiches a little while ago—a reward for all their hard work. Now she sat on one end of the sofa, her long legs tucked beneath her, her shoes on the floor, a soft, relaxed look on her face.

Jim sat at the other end, the cup between his square hands. Everything seemed perfect to him—the quiet, the snowflakes gently falling outside, the beauty of a woman he was drawn more and more by the hour, the snap and crackle of the fire, the intimacy of the dimly lit room. Yes, he was happy, he realized—in a way he'd never been before.

Rachel studied Jim's pensive features, profiled

against the dark. He had a strong face, yet his sense of humor was wonderful. The kind of face that shouted of his responsible nature. Her stomach still hurt, they had laughed so much while working together. Really, Rachel admitted to herself, he was terribly desirable to her in every way. Rarely had she seen such a gentle nature in a man. Maybe it was because he was an EMT and dealt with people in crisis all the time. He was a far cry from her father, who had always been full of rage. Maybe her new relationship with Jim was a good sign of her health—she was reaching out to a man of peace, not violence.

Pulling herself from her reverie, she said, "Did I ever tell you what made me slam on my brakes up there in the canyon?"

Jim turned and placed his arm across the back of the couch. "No. I think you said it was a cat."

Rachel rolled her eyes. "It wasn't a cougar. When I got home from ER, I asked Jessica to bring me an encyclopedia. I lay there in bed with books surrounding me. I looked under *L* for leopard, and that wasn't what I saw. When I looked under *J* for jaguar…" She gave him a bemused look. "That was what I saw out there, Jim, in the middle of an ice-covered highway that morning—a jaguar." She saw the surprise flare in his eyes. "I thought I was hallucinating, of course, but then something very unusual—strange—happened."

"Oh?" Jim replied with a smile. He liked the way her mouth curved into a self-deprecating line. Rachel had no problem poking fun at herself—she was confident enough to do so. As she moved her hand to punctuate her story, he marveled at her effortless grace. She was like a ballet dancer. He wanted to say that she had the grace of a jungle cat—a boneless, rhythmic way of moving that simply entranced him.

"Jessica and Kate came in about an hour later to check on me, and when I showed them the picture in the encyclopedia, well, Jessica went bonkers!" Rachel chuckled. "She began babbling a mile a minute—you know how Jess can get when she's excited—and she told me the following story, which I've been meaning to share with you."

Interested, Jim placed his empty coffee cup on the table. The peacefulness that surrounded Rachel was something he'd craved. Any excuse to remain in her company just a few minutes longer he'd take without apology. "Let's hear it. I like stories. I recall Mom always had a story for me at bedtime," he said wistfully, remembering those special times.

Sipping her coffee thoughtfully, Rachel decided to give Jim all the details Jessica had filled her in on since the day she'd come home from the hospital. "Awhile back, Morgan Trayhern and his wife, Laura, visited with us. They were trying to put the pieces of their lives back together after being kidnapped by drug lords from South America. An Army Special Forces officer by the name of Mike Houston was asked to come and stay with them and be their 'guard dog' while they were here with us. Dr. Ann Parsons, an MD and psychiatrist who worked for Morgan's company, Perseus, also stayed here." Rachel gestured to the north. "They each stayed in one of the houses here at the ranch.

"Jessica made good friends with Mike and Ann while we were here for the week following Kelly's funeral. At the time, I was too busy helping Kate to really get to know them, although we shared a couple of meals with them and I helped Morgan and Laura move into the cabin up in the canyon, where they stayed." She frowned slightly. "One of the things Jessica said was that she confided in Mike. She asked how he, one man, could possibly protect anyone from sneaking up on Morgan and Laura if they wanted to, the ranch was so large. I guess Mike laughed and said that he had a little help. Jessica pressed him on that point, and he said that his mother's people, the Quechua Indians, had certain people within their nation who had a special kind of medicine. 'Medicine,' as you know, means a skill or talent. He said he was born with jaguar medicine."

Laughing, Rachel placed her cup on the coffee table. The intent look in Jim's eyes told her he was fascinated with her story. He wasn't making fun of her or sitting there with disbelief written across his face, so she continued. "Well, this little piece of information really spurred Jessica on to ask more questions. You know how she is." Rachel smiled fondly. "As 'fate' would have it, Jessica's good friend, Moyra, who lived up in Vancouver, was also a member of a Jaguar Clan down in Peru. And, of course, Mike was stationed in Peru as a trainer for Peruvian soldiers who went after the drug lords and stopped cocaine shipments from coming north to the U.S. Jessica couldn't let this little development go, so she really nagged Mike to give her more information.

"Mike told her that he was a member of the Jaguar Clan. He teasingly said that down there, in Peru, they called him the Jaguar god. Of course, this really excited Jessica, who is into paranormal things big-time." Again, Rachel laughed softly. "She told Mike that Moyra had *hinted* that members of the Jaguar Clan possessed certain special 'powers.' Did he? Mike tried to tease her and deflect her, but she just kept coming back and pushing him for answers. Finally, one night, just before she left to go home to Canada, Mike told her that people born with Jaguar Clan blood could do certain things most other people could not. They could heal, for one thing. And when they touched someone they cared about or loved, that person could be saved—regardless of how sick or wounded he or she was. Mike admitted that he'd gotten his nickname out in the jungles fighting cocaine soldiers and drug lords. He told her that one time, one of his men got hit by a bullet and was bleeding to death. Mike placed his hand over the wound and, miraculously, it stopped bleeding. The man lived. Mike's legend grew. They said he could bring the dying back to life."

Fascinated, Jim rested his elbows on his knees and watched her shadowed features. "Interesting," he murmured.

"I thought so. But here's the really interesting part, Jim." She moved to where he was sitting, keeping barely a foot between them. Opening her hands, she whispered. "Jessica also told me more than once that Moyra had a jaguar spirit guardian. Jessica is very clairvoyant and she can 'see' things most of us can't. She told me that when Carl, her ex-husband, was stalking her, Moyra would know he was nearby. One afternoon, Jessica was taking a walk in the woods when she came to a creek and saw Moyra." Rachel shook her head. "This is going to sound really off-the-wall, Jim."

He grinned a little. "Hey, remember my mother was Apache. I was raised with a pretty spiritually based system of beliefs."

Rachel nodded. "Well, Jessica swears she saw Moyra

standing in the middle of the creek, and then the next moment she saw a jaguar there instead!"

"Moyra turned into a jaguar?"

Rachel shrugged. "Jessica swears she wasn't seeing things. She watched this jaguar trot off across the meadow and into the woods. Jessica was so stunned and shocked that she ran back to the cabin, scared to death! When Moyra came in a couple hours later, Jessica confronted her on it. Moyra laughed, shrugged it off and said that shape shifting was as natural as breathing to her clan. And wasn't it more important that she and her jaguar guardian be out, protecting Jessica from Carl?"

With a shake of his head, Jim studied Rachel in the firelight. How beautiful she looked! He wanted to kiss her, feel her ripe, soft lips beneath his mouth. Never had he wanted anything more than that, but he placed steely control over that desire. He liked the intimacy that was being established between them. If he was to kiss her, it might destroy that. Instead, he asked, "How does this story dovetail into your seeing that jaguar?"

Rachel laughed a little, embarrassed. "Well, what you didn't tell me was that there was a terrible accident a mile below where I'd crashed!"

He nodded. "That's right, there was. I didn't want to upset you."

Rachel reached out and laid her hand on his arm. She felt his muscle tense beneath her touch. Tingles flowed up her fingers and she absorbed the warmth of his flesh. Reluctantly, she withdrew her hand. The shadows played against his strong face, and she felt the heat of his gaze upon her, making her feel desired. Heat pooled within her, warm and evocative.

Clearing her throat, she went on. "Jessica was the one

who put it all together. She thinks that the jaguar was protecting me from becoming a part of that awful wreck down the road. We calculated later that if I hadn't spun out where I did, I could easily have been involved in that fiery wreck where everyone was burned to death." Rachel placed her arms around herself. "I know it sounds crazy, but Jessica thinks the jaguar showed up to stop me from dying."

"You almost did, anyway," Jim said, scowling.

She relaxed her arms and opened her hands. "I never told you this, Jim. I guess I was afraid to—afraid you'd laugh at me. But I did share it with my sisters. Until you arrived, I kept seeing this jaguar. I saw it circle my car. I thought I was seeing things, of course." She frowned. "Did *you* see any tracks around the car?"

"I wasn't really paying attention," he said apologetically. "All my focus was on you, the stability of the car, and if there were any gas leaks."

Nodding, Rachel said, "Of course…"

"Well…" Jim sighed. "I don't disbelieve you, Rachel."

She studied him in the growing silence. "I thought you might think I was hallucinating. I *had* lost a lot of blood."

"My mother's people have a deep belief in shape-shifters—people who can turn from human into animal, reptile or insect form, and then change back into a human one again. I remember her sitting me on her knee and telling me stories about those special medicine people."

"Jessica thinks it was Moyra who came in the form of a jaguar to protect me until you could arrive on scene." She laughed a little, embarrassed over her explanation.

Jim smiled thoughtfully. "I think because we're part

Indian and raised to know that there is an unseen, invisible world of spirits around us, that it's not really that crazy an explanation. Do you?"

Somberly, Rachel shook her head. "Thanks for not laughing at me about this, Jim. There's no question you helped save my life." She held his dark stare. "If it wasn't for you, I wouldn't be sitting here right now." She eased her hand over his. "I wish there was some way I could truly pay you back for what you did."

His fingers curled around her slender ones, as his heart pounded fiercely in his chest. "You're doing it right now," he rasped, holding her soft, glistening gaze. The fact that Rachel could be so damned open and vulnerable shook Jim. He'd met so few people capable of such honest emotions. Most people, including himself, hid behind protective walls. Like Kate Donovan did, although she was changing, most likely softened because of her love for Sam McGuire.

Rachel liked the tender smile on his mouth. "Now that the weddings are over, I have a big job ahead of me," she admitted in a low voice. "My sisters are counting on me to bring in some desperately needed money to keep the ranch afloat." Looking up, she stared out the window. A few snowflakes twirled by. "If we don't get good snowfall this winter, and spring rains, we're doomed, Jim. There's just no money to keep buying the hay we need to feed the cattle because of the continued drought."

"It's bad for every rancher," he agreed. "How are you going to make money?"

She leaned back on the couch and closed her eyes, feeling content despite her worry. The natural intimacy she felt with Jim was soothing. "I'm going to go into

Sedona on Monday to find an office to rent. I'm going to set up my practice as a homeopath."

"If you need patients, I'll be the first to make an appointment."

She opened her eyes and looked at him. He was serious. "I don't see anything wrong with you."

Grinning a little, he said, "Actually, it will be for my father, who has diabetes. Since meeting you, I did a little research on what homeopathy is and how it works. My father refuses to take his meds most of the time, unless I hand them to him morning and night."

"Can't your two brothers help out?" She saw his scowl, the banked anger in his eyes. Automatically, Rachel closed her fingers over his. She enjoyed his closeness, craved it, telling herself that it was all right. Part of her, however, was scared to death.

"Bo and Chet aren't responsible in that way," he muttered, sitting up suddenly. He knew he had to get home. He could almost feel his father's upset that he was still at the Donovan Ranch. Moving his shoulders as if to get rid of the invisible loads he carried, he turned toward Rachel. Their knees met and touched. He released her hand and slid his arm to the back of the couch behind her. The concern in her eyes for his father was genuine. It was refreshing to see that she could still feel compassion for his father, in spite of the feud.

"Your father's diabetes can worsen to a dangerous level if he doesn't consistently take his meds."

"I know that," Jim said wearily.

"You're carrying a lot of loads for your family, aren't you?"

Rachel's quietly spoken words eased some of the pain he felt at the entire situation. "Yes…"

"It's very hard to change three people's minds about life, Jim," she said gently.

One corner of his mouth lifted in a grimace. "I know it sounds impossible, but I have to try."

Feeling his pain and keeping herself from reacting to it the way she wanted to was one of the hardest things Rachel had ever done. In that moment, she saw the exhaustion mirrored in Jim's face, the grief in his darkened eyes.

"You go through hell over there, don't you?"

He shrugged. "Sometimes."

Rachel sat up. "You'll catch a lot of hell being over here for the wedding."

"Yes," he muttered, slowly standing up, unwinding his long, lean frame. It was time to go, because if he didn't, he was going to do the unpardonable: he was going to kiss Rachel senseless. The powerful intimacy that had sprung up between them was throbbing and alive. Jim could feel his control disintegrating moment by moment. If he didn't leave—

Rachel stood up and slipped her shoes back on her feet. "I'll walk you to the door," she said gently. Just the way Jim moved, she could tell he wasn't looking forward to going home. Her heart bled for him. She knew how angry and spiteful Old Man Cunningham could be. As Jim picked up his suit coat and shrugged it across his broad shoulder, Rachel opened the door for him, noticing how boyish he looked despite the suit he wore. He'd taken off the tie a long time ago, his open collar revealing dark hair on his chest.

They stood in the foyer together, a few inches apart. Rachel felt the power of desire flow through her as she looked up into his burning, searching gaze. Automatically, she placed her hand against his chest and leaned upward. In all her life she had never been so bold or honest about her feelings. Maybe it was because she was home, and that gave her a dose of security and confidence she wouldn't have elsewhere. Whatever it was, Rachel followed her heart and pressed her lips to the hard line of his mouth.

She had expected nothing in return from Jim. The kiss was one to assuage the pain she saw banked in his eyes—the worry for his father and the war that was ongoing in his family. Somehow, she wanted to soothe and heal Jim. He had, after all, unselfishly saved her life, giving his blood so that she might live. She told her frightened heart that this was her reason for kissing him.

As Rachel's soft lips touched his mouth, something wild and primal exploded within Jim. He reached out and captured her against him. For an instant, as if in shock, she stiffened. And then, just as quickly, she melted against him like a stream flowing gently against hard rock. Her kiss was unexpected. Beautiful. Necessary. He opened his mouth and melded her lips more fully against his. Framing her face with his hands, he breathed her sweet breath deep into his lungs. The knots in his gut, the worry over what was waiting for him when he got home tonight, miraculously dissolved. She tasted of sweet, honeyed coffee, of the spicy perfume she'd put on earlier for the wedding. Her mouth was pliant, giving and taking. He ran his tongue across her lower lip and felt her tremble like a leaf in a storm beneath his tentative exploration.

How long had it been since he'd had a woman he wanted to love? Too long, his lonely heart cried out. Too long. His craving for her warmth, compassion and care overrode his normal control mechanisms. Hungrily, Jim captured Rachel more fully against him. Her arms slid around his shoulders and he felt good and strong and needed once again. Just caressing the soft firmness of her cheek, his fingers trailing across her temple into the softness of her hairline, made him hot and burning all over. He felt her quiver as he grazed the outside curve of her breast, felt her melting even more into his arms, into his searching mouth as it slid wetly across her giving lips. He was a starving thief and he needed her. Every part and cell of her. His pulse pounded through him, the pain in his lower body building to an excruciating level.

Rachel spun mindlessly, enjoying the texture of his searching mouth as it skimmed and cajoled, his hands framing her face, his hard body pressing her against the door. She felt him trembling, felt his arousal against her lower body, and a sweet, hot ache filled her. It would be so easy to surrender to Jim in all ways. So easy! Her heart, however, was reminding her of the last time she'd given herself away. Fear began to encroach upon her joy. Fear ate away at the hot yearning of her body, her burning need for Jim.

"No…"

Jim heard Rachel whisper the word. Easing away from her lips, which were now wet and soft from his onslaught, he opened his eyes and looked down at her. Though her eyes were barely opened, he saw the need in them. And the fear. Why? Had he hurt her? Instantly, he pulled back. The tears in her eyes stunned him. He *had* hurt her! *Damn!* He felt her hands pressing against his chest, pushing him away. She swayed unsteadily and he cupped her shoulders. Breathing erratically, he held her gently. She lifted her hand to touch her glistening lips. A deep flush covered her cheeks and she refused to look up at him.

Angry with himself for placing his own selfish needs before hers, he rasped, "I'm sorry, Rachel...."

Still spinning from the power of his kiss, Rachel couldn't find the right words to reply. Her heart had opened and she'd felt the power of her feelings toward Jim. Stunned in the aftermath of his unexpected response, she whispered, "No...." and then she couldn't say anything else. Rocking between the past and the present, she closed her eyes and leaned against the door.

"I shouldn't have done it," Jim said thickly. "I took advantage.... I'm sorry, Rachel...." Then he opened the door and disappeared into the dark, cold night.

Rachel was unable to protest Jim's sudden departure. She could only press her hand against her wildly beating heart and try to catch her breath. One kiss! Just one kiss had made her knees feel like jelly! Her heart had opened up like a flower, greedy for love, and she was left speechless in the wake of his branding kiss. When had *any* man ever made her feel like that? At the sound of the engine of a pickup in the distance, her eyes flew open. She forced herself to go out to the front porch. Wanting to shout at Jim, Rachel realized it was too late. He was already on the road leading away from the ranch, away from her.

She stood on the porch, the light surrounding her, the chill making her wrap her arms around herself. A few snowflakes twirled lazily down out of an ebony sky as she watched Jim drive up and out of the valley, the headlights stabbing the darkness. What had she done? Was she crazy? Sighing raggedly, she turned on her heel and went back into the ranch house.

As she quietly shut the huge oak door, she felt trembly inside. Her mouth throbbed with the stamp of Jim's kiss and she could still taste him on her lips. Moving slowly to the couch, she sat down before she fell down, her knees still weak in the aftermath of that explosive, unexpected joining. Hiding her face in her hands, Rachel wondered what was wrong with her. She couldn't risk getting involved again. She couldn't stand the possible loss; remembered how badly things had ended the last time—all the fears that had kept her from happiness before threatened to ruin her relationship again. But Jim was so compelling she ached to have him, explore him and know him on every level. He was so unlike the rest of his family. He was a decent human being, a man struggling to do the right thing not only for himself, but for his misguided, dysfunctional family. With a sigh, she raised her head and stared into the bright flames of the fire. Remembering the hurt in his eyes when she'd stopped the kiss, she knew he didn't know why she'd called things to a halt. He probably thought it had to do with him, but it hadn't. Somehow, Rachel knew she had to see him, to tell him the truth, so that Jim didn't take the guilt that wasn't his.

Worriedly, Rachel sat there, knowing that he would be driving home to a nasty situation. Earlier, she'd seen the anguish in his eyes over his family. Taking a pillow, she pressed it against her torso, her arms wrapped around it. How she ached to have Jim against her once again! Yet a niggling voice reminded her that he had a dangerous job as an EMT. He went out on calls with the firefighters. Anything could happen to him, and he could die, just like… Rachel shut off the flow of her thoughts. Oh, why did she have such an overactive imagination? She sighed, wishing she had handled things better between her and Jim. He probably felt bad enough about her pushing him away in the middle of their wonderful, melting kiss. Now he was going to be facing a very angry father because he had been here, on Donovan property. Closing her eyes, Rachel released another ragged sigh, wanting somehow to protect Jim. But there was nothing she could do for him right now. Absolutely nothing.

"Just where the hell have you been?" Frank Cunningham snarled, wheeling his chair into the living room as Jim entered the ranch house at 9:00 p.m.

Trying to quell his ragged emotions, Jim quietly shut the door. He turned and faced his father. The hatred in Frank's eyes slapped at him. Jim stood in silence, his hands at his side, waiting for the tirade he knew was coming. Glancing over at the kitchen entrance, he saw Bo and Chet standing on alert. Bo had a smirk on his face and Chet looked drunker than hell. Inhaling deeply, Jim could smell the odor of whiskey in the air. What had they been doing? Plying their father with liquor all night? Feeding his fury? Playing on his self-righteous belief that Jim had transgressed and committed an unpardonable sin by spending time at the Donovans? Placing a hold on his building anger toward his two manipulative brothers, Jim calmly met his father's furious look.

"You knew where I was. I called you at five-thirty and told you I wouldn't be home for dinner."

Frank glared up at him. His long, weather-beaten fingers opened and closed like claws around the arms of the chair he was imprisoned in. "Damn you, Jim.

You know better! I've begged you not to consort with those Donovan girls."

Jim shrugged tensely out of his coat. "They aren't girls, father. They're grown women. Adults." He saw Bo grin a little as he leaned against the door, a glass of liquor in his long fingers. "And you know drinking whiskey isn't good for your diabetes."

"You don't care!" Frank retorted explosively. "I drank because you went over there!"

"That's crap," Jim snarled back. "I'm not responsible for what you do. I'm responsible for myself. You're not going to push that kind of blame on me. Guilt might have worked when we were kids growing up, Father, but it doesn't cut it now." His nostrils quivered as he tried to withhold his anger. He saw his father's face grow stormy and tried to shield himself against what would come next. A part of him was so tired of trying to make things better around here. He'd been home nearly a year, and nothing had changed except that he was the scapegoat for the three of them now—just as he had been as a kid growing up after their mother's death.

"Word games!" Frank declared. He wiped the back of his mouth with a trembling hand. "You aren't one of us. You are deliberately going over to the Donovan place and consorting with them to get at me!"

Jim raised his gaze to Bo. "Who told you that, Father? Did Bo?"

Bo's grin disappeared. He stood up straight, tense.

Frank waved his hand in a cutting motion. "Bo and Chet are my eyes and ears, since I can't get around like I used to. You're sweet on Rachel Donovan, aren't you?"

Bo and Chet were both smiling now. Anger shredded Jim's composure as he held his father's accusing gaze.

"My private life is none of your—or their—business." He turned and walked down the hall toward his bedroom.

"You go out with her," Frank thundered down the hall, "and I'll disown you! Only this time for good, damn you!"

Jim shut the door to his bedroom, his only refuge. In disgust, he hung up his suit coat and looped the tie over the hangar. Breathing hard, he realized his hands were shaking—with fury. It was obvious that Bo and Chet had plied their father with whiskey, nursing all his anger and making him even more furious. Sitting down on the edge of his old brass bed, which creaked with his sudden weight, Jim slipped off his cowboy boots. Beginning at noon tomorrow, he was on duty for the next forty-eight hours. At least he'd be out of here and away from his father's simmering, scalding anger, his constant sniping and glares over his youngest son's latest transgression.

Undressing, Jim went to the bathroom across the hall and took a long, hot shower. He could hear the three men talking in the living room. Without even bothering to try and listen, Jim was sure it was about him. He wanted to say to hell with them, but it wasn't that easy. As he soaped down beneath the hot, massaging streams of water, his heart, his mind, revolved back to Rachel, to the kiss she'd initiated with him. He hadn't expected it. So why had she suddenly pushed him away? He didn't want to think it was because his last name was Cunningham. That would hurt more than anything else. Yet if he tried to see her when he got off duty, his family would damn him because she was a Donovan.

Scrubbing his hair, he wondered how serious Frank

was about disowning him. The first time his father had spoken those words to him, when he was eighteen, Jim had felt as if a huge, black hole had opened up and swallowed him. He'd taken his father's words seriously and he'd left for over a decade, attempting to remake his life. Frank had asked him to come home for Christmas—and that was all.

Snorting softly, Jim shut off the shower. He opened the door, grabbed a soft yellow towel and stepped out. He knew Frank would follow through on his threat to kick him out of his life—again. This time Jim was really worried, because neither Bo nor Chet would make sure Frank took his meds for his diabetic condition. If Jim wasn't around on a daily basis to see to that, his father's health would seriously decline in a very short time. He didn't want his father to die. But he didn't want to lose Rachel, either.

Rubbing his face, he drew in a ragged breath. Yes, he liked her—one helluva lot. Too much. How did a man stop his heart from feeling? From wanting? Rachel fit every part of him and he knew it. He sensed it. Could he give her up so that his father could live? What the hell was he going to do?

Chapter 7

"Dammit all to hell," Chet shouted as he entered the ranch house. He jerked off his Stetson and slammed the door behind him. Dressed in a sheepskin coat, red muffler and thick, protective leather gloves, he headed toward his father, who had just wheeled into the living room.

Jim was rubbing his hands in the warmth of the huge, open fireplace at one end of the living room when Chet stormed in. His older brother had a glazed look in his eyes, a two-day beard on his cheeks and an agitated expression on his face.

"Pa, that dammed cougar has killed another of our cows up in the north pasture!" Chet growled, throwing his coat and gloves on the leather couch. "Half of her is missing. She was pregnant, too."

Frank frowned, stopped his wheelchair near the fireplace where Jim was standing. "We've lost a cow every two weeks for the last four months this way," he said, running his long, large-knuckled hands through his thick white hair.

As Jim turned to warm his back, Chet joined them at the fireplace, opening his own cold hands toward the flames. Chet's eyes were red and Jim could smell liquor on his breath. His brother was drinking like Frank used to drink before contracting diabetes, he realized with concern. Jim sighed. The last three days, since he'd come back from the Donovan wedding party, things had been tense around the house. He was glad his forty-eight hours of duty had begun shortly thereafter, keeping him on call for two days with the ambulance and allowing him to eat and sleep at the fire station down at Sedona. Luckily, things had been quiet, and he'd been able to settle down from the last major confrontation with his father.

"Have you seen the spoor, Chet?" Jim asked.

"Well, shore I have!" he said, wiping his running nose with the back of his flannel sleeve. "Got spoor all over the place. There's about a foot of snow up there. The tracks are good this time."

"We need to get a hunting party together," Frank growled at them. "I'm tired of losing a beef every other week to this cat."

"Humph, we're losin' two of 'em, Pa. That cat's smart—picks on two for one."

"You were always good at hunting cougar," Frank said, looking up at Jim. "Why don't you drive up there and see what you can find out? Arrange a hunting party?"

Jim was relieved to have something to do outside the house. Usually he rode fence line, did repairs and helped out wherever he could with ranching duties. His father had ten wranglers who did most of the hard work, but Jim always looked for ways to stay out of the house when he was home between his bouts of duty at the fire station.

"Okay. How's the road back into that north pasture, Chet?"

"Pretty solid," he answered, rubbing his hands briskly. "The temps was around twenty degrees out there midday. Colder than hell. No snow, but cold. We need the snow for the water or we're going to have drought again," he muttered, his brows moving downward.

"I'll get out of my uniform and go check on it," Jim told his father.

With a brisk nod, Frank added, "You find that son of a bitch, you shoot it on sight, you hear me? I don't want any of that hearts and flower stuff you try to pull."

Jim ignored the cutting jab as he walked down the darkened hall to his bedroom. Moving his shoulders, he felt the tension in them ease a little. In his bedroom, he quickly shed his firefighter's uniform and climbed into a pair of thermal underwear, a well-worn set of Levi's, a dark blue flannel shirt and thick socks. As he sat on the bed, pulling on his cowboy boots, his mind—and if he were honest, his heart—drifted back to Rachel and that sweet, sweet kiss he'd shared with her. It had been three days since then.

He'd wanted to call her, but he hadn't. He was a coward. The way she'd pulled away from him, the fear in her eyes, had told him she didn't like what they'd shared. He felt rebuffed and hurt. Anyone would. She was a beautiful, desirable woman, and Jim was sure that now that she was home for good, every available male in Sedona would soon be tripping over themselves to ask her out. Shrugging into his sheepskin coat, he picked up the black Stetson that hung on one of the bedposts, and settled it on his head.

As he walked out into the living room, he saw Chet and his father talking. In another corner of the room was a huge, fifteen-foot-tall Christmas tree. It would be another lonely Christmas for the four of them. As he headed out the door, gloves in hand, he thought about Christmas over at the Donovan Ranch. In years past, they'd invited in the homeless and fed them a turkey dinner with all the trimmings. Odula, their mother, had coordinated such plans with the agencies around the county, and her bigheartedness was still remembered. Now her daughters were carrying on in her footsteps. Rachel had mentioned that her sisters would be coming back on Christmas Eve to help in the kitchen and to make that celebration happen once again.

Settling into the Dodge pickup, Jim looked around. The sky was a heavy, gunmetal gray, hanging low over the Rim country. It looked like it might snow. He hoped it would. Arizona high country desperately needed a huge snow this winter to fill the reservoirs so that the city of Phoenix would have enough water for the coming year. Hell, they needed groundwater to fill the aquifer below Sedona or they would lose thousands of head of cattle this spring. His father would have to sell some of his herd off cheap—probably at a loss—so that the cattle wouldn't die of starvation out on the desert range.

Driving over a cattle guard, Jim noticed the white snow lying like a clean blanket across the red, sandy desert and clay soil. He enjoyed his time out here alone. Off to his left, he saw a couple of wranglers on horseback in another pasture, moving a number of cows. His thoughts wandered as he drove and soon Rachel's soft face danced before his mind's eye. His hands tightened momentarily on the wheel. More than anything, Jim wanted to see Rachel again. He could use Christmas as an excuse to drop over and see her, apologize in person for kissing her unexpectedly. Though he knew he'd been out of line, his mouth tingled in memory of her lips skimming his. She'd been warm, soft and hungry. So why had she suddenly pushed away? Was it him? Was it the fact that he was a Cunningham? Jim thought so.

Ten miles down the winding, snow-smattered road, Jim saw the carcass in the distance. Braking, he eased up next to the partially eaten cow. The wind was blowing in fierce gusts down off the Rim and he pulled his hat down a little more tightly as he stepped out and walked around the front of the truck.

As he leaned down, he saw that the cow's throat was mangled, and he scowled, realizing the cat had killed the cow by grabbing her throat and suffocating her. There was evidence of a struggle, but little blood in the snow around her. Putting his hand on her, he found that she was frozen solid. The kill had to have occurred last night.

Easing up to his full height, he moved carefully around the carcass and found the spoor. Leaning down, his eyes narrowing, he studied them intently. The tracks moved north, back up the two-thousand-foot-high limestone and sandstone cliff above him. Somewhere up there the cat made his home.

Studying the carcass once again, Jim realized that though the cat had gutted her and eaten his fill, almost ninety percent of the animal was left intact and unmolested. That gave him an idea. Getting to his feet, he went back to the pickup, opened the door and picked up the mike on his radio to call the foreman, Randy Parker.

"Get a couple of the boys out here," Jim ordered when Randy answered, "to pick up this cow carcass. Put it in the back of a pickup and bring it to the homestead. When it gets there, let me know."

"Sure thing," Randy answered promptly.

Satisfied, Jim replaced the mike on the console. He smiled a little to himself. Yes, his plan would work—he hoped. Soon enough, he'd know if it was going to.

Rachel was in the kitchen, up to her wrists in mashed potatoes, when she heard a heavy knock at the front door. Expecting no one, she frowned. "I'm coming!" she called out, quickly rinsing her hands, grabbing a towel and running through the living room. It was December 23, and she had been working for three days solid preparing all the dishes for the homeless people's Christmas feast. Her sisters would be home tomorrow, to help with warming and serving the meal for thirty people the following day.

When she opened the door, her eyes widened enormously. "Jim!"

He stood there, hat in hand, a sheepish look on his face. "Hi, Rachel."

Stunned, she felt color race up her throat and into her face. How handsome he looked. His face was flushed, too, but more than likely it was from being outdoors in this freezing cold weather. "Hi…." she whispered. The memory of his meltingly hot kiss, which was never far from her heart or mind, burned through her. She saw his eyes narrow on her and she felt like he was looking through her.

"Come in, it's cold out there," she said apologetically, moving to one side.

"Uh...in a minute." He pointed to his truck, parked near the porch. "Listen, we had a cow killed last night by a cat. Ninety percent of it is still good meat. It's frozen and clean. I had some of our hands bring it down in a pickup. I brought it here, thinking that you might be able to use the meat for your meal for the homeless on Christmas Day."

His thoughtfulness touched her. "That's wonderful! I mean, I'm sorry a cougar killed your cow...but what a great idea."

Grinning a little, and relieved that she wasn't going to slam the door in his face, he nervously moved his felt hat between his gloved fingers. "Good. Look, I know you have a slaughter-freezing-and-packing area in that building over there. I'm not the world's best at carving and cutting, but with a couple of sharp knives, I can get the steaks, the roasts and things like that, in a couple of hours for you."

Rachel smiled a little. "Since we don't have any other hands around, I'd have to ask you to do it." She looked at him intently. "Are you *sure* you want to do that? It's an awful lot of work."

Shrugging, Jim said, "Want the truth?"

She saw the wry lift of one corner of his mouth. Joy surged through her. She was happy to see Jim again, thrilled that her display the other night hadn't chased him away permanently. "Always the truth," she answered softly.

Looking down at his muddy boots for a moment, Jim rasped, "I was looking for a way to get out of the house. My old man is on the warpath again and I didn't want to be under the same roof." He took a deep breath and then met and held her compassionate gaze. "More important, I wanted to come over here and apologize to you in person, and I had to find an excuse to do it."

Fierce heat flowed through Rachel. She saw the uncertainty in Jim's eyes and heard the sorrow in his voice. Pressing her hand against her heart, which pounded with happiness at his appearance, she stepped out onto the porch. The wind was cold and sharp.

"No," she whispered unsteadily, "you don't need to apologize for anything, Jim. It's me. I mean...when we kissed. It wasn't your fault." She looked away, her voice becoming low. "It was me...my past...."

Stymied, Jim knew this wasn't the time or place to question her response. Still, relief flooded through him. "I thought I'd overstepped my bounds with you," he said. "I wanted to come over and apologize."

Reaching out, Rachel gripped his lower arm, finding the thick sheepskin of his coat soft and warm. "I've got some ghosts from my past that still haunt me, Jim."

The desire to step forward and simply gather her slender form against him was nearly his undoing. His arm tingled where she'd briefly touched him. But when he saw her nervousness, he held himself in check, understood it. Managing a lopsided, boyish smile, he said, "Fair enough. Ghosts I can handle."

"I wish I could," Rachel said, rolling her eyes. "I'm not doing so well at it."

Settling his hat back on his head, he turned and pointed toward a building near the barn. "How about I get started on this carcass? I'll wrap the meat in butcher paper and put it in your freezer."

She nodded. "Fine. I'm up to my elbows in about

thirty gallons of mashed potatoes right now, or I'd come over to help you."

He held up his hand. "Tell you what." Looking at the watch on his dark-haired wrist, he said, "How about if I get done in time for dinner, I take you out to a restaurant? You're probably tired of cooking at this point and you deserve a break."

Thrilled, Rachel smiled. "I'd love that, Jim. What a wonderful idea! And I can fill you in on my new office, which I rented today!"

He saw the flush of happiness on her face. It made him feel good, and he smiled shyly. "Okay," he rasped, "it's a date. It's going to take me about four hours to carve up that beef." By then, it would be 7:00 p.m.

"That's about how much time I'll need to finish up in the kitchen." Rachel turned. "I've got sweet potatoes baking right now. Fifty of them! And then I've got to mash them up, mix in the brown sugar, top them with marshmallows and let them bake a little more."

"You're making me hungry!" he teased with a grin. How young Rachel looked at that moment. Not like a thirty-year-old homeopath, but like the girl with thick, long braids he remembered from junior high. Her eyes danced with gold flecks and he absorbed her happiness into his heart. The fact that Rachel would go to dinner with him made him feel like he was walking on air. "I'll come over here when I'm done?"

Rachel nodded. "Yes, and I'm sure you'll want to shower before we go."

"I'm going to have to." Now he was sorry he hadn't brought a change of clothes.

"Sam McGuire didn't take all his shirts with him

on his honeymoon. I'll bet he'd let you borrow a clean one," she hinted with a broadening smile.

"I'm not going to fight a good idea," Jim said. He turned and made his way off the porch. He didn't even feel the cold wind and snow as he headed back to his truck. Rachel was going to have dinner with him. Never had he expected that. The words, the invitation, had just slipped spontaneously out of his mouth. Suddenly, all the weight he carried on his shoulders disappeared. By 7:00 p.m. he was going to be with Rachel in an intimate, quiet place. Never had he looked forward to anything more than that. And Jim didn't give a damn what the locals might think.

Jim took Rachel to the Sun and Moon Restaurant. He liked this place because it was quiet, the service was unobtrusive and the huge, black-and-white leather booths surrounded them like a mother's embrace. They sat in a corner booth; no one could see them and the sense of privacy made him relax.

Rachel sat next to him, less than twelve inches away, in a simple burgundy velvet dress that hung to her ankles. It sported a scoop neck and formfitting long sleeves, and she wore a simple amethyst pendant and matching earrings. Her hair, thick and slightly curly, hung well below her shoulders, framing her face and accenting her full lips and glorious, forest green eyes.

Jim had taken a hot shower and borrowed one of Sam's white, long-sleeved work shirts. Jim had wanted to shave but couldn't, so knew he had a dark shadow on his face. Rachel didn't seem to care about that, however.

After the waitress gave them glasses of water and

cups of mocha latte, she left so they could look over the menu.

"That burgundy dress looks good on you," Jim said, complimenting Rachel.

She touched the sleeve of her nubby velvet dress. "Thanks. It's warm and I feel very feminine in this. I bought it over in England many years ago. It's like a good friend. I can't bear to part with it." She liked the burning look in his eyes—it made her feel desirable. But she was scared, too, though. Jim was being every bit the gentleman. She hungered for his quiet, steady male energy. His quick wit always engaged her more serious side and he never failed to make her laugh.

"I'm glad we have this time with each other," he told her as he laid the menu aside. "I'd like to hear about your years over in England. What you did. What it was like to live in a foreign country."

She smiled a little and sipped the frothy mocha latte, which was topped with whipped cream and cinnamon sprinkles. "First I want to hear how we came by this gift of beef you brought us." She set her cup aside.

Jim opened his hands. "It's the strangest thing, Rachel. For the last four months, about once every two weeks, a cat's been coming down off the Rim and killing one of the cows. My father's upset about it and he wants me to put together a hunting party and kill it."

"This isn't the first time we've had a cougar kill stock," Rachel said.

"That's true." He frowned and glanced at her. Even in the shadows, nothing could mar Rachel's beauty. He saw Odula's face in hers, those wide-set eyes, the broadness of her cheekbones. "But I'm not sure it's a cougar."

"What?"

Shaking his head, Jim muttered, "I saw the spoor for myself earlier today. We finally got enough snow up there so we had some good imprints of the cat's paws." He held up his hand. "I know cougar." Smiling slighty, he said, "My friends call me Cougar. I got that name when I was a teenager because I tracked down one of the largest cougars in the state. He had been killing off our stock for nearly a year before my father let me track him for days on end up in the Rim country." Scowling, he continued, "I didn't like killing him. In fact, after I did it, I swore I'd never kill another one. He was a magnificent animal."

"I saw the other night that you wear a leather thong around your neck," Rachel noted, gesturing toward the open collar of his shirt, which revealed not only the thong, but strands of the dark hair of his upper chest.

Jim pulled up the thong, revealing a huge cougar claw set in a sterling silver cap and a small medicine bag. "Yeah, my father had me take one of the claws to a Navajo silversmith. He said I should wear it. My mother's uncle, who used to come and visit us as kids, was a full-blood Apache medicine man. He told me that the spirit of that cougar now lived in me."

"Makes sense."

"Maybe to those of us who are part Indian," he agreed.

Rachel smiled and gazed at the fearsome claw. It was a good inch in length. She shivered as she thought of the power of such a cougar. "How old were you when you hunted that cougar?"

"Fifteen. And I was scared." Jim chuckled as he closed his hands around the latte. "Scared spitless, actually. My father sent me out alone with a 30.06 rifle, my horse and five days' worth of food. He told me to find the cougar and kill it."

"Your father had a lot of faith in you."

"Back then," Jim said wistfully. "Maybe too much." He gave her a wry look. "If I had a fifteen-year-old kid, I wouldn't be sending him out into the Rim country by himself. I'd want to be there with him, to protect him."

"Maybe your father knew you could handle the situation?"

Shrugging painfully, Jim sipped the latte. "Maybe." He wanted to get off the topic of his sordid past. "That spoor I saw today?"

"Yes?"

"I'm sure it wasn't a cougar's."

Rachel stared at him, her cup halfway to her lips. "What then?"

"I don't know *what* it is, but I know it's not what my father thinks. I took some photos of the spoor, measured it and faxed copies of everything to a friend of mine who works for the fish and game department. He'll make some inquiries and maybe I can find out what it really is."

Setting the cup down, Rachel stared at him. "This is going to sound silly, but I had a dream the other night after we…kissed…."

"At least it wasn't a nightmare."

She smiled a little nervously. "No…it wasn't, Jim. It never would be." She saw the strain in his features diminish a little.

"What about this dream you had?"

"Being part Indian, you know how we put great stock in our dreams?"

"Sure," he murmured. "My uncle Bradford taught all of us boys the power of dreams and dreaming." Jim held her gaze. Reaching out, he slipped his hand over hers, to soothe her nervousness. "So, tell me about this dream you had."

Rachel sighed. His hand was warm and strong. "My mother, Odula, was a great dreamer. Like your uncle, she taught us that dreaming was very important. That our dreams were symbols trying to talk to us. Of course," she whispered, amused, "the big trick was figuring out what the dream symbology meant."

"No kidding," Jim chortled. He liked the fact that Rachel was allowing him to hold her hand. He didn't care who saw them. And he didn't care what gossip got back to his father. For the first time, Jim felt hopeful that his father wouldn't disown him again. Frank Cunningham was too old, too frail and in poor health. Jim was hoping that time had healed some of the old wounds between them and that his father would accept that Rachel was a very necessary part of his life.

"Well," Rachel said tentatively, "I was riding up in the Rim country on horseback. I was alone. I was looking for something—someone… I'm not sure. It was a winter day, and it was cold and I was freezing. I was in this red sandstone canyon. As we rode to the end of it, it turned out to be a box canyon. I was really disappointed and I felt fear. A lot of fear. I was looking around for something. My horse was nervous, too. Then I heard this noise. My horse jumped sideways, dumping me in the snow. When I got to my feet, the horse was galloping off into the distance. I felt this incredible power surround me, like invisible arms embracing me. I looked up…" she held his intense gaze "…and you won't believe what I saw."

"Try me. I'm open to anything."

"That same jaguar that caused me to wreck the car,

Jim." Leaning back, Rachel felt his fingers tighten slightly around her hand. "The jaguar was there, no more than twenty feet away from me. Only this time, I realized a lot more. I knew the jaguar was a she, not a he. And I saw that she was in front of a cave, which she had made into a lair. She was just standing there and looking at me. I was scared, but I didn't feel like she was going to attack me or anything."

"Interesting," Jim murmured. "Then what happened?" Noting the awe in Rachel's eyes as she spoke, he knew her story was more than just a dream; he sensed it.

"I felt as if I were in some sort of silent communication with her. I *felt* it here, in my heart. I know how strange that sounds, but I sensed no danger while I was with her. I could feel her thoughts, her emotions. It was weird."

"Sort of like..." he searched for the right words "...mental telepathy?"

"Why, yes!" Rachel stared at him. "Have you been dreaming about this jaguar, too?"

He grinned a little and shook his head. "No, but when I finally met and confronted that big male cougar, we stared at one another for a long moment before I fired the gun and killed him. I *felt* him. I felt his thoughts and emotions. It was strange. Unsettling. After I shot him, I sank to my knees and I cried. I felt terrible about killing him. I knew I'd done something very wrong. Looking back on it, if I had it to do all over again, I wouldn't have killed him. I'd have let him escape."

"But then your father, who's famous for his hunting parties, would have gotten a bunch of men together and hunted him down and treed him with dogs." Rachel shook her head. "No, Jim, you gave him an honorable death compared to what your father would have done. He'd have wounded the cat, and then, when the cougar dropped from the tree, he'd have let his hounds tear him apart." Grimly, she saw the pain in Jim's eyes and she tightened her fingers around his hand. "Mom always said that if we prayed for the spirit of the animal, and asked for it to be released over the rainbow bridge, that made things right."

He snorted softly. "I did that. I went over to the cougar, held him in my skinny arms and cried my heart out. He was a magnificent animal, Rachel. He knew I was going to kill him and he just stood there looking at me with those big yellow eyes. I swear to this day that I felt embraced by this powerful sense of love from him. I *felt* it."

"Interesting," she murmured, "because in my dream about this jaguar, I felt embraced by her love, too."

"Was that the end of your dream?"

"No," she said. "I saw the jaguar begin to change."

"Change?"

Rachel pulled her hand from his. She didn't want to, but she saw the waitress was taking an order at the next table and knew she'd soon come to take theirs. "Change as in shape shifting. You told me last time we spoke that you knew something about that."

"A little. My uncle, the Apache medicine man, said that he was a shape-shifter. He said that he could change from a man into a hawk and fly anywhere he wanted, that he could see things all over the world."

"The Navajo have their skin-walkers," Rachel said in agreement, "sorcerers who change into coyotes and stalk the poor Navajo who are caught out after dark."

"That's the nasty side of shape shifting," Jim said.

"My uncle was a good man, and he said he used this power and ability to help heal people."

"My mother told us many stories of shape-shifters among her people, too. But this jaguar, Jim, changed into a woman!" Her voice lowered with awe. "She was an incredibly beautiful woman. Her skin was a golden color. She had long black hair and these incredible green eyes. You know how when leaves come out on a tree in early spring they're that pale green color?"

He nodded. "Sure."

"Her eyes were like that. And what's even more strange, she wore Army camouflage pants, black military boots, an olive green, sleeveless T-shirt. Across her shoulders were bandoliers of ammunition. I kid you not! Isn't that a wild dream?"

He agreed. "Did she say anything to you?"

"Not verbally, no. She stood there and I could see her black boots shifting and changing back into the feet of the jaguar. She was almost like an apparition. I was so stunned by her powerful presence that I just stood there, too, my mouth hanging open." Rachel laughed. "I felt her looking *through* me. I felt as if she were looking for someone. But it wasn't me. I could feel her probing me mentally. This woman was very powerful, Jim. I'm sure she was a medicine woman. Maybe from South America. Then I saw her change back into the jaguar. And she was gone!" She snapped her fingers. "Just like that. Into thin air."

"What happened next?"

"I woke up." Rachel sighed. "I got up, made myself some hot tea and sat out in the living room next to the fireplace, trying to feel my way through the dream.

You had kissed me hours before. I was wondering if my dream was somehow linked to that, to you."

Shrugging, Jim murmured, "I don't know. Maybe my friend at the fish and game department will shed some light on that spoor print. Maybe it's from a jaguar." He gauged her steadily. "Maybe what you saw on the highway that day was real, and not a hallucination."

Rachel gave a little laugh. "It looked pretty physical and real to me. *If* it is a jaguar, what are you going to do?"

Grimly, Jim said, "Number one, I'm not going to kill it. Number two, I'll enlist the help of the fish and game department to track the cat, locate its lair and then lay a trap to harmlessly capture it. Then they can take the cat out of the area, like they do the black bears that get too close to civilization."

Rachel felt happiness over his decision. "That's wonderful. If it is a jaguar, it would be a crying shame to shoot her."

He couldn't agree more. The waitress came to their table then, and once they gave her their orders, Jim folded his hands in front of him and caught Rachel's sparkling gaze. Gathering up his courage, he asked, "Could you use another hand on Christmas Day to help feed the homeless? Things are pretty tense around home. I'll spend Christmas morning with my father and brothers, but around noon, I want to be elsewhere."

"You don't have to work at the fire department?" Rachel's heart picked up in beat. More than anything, she'd love to have Jim's company. Kate would have Sam at her side, and Jessica would be working with Dan. It would be wonderful to have Jim with her. She knew Kate was settling her differences with Jim, so it wouldn't cause a lot of tension among them. Never had Rachel wanted anything more than to spend Christmas with Jim.

"I have the next three days off," he said. He saw hope burning brightly in Rachel's eyes. The genuine happiness in her expression made him feel strong and very sure of himself. "So, you can stand for me to be underfoot for part of Christmas Day?"

Clapping her hands enthusiastically, Rachel whispered, "Oh, yes. I'd love to have you with us!"

Moving the cup of latte in his hands, Jim nodded. "Good," he rasped. He didn't add that he'd catch hell for this decision. His father would explode in a rage. Bo and Chet would both ride him mercilessly about it. Well, Jim didn't care. All his life, he'd try to follow his heart and not his head. His heart had led him into wildfire fighting for nearly ten years. And then it had led him home, into a cauldron of boiling strife with his family. Now it whispered that with Rachel was where he longed to be.

As he saw the gold flecks in her eyes, he wanted to kiss her again—only this time he wanted to kiss her senseless and lose himself completely in her. She was a woman of the earth, no question. He was glad they shared a Native American background. They spoke the same language about the invisible realms, the world of spirit and the unseen. Jim never believed in accidents; he felt that everything, no matter what it was, had a purpose, a reason for happening. And the best thing in his life was occurring right now.

A powerful emotion moved through him, rocking him to the core. Could it be love? Studying Rachel as she delicately sipped her latte, her slender fingers wrapped around the cup, he smiled to himself. There was no doubt he loved her. The real question was did she love him? Could she? Or would she never be able to because she was a Donovan and he a Cunningham? Would Rachel always push him away, because of all the old baggage and scars between their two families?

Jim had no answers. Only questions that ate at him, gnawed away at the burgeoning love he felt toward Rachel. He knew he had to take it a day at a time with her. He had to let her adjust to her new life here in Sedona. He had to use that Apache patience of his and slow down. Let her set the pace so she would be comfortable with him. Only then, Jim hoped, over time, she would grow to love him, and want him in her life as much as he wanted her.

Chapter 8

Rachel tried to appear unaffected by the fact that Jim Cunningham was in the kitchen of their home on Christmas Day. Both Kate and Jessica kept grinning hugely with those Cheshirelike smiles they always gave her when they knew something she didn't. Jim had arrived promptly at noon and set to work in the kitchen with the two men while the Donovan sisters served the sumptuous meal to thirty homeless people in their huge living room.

Christmas music played softly in the background and there was a roaring blaze in the fireplace. The tall timbers were wreathed in fresh pine boughs, and the noise of people laughing, talking and sharing filled the air. Rachel had never felt so happy as she passed from one table to another with coffeepot in hand, refilling cups. Among the people who had come were several families with children. Kate and Sam had gone to stores in Flagstaff and asked for donations of presents for the children. They'd spent part of their honeymoon collecting the gifts and then wrapping them.

Each child had a gift beside his or her plate. Each family would receive a sizable portion of Jim's beef to take back to the shelter where they were living. Jessica and Dan had worked with the various county agencies to see that those who had nowhere to go would have a roof over their head for the winter. Yes, this was what Christmas was *really* all about. And it was a tradition their generous, loving mother had started. It brought tears to Rachel's eyes to know that Odula's spirit still flowed strongly through them. Like their mother, the three daughters felt this was the way to gift humanity during this very special season.

The delight on the children's faces always touched Rachel deeply. For some odd reason, whenever she looked at a tiny baby in the arms of its mother, she thought of Jim. She felt a warm feeling in her lower body, and the errant, surprising thought of what it might be like to have Jim's baby flowed deliciously through her. With that thought, Rachel almost stumbled and fell on a rug that had been rolled to one side. She felt her face suffuse with heat. When she went back to the kitchen to refill her coffee urn, she avoided the look that Jim gave her as he busily carved up one of the many turkeys. Dan was spooning up mash potatoes, gravy and stuffing onto each plate that was passed down the line. Sam added cranberries, Waldorf salad and candied yams topped with browned marshmallows.

Rachel wished for some quiet time alone with Jim. When he'd arrived, they were already in full swing with the start of the dinner. The kiss they'd shared, the intimacy of their last meal together, all came back to her. She found herself wanting to kiss him again. And again. Oh, how she wished her past would disappear! If she could somehow move it aside.... There was no question she desired Jim. And she knew she wanted to pursue some kind of relationship with him. But fear was stopping her. And it was giving him mixed signals. Sighing, Rachel looked forward to the evening, when things would quiet down and they would at last be alone. She had her own house at the ranch, and she could invite Jim over for coffee later and they could talk.

"Heck of a day," Jim said, sipping coffee at Rachel's kitchen table. Her house, which had been built many years ago by Kelly Donovan, was smaller than the other two he'd built for his daughters, but it was intimate and Jim liked that. Although Rachel had only recently moved into it, he could see her feminine touches to the pale pink kitchen. There were some pots on the windowsill above the sink where she had planted some parsley, chives and basil. The table was covered with a creamy lace cloth—from England, she'd told him.

"Wasn't it though?" Rachel moved from the stove, bringing her coffee with her. She felt nervous and ruffled as she looked at Jim. How handsome he was in his dark brown slacks, white cowboy shirt and bolo tie made of a cougar's head with a turquoise inset for the eye. His sleeves were rolled up from all the kitchen duty, the dark hair on his arms bringing out the deep gold color of his weathered skin.

"When you came in at noon, you looked pretty stressed out," Rachel said, sitting down. Their elbows nearly touched at the oval table. She liked sitting close to him.

With a shrug, Jim nodded. "Family squabble just before I left," he muttered.

"Your father didn't want you to come over here, right?" She saw the shadowy pain in his eyes as he avoided her direct look.

"Yeah, you could say that." Jim sipped his coffee grimly.

"And you have dark shadows under your eyes."

He grinned a little and looked at her. "You don't miss much, do you?"

"I'm trained to observe," Rachel teased. Placing her hands around the fine, bone china cup, she lost her smile. "Why do you stay at your father's house if it's so hard on you?"

Pain serrated Jim. His brows dipped. "I don't know anymore," he rasped. "I thought I could help make a difference, turn the family around, but no one wants to change. They want me to change into one of them and I'm not going to do it."

"In homeopathy, it's known as an obstacle to cure," Rachel said. "They don't want to change their dysfunctional way of living because it suits their purposes to stay that way." She gave Jim a tender look. "You wanted to be healthy, not dysfunctional, so you left as soon as you could and you stayed away until just recently. I've treated thousands of people over the years and I know from experience that if they don't want to leave the job, the spouse or the family that is causing them to remain sick or unhealthy, there's little I, a homeopathic remedy or anything else can do about it."

"Sort of like the old saying you can lead a horse to water but you can't make her drink?"

"Yes," Rachel replied with a sigh, trying to give him a smile. Jim looked exhausted. She had seen that look before when a person was tired to the bones with a struggle they were losing, not winning. She opened her hands tentatively. "So, what are your options? Could you move out and maybe see your father, whom you're worried about, from time to time?"

Rearing back on two legs of the chair, Jim gazed over at her. The lamp above the table softly lit Rachel's features. He was hungry for her compassion, her understanding of the circumstances that had him caught like a vise. He valued her insights, which were wise and deep. "I've been thinking about that," he admitted reluctantly. "Only, who will make sure my father takes his meds twice daily?"

"How long has your father had diabetes?"

"Ten years."

"And how did he survive that long without you being there to make sure he took his meds?"

Wryly, he studied her in the ensuing silence. "Touché."

"Could you find a house to rent in Sedona?"

"Maybe," he said. "I'll just have to see how it goes."

"What was the fight about before you left to come to our ranch?"

His mouth quirked. "Chet's all up in arms about this cat that killed the beef. He's whipping up Bo and my father into forming a hunting party tomorrow to go track the cat, tree it and kill it. I argued not to do that, to call the fish and game department and work with them to trap the cat and take it somewhere else, into a less-populated area."

Rachel felt sudden fear grip her heart. "And what did they decide?"

Easing the chair down on all four legs, Jim muttered, "They're going out tomorrow morning to hunt the cat down and kill it."

She gasped. "No!"

"I'm with you on this." Again, he studied her. "After hearing your dream, and talking more to Jessica today, I'm convinced it's a jaguar up there on the Rim, not a cougar, Rachel. Jessica's sure that it's a shape-shifter. She's worried that it's Moyra, her friend, coming to check on her, on the family." Shrugging, he eased out of the chair and stood up, coffee cup in hand. "I don't know if I believe her or not, but it really doesn't matter. I don't care if it's a cougar or a jaguar—I don't want to see it treed and killed." Leaning his hip against the counter, he asked, "Want to come with me tomorrow to track the cat? I've got the day off. I called Bob Granby, my friend from the fish and game department, and told him I was going to ride out early tomorrow, get a jump on my brothers' plan, and try to find the cat first. I'll be carrying a walkie-talkie with me. Bob promised that if I could locate the cat, he'd meet us, establish jurisdiction and make my family stop the hunt. Then we could lay out bait to lure the cat into a humane device."

Her heartbeat soared. "Yes, I'd love to go with you." Then she laughed a little. "I haven't thrown a leg over a horse in a long time, but that's okay. You know, Sam and Dan are good trackers, too. They could help."

Jim shook his head. "No. If my brothers saw them, they'd probably open fire on them. Besides, this is on

Cunningham land and they don't want them trespassing. I can't risk a confrontation, Rachel."

"What about me? What if they see me with you?"

"That's a little different. They don't get riled with a woman. They will with a man, though. Some of the Old West ethics are still alive and well in them." He smiled briefly.

"Just tell me your plans," she said, "and I'll come with you."

"If you can pack us a lunch and dinner, I hope to be able to track the cat and locate it by no later than tomorrow afternoon. We'll have a two-hour head start on their hunting party. If we could use Donovan horses, that would keep what I'm doing a secret."

Rachel felt her stomach knot a little. "What will your brothers do if they find out you've beat them to the punch on this?"

"Scream bloody blue murder, but that's all." Jim chuckled. "They've had enough tangles with the law of late. Neither of them wants to see the inside of a county jail again for a long time. Once they know I'm working for the fish and game department, they'll slink off."

Sighing, Rachel nodded. "Okay, I'll let Kate know. I'm sure Sam will make sure we've got two excellent trail and hunting horses. I'll pack our food."

Jim nodded, then looked at his watch. It was nearly midnight. "I need to get going," he said reluctantly, not wanting to leave. Setting the coffee cup on the table, he reached into his back pocket and brought out a small, wrapped gift. "It's not much, but I wanted to give you something for Christmas."

Touched, Rachel took the gift, thrilling as their fingers met. "Why, thank you! I didn't expect anything…."

She removed the bright red ribbon and the gold foil wrapping.

Jim felt nervous. Settling his hands on his hips, he watched the joy cross Rachel's face. Her eyes, her beautiful forest green eyes, sparkled. It made him feel good. Better than he'd felt all day. Would Rachel like his gift? He hadn't had much time to find something in Sedona that he thought she might want. He hoped she'd like it at least.

Rachel gasped as the paper fell away. Inside were two combs for her hair. They were made of tortoise shell, and each one had twelve tiny, rounded beads of turquoise across the top. Sliding her fingers over them, she saw they were obviously well crafted.

"These are beautiful," she whispered, as she gazed up at his shadowed, worried features. "I've never seen anything like them…."

Shyly, Jim murmured, "I have a Navajo silversmith friend, and I went over to his house yesterday. You have such beautiful hair," he continued, gesturing toward her head. "And I knew he was working on a new design with hair combs." He smiled a little as he saw that she truly did treasure his gift. "When I saw these, I knew they belonged to you."

Without a word, Rachel got up and threw her arms around his neck, pressing herself to him. "Thank you," she quavered near his ear. She felt Jim tense for a moment, as if surprised, and then his arms flowed around her, holding her tightly, his hand sliding up her spine. Heat flared in her and she lifted her face from his shoulder to look up at him. His eyes were hooded and burning—with desire. Breathless and scared, Rachel felt the old fear coming up. She didn't care. She was in the arms of a man who was strong and good and caring. Although his gift was small, it was thoughtful and it touched her like little else could.

Closing her eyes, Rachel knew he was going to kiss her. Nothing had ever seemed so right! As her lips parted, she felt the powerful stamp of his mouth settle firmly upon hers and she surrendered completely to him, to his strong, caring arms and to the heat that exploded violently within her. His lips were cajoling and skimmed hers teasingly at first. She felt his moist breath against her cheek. The taste of coffee was present on his lips. His beard scraped her softer skin, sending wild tingles through her. His fingers moved upward, following the line of her torso, barely brushing the curvature of her firm breasts.

More heat built within her and she felt an ache between her thighs. How long had it been since she'd made love? Far too long. Her body screamed out for Jim's continued touch, for his hands to cup her breasts more fully, to touch and tease them. Instead, he slid his hand across her shoulders, up the slender expanse of her neck to frame her face. He angled her jaw slightly so that he could have more contact with her mouth. His tongue trailed a languid pattern of fire across her lower lip. She quivered violently. He groaned. Their breaths mingled, hot, wild and swift. Her heart pounded in her breast as his mouth settled firmly over hers. She lost herself in the power of him as a man, in the cajoling tenderness he bestowed upon her, the give and take of his mouth upon hers and the sweet, hot wetness that was created between them.

Slowly, ever so slowly, Jim eased away from her mouth. Rachel wanted to cry out that she wanted more of him, of his touch. The dark gleam in his eyes showed the primal side of him, and she shivered out of need, wondering what it would be like to go all the way with Jim. She felt his barely leashed control, felt it in the tremble of his hands along the sides of her face as he continued to hungrily press her into himself in those fragile moments strung between them.

"If I don't go now," he told her thickly, "I won't leave...." The pain in his lower body attested to his need of Rachel. She was soft, supple and warm in his arms. He saw the drowsy look in her eyes, how much his capturing kiss had affected her. Gently, he ran his hands across her crown and down the long, thick strands of her hair. She swayed unsteadily, and he held her carefully in his arms. It was too soon, his mind shrilled at him. Rachel had to have time to get to know him. And vice versa. He'd learned patience a long time ago when it came to relationships. And more than anything, Jim wanted his relationship with Rachel to develop naturally, and not become a pressure to her. When he saw the question in her gaze, he knew he'd made the right decision. Despite the desire burning in her eyes, he also saw fear banked in their depths. She was afraid of something. Him? Her past? Maybe a man she had known in England. That thought shattered him more than any other. Yes, he had to back off and find out more about her and what she wanted out of life—and if he figured in her dream at all.

Easing away, he smiled a little. "We're going to be getting up at the crack of dawn to leave. We need to get some sleep." What Jim really wanted was to sleep with Rachel in his arms. But he didn't say that.

"Yes..." Rachel whispered, her voice faint and husky.

She wanted Jim to stay, and the words were almost torn from her. But it wouldn't be fair to him—or her. If she was lucky, maybe tomorrow, as they tracked the cat, she could share her fears, her hopes and dreams with him.

The snort of the horses, the jets of white steam coming from their nostrils, were quickly absorbed by the thick pine forest that surrounded them as Rachel rode beside Jim. They had been in the saddle for nearly three hours and the temperature hovered in the low thirties up on the Rim. Bundled up, Rachel had never felt happier. And she knew why. It was because she was with Jim. They had spoken little since he'd started tracking. The spoor was still visible, thanks to the snow that hadn't yet melted off the Rim. Down below on the desert floor, the drifts had already disappeared.

Jim rode slightly ahead on a big black Arabian gelding. There was a rifle in the leather case along the right side of his saddle, beneath his leg. Rachel knew he didn't want to use it, but if the cat attacked, they had to defend themselves. It was a last resort. His black Stetson was drawn low across his brow as he leaned over the horse, looking for spoor. There weren't many, and Rachel was amazed at how well he could track on seemingly nothing. Occasionally he'd point out a tiny broken twig on a bush, a place where the snow had melted, a part of an imprint left in the pine needles—rocks that she wouldn't have seen without Jim's expertise.

Unable to get their heated kiss out of her head, Rachel waited for the right time to talk to him. Right now, he needed silence in order to concentrate. They were two hours ahead of his family's hunting party. Bo and

Chet weren't great at tracking, and Jim hoped his brothers would lose the trail, anyway.

He held up his hand. "Let's stop here for a bite to eat." He twisted around in the saddle, resting his hand on the rump of his gelding. Rachel was beautiful in her dark brown Stetson. She had a red wool muffler wrapped around her neck, and she wore a sheepskin jacket, Levi's, boots and thick, protective gloves. He was glad she'd dressed warmly, even though the temperature was rising and he was sure it would get over thirty-two degrees in the bright sunshine. Dismounting, he dropped the reins on the gelding, knowing that a ground-tied horse, once the reins were dropped, would not move.

Coming around, he held out his hands to Rachel, placing them around her waist and lifting her off the little gray Arabian mare she rode. He saw surprise and then pleasure in her eyes as she settled her own hands trustingly on his upper arms while he gently placed her feet on the ground. It would have been so easy to lean down and take her ripe, parted lips, so easy... Tearing himself out of that mode, Jim released her.

"What have you brought for us to eat?" He took the horses and tied them to a nearby tree. The trail had led them into a huge, jagged canyon of red-and-white rock. Noticing a limestone cave halfway up on one wall, he realized it was a perfect place for a cat to have a lair.

Rachel felt giddy. Jim's unexpected touch was exhilarating to her. Taking off her gloves, she opened up one of the bulging saddlebags. "I know this isn't going to be a surprise to you. Turkey sandwiches?"

Chuckling, Jim grinned and came and stood next to her. "We'll sit over there," he said. There were some black lava rocks free of snow that had dried in the sunlight. "I like turkey."

"I hope so." Rachel laughed softly. She purposely kept her voice low. When tracking, making noise wasn't a good idea.

"Come on," he urged, taking the sandwich wrapped in tinfoil. "Let's rest a bit. Your legs have to be killing you."

Rachel was happy to sit with her back against his on the smooth, rounded surface of the lava boulder. It was a perfect spot, the sunlight lancing down through the fir, spotlighting them with warmth. She removed her hat and muffler and opened up her coat because it was getting warmer. Picking up her sandwich, she found herself starved. Between bites, she said, "My legs feel pretty good. I'm surprised."

"By tonight," he warned wryly, "your legs will be seriously bowed."

She chortled. "That's when I take Arnica for sore muscles."

He grinned and ate with a contentment he'd rarely felt. The turkey tasted good. Rachel had used a seven-grain, homemade brown bread. Slathered with a lot of mayonnaise and a little salt on the turkey, the sandwich tasted wonderful. Savoring in the silence of the forest, the warmth of the sun, the feel of her resting against his back and left shoulder, he smiled.

"This is the good life."

Rachel nodded. "I love the peace of the forest. As a kid, I loved coming up on the Rim with my horse and just hanging out. When I was in junior high and high school, I was in the photography club, so I used to shoot a lot of what I thought were 'artistic' shots up here."

She laughed and shook her head. "The club advisor, a teacher, was more than kind about my fledgling efforts."

Smiling, Jim said, "I almost joined the photography club because you were in it."

Her brows arched and she twisted around and caught his amused gaze. "You're kidding me!"

"No," he said, holding up his hand. "Honest, I had a crush on you for six years. Did you know that?"

Even though he'd already confessed his boyhood crush, his words still stunned her. Maneuvering around so that she sat next to him, their elbows touching, she finished off her sandwich and leaned down to wipe her fingers in the snow and pine needles to clean them off. "I still can't believe you had a crush on me."

"Why is that so hard to believe? I thought you were the prettiest girl I'd ever seen." And then his smile softened. "You still are, Rachel."

Her heart thumped at the sincerity she heard in Jim's voice, and the serious look she saw on his face. "Oh," she said in a whisper, "I never knew back then, Jim…."

Chuckling, he took a second sandwich and unwrapped it. "Well, who was going to look at a pimply faced teenager? I wasn't the star running back of the football team like Sam was. I was shy. Not exactly good-looking. More the nerd than the sports-hero type." He chuckled again. "You always had suitors who wanted your attention."

"Well," she began helplessly, "I didn't know…"

He caught and held her gaze. "Let's face it," he said heavily, "back then, as kids, we wouldn't have stood a chance anyway. You were a hated Donovan. If my father had seen me get interested in you, all hell would've broken loose."

Glumly, Rachel agreed. "He'd have probably beaten you within an inch of your life. Come to think of it, so would my dad."

"Yeah, two rogue stallions against one scrawny teenage kid with acne isn't exactly good odds, is it?"

Laughing a little, Rachel offered him some of the corn chips she'd bagged up for them. Munching on the salty treat, she murmured, "No, that's not good odds. Maybe it's just as well I didn't know, then...."

The silence enveloped them for a full five minutes before either spoke again. Rachel wiped the last of the salt and grease from the chips off on her Levi's. There was something lulling and healing about being in a forest. It made what she wanted to share with Jim a little easier to undertake. Folding her hands against her knees, she drew them up against her.

"When I moved to England, a long time ago, Jim, I went over there to get the very best training possible to become a homeopath. I had no desire to live at the ranch. I knew my mother wanted all of us girls to come home, but none of us could stomach Kelly's drinking habits." She shook her head and glanced at Jim. His eyes were dark and understanding. "I loved my mother so much, but I just couldn't bring myself to come back home after I graduated from four years' training at Sheffield College. I went on to become a member of the Royal Society of Homeopaths and worked with several MDs at a clinic in London. I really loved my work, and how homeopathy, which was a natural medicine, could cure terrible illnesses and chronic diseases.

"I was very good at what I did, and eventually, the administrator at Sheffield College asked me to come back and teach. They offered me not only a teaching position, but said I could write a book on the topic and keep practicing through clinic work at their facility."

"It sounds like a dream come true for you," Jim said.

"Well, it was even more than that," she said ruefully, leaning down and picking up a damp, brown pine needle. Stroking it slowly with her fingertip, she continued, "I met Dr. Anthony Armstrong at the clinic. He was an MD. Over time, we fell in love." She frowned. "Because of my past, my father, I was really leery of marriage. I didn't want to get trapped like my mother had been. Tony was a wonderful homeopath and healer. We had so much in common. But I kept balking at setting a wedding date. This went on for five years." Rachel shook her head. "I guess you could say I was gun-shy."

Jim's heart sank. "You had good reason to be," he answered honestly. "Living with Kelly was enough to make all three of you women gun-shy of marriage and of men in general." And it was. Jim had feared Kelly himself. Nearly anyone with any sense had. The man had been unstable. He'd blow up and rage at the slightest indiscretion, over things that didn't warrant such a violent reaction. As much as Jim tried to imagine what it had been like for Rachel and her sisters, he could not. What he did see, however, was the damage that it had done to each of them, and he realized for the first time how deeply wounded Rachel had been by it as well.

"I was scared, Jim," she said finally, the words forced out from between her set lips. "Tony was a wonderful friend. We loved homeopathy. We loved helping people get well at the clinic. We had so much in common," she said again.

"But did you love him?"

Rachel closed her eyes. Her lips compressed. "Do

you always ask the right question?" She opened her eyes and studied Jim's grave face. His ability to see straight through her, to her core, was unsettling but wonderful. Rachel had never met a man who could see that deep inside her. And she knew her secret vulnerabilities were safe with Jim.

"Not always," Jim murmured, one corner of his mouth lifting slightly, "but I try, and that's what counts." Seeing the fear and grief in Rachel's eyes, he asked gently, "So what happened? Did you eventually marry him?"

Allowing the pine needle to drop, she whispered, "No... I was too scared, Jim. Tony and I—well, we were good friends. I gradually realized I really didn't love him—not like he loved me. Maybe, in my late twenties, I was still gun-shy and wasn't sure about love, or what it was really supposed to be. I had a lot of phone conversations with my mother about that. I just wasn't sure what love was."

Seeing the devastation on Rachel's face, hearing the apology in her husky voice, he bit back the question that whirled in his head: *And now? Do you know what love is? Do you know that what we have is love?* "Time heals old wounds," he soothed. "I've seen it for myself with my father. When I left at age eighteen, I hated him. It took me ten years to realize a lot of things, and growing up, maturing, really helped."

"Doesn't it?" Rachel laughed softly as she lifted her head and looked up at the bright blue sky. The sunlight filtered delicately down among the fir boughs, dancing over the snow patches and pine needles.

"That's why I came home. Blood is thicker than water. I thought I could help, but I haven't been able to do a damned thing." Ruefully, he held her tender gaze. "The only good thing that's happened out of it is meeting you again."

Her throat tightened with sudden emotion and she felt tears sting the backs of her eyes. Her voice was off-key when she spoke. "When I became conscious in that wreck and saw you, your face, I knew I was going to be okay. I didn't know how, but I knew that. You had such confidence and I could feel your care. You made me feel safe, Jim, in a way I've never felt safe in my life." She tried to smile, but failed. Opening her hands, Rachel pushed on, because if she didn't get the words out, the fear would stop her from ever trying again.

"I know we haven't known each other long, but I feel so good around you. I like your touch, your kindness, the way you treat others. There's nothing not to like about you." She laughed shyly. Unable to meet his gaze because she was afraid of what she might see, she went on. "I'm so afraid to reach out…to—to like you… because of my past. I hurt Tony terribly. I kept the poor guy hanging on for five years thinking that I could remake myself, or let go of my paranoia about marriage, my fear of being trapped by it. I thought it would go away with time, but that didn't happen. I felt horrible about it. That poor man waited in hope for five years for me to get my act together—and I never did." Sorrowfully, Rachel turned and met Jim's gaze. It took the last of her courage to do that because he deserved no less than honesty from her.

"Now I've met you. And what I feel here—" she touched her heart with her hand "—is so strong and good and clean that I wake up every morning happy, so happy that I'm afraid it's all a dream and will end.

That's stupid, I know. I know better than that. It's not a dream…."

Gently, Jim turned and captured her hands in his. "Maybe it's a dream that's been there all along, but due to life and circumstances, you couldn't dream it—until now?"

Just the tenderness of his low voice made her vision blur with tears. Rachel hung her head. She felt Jim's hands tighten a little around hers. "I'm so scared, Jim… of myself, of how I feel about you…of the fact that your family would come unglued if—if I let myself go and allow the feelings I have for you to grow. I'm scared of myself. I wonder if I'll freeze again like I did with Tony. I don't want to hurt anyone. I don't want to make you suffer like I did him."

"Listen to me," Jim commanded gruffly as he placed his finger beneath Rachel's chin, making her look up at him. Tears beaded her thick, dark lashes and there was such misery in her forest green eyes. "Tony was a big boy. He knew the score. You weren't teenagers. You were adults. And so are we, Rachel." Jim slid his hand across the smooth slope of her cheek. "I know you're scared. Now I know why. That's information that can help us make decisions with each other." He brushed several strands of dark hair away from her delicate ear. "I couldn't give a damn that my last name is Cunningham and yours is Donovan. The feud our fathers and grandfathers waged with one another stops here, with us. We aren't going to fight anymore. It's this generation that has to begin the healing. I know you know that. So does Kate and Jessica. My family doesn't—not yet. And maybe they never will. But I can't live my life for them. I have to live my life the way I think it should go."

Rachel closed her eyes as he stroked her cheek. His hand was roughened from hard work, from the outdoors, and she relished his closeness, his warmth.

"I guess," Jim rasped in a low voice, "I never got over my crush on you, Rachel." He saw her eyes open. "What I felt as an awkward, gawky teenager, I feel right now. When I saw it was you trapped in that car, I almost lost it. I almost panicked. I was so afraid that you were going to die. I didn't want you to leave me." He shook his head and placed his hand over hers again. "When you needed that rare blood type, and I had the same type, I knew something special was going down. I knew it here, in my heart. I was glad to give my blood to you. For me, with my Apache upbringing, I saw it symbolically, as if the blood from our two families was now one, in you." He gazed into her green eyes and hoped she understood the depth of what he was trying to share with her.

"In a way, we're already joined. And I want to pursue what we have, Rachel—if you want to. I'm not here to push you or shove you. You need to tell me if I have a chance with you."

Chapter 9

Before Rachel could answer, both horses suddenly snorted and started violently. Jim and Rachel jumped to their feet and turned toward the fir tree, where the horses were firmly tied and standing frozen, their attention drawn deeper into the canyon.

Rachel's eyes widened enormously and her heart thudded hard in her chest. There, no more than a hundred feet away on the wall of the canyon next to the cave, stood a huge, stocky jaguar. The cat switched its tail, watching them.

Jim moved in front of her, as if to protect her. She could feel the fine tension in his body, and she gasped. The jaguar was real! Though the cat was a hundred feet above them and unable to leap toward them, her emotions were screaming in fear.

"Don't move," Jim rasped. His eyes narrowed as he slowly turned and fully faced the jaguar. For some reason, he sensed it was a female, just as in Rachel's dream. The cat was positively huge! He'd seen photos and films of jaguars, but never one in the wild. They were a lot stockier than the lithe cougar and weighed a helluva lot more. The cat's gold-and-black fur looked magnificent against the white limestone cliff. Between her jaws was a limp jackrabbit she'd obviously brought back to her lair to enjoy.

The snort of the horses echoed warningly down the canyon walls and Jim automatically put his arm out, as if to stop Rachel from any forward movement. He felt her hand on the back of his shoulder.

Rachel was mesmerized by the stark beauty of the jaguar as the cat lowered her broad, massive head and gently placed the dead rabbit at her feet. Looking down at them as if she were queen of all she surveyed and they mere subjects within her domain.

"She's beautiful!" Rachel whispered excitedly. "Look at her!"

Jim barely nodded. He was concerned she would attack. Fortunately, both horses were trained for hunting and were able to stand their ground rather than tear at their reins to get away—which any horse in its right mind would have done under the present circumstances. He estimated how long it would take to reach his gelding, unsnap the leather scabbard, pull out the rifle, load it and aim it. The odds weren't in his favor.

"She's not going to harm us," Rachel whispered. Moving closer to Jim, their bodies nearly touching as she dug her fingers into his broad shoulder. "This is so odd, Jim. I feel like she's trying to communicate with us. Look at her!"

He couldn't deny what Rachel had voiced. The cat

lazily switched her tail, but showed no sign of alarm at being so near to them. Instead, she eased to the ground, the rabbit between her massive front paws. Sniffing the morsel, she raised her head and viewed them again.

"Listen to me, Rachel," Jim said in a very low voice, keeping his eyes on the jaguar. "I want you to slowly back away from me. Mount your horse and, as quietly as you can, *walk* it out of the canyon. Once you get down the hill, take the walkie-talkie you have in the saddle-bag and make a call to Bob. Tell him we've located the cat and it's a jaguar. The walkie-talkie won't work up here in the fir trees. You need an open area. It might take you fifteen minutes to ride down this slope to the meadow below. Call him and then wait for him down there. I know he's on 89A waiting for us. He can drive through the Cunningham ranch. Tell him to go to the northernmost pasture. We'll meet him there."

"What are you going to do?"

"Stay here."

Alarmed, Rachel asked, "Why? Why not come with me?"

"Because if she wants to charge someone, I'd rather it be me, not you." He reached behind him and his hand found her jean-clad thigh. Patting her gently, he said, "Go on. I'll come down the hill fifteen minutes from now. I just want to give you a head start. The cat isn't going to follow you if she has me here. Besides, she's eating her lunch right now. If she's starving, that rabbit will put a dent in her appetite and she'll be far less likely to think of us as a meal."

Rachel understood his logic. "Okay, I'll do it." Her heart still pounded, but it wasn't fear she felt in the jaguar's presence, just a thrilling excitement.

He nodded slowly. "I'll see you in about twenty minutes down below in that meadow?"

Compressing her lips, Rachel reached out and squeezed his hand. "Yes," she said. "*You* be careful."

He smiled tensely. "I don't get any sense she's going to attack us."

"Me neither." Rachel released his hand. "She's so beautiful, Jim! And she's the one I saw standing in the middle of 89A. I'd swear it because I remember that black crescent on her forehead. I thought it looked odd, out of place there. It's impossible that two jaguars would have that same identical marking, isn't it?"

"Yeah, they're all marked slightly different," he agreed. "Sort of like fingerprints, you know?" He felt safe enough to turn his head slightly. Rachel's eyes were huge and full of awe as she gazed up on the cliff wall at the cat. Her cheeks were deeply flushed with excitement. Hell, he was excited, too.

"I think this is wonderful!" she gushed in a low voice. "The jaguars are back in Arizona!"

Chuckling a little, Jim said, "Well, *some* people will be thrilled with this discovery and others won't be. Like my family. Now we know who's been eating a beef every two weeks."

Frowning, Rachel sighed. "Thank goodness the fish and game department will capture her and take her someplace where she won't get killed by man."

"I talked to Bob this morning. He said jaguars were not only protected in South and Central America, but that they would be federally protected here if they ever migrated far enough north to cross the border."

"Well," Rachel said, "she certainly has. It's nice to know she can't be shot by your brothers, though they'd probably do it anyway if they had the chance, I'm sorry to say."

Glumly, Jim agreed. "No argument there. Better get going."

She patted his shoulder. "This whole day has been an incredible gift. I'll see you in about twenty minutes." Then she slowly backed away from him.

Jim tensed when the jaguar snapped up her head as Rachel began to move. Would the cat attack? Run away? He watched, awed by the beauty and throbbing power that seemed to emanate from the animal. She was a magnificent beast—so proud and queenly in the way she lifted her head to observe them. As Rachel mounted her horse and walked it out of the canyon, the cat flicked its tail once and then resumed eating her kill.

Recalling the time he'd hunted and trapped the mountain lion up here on the Rim, Jim realized this was a far cry from that traumatic event. Glancing down at his watch, he decided to give Rachel twenty minutes before he mounted up to go back down the slope and join her in the meadow. If the truth be known, he savored this time with the jaguar. He felt privileged and excited. This time he didn't have to kill, as he had with the mountain lion. The memory caused shame to creep through him as he stood there observing the jaguar. After he'd killed the cougar, his father had slapped him on the back, congratulating him heartily. Jim had felt like crying. He'd killed something wild and beautiful and had seen no sense to it.

His Apache mother had given each of her sons an Apache name when they were born. Even though it wasn't on his birth certificate, she'd called him Cougar. He remembered how she had extolled his cougar medicine, and how she made him realize how important it was. Even though he'd only been six years old when she died, her passionate remarks had made a lasting impression on him.

The past unfolded gently before him as he stood there. His mother had always called him Cougar because Jim was a white man's name, she'd told him teasingly. In her eyes and heart, he was like the cougar, and he knew he would learn how to become one because the cougar was the guardian spirit that had come into this life with him. Jim recalled the special ceremony his mother's people had had for him when he was five years old. Since she was Chiricahua, they'd traveled back to that reservation and her people had honored him. The old, crippled medicine man had given him a leather thong with a small beaded pouch attached to it. Inside the pouch was his "medicine."

To this day, Jim wore that medicine bag around his neck. The beading had long ago fallen off and he'd had to change the leather thong yearly. Whether it was crazy or not, Jim had worn that medicine bag from the day it had been placed on him during that ceremony. The medicine man head told him that the fur of a cougar was in the bag, that it was his protector, teacher and guardian. Sighing, Jim looked down at the rapidly melting midday snow. Maybe that was why that mountain lion never charged him when he came upon him that fateful day so long ago. The cat had simply looked at him through wise, yellow eyes and waited. It was as if he knew Jim had to kill him, so he stood there, magnificent and proud, awaiting his fate.

Suddenly Jim felt as if the claw he wore next to his small medicine bag was burning in his chest. Without thinking, Jim rubbed that area of his chest. He wondered if this jaguar sensed his cougar medicine. He knew that the great cats were related to one another. Was that why she chose not to charge him? His Anglo side said that was foolish, but his Apache blood said that he was correct in this assumption. The jaguar saw him as one of them. She would not kill one of her own kind. And then a crazy smile tugged at a corner of Jim's mouth. Rachel must have jaguar medicine, for it was this cat that had saved her from a fiery death at the accident that occurred less than a mile down the road. It was this cat that had leaped into the middle of the highway to stop her.

With a shake of his head, he knew life was more mystical than practical at times. He recalled the dream Rachel had had of the jaguar turning into a warrior woman. Gazing up at the animal, he smiled. There was no question he was being given a second chance. This time he wasn't going to kill. He was going to trap her and have her taken to an area where no Anglo's rifle could rip into her beautiful gold-and-black fur.

Remembering Rachel, he glanced at his watch. To his surprise, fifteen minutes had already flown by! Jim wished he could slow down time and remain here, just watching the jaguar, who had finished her meal and was licking one paw with her long, pink tongue.

Rachel had just reached the snow-covered meadow when to her horror she saw two cowboys emerge from the other end of it. Halting her horse, she realized it was Bo and Chet Cunningham and they had spotted her. Hands tightening on the reins, Rachel was torn by indecision. Should she try and outrun them? Her horse danced nervously beneath her, which wasn't like the animal at all. When she saw the rifles they carried on their saddles and the grim looks on their unshaven faces, she felt leery and decided to stand her ground. When the two men saw her, they spurred their mounts forward, the horses slipping and sliding as they thundered across the small meadow.

"Who the hell are you?" Bo demanded, jerking hard on the reins when he reached her. His horse grunted, opened its mouth to escape the pain of the bit and slid down on its hindquarters momentarily.

Rachel's horse leaped sideways. Steadying the animal, she glared at Bo. The larger of the two brothers, he looked formidable in his black Stetson, sheepskin coat and red bandanna. Danger prickled at Rachel and she put a hand on her horse's neck to keep him calm.

"I'm Rachel Donovan. Your brother—"

"A Donovan!" Chet snarled, pulling up on the other side of her horse.

Suddenly Rachel and her lightweight Arabian were trapped by two beefy thirteen-hundred-pound quarter horses. Bo's eyes turned merciless. "What the hell you doin' on our property, bitch?" he growled. His hand shot out.

Giving a small cry of surprise, Rachel felt his fingers tangle in her long, thick hair. Her scalp radiated with pain as he gave her a yank, nearly unseating her from the saddle. She pulled back on the reins so her gelding wouldn't leap forward.

"Oww!" she cried, "Let me go!"

Breathing savagely, Bo wrapped his fingers a little tighter in her hair. "You bossy bitch. What the hell you doin' on Cunningham property? You're not welcomed over here."

She could smell whiskey on his breath as he leaned over, his face inches from hers. Hanging at an angle, with only her legs keeping her aboard her nervous horse, Rachel tried to think. As the pain in her scalp intensified, the feral quality in Bo's eyes sent a sheet of fear through her.

"Let's get 'er down," Chet snapped. "Let's teach her a lesson she won't forget, Bo. A little rape oughta keep her in line, wouldn't ya say?"

Rachel cried out in terror. Without thinking, she raised her hand to slap Bo's away. Knocking her arm away, Bo cursed and balled his right hand into a fist. Before she could protect herself, she saw his fist swing forward. Suddenly the side of her head exploded in stars, light and pain.

She was falling. Semiconscious, she felt the horse bolt from beneath her. Landing on her back, she hit the ground hard, and her breath was torn from her. She saw Chet leap from his horse, his face twisted into a savage grin of confidence as he approached her. She struggled to sit up but he straddled her with his long, powerful legs, slamming her back down into the red mud and snow. She felt his hands like vises on her wrists, pulling them above her head. Screaming and kicking out, she tried to buck him off her body, but he had her securely pinned. Grinning triumphantly at her, he placed his hand on the open throat of her shirt and gave a savage yank. The material ripped with a sickening sound.

"No!" Rachel shrieked. "Get off me!" She managed to get one hand free and she struck at Chet. She heard Bo laugh as the blow landed on the side of Chet's head.

"Ride 'er strong, brother. Hold on, I'll dismount and come and help you."

Panic turned to overwhelming terror. Sobbing, Rachel fought on, pummeling Chet's face repeatedly until he lifted his arms to protect himself.

At the same time, she heard Bo give a warning scream.

"Look out! A cougar! There's that cougar comin'!"

As Chet slammed Rachel down to the ground again, her head snapped back. Blood flowed from her nose and as she tried to move, she felt darkness claiming her. Chet dragged himself off her and ran for his horse, which danced nervously next to where she lay in the snow.

Bo cursed and jerked his horse around as the large cat hurtled toward them.

"Son of a bitch!" he yelled to Chet, and he made a grab for his rifle. His horse shied sideways once it caught sight of the charging cat coming directly at him.

Chet gave a cry as he remounted, his horse bucking violently beneath him as he clung to the saddle horn. The animal was wild with fear and trying to run.

Rachel rolled onto her stomach, dazed. The jaguar was charging directly down upon them. For a moment, she thought she was seeing things, but there was no way she could deny the reality of the huge cat's remarkable agility and speed, the massive power in her thick, short body as she made ground-covering strides right at them.

Snow and mud flew in sheets around the cat as she ran. Then suddenly the jaguar growled, and Rachel cried out as the sound reverberated through her entire being.

"Kill it!" Chet screeched, trying to stop his horse.

He yanked savagely on one rein, causing his horse to begin to circle. *"Kill it!"* he howled again.

Bo pulled his horse to a standstill and made a grab for his rifle. But before he could clear the weapon from the scabbard, the jaguar leaped directly at him.

Rachel saw the cat's thick back legs flex as she leaped, saw the primal intent in her gold eyes rimmed in black. Everything seemed to move in slow motion. Rachel heard herself gasp and she raised her arms to protect herself from Bo's horse, which was dancing side-ways next to her in order to escape the charge. Mud and snow flew everywhere, pelting Rachel as she watched the cat arch gracefully through the air directly at Bo, her huge claws bared like knives pulled from sheaths.

Bo gave a cry of surprise as the jaguar landed on the side of his horse. His mount reared and went over backward, carrying rider and cat with him. As Rachel rolled out of the way and jumped to her feet, she heard another shout. It was Jim's voice!

Staggering dazedly, Rachel looked toward where Jim was flying down the snow-covered slope at a hard gallop, his face stony with anger. The snarl of the jag-uar behind her snagged Rachel's failing attention. Her knees weakened as she turned. To her horror, she saw the jaguar take one vicious swipe at the downed horse and rider. Bo cried out and the horse screamed, its legs flailing wildly as it tried to avoid another attack by the infuriated jaguar.

Within seconds, the jaguar leaped away, taking off toward the timberline at a dead run. Though Bo was on the ground his horse had managed to get to its feet and run away, back toward the ranch. Chet had gotten his horse under control finally, but his hands were shaking so badly he couldn't get his rifle out of its sheath.

Bo leaped to his feet with a curse. He glared as Jim slid his horse to a stop and dismounted. "Get that damn cougar before he gets away!" Bo shouted, pointing toward the forest where the cat had disappeared once again.

Ignoring his brother, Jim ran up to Rachel. When he saw the blood flowing down across her lips and chin, the bruise marks along her throat, her shirt torn and hanging open, rage tunneled up through him. He reached out to steady her and she sagged into his arms with a small, helpless cry. Gripping her hard, he eased her to the ground. Breathing raggedly he glanced up at Bo, who was looking down at his left leg, where one of his leather chaps had been ripped away. The meadow looked like a battlefield. Blood was all over the place.

"Are you all right, Rachel?" Jim asked urgently, touching her head and examining her.

"Y-yes…." Rachel whispered faintly.

"What happened? Did the jaguar—"

"No," she rattled, her voice cracking. "Bo hit me. They saw me, trapped me between their horses. Your brother jerked me by my hair. When he went for my throat to haul me off my horse, I tried to shove his arm away. That's when Bo hit me." Blinking, Rachel held Jim's darkening gaze. "Chet tried to rape me. Bo was coming to help him until the jaguar charged…." Gripping his hand, she rasped, "Jim, that jaguar came out of nowhere. She protected me. I—I…they were going to rape me…. They thought I was alone. They didn't give me a chance to explain why I was on their property. Bo and Chet just attacked."

"Don't move," Jim rasped.

Rachel watched dazedly as Jim leaped to his feet. The attack of the jaguar had left her shaking. Terror still pounded through her and she didn't want Jim to leave. In four strides, he approached Bo, grabbing him by the collar of his sheepskin coat.

"What the hell do you think you were doing?" Jim snarled, yanking Bo so hard that his neck snapped back. He saw his brother's face go stormy.

"Get your hands off me!"

"Not a chance," Jim breathed savagely. Then he doubled his fist and hit Bo with every ounce of strength he had. Fury pumped through him as he felt Bo's nose crack beneath the power of his assault. His brother crumpled like a rag doll.

Chet yelled at him to stop, but kept his fractious horse at a distance. "You can't hit him!" he shrieked.

Jim hunkered over Bo, who sat up, holding his badly bleeding nose. "You stay down or next time it'll be your jaw," he warned thickly. Bo remained on the ground.

Straightening up, Jim glared at Chet. "Get the hell out of here," he ordered.

"But—"

"Now!" Jim thundered, his voice echoing around the small meadow. Jabbing his finger at Chet, he snarled, "You tell Father that this cat is under federal protection. The fish and game department is going to come in and trap it and take it to another area. If either of you think you're going to kill that jaguar, I'll make sure it doesn't happen. You got that?"

Chet glared at him, trying to hold his dancing horse in place. "Jaguar? You're crazy! That was a cougar. We saw it with our own eyes!"

Blinking in confusion, Jim looked over at Rachel.

When he saw her sitting in the snow, packing some of it against the right side of her swollen face and bleeding nose, he wanted to kill Bo for hurting her. Leaning down, he grabbed his brother by his black hair. "You sick son of a bitch," he snarled in his face. "You had no *right* to do that to Rachel—to any woman!" He saw Bo's face tighten in pain as he gripped his hair hard. "How does it feel?" Jim rasped. "Hurts, doesn't it? You ever think about that before you beat up on someone, Bo?"

"Let go of me!"

"You bastard." Jim shoved him back into the snow. "Now you lay there and don't you move!" He turned and strode back to Rachel. Leaning down, his hands on her shoulders, he met her tear-filled eyes.

"Hang on," he whispered unsteadily, "I'm calling for help."

"Just get Bob Granby. I didn't make the call yet, Jim...."

Nodding, he went over to his horse and opened one of his saddlebags. His gaze nailed Bo, who was sitting up, nursing his bloody nose and sulking. Pulling out a small first-aid kit, he went back to Rachel.

"Get my homeopathic first-aid kit," she begged. "I can stop the bleeding and the swelling with it."

He went to her horse and got the small plastic kit. Kneeling beside her, his hand still shaking with rage, he opened the kit for her. "I'm sorry," he rasped, meaning it. As she opened one of the vials and poured several white pellets into her hand, he felt a desire to kill Bo and Chet for what they'd done to her. Rachel's cheek was swollen and he knew she'd have a black eye soon. Worse, her nose looked puffy, too, and he wondered if it was broken. Setting the kits down, he waited until she put the pellets in her mouth.

"Let me see if your nose is broken," he urged as he placed one hand behind her head. It was so easy, so natural between them. The tension he'd seen in her, the wariness in her eyes fled the moment he touched her. A fierce love for her swept through him. As gently as possible, he examined her fine, thin nose.

"Good," he whispered huskily, trying to smile down at her. "I don't think it's broken."

Rachel shut her eyes. With Jim close, she felt safe. "Did you see what happened?" she quavered.

"Yeah, I saw all of it," he told her grimly. Placing a dressing against her nose, he showed her how to hold it in place. "Stay here. I want to make that call to Bob and a second one to the sheriff."

Eyes widening, Rachel looked up at the grim set of his face. "The sheriff?"

"Damn straight. Bo's going up on assault charges. He's not going to hit you and get away with it," he growled as he rose to his feet.

Rachel closed her eyes once again. Her head, cheek and nose were throbbing. Within minutes, the homeopathic remedy stopped the bleeding and took away most of the pain in her cheekbone area. As she sat there in the wet snow, she began to shiver and realized shock was setting in. Lying down, she closed her eyes and tried to concentrate on taking slow, deep breaths to ward it off. The snort and stomp of nervous horses snagged her consciousness. She heard Jim's low, taut voice on the walkie-talkie, Chet's high, nervous voice as he talked to Bo in the background.

What had happened? Chet said a cougar had charged them. Yet Rachel had seen the female jaguar. And how had Jim known she was in trouble? He'd come off that mountain at a dangerous rate of speed. It was all so crazy and confusing, she thought, feeling blackness rim her vision. She hoped the homeopathic remedy would pull her out of the shock soon. It should. All she had to do was lie quietly for a few minutes and let it help her body heal itself from the trauma.

More than anything, Rachel wanted to be home. The violence in Bo's eyes had scared her as nothing else ever had. She knew that if the jaguar had not charged him, if Jim hadn't arrived when he did, they would have raped her—simply because she was a Donovan. The thought sickened her. Jim was right—the sheriff must be called. She had no problem laying charges against Bo and Chet. If she had her way, it would be the last time Bo ever cocked his fist at a woman. The last time. Judging from the murderous look in Jim's eyes, he was ready to beat his older brother to a pulp. Rachel had seen the savagery in Jim's face, but she knew he wasn't like his two older brothers. He'd hit Bo just enough to disable him so he couldn't hurt either of them in the meantime. Unlike his brothers, Jim had shown remarkable restraint.

A fierce love welled up through Rachel as she lay there in the cooling snow. Though she felt very cold and emotionally fragile at the moment, the heat of the sun upon her felt good. No one had ever hurt her like this in her life. The shock had gone deep within her psyche. The last thing Rachel expected was to be physically attacked. Now all she wanted to do was get Bob Granby up here with the humane trap. And then she wanted to go home—and heal. More than anything, Rachel needed Jim right now, his arms around her, making a safe place for her in a world gone suddenly mad.

Chapter 10

Rachel's head ached as she sat on the edge of the gurney in the emergency room at the Flagstaff Hospital. If it weren't for Jim's presence and soothing stability through a host of X rays and numerous examinations by doctor and nurses who came into her cubical from time to time, her frayed nerves would be completely shot. Luckily, Jim knew everyone in the ER, making it easier for her to tolerate the busy, hectic place.

Rachel closed her eyes and held the ice pack against her badly swollen cheek. She'd found out moments earlier that her cheekbone had sustained a hairline fracture. At least her nose wasn't broken, she thought with a slight smile. Jim's hand rarely left hers. She could tell he was trying to hide his anger and upset from her. Bob Granby from the fish and game department had come out and met them on the Cunningham land about the same time a deputy sheriff, Scott Maitland, had rolled up. Chet and Bo were taken into custody and transported to the Flagstaff jail, awaiting charges.

Rachel was about to speak when the green curtains surrounding her cubical parted. She felt Jim's hand tighten slightly around hers as Deputy Scott Maitland approached the gurney. She knew Maitland was going to ask for a statement. Her head ached so badly that all she wanted to do was crawl off alone to a quiet place and just rest.

Maitland tipped his gray Stetson in her direction. "Ms. Donovan?"

Rachel sat up a little and tried to smile, but wasn't successful. "Yes?"

Apologetically, Maitland looked over at Jim and reached out to shake his hand. "Sorry about this, Jim."

"Thanks, Scott." He looked worriedly at Rachel. "She's in a lot of pain right now and some shock. Can you take her statement later?"

Maitland shook his head. He held a clipboard in his large hands. "I'm afraid not. Your father already has his attorney, Stuart Applebaum, up at the jail demanding bail information for your brothers. We can't do anything until I take your statements."

Rachel removed the ice pack and tried to focus on the very tall, broad-shouldered deputy. The Maitlands owned the third largest cattle ranch in Arizona. The spread was run by two brothers and two sisters and Scott was the second oldest, about twenty-eight years old. The history of the Maitland dynasty was a long and honorable one that Rachel, who was a history buff, knew well. For her senior thesis, she'd written up the history of cattle ranching for Arizona. She knew from her research that Cathan Maitland had come from Ireland during the Potato Famine in the mid-1800s and claimed acreage up around Flagstaff. He'd then married a woman Comanche warrior, whose raiding parties used to keep the area up in arms, as did the Apache attacks.

As Rachel looked up into Scott's clear gray eyes, she saw some of that Comanche heritage in him, from his thick, short black hair to his high cheekbones and golden skin. He had a kind face, not a stern one, so she relaxed a little, grateful for his gentle demeanor as he walked over and stood in front of her. His mouth was pulled into an apologetic line.

"Looks like you're going to be a raccoon pretty soon," he teased.

Rachel touched her right eye, which she knew was bruised and darkening. "You're right," she said huskily.

"I'll try and make this as painless and fast as possible," he told her. "I think the docs have pretty much wrapped you up and are ready to sign you out of here so you can go home and rest." His eyes sparkled. "I'll see if I can beat their discharge time for you."

"Thanks," Rachel whispered, and placed the ice pack back on her cheek very gently.

"Just tell me in your own words what happened," Maitland urged, "and I'll fill out this report."

Rachel tried to be as clear and specific as possible as she told the story. When she said that she had seen the jaguar, Scott's eyes widened.

"A jaguar?"

"Yes," Rachel murmured. She looked at Jim, who continued to hold her hand as she leaned against his strong, unyielding frame. "Jim saw it, too."

"I did, Scott. A big, beautiful female jaguar."

"I'll be damned," he said, writing it down.

"Why are you acting so surprised?" Jim inquired.

"Well, your brothers swear they were attacked by a cougar." Maitland studied Rachel. "And you're saying you saw a jaguar come running down that hill and attack Bo?"

"I'm positive it was a jaguar," Rachel said.

"Scott, let me break in here and tell you something Rachel doesn't know yet. When she left to head down to the meadow, that female jaguar just sat at the opening to her lair, cleaning off her paws after finishing her jackrabbit. And then suddenly she jumped up, leaped off that ledge and ran right by me." Jim scratched his head. "She stopped about a hundred feet away from me, growled, looked down the mountain and then back at me. As crazy as this sounds, I got the impression I had to hurry—that something was wrong." Grimly, his eyes flashing, he added, "I leaped into the saddle and rode hell-bent-for-leather down that mountain. That jaguar was right in front of me, never more than a hundred yards away. She was running full bore. So were we. When I came out of the woods, I saw my brothers had Rachel down on the ground. That was when the jaguar really sped up. She was like a blur of motion as she ran right for Bo."

"I saw the jaguar leap," Rachel told Scott in a low voice. "I heard her growl and saw her jump. I saw her slash out with her claws at Bo." She frowned. "You saw Bo's chaps, didn't you?"

"Yeah." Scott chuckled. "No way around that. That cat slashed the hell out of them and that's thick cowhide leather." He scratched his jaw in thought. "The only disagreement we've got here is that two witnesses say it was a cougar and you both say it was a jaguar."

"Does it really matter?" Rachel asked grimly.

"No, I guess it doesn't. The fact that Bo assaulted you and Chet threatened you with rape is the real point of this report."

Shivering, Rachel closed her eyes. She felt Jim place his arm around her and draw her against him more tightly. Right now she felt cold and tired, and all she wanted was rest and quiet, not this interrogation.

"Let's try and get this done as soon as possible," Jim urged his friend. "She's getting paler by the moment and I want to get her home so she can rest."

"Sure," Maitland murmured.

Rachel never thought that being home—her new home on her family ranch—would ever feel so good. But it did. Kate and Jessica had come over as soon as Jim had driven into the homestead. They'd fussed over her like two broody hens. Kate got the fire going in the fireplace out in the living room and Jessica made her some chamomile tea to soothe her jangled nerves. Jim had gotten her two high-potency homeopathic remedies, one for her fracture and the other for her swollen cheek and black eye. She drank the tea and took the remedies. Five minutes later, she was so tired due to the healing effects of the remedies that she dropped off asleep on her bed, covered by the colorful afghan knit by her mother many years before.

Jim moved quietly down the carpeted hall to Rachel's bedroom. The door was open and Kate and Jessica had just left. He'd told them he was going to stay with Rachel for a while just to make sure she was all right. The truth was he didn't want to leave her at all. Torn between going home and facing his infuriated father and remaining with her, he stood poised at the door.

Rachel lay on her right side, her hands beneath the pillow where her dark hair lay like a halo around her head. The colorful afghan wasn't large enough to cover her fully and he was concerned about the coolness in the house. The only heat supply was from the fireplace, and it would take awhile to warm the small adobe home. Moving quietly, he went to the other side of the old brass bed, pulled up a dark pink, cotton goose down bedspread and gently eased it over her. Snugging it gently over her shoulders, he smiled down at Rachel as she slept.

Her golden skin looked washed out, almost pasty. Reaching down, he grazed her left cheek, which was soft and firm beneath his touch. Her lips were slightly parted. She looked so vulnerable. Rage flowed through him as he straightened. His right hand still throbbed and he was sure he'd probably fractured one of his fingers in the process of slugging Bo. Flexing his fingers, Jim felt satisfaction thrum through him. At least Bo was suffering just a little from hurting Rachel. If Jim had his way, his brother was going to suffer a lot more. This was one time that neither his father's lawyer nor his money would dissuade Rachel from putting both his brothers up on charges that would stick. With their past criminal record, they were looking at federal prison time.

Jim needed to get home and he knew it. Leaning over, he cupped her shoulder and placed a light kiss on her unmarred brow.

"Sleep, princess," he whispered. *I love you*. And he did. A lump formed in his throat as he left the bedroom and walked quietly down the hall. Shrugging into his sheepskin coat and settling the black Stetson on his head, he left her house. Outside, the sun was hanging low in the west, the day nearly spent. What a hell of a day it had been. As he drove his pickup down the muddy red road, Jim's thoughts revolved around his love for Rachel. He knew it was too soon to share it with her. Time was needed to cultivate a relationship with her. If he'd had any doubt about his feelings for her, he'd lost them all out there in that meadow.

Working his mouth, Jim drove down 89A toward Sedona. Just before town was the turnoff for the Bar C. His hands tightened on the steering wheel as he wound down Oak Creek Canyon. The world-famous beauty of the tall Douglas firs, the red and white cliffs rising thousands of feet on both sides of the slash of asphalt, did not move him today as they normally did.

Would Rachel allow him to remain in her life after what had happened? Would his Cunningham blood taint her so that she retreated from him, from the love he held for her? He sighed. There would be a trial. And Jim was going to testify with Rachel against his brothers. Everything was so tenuous. So unsure. He felt fear. Fear of losing Rachel before he'd ever had her, before she could know his love for her.

Jim tried to gather his strewn emotions, knowing all hell would break loose once he stepped into the main ranch house when he got home. His father, because he was wheelchair bound, relied on one of them to drive him wherever he wanted to go. Jim was sure Frank was seething with anger and worry over Bo and Chet. But his father ought to be concerned about Rachel, and what they had done to her—and what they would have done had it not been for that jaguar attacking.

Shaking his head as he drove slowly down the dirt road toward home, Jim wondered about the discrepancy in the police report. How could Bo and Chet have seen a cougar when it was a jaguar? What the hell was going on here? No matter, the fish and game expert would see the tracks, would capture the jaguar in a special cage, and that would be proof enough. His brothers were well known for their lies. This was just one more.

"What the hell is going on?" Frank roared as Jim stepped through the door into the living room. He angrily wheeled his chair forward, his face livid.

Quietly shutting the door, Jim took off his hat and coat and hung them on hooks beside it. "Bo and Chet are up on assault charges," he said quietly as he turned and faced his father.

"Applebaum tells me Rachel Donovan is pressing charges. Is that true?"

Allowing his hands to rest tensely on his hips, Jim nodded. "Yes, and she's not going to withdraw them, either. And even if she did," he said in a level tone, holding his father's dark gaze, "I would keep my charges against them, anyway."

"How could you? Dammit!" Frank snarled, balling up his fist and striking the chair arm. "How can you do this to your own family? Blood's thicker than water, Jim. You *know* that! When there's a storm, the family goes through it together. We're supposed to help and protect one another, not—"

"Dammit, Father," he breathed savagely, "Bo hit Rachel. She's got a fractured cheekbone. Not that you care." His nostrils flared and his voice lowered to a growl. "You don't care because she's a Donovan. And you couldn't care less what happens to anyone with that last name." Punching his finger toward his father, he continued, "I happen to love her. And I don't know if she loves me. This situation isn't going to help at all. But whatever happens, I'll tell you one thing—they aren't getting away with it this time. All your money, your influence peddling and the political strings you pull aren't going to make the charges against them go away. Chet and Bo were going to rape her. Did you know that? Is that something you condone?" He straightened, fury in his voice. "Knowing you, you'd condone it because her last name was Donovan."

Stunned, Frank looked up at him. "They said nothing about rape. Applebaum said Bo threw a punch her way because she lashed out at him."

"Yeah, well, it connected, Father. Big-time." Jim pushed his fingers angrily through his short hair and moved over to the fireplace. He felt his father's glare follow him. Jim's stomach was in knots. He was breathing hard. A burning sensation in the middle of his chest told him just how much he wanted to cry with pure rage over this whole fiasco.

Frank slowly turned his wheelchair around. Scowling at Jim. "What's this you said about loving this woman?"

"Her name is Rachel Donovan, Father. And yes, I love her."

"She love you?" he asked, his voice suddenly weary and old sounding.

Jim pushed his shoulders back to release the terrible tension in them. "I don't know. It's too soon. And too damn much has happened. I'll be lucky if she doesn't tar and feather me with the same brush as Bo and Chet."

"My own son...falling in love with a Donovan.... My God, how could you do this to me, Jim? How?"

Looking into his father's eyes, Jim saw tears in them. That shook him. He'd never seen his father cry—ever. "You know," Jim rasped, "I would hope the tears I see in your eyes are for what Rachel suffered at their hands and not the fact that I love her."

Frank's mouth tightened. "Get out of here. Get out and don't ever come back. You're a turncoat, Jim. I'm ashamed of you. My youngest boy, a boy I'd hoped would someday run the Bar C with his brothers...." He shook his head. His voice cracked with raw emotion. "Just when I need you the most, you turn traitor on me. And you're willing to sell your brothers out, too. How could you? Your own family!"

Fighting back tears, Jim held his father's accusing gaze as a lump formed in his throat. He wanted to scream at the unfairness of it all. Suddenly, he didn't care anymore. "I've spent nearly a year here, trying to straighten out things between you, me, and my brothers," he said thickly, "and it backfired on me. I got warned more times than not that I can't fix three people who'd like to stay the way they are." He headed slowly to his coat and hat. "You can't see anything because you're blinded by hate, Father. The word *Donovan* makes you like a rabid dog. Well," he said, jerking his coat off the hook, "I won't be part and parcel of what you, Bo or Chet want to do. I don't give a damn about this ranch, either, if it means others will suffer in order to claim it." He shrugged on his coat. "You're willing to do anything to get revenge for transgressions that died with Kelly."

His heart hurt in his chest and his voice wobbled dangerously as he jerked open the door. Settling his hat on his head, he rasped unevenly, "I'll be moving out. In the next week, I'll come over and pick up my stuff. I'll be seeing you in court."

"Rachel, you look so sad," Jessica said with a sigh. She touched her sister's shoulder as she headed for the stove in Rachel's kitchen. "The homeopathy sure helped get rid of that shiner you had and there's hardly any swelling left on your cheek. But nothing has cheered you up yet." She smiled brightly and poured some tea for both of them. Sunlight lanced through the curtains, flooding the cheery kitchen.

Thanking Jessica for the tea, Rachel squeezed a bit of fresh lemon into it. "I'm okay…really, I am."

Jessica sat down across from her and frowned. "It's been four days now since it happened. You just mope around. Something's wrong. I can feel it around you."

The tart, sweet tea tasted good to Rachel. Gently setting the china cup down on the saucer, she stared at it and said softly, "I wonder why Jim hasn't come by?"

"Ahh," Jessica said with a burgeoning smile, "that's it, isn't it? Why, I didn't know you were sweet on him, Rachel."

Looking up at her youngest sister, Rachel whispered, "I guess what happened out there in the meadow did something to me—ripped something away so I could see or feel more…." Lamely, she opened her hands. "I know he probably thinks I think less of him because of what his two brothers did to me."

"Hmm," Jessica murmured, "I don't sense that." She laughed, pressing her hand to the front of her green plaid, flannel, long-sleeved shirt.

"Your intuition?" Rachel valued Jessica's clairvoyant abilities.

"Maybe Jim hasn't come around because he's busy. You know, with two brothers in jail, someone has to run the Bar C, and he's got a part-time job as an EMT with the Sedona Fire Department. I imagine between the two, it has kept him hopping."

"Always the idealist."

Chortling, Jessica asked, "Do you like the alternative?"

"No," Rachel admitted sadly, sipping her tea. "I think Jim's avoiding me."

"I don't."

There was a knock on the front door. Jessica grinned and quickly stood up, her long blond braids swinging. "Are you expecting anyone?"

"No," Rachel said.

"I'll get it. You stay here."

Rachel was about to protest that she wasn't an invalid—and that Kate and Jessica were doting too much over her—when she heard a man's low, husky voice. *Jim.* Instantly, her heart began to beat hard in her chest and she nearly spilled the contents of her cup as she set it askew on the saucer.

"Look who's here!" Jessica announced breathlessly as she hurried back into the kitchen, her eyes shining with laughter.

Jim took off the baseball cap he wore when he was on EMT duty. He saw Rachel stand, her fingertips resting tentatively on the table, her cheeks flushed a dull red. Would she rebuff him? Tell him to leave? He was unsure as he held her widening eyes.

"Hi," he said with a broken smile. "I just thought I'd drop over and see how you were coming along."

Jessica patted his arm in a motherly fashion. "Believe me, you're just what the doctor ordered, Jim. Listen, I gotta go! Dan is helping me repot several of my orchid girls over in the greenhouse and he needs my guidance." She flashed them both a smile, raised her hand and was gone, like the little whirlwind she was.

When Jim heard the front door close, he met and held Rachel's assessing, forest green gaze. "I wasn't sure if I should drop over unannounced or not," he began, the cap in his right hand.

"I—I'm glad to see you," she said. "Would you like to have some tea? Jessica just made some a little while ago." The look on his face tore at her. She saw dark smudges beneath his bloodshot eyes and a strain around his mouth. He looked as if he hadn't slept well at all.

"Uh...tea sounds great," he replied, maneuvering around to a chair and pulling it out. He placed his dark blue cap on the table and said, "I can't stay long." He patted the pager on his belt. "I'm on duty."

Nervously, Rachel went over to the kitchen cabinet and pulled out another cup and saucer. Jim was here. Here! How could she tell him how much she missed his presence in her life? Compressing her lips, she poured him some tea and placed it in front of him.

"Kate brought over some fresh doughnuts that Sam picked up from the bakery this morning. You look a little pasty. Maybe some food might help?"

Jim looked up. "That sounds good," he said. "I'll take a couple if you have them handy." He studied the woman before him. Rachel's hair was combed and hung well below her shoulders, glinting with red-gold highlights. She wore a pale yellow, long-sleeved blouse, tan slacks and dark brown loafers. In his eyes, she'd never looked more beautiful. Her black eye was gone and he saw only the slightest swelling along her right cheekbone. She almost looked as if nothing had happened. But it had.

Thanking her for the chocolate-covered doughnuts, he watched as she sat down next to him after pouring herself more hot tea. He gauged the guarded look on her features.

"How are you surviving?" he asked, munching on a doughnut. For the first time in four days, he found himself hungry. Ravenous, in fact—but even more, he was starved for her company, her voice, her presence.

"Oh, fine…fine…." Rachel waved her hands in a nervous gesture. "But you don't look too good." She avoided his eyes. "I've been worried about you, Jim. About you having to go over to your father's home and live there and take the heat from him about your brothers." She gestured toward his face. "You look like you haven't been sleeping well, either."

With a grimace, he wiped his mouth with a napkin. "A lot's changed since we last were together," he admitted slowly.

"Is your father okay?"

He heard the genuine worry in Rachel's voice. Her insight, her care of others was one of the many things he loved fiercely about her. Putting the cup aside, he laid his arms on the table and held her gaze.

"He had a stroke four days ago."

"Oh, no!" Rachel cried.

Scowling, Jim rasped, "Yeah…."

"And what's his prognosis?"

He shook his head and avoided her eyes. "The docs up in Flag say he's going to make it. His whole right side is paralyzed, though, and he can't talk anymore."

Squeezing her eyes shut, Rachel whispered, "Oh, Jim, I'm so sorry. This is awful." She opened her eyes. "Why didn't you call and tell me about it?"

Shrugging painfully, he put the doughnuts aside. "Honestly?"

"Always," she whispered, reaching out and slipping her fingers into his hand.

"I was afraid after what happened that you wouldn't want to be around me anymore...because of my brothers. You know, the Cunningham name and all...."

Rachel felt her heart break. Tears gathered in her eyes. "Oh, Jim, no! Never...not ever would I let how I feel toward you change just because of your last name." She reached out and took his other hand. "Is there anything we can do to help you? Or your father?" She knew Frank Cunningham would be an invalid now, confined to bed unless he went through therapy. And even then, Frank would be bound to a wheelchair for the rest of his life. She saw tears glimmer in Jim's eyes and then he forced them away. His hands felt strong and good on hers.

Without a word, she released his hands, stood up and came around the table. Moving behind him, she slid her arms around him and pressed her uninjured cheek against his and just held him. She felt so much tension in him, and as she squeezed him gently, he released a ragged sigh. His hands slid across her lower arms, and she closed her eyes.

"I feel so awful for all of you," she whispered brokenly. "I'm sorry all this happened."

The firmness of her flesh made him need her even more. Without a word, Jim eased out of her arms and stood up. Putting the chair aside, he faced Rachel. Tears ran down her cheeks. She was crying for his father, for him and for the whole, ugly situation. Her generosity, her compassion, shook him as nothing else ever could.

"What I need," he said unsteadily as he held out his hand toward Rachel, "is you...just you...."

Chapter 11

Ａs Rachel pressed herself to Jim, his arms went around her like steel bands. The air rushed out of her lungs, and she felt his shaven cheek against her own. A shudder went through him as he buried his face in her thick, dark hair. Clinging to her like a man who was dying and could be saved only by her. Her heart opened and she sniffled, the tears coming more and more quickly.

"I'm sorry, so sorry," she sobbed. "I didn't mean to cause this kind of trouble…and your father—"

"Hush," Jim whispered thickly, framing her face with his hands. He was mindful of her fractured right cheekbone, and he barely touched that area of her face. He looked deeply into her dark, pain-filled eyes. Tears beaded on her dark lashes. Her mouth was a tortured line. "This isn't your fault. None of it, princess."

He winced inwardly as he realized he'd allowed his

endearment for her to slip out. Rachel blinked once, as if assimilating the word. She gulped, her hands caressing the back of his neck and shoulders.

"There's been so much misery between our families," she whispered unsteadily. "I was hoping…oh, how I was hoping things would settle down now that Kelly was gone."

Caressing her uninjured cheek, Jim wiped the tears away with his fingers. "We aren't going to pay the price that those two decided to pay one another, Rachel. We aren't. You and I—" he looked deeply into her eyes, his voice low and fervent "—can have a better life. A happier one if we want it. We can make better decisions than they ever have. We should learn from them, not duplicate their actions."

Closing her eyes, she felt a fine quiver go through her. "Not like Chet and Bo," she admitted painfully.

He nodded grimly. "We're nothing like those two. They have to find their own way now. Father is mute. He'll never speak again. He'll never be able to wield the power or call in the chips like he did before his stroke." Caressing her hair, Jim added wearily, "Chet and Bo will go to prison for at least a couple of years. I've talked to the district attorney for Coconino County, and he said that, based upon the evidence and our testimony and their past jail records, the judge won't be lenient. He shouldn't be."

Numbly, Rachel rested her brow against his chin. She felt the caress of his fingers through her hair and relaxed as he gently massaged her tense neck and shoulders. "It's all so stupid," she said. "They could have done so many other things with their lives—good things."

"They made their bed," Jim told her harshly, flattening his hands against her supple back, "now let them lie in it."

Surrendering to his strength, Rachel flowed against him. She heard Jim groan in utter pleasure. Breathing in his masculine scent, she reveled in his warm, tender embrace. As the moments flowed by, she closed her eyes and simply absorbed his gentle and protective nature.

Pressing a kiss to her hair, Jim finally eased Rachel away just enough to look into her languid eyes. There was a sweet, spicy fragrance to her hair and he inhaled it deeply. Rachel was life. *His* life. He saw the gold flecks in the forest green depths of her eyes, and he fought the urge to lean down and take her delicious, parted lips. Instead, he asked wryly, "We never got to finish our conversation up on the Rim, do you realize that?"

Heat burned in Rachel's cheeks as she stood in his arms, her hands on his hard biceps. "You're right...we didn't."

"What do you think? Am I worth the risk? I know you are."

Shyly, Rachel searched his serious features. "Yesterday," she whispered, "I thought a lot about you...how long I've known you, and how I hadn't realized you had a crush on me back then."

"My crush on you," Jim told her, moving a strand of hair away from her flushed cheek, "never ended."

Swallowing hard, Rachel nodded. "I began to understand that."

"I'm scared. Are you?"

"Very," Rachel admitted in a strained voice, her fingers digging a little more firmly into his arms. "When Bo dragged me off the horse, I thought I was going to die, Jim. I could see the hatred in both your brothers' eyes and I knew…" She swallowed painfully. Her eyes misted and her voice softened. "I knew I loved you and I didn't have the courage to tell you I did. And I was sorry because I thought I'd never see you again." A sob stuck in her throat, and she felt hot tears spilling down her cheeks again.

Jim held her hard against him and gently rocked her back and forth. "It's okay, princess. I know you love me." He laughed a little shakily. "What a crazy time this is." He kissed her hair and then carefully cupped her face. "I love you, Rachel Donovan. And ten thousand stampeding horses aren't going to stop me from seeing you whenever I can."

His mouth was warm and strong as it settled against her tear-bathed lips. Rachel moaned, but it was a moan of surrender, of need of him. She tasted the sweet tartness of the lemon and sugar on his lips, the scent of juniper around him as he deepened his exploration of her. Her breath became ragged and her heart pounded. The power of his mouth, the searching heat of him surrounded her, drugged her, and she bent like a willow in his arms.

Just then, his beeper went off.

"Damn," he growled, tearing his mouth from hers. Apologetically, he eased Rachel into the nearest chair. "I'm sorry," he said, looking down at the pager. "Larry and I are on duty. It's probably an EMT call."

"The phone's in the living room," Rachel whispered, dizzy from his unexpected, tender kiss. Touching her tingling lower lip, she felt euphoria sweep through her. Just the sound of his steady, low voice as he talked on the phone, was comforting to her. He loved her. The admission was sweet, filled with promise. And filled with terror. But as she sat there remembering the taste and touch of Jim, Rachel realized her terror hadn't won. It was still there, but not as overwhelming as before. Maybe the fact that she had almost died made her realize how good life was with Jim in it.

Jim walked back into the kitchen, his brow knitted. "I've got to go. There's been a multiple accident about a mile down 89A from here."

Rachel nodded and stood up. Her knees felt weak. Before she could speak, he slid his arm around her, drew her against him and captured her parted lips with his mouth. It was a hot, searching, almost desperate kiss. Before she could respond, he released her and rasped, "I get off tomorrow at noon. I'll bring lunch."

Then he was gone. Rachel swayed. Touching her lips gently, she felt a stab of fear—only this time she was worried over Jim and the accident scene. She remembered his promise of lunch tomorrow and the thought blanketed her, filling her with warmth. Never had she felt this way before. Her heart throbbed with a joy she'd never known. Love. She was in love with Jim Cunningham.

A little in shock over the realization, Rachel sat down before she fell down. She heard a knock at the front door, and then Kate's voice rang through the house.

"Rachel?"

"In here," she called. "Come on in."

Kate took off her cowboy hat and ran her fingers through her dark, tangled hair. She grinned as she came into the kitchen.

"I just saw Jim leaving in a hurry. He on call?"

"Yes. There's been a bad accident a mile down from our ranch on 89A. Are Dan and Sam here?"

"Yep," she said with a sigh, going over to the kitchen counter and pouring herself a cup of tea. "It's really nice," she murmured, "that you're home now. I like having an excuse to escape from vetting horses and cattle and to come over here and see you."

Smiling up at her older sister, Rachel patted the chair next to her own. "Isn't it great? Come, sit down. You're working too hard, Kate." Rachel knew her sister was up well before daybreak everyday, and rarely did she and Sam hit the sack until around midnight. She didn't know how Kate did it. Perhaps she had Kelly's drive and passion for the ranch more than any of the sisters.

Flopping down on the chair, Kate sipped her tea. "Mmm, this hits the spot on a cold day." She crossed her legs. Her cowboy boots were scuffed and dusty. "Did you hear the latest? Sam and I just came in from Sedona."

"No." Rachel rolled her eyes. "I hate town gossip. You know that."

"Mmm, you'll be interested in this," Kate said. She took another gulp of the steaming coffee and sat up. Tapping the table with her finger, she said, "We heard from Deputy Scott Maitland that Bo and Chet are probably going away to do federal prison time."

Rachel nodded. "Yes, Jim just told me the same thing."

"They deserve it," she growled. "If I'd been there, I'd probably have blown their heads off with my rifle, and then I'd never live outside of prison bars again."

Rachel grimaced. "Thank goodness you weren't there, then. You've seen enough of that place."

Kate made a face. "No kidding."

"Did you hear that Jim's father had a stroke? He's up at the Flag hospital recovering."

Shocked, Kate sat up. "No. What happened?"

"I'm not sure. Maybe it was the shock of Bo and Chet being in jail."

"Or you pressing charges," Kate muttered angrily. "I'm surprised that Old Man Cunningham didn't keel over of a stroke a decade ago. He's always blowing his top over some little thing."

"Two of your sons going to prison isn't little," Rachel said softly. "The ranch, from what Jim said, is in his brothers' names."

"Is Old Man Cunningham paralyzed?"

"Yes. He's pretty bad," Rachel murmured worriedly.

"Well," Kate said, pushing several strands of hair away from her flushed cheek, "that means Jim is going to have to assume the running of the Bar C."

Surprised, Rachel bolted upright. She stared at Kate. "What?"

"Sure," she said, leaning back in the chair and sipping her coffee, "someone's got to run it now that the old man can't. Chet and Bo are probably looking at five years in the pen. Maybe they'll get off in two and a half for good behavior. If Jim doesn't quit his job as an EMT and return to the ranch, it will fall apart. Who will be there to pay the bills? Give the wranglers their checks? Or manage the place?" With a shake of her head, Kate said, "Boy, what goes around comes around, doesn't it? Cunningham was trying to put us out of business and look what's happened to him." She brightened a little. "Come to think of it, that trumped-up lawsuit he's got against us will die on the vine, too." Smiling grimly, she got up and poured herself another cup of tea. "This disaster might be a blessing in disguise. If we can get his lawyer off our backs, we won't have to spend money filing—money we don't have."

Rachel nodded and watched her sister sit back down. She wondered about everything Kate had told her. Would Jim really settle down to ranching life on his father's spread? For the first time, she saw hope for a future with Jim.

The noontime sun streamed into Rachel's small but cozy kitchen as Jim sat sharing the lunch he'd promised with her. He'd stopped at a deli in town and gotten tuna sandwiches, sweet pickles and two thick slices of chocolate cake. Ever since he'd arrived, he'd been longing to take her in his arms again, to finish what they'd only started yesterday. But he could still see a slight swelling along her right cheekbone where it had been fractured. As badly as he wanted to make love to her, he would wait until she was healed. The way she carefully ate told him that moving her jaw caused her pain. Instead, he decided to tell her his news. "I quit my job at the fire department."

"To run the ranch?" Rachel asked, carefully chewing her sandwich and studying the man before her. Jim wore his dark blue uniform, leaving his baseball cap on the side of the table as he ate. He looked exhausted, and Rachel knew it was due to worrying over his father's condition. She was glad he'd come by, though—how she had looked forward to seeing him again!

"Yes," he said, sipping the hot coffee. "I talked to the hospital and they're beginning recovery therapy for my father. He's got all kinds of medical insurance, so it won't be a problem that way, thank God."

Rachel raised her brows. "It's a good thing he has insurance. We have none. Can't afford it."

"Like about one-third of all Americans," Jim agreed somberly.

"When will you bring him home?"

"In about a week, from the looks of it."

"How do you feel about running the Bar C?" she asked tentatively.

"Odd, I guess." He exchanged a warm look with her. "When I left after high school, I figured I'd never be back. When I did come home, Father told me Bo and Chet would take over the ranch after he died."

"How did you feel about that?"

"I didn't care."

"And now?"

He grinned a little. "I still don't." Reaching out, he captured her hand briefly. "I've got my priorities straight. I want a life with the woman who stole my heart when I was a teenager."

She smiled softly at the tenderness that burned in his eyes. "I still can't believe you loved me all those years, Jim. You never said a thing."

"I was a shy kid," he said with a laugh. "And I had the curse of my father's Donovan-hating on top of it. That was the best reason not to approach you."

Rachel nodded and reluctantly released his hand. "I know," she whispered sadly. Holding his gaze, she asked, "Have you ever wondered what our lives might have been like if our fathers hadn't been carrying on that stupid feud?"

"Yeah," he said fondly, finishing off his second sandwich. Being around Rachel made him famished. "We'd probably have married at eighteen, had a brood of kids and been happy as hell."

Rachel couldn't deny the possible scenario. "And now? What do you want out of life, Jim?"

Somberly, he picked up her hand as she laid her own half-eaten sandwich aside. "You. Just you, princess."

Coloring, she smiled. "That's a beautiful endearment."

"Good, because as an awkward, shy teenager, I used to fantasize that you were a princess from a foreign country—so beautiful and yet untouchable."

Her voice grew strained with tears. "What a positive way to look at it, at the situation." Rachel gently pressed the back of his hand to her left cheek. The coals of desire burned in his eyes and she ached to love Jim. He'd made it clear earlier that, because her cheekbone was fractured, they should wait, and she'd agreed. To even try and kiss him was painful. Waiting was tough, but not impossible for Rachel. She understood on a deeper level that they needed the time to reacquaint themselves with one another, without all the family fireworks and dramatics going on around them.

He eased his hand from hers. "I brought something with me that I've been saving for a long, long time." He grinned sheepishly and dug into the left pocket of his dark blue shirt. "Now," he cautioned her lightly, "you have to keep this in perspective, okay?"

Rachel smiled with him. Jim suddenly was boyish, looking years younger. His eyes sparkled mischievously as he pulled something wrapped in a tissue from his pocket. "Well, sure. What is it, Jim?"

Chuckling, he laid the lump of tissue on the table between them. "I had such a crush on you that I saved my money and I went to Mr. Foglesong's jewelry store and bought you this. I kept dreaming that someday you'd look at me, or give me a smile, and we would meet, and at the right moment, I could give you this." He gestured toward it. "Go ahead, it's yours. A few years late, but it's yours, anyway."

Jim saw Rachel's cheeks flush with pleasure as she carefully unwrapped the tissue on the table. He heard her audible gasp and saw her dark green eyes widen beautifully.

"Now, it's nothing expensive," he warned as she picked up a ring encrusted with colorful gems on a silver band. "It's base metal covered with electroplated silver. The stones are nothing more than cut glass."

Touched beyond words, Rachel gently held the ring encircled with sparkling, colorful "diamonds."

"Back then, every girl wore her boyfriend's ring around her neck on a chain."

He laughed. "Yeah, going steady."

"And you were going to give this to me?" She held it up in a slash of sunlight that crossed the table where they sat. The ring sparkled like a rainbow.

"I wanted to," Jim told her ruefully. "I saved my money and bought it the first year I saw you in junior high."

The realization that Jim had kept this ring through six years of school and never once had she even said hello to him or smiled at him broke her heart. No, he was a Cunningham, and Rachel, like her sisters, had avoided anyone with that name like the plague. She felt deep sadness move through her as she slipped the ring on the fourth finger of her right hand. It fit perfectly.

Tears burned in her eyes as she held out her hand for him to inspect.

"How does it look?" she quavered.

Words choked in Jim's throat as he slid his hands around hers. "Nice. But what I'm looking at is beautiful."

Sniffing, Rachel wiped the tears from her eyes with trembling fingers. "This is so sad, Jim. You carried this ring for six years in school hoping I'd say hello to you, or at least look you in the eye. Every time I saw a Cunningham coming, I'd turn the other way and leave. I'm so sorry! I didn't know…. I really didn't know…."

"Hush, princess, it doesn't matter. You came home and so did I, and look what happened." His mouth curved into a gentle smile as he held her tear-filled eyes. "We have a chance to start over, Rachel. That's how I see it." Gripping her hand more firmly, he continued, "Life isn't exactly going to be a lot of fun this next six weeks, but after that, things should settle out a little."

"I know," she agreed. Six weeks. The trial would be coming up in a month and then Chet and Bo would get from the judge what they deserved. It would take six weeks for her fractured cheekbone to heal. And then… Her heart took off at a gallop. Then she could make love to Jim. The thought was hot, melting and full of promise. She ached to have him, love him and join with him in that beautiful oneness.

"I'm sure my brothers will be going to prison," Jim said in a low voice. "And my father is going to take up a lot of my time. I'll have to get used to running the ranch. I was thinking of asking Sam for some help and guidance. He was the manager of the Bar C for a while, and he knows the inner workings of it. He can kind of shadow me until I get into the full swing of things."

Rachel nodded. "I know Sam would do anything to help out. We all will, Jim."

"Do you know how good that is to hear?" he rasped. "No more fighting between the Donovans and the Cunninghams. Now we'll have peace. Isn't that something?"

It was. Rachel sat there in awe over the realization. "I never thought of it in those terms before, but you're right." She gave a little laugh. "Just think, the next time your cattle stray onto our land or vice versa, no nasty phone calls. Just a call saying, 'hey, your cows are straying again.'" She laughed. "Do you know how *good* that will be?"

"The range war between us is over," he said, patting her hand and admiring the ring on her finger once again. It was a child's innocent love that had bought that present for her, but Jim felt his heart swell with pride that Rachel had put it on, nevertheless.

"There's something I want to tell you," he said. "When I left here the other day after Bo and Chet assaulted you, I went home and had it out with my father." He frowned. "It probably contributed to him having a stroke, but I can't be sorry for what I told him." He held Rachel's soft green eyes. "I told him I was in love with you."

"Oh, dear, Jim."

"He needed to hear it from me," he rasped. "He didn't like it, but that's life."

"And he accused you of being a traitor?"

"Yes," Jim replied, amazed by her insight. But then, he shouldn't be surprised. She had always been a deep and caring person. "He said I was being a traitor to the family."

"What else? I can see it in your eyes."

Ordinarily, Jim would feel uncomfortable revealing so much of himself, but with Rachel, he felt not only safe in showing those depths within him, but he wanted to. "My father disowned me—for the second time."

"No...." Rachel pressed her hand against her heart as she felt and heard the pain in his voice, saw it clearly in his face and eyes. "And then he had that stroke?"

"He had one of the wranglers drive him up to the Flag jail. From what I hear from Scott Maitland, who was there when my father entered into the jail facility, he got into a hell of a fight with the sheriff of Coconino Country, Slade Cameron. That's when he had the stroke. They called 911 and he was taken right over to the hospital from there. Scott told me at the hospital, after I arrived, that my father was demanding that Cameron let my brothers go on bail. The judge had refused them bail, too, and Cameron was backing the judge's decision to the hilt."

Inwardly, Rachel shivered. She knew why the judge had not given them bail. The Cunningham brothers had a notorious history of taking revenge on people who pressed charges against them. That was why they had gotten away without punishment until now—they'd threatened their victims until they dropped the charges. But not this time. Rachel would have kept pressing charges even if they had gotten bail.

"So his anger blew a blood vessel in his brain," Jim told her quietly. "I'm surprised it hadn't happened before this, to tell you the truth."

She nodded and got up. Leaning against the counter,

she studied him in the gathering warmth and silence. "How are you feeling about all this?"

Shrugging, Jim eased out of the chair and came to her side. He slid his arm around her shoulders and guided her into the living room. "Guilty. I can't help but feel that way, but I wasn't going to live a lie with my father, either. He had to know I loved you and that I was going to testify in your defense at Chet and Bo's trial."

She moved with him to the purple-pink-and-cream-colored couch near the fireplace. Sitting down, she leaned against him, contented as never before. "And even though he's disowned you a second time, you're going to stay and run the ranch?"

Jim absorbed the feel of her slender form. How natural, how good it felt to have Rachel in his arms. Outside the picture window, he saw snowflakes twirling down again. The fire crackled pleasantly, and he'd never felt happier—or sadder. "Yes. This disowning thing is a game with my father. I know he meant it, but now it doesn't matter."

Rachel rested her head against his strong, capable shoulder. "And you really want to run the Bar C?"

"Sure." He grinned down at her. "Once a cowboy, always a cowboy."

"An EMT cowboy. And a firefighter."

"All those things," Jim agreed.

"And when Bo and Chet get out of prison, what will you do? Hand the ranch over to them to run?"

Sobering, Jim nodded. He moved his fingers languidly down her shoulder and upper arm. "Yes," he said grimly, "I will."

"He'll never be able to run it," Rachel said worriedly.

"Bo and Chet are the owners, technically. I know they aren't going to want me around when they get out."

"And your father? What will you do? Continue to live there?"

Gently, he turned Rachel around so that she faced him. "When the time's right, I'm going to propose to you. And if you say yes, you'll live over on the Bar C with me. We have several other homes. I'll put my father in one of them and we'll live at the main ranch house. Even though he disowned me, he's going to need me now. And I'm hoping we can mend fences, at least for the sake of his health. When Bo and Chet get out, you and I will leave."

Rachel thrilled to the idea of being Jim's wife. His partner for life. All her previous fears were gone and she knew that was because she was certain of her love for Jim. Heat burned in her cheeks and she held his hopeful gaze. "Kate wants us to live here. In this house, Jim. She already told me we were welcome here in case we got 'serious' about one another."

Grinning, he caressed her hair and followed the sweep of it down her shoulder. "Kate saw us getting together?"

"Kate's not a dumb post."

Chuckling, Jim nodded. "No, I'd never accuse her of being that, ever."

Sliding her hand up his cheek, Rachel felt the sandpaper quality of his skin beneath her palm. She saw Jim's eyes go dark with longing—for her. It was such a delicious feeling to be wanted by him. "Then you wouldn't mind living here and working on the Donovan Ranch instead when the time came?"

"No," he whispered, leaning over and placing a very

light kiss on the tip of her nose, "why should I? I'll have you. That's all I'll ever need, princess. Where I live with you doesn't matter at all. It never did."

Sliding into his waiting arms, Rachel closed her eyes and rested her head against Jim's shoulder. A broken sigh escaped her. The next six weeks were going to be a special hell for all of them on many levels. The trial would tear them all apart, she knew. And Jim would be away from her more than with her because he would have to be at the Bar C learning how to manage the huge ranch. And she, well, she had just rented an office in Sedona and there was a lot of pressure on her to get patients and start making money and contributing to paying off that huge debt against the ranch.

"I can hardly wait," Rachel quavered, "for these next six weeks to be done and gone."

Holding her tightly, Jim ran his hand along the line of her graceful back. Pressing a kiss to her hair, he murmured fervently, "I know, princess. Believe me, I know…"

Chapter 12

The mid-February sunlight was strong and bright as Rachel sat on her horse, her leg occasionally touching Jim's as the gelding moved to nibble the green grass shoots that surrounded them. The patches of snow here and there on the red clay soil of the Cunningham pasture was strong evidence of the fact that the steady snowfall would break some of the drought conditions that had held everyone captive.

"The cattle are going to eat well," Jim commented as he moved his hat up on his brow and gazed at Rachel. She looked beautiful in Levi's, a long-sleeved white blouse, leather vest and black Stetson cowboy hat. Her hair was caught up in a single braid that lay down the middle of her back.

Nodding, she leaned down and stroked the neck of her black Arabian mare. "For once."

They sat on their horses on a hill that overlooked

both Donovan and Cunningham ranch land, a barbed wire fence marking the division line. Down below, on the Donovan side, Kate and Sam were working to repair fence so that their cattle wouldn't wander over onto Cunningham property. At least, Jim thought, this time there was going to be teamwork between the two families, and not angry words followed by violence.

"How's your father?" Rachel asked. Jim's face took on a pained expression. Frank Cunningham had never recovered after the stroke as the doctors had hoped. He was now bedridden, with twenty-four-hour nursing care at the ranch house. Jim divided his duties between managing the huge ranch and trying to help his father, who had given up on living. She knew it was just a matter of time. Frank hadn't been doing well since he'd found out that his two sons were going to prison. Bo got a year and Chet two years.

"Father's a little better today," he said, wiping the sweat off his brow. "That's why I came out with the line crew."

"It does you good to get out of that office you've been living in."

Grinning a little, he held Rachel's dancing, lively gaze. "I was going stir-crazy in there, if you want the truth." Jim knew that ever since the trial, which had taken place two weeks earlier, Rachel had been upset and strained. For the first time, he was seeing her more relaxed. Now she had a thriving office filled with patients who wanted natural medicine, like homeopathy, instead of drugs. To say she was a little busy was an understatement. Income from her growing business was helping to pay off some bills on the Donovan Ranch.

"What's the chances of you coming over for dinner

tonight?" Rachel asked, her heart beating a little harder. The ache to be with Jim, to share more time with him, never left her. The last six weeks had been a hell for them. They needed a break. She needed him. The stolen kisses, the hot, lingering touches, weren't enough for her anymore.

Frowning, Jim said, "How about a picnic tomorrow? I wanted to go back up on the Rim and explore where they captured that jaguar and took her away." Reaching over, he closed his hand over hers. "Want to come along?"

"I'll provide the lunch?" Rachel asked, thrilling at his strong, steady grip on her hand. The burning hunger in his eyes matched her own feelings. How she hungered to have a few moments alone with Jim! The demands in their lives had kept them apart and she wanted to change that.

"You bet," he murmured with a smile.

"Have you heard from Bob Granby in the fish and game department about how the jaguar is getting along in her new haunt?"

Jim shifted in the saddle, the leather creaking pleasantly beneath him. "Matter of fact, I did. She's been taken over to the White Mountain area and is getting along fine there. He said two more jaguars have been spotted in the mountains north of Tucson, so they are migrating north for sure."

"I love how things in nature, if they are disturbed, will come back into harmony over time."

Reluctantly releasing Rachel's hand, Jim nodded. "I like the harmony we're establishing right now between the two ranches."

"It will last only a year," she commented sadly.

He studied her. "Not if you agree to marry me, Rachel."

Her heart thudded. She stared at Jim. "What?"

He grinned a little. "Well? Will you?"

She saw that boyish grin on his face, his eyes tender with love—for her. Lips parting, she tried to find the words to go along with her feelings.

"Is your stunned look a no or a yes?" he teased, his grin widening. Over the last six weeks, they had grown incredibly close. Nothing had ever felt so right or so good to Jim. He prayed silently that Rachel wanted marriage as much as he did.

Touching her flaming cheeks, Rachel said, "Let me think about it? I'll give you an answer tomorrow at lunch, okay?"

Nodding, he picked up the reins from the neck of the quarter horse he rode. A part of him felt terror that she'd say no. Another part whispered that Rachel truly needed the time. But that was something he could give her. Leaning over, he curved his hand behind her neck and drew her to him.

"What we have," he told her, his face inches from hers, "is good and beautiful, princess. I'll wait as long as you want me to." He smiled a little, recalling that she had made the other man in her life wait five years and even then she couldn't marry him. Things were different this time around and Jim knew it. Over the last six weeks, he'd watched Rachel's fear dissolve more and more. The fact that he'd loved her since he was a teenager, he was sure, had something to do with it. Leaning over a little more, he crushed her lips to his and tasted sunlight, the clean, fresh air on them. It was so easy to kiss Rachel. And how wonderful it would be to love her fully. Her cheek was healed now, and he didn't have to worry about possibly hurting her when he kissed her hard and swiftly. And he knew she wanted him, too, noting her warm, hot response to his mouth skimming hers.

Easing away, Jim reluctantly released her. There was a delicious cloudiness in Rachel's eyes, and he read it as longing—for him. "I'll meet you at the north pasture at ten tomorrow morning?" he asked huskily.

Rachel felt dizzy with heat, with an aching longing for Jim. Every time he stole a kiss unexpectedly from her, she wanted him just that much more. Touching her lips, she nodded. He look so handsome and confident, sitting astride his bay gelding with that dangerous look glittering in his eyes, one corner of his mouth pulled into a slight, confident smile.

"Yes—tomorrow...."

Rachel found Kate out in the barn, feeding the broodmares for the evening. She helped her older sister finish off the feeding by giving the pregnant Arabian mares a ration of oats. When they were done, Rachel sat down on a bale of hay at one end of the barn. Kate walked up, took off her hat and, wiping her brow with the back of her hand, joined her.

"Thanks for the help."

Rachel nodded. "I need to share something with you, Kate, and I wanted you to hear it from me and not secondhand."

She saw Kate's face go on guard. Rachel smiled a little. "It's good news, Kate."

"Whew. Okay, what is it?" she asked, running her fingers through her hair. "I could use good news."

Wasn't that the truth? Rachel smiled tentatively. "Jim asked me to marry me today." She watched Kate's expression carefully. "I've already told Jessica and Dan. Now I want to tell you and Sam. I'd like to know how you feel about the possibility." Her gut clenched a little as she waited for Kate to speak.

"Jim's a good man," Kate said finally, in a low voice. She picked at some of the alfalfa hay between her legs where she'd straddled the bale. Her brows knitted as she chose her words. "I didn't like him before. But that's because his last name is Cunningham." Looking up, she smiled apologetically. "I'm the last one who should be holding a grudge. The more I saw of Jim in different circumstances, the more I realized that he was genuine. He's not like the others in his family. And he's trying to straighten things out between the two families."

"If I tell him yes," Rachel whispered, a catch in her voice, "that means I'll be living over there for a while, at least until Bo and Chet come back to claim the ranch."

"And then," Kate said, straightening and moving her shoulders a little, "you can come home and have your house back if you want."

"Then you don't mind if I tell Jim yes?"

Kate gave her a silly grin. Leaning over, she hugged Rachel tightly for a moment. "You love each other! Why should I stand in the way? Jim's a good person. He means to do right by others. He can't help it if he's got rattlesnakes for brothers."

Grinning, Rachel gripped Kate's long, callused hand. "Thanks, Kate. Your blessing means everything to me. I—I didn't want to come back here and not be welcomed."

Tears formed in Kate's eyes and she wiped them away self-consciously. "Listen, I've committed enough mistakes for the whole family. You've both forgiven me.

Why can't I do the same for you and Jim? So, when's the big day?"

"I don't know—yet. Jim and I are going to ride up on the Rim tomorrow morning where we found the jaguar's den. I'm packing a lunch."

Rising, Kate said, "Great! I'm sure you'll know a lot more when you come down." Holding her hand out to Rachel, she sighed. "Isn't it wonderful? We've all come home from various parts of the world and we're getting our ranch back on its feet. Together."

Rachel released Kate's hand and walked slowly down the aisle with her. She slipped her arm around her sister's slender waist. "Dreams do come true," she agreed. "I hated leaving here when I did. I cried so much that first year I was gone. I was so homesick for Mama, for this wonderful land…."

Sighing, Kate wrapped her arm around Rachel's waist. The gloom of the barn cast long shadows down the aisle as they slowly walked together. "All three of us were. At least we had the guts to come back and work to save our ranch."

"And we're finally coming out from under the bank's thumb!" Rachel laughed, feeling almost giddy about their good fortune. Kate and Sam had sold off half the Herefords for a good price. With the bank loan paid off, they now had a clear shot at keeping the ranch once and for all.

Kate looked down at her, smiling. "Want another piece of good news?"

"Sure? Gosh, two in a row, Katie. I don't know if I can handle it or not!"

She laughed huskily. Patting her abdomen, she said, "I'm pregnant."

Stunned, Rachel released her and turned, her mouth dropping open. "What?"

Coloring prettily, Kate kept her hand across her abdomen. "I just found out this afternoon. Doc Kaldenbaugh said I was two and a half months along. Isn't that wonderful?"

"And Sam? Does he know about it?" Rachel asked, feeling thrilled. She saw the shyness in Kate's face and the joy in it, too.

"Sure, he was with me."

"Oh!" Rachel cried, throwing her arms around Kate and hugging her. "This is so wonderful! I'm gonna be an aunt!"

Kate laughed self-consciously. "Hey, I'm going to need all the help I can get. This mothering role isn't one I know a whole lot about."

Tears trickled down Rachel's cheeks. "Don't worry," she whispered, choking up, "Jessica and I will love being aunts and helping you out. I think among the three of us, we can do the job, don't you?"

Kate grinned mischievously. "You mean Jessica hasn't told you yet?"

"Told me what?"

"She's expecting, too."

Stunned, Rachel stared. "What? When did this all happen? Where was I?"

Chuckling, Kate said, "We both went to Doc Kaldenbaugh today. Seems Jessica is expecting twins. They run in Dan Black's family, you know."

Rachel pressed her hands to her cheeks, dumbfounded. She saw Kate's eyes sparkle with laughter over her reaction.

"So, little sis, you and Jim had better get busy, eh? I'm assuming you want children?"

"More than anything," Rachel said, her voice soft and in awe. "You're *both* pregnant!"

"Yes." Kate gave her a satisfied smile. She turned and shut the barn doors for the night with Rachel's help. "Sam is going to hire a couple more wranglers now that we have some money. Then I can ease off on some of the work I've been doing. He wants me to take it easy." She laughed as she brought the latch down on the door. "I can't exactly see me knitting and crocheting in the house all day, can you?"

Rachel shook her head. "No, but Sam's right—you do need to ease off on some of that hard, physical labor you do on the ranch. I'm sure Jessica could use some help in her flower essence business. You like the greenhouse."

"I was thinking I would help her," Kate said. Patting Rachel on the shoulder, she said, "I'll let Jessica know I told you the big news. When you see Jim tomorrow, and say yes, tell him from me that I'm glad he's going to be a part of our family."

Rachel nodded and gripped her sister's hand for a moment. Kate's blessing made things right. "I will," she whispered. "And thanks for understanding."

"Around here," Kate said, looking up at the bright coverlet of stars in the black night above them, "everything is heart centered, Rachel. I like living out of my heart again. This ranch is our heart, our soul. I'm looking forward to having kids running around again. I'm really looking forward to seeing life and discoveries through their eyes. You know?"

Rachel did know. She lifted her hand. "Good night, Kate. That baby you're carrying will be one of the most loved children on the face of this earth." And it would be. As Rachel made her way through the darkness, broken by patches of light from the sulfur lamps placed here and there around the ranch, she smiled softly. They had suffered so much—each of them, and now life was giving them gifts in return for their courage. Her heart expanded and she longed to see Jim. Rachel could hardly wait for morning to arrive.

"Isn't that wonderful news?" Rachel asked as she sat on the red-and-white checkered blanket. Jim had spread the picnic blanket out at the mouth to the canyon, beneath an alligator juniper that was probably well over two hundred years old. Above them was the empty lair where the jaguar had once lived.

He munched thoughtfully on an apple. Lying on his side, his cowboy hat hung on a low tree limb, he nodded. "Twins. Wow. Jessica and Dan are going to be busy."

Chuckling, Rachel put the last of the chocolate cake and the half-empty bottle of sparkling grape juice back into the saddlebags. "No kidding."

"You like the idea of being an aunt?" Jim asked, slowly easing into a sitting position. He watched as Rachel put the items away. No matter what she did, there was always grace about her movements. Today she wore her hair loose and free, with dark strands cascading across her pale pink cowboy shirt.

"I love the idea."

He caught her hand. "What do you think about having children?"

His hand was warm and dry as she met and held his tender gaze. "I've always wanted them. And you?"

"They're a natural part of life—and love," he said

slowly as he pulled a small box from his pocket. Placing the gray velvet box in the palm of her hand, he whispered, "Open it, Rachel...."

Heart pounding, she smiled tremulously. Rachel knew it was a wedding ring. She loved the idea of him asking to marry her here, in this special canyon the jaguar had come home to. In many ways, the Donovan women were like that jaguar—chased away by a man. And they, too, had finally returned home.

Her fingers trembled as she opened the tiny brass latch. Inside was a gold band. Instead of a diamond, however, there were eight channel-cut stones the same height as the surface of the ring so they wouldn't snag or catch on anything. Each stone was a different color, and as Rachel removed the ring, they sparkled wildly in the sunlight.

"This is so beautiful, Jim," she whispered. Tears stung her eyes as she held it up to him. "It's like this ring." She held up her hand, showing him the "going steady" ring he'd bought so long ago and that she'd faithfully worn since he'd gotten up the courage to give it to her.

Touched, Jim nodded. "Do you like it?"

"Like it?" Rachel stroked the new ring. "I love it...."

"I had it made by a jeweler in Sedona. He's well known for one-of-a-kind pieces. I drew him a picture of the other ring and he said he could do it. Instead of cut glass, though, each of those are gemstones. There's a small emerald, topaz, pink tourmaline, ruby, white moonstone and opal set in it."

Amazed at the simple beauty of the wedding ring, Rachel sighed. "Oh, Jim, this is beyond anything I could imagine."

Wryly, he said, "Can you imagine being my wife?"

Lifting her chin, Rachel met and held his very serious gaze. "Yes, I can."

Satisfaction soared through him. "Let's see if it fits." He took the ring and slid it onto her finger. The fit was perfect. Holding her hand, he added huskily, "You name the date, okay?"

Sniffing, she wiped the tears from her cheeks with her fingers. "My mother's birthday was March 21. I'd love to get married on that day and honor her spirit, honor what she's given the three of us. Is that too soon?"

Grinning, Jim brought her into the circle of his arms. "Too soon?" He pressed a kiss to her hair as she settled against his tall, hard frame. "I was thinking, like, tomorrow?"

Rachel laughed giddily. "Jim! You don't mean that, do you?"

He leaned down and held Rachel in his arms, taking her mouth gently. She was soft and warm and giving. As her hand slid around his neck, a hot, trembling need poured through him. He skimmed her lips with his and felt her quiver in response. She tasted of sweet cherries and chocolate from the cake she'd just eaten. Running his hands through her thick, unbound hair, he was reminded of the strength that Rachel possessed.

Drawing her onto the blanket, he met her eyes, dazed with joy and need. "I want to love you," he rasped, threading his fingers through her hair as it fell against the blanket like a dark halo. Sunlight filtering through the juniper above them dappled the ground with gold. The breeze was warm and pine scented. Everything was perfect with Rachel beside him. Nothing had ever felt so right to Jim as this moment.

"Yes…" Rachel whispered as she moved her hands to

his light blue chambray shirt. She began to unsnap the pearl buttons one at a time until the shirt fell away, exposing his darkly haired chest. Closing her eyes, Rachel spread her hands out across his torso, the thick, wiry hair beneath her palms sending tingles up her limbs. There was such strength to Jim, she realized, as she continued to languidly explore his deep, well-formed body. At the same time, she felt his fingers undoing the buttons on her blouse. Each touch was featherlight, evocative and teasing. Her nipples hardened in anticipation as he moved the material aside, easing it off her shoulders. The sunlight felt warm against her exposed skin as her bra was shed.

The first, skimming touch of his work-roughened fingers along her collarbone made her inhale sharply. Opening her eyes, she drowned in his stormy ones. They had always called him Cougar and she could see and feel his desire stalking her now. As he spread his hand outward to follow the curve of her breast, her lashes fluttered closed. Hot, wild tingling sped through her and she moaned as his fingers cupped her flesh.

Moments later, she felt his lips capture one hardened nipple and a cry of pleasure escaped her lips. Instinctively, she arched against him. His naked chest met hers. A galvanizing fire sizzled through her as he suckled her. The heat burned down her to her lower abdomen, an ache building so fiercely between her thighs that she moaned as his hand moved to release the snap on her Levi's. Never had Rachel felt so wanted and desired as now. As he lifted his head, he smiled down at her. His gaze burned through her, straight to her heart, to her soul. This was the man she wanted forever, she realized dazedly.

As he slipped out of his Levi's, after pulling hers from

her legs, Rachel felt shaky with need. Her mind wasn't functioning; she was solely captive to her emotions, to the love she felt for Jim as he eased her back down on the blanket. As his strong, sun-darkened body met and flowed against hers, she released a ragged little sigh. Automatically, she pressed herself wantonly against him. His hand ranged down across her hip to her thigh. As she met his mouth, and he plundered her depths hotly, she slid her hand up and over his chest. Their breathing was hot and shallow. Their hearts pounded in fury and need.

The moment his hand slid between her thighs, silently asking her to open to him, she felt his tongue move into her mouth. Where did rapture begin and end? Rachel wasn't sure as his tongue stroked hers at the same time his fingers sought and found the moist opening to her womanhood. Sharp jolts of heat moved up through her. The cry in her throat turned to a moan of utter need. In moments, she felt him move across her, felt his knee guide her thighs open to receive all of him, and she clung to his capturing, cajoling mouth.

She throbbed with desire. She couldn't wait any longer. Thrusting her hips upward, she met him fearlessly, with equal passion. The moment he plunged into her, she gave a startled cry, but it was one of utter pleasure, not pain. His other hand settled beneath her hips and he moved rhythmically with her. The ache dissolved into hot honey within her. This warmth of the sunlight on her flesh, his mouth seeking and molding, their breaths wild and chaotic, all blended into an incredible collage of movement, sound, taste and pleasure. A white-hot explosion occurred deep within her, and Rachel threw back her head with a cry and arched hard against him. Through the haze of sensations she heard him growl like the cougar he really was. His hands were hard on her shoulders as he thrust repeatedly into her, heightening her pleasure as the volcanic release flowed wildly through her. In those moments, the world spun around them. There was only Jim, his powerful embrace, his heart thundering against hers as they clung to one another in that beautiful moment of creation between them.

Languidly, Rachel relaxed in his arms in the aftermath. Barely opening her eyes, she smiled tremulously up at him. His face glistened with perspiration; his eyes were banked with desire and love for her alone. Stretching fully, Rachel lay against his muscular length, his arms around her, holding her close to him.

"I love you," Jim rasped as he kissed her hair, her temple and her flushed cheek. "I always have, sweet woman of mine." And she was his. In every way. Never had Jim felt more powerful, more sure of himself as a man, as now. She was like sweet, hot honey in his arms, her body lithe, warm and trembling. How alive Rachel was! Not only was there such compassion in her, he was lucky to be able to share her passion as well. Moving several damp strands of hair from her brow, he drowned in her forest green eyes, which danced with gold flecks. Her lips were parted, glistening and well kissed. She had a mouth he wanted to kiss forever.

His words fell softly against her ears. Rachel sighed and closed her eyes, resting her brow against his jaw. Somewhere in the background, she heard the call of a raven far above the canyon where they lay. She felt the dappled sunlight dancing across her sated form. The breeze was like invisible hands drying and softly caressing her. More than anything, she absorbed Jim's love, the protectiveness he naturally accorded her as she lay in his arms. This was a man whose heart, whose morals and values were worth everything to her—and then some. It didn't matter that his last name was Cunningham. By them loving one another, Rachel thought dazedly, still lost in the memory of their lovemaking, a hundred-year-old feud no longer existed between their families.

Moving her hand in a weak motion across his damp chest, she smiled softly. "I love you so much, darling." She looked up into his eyes. "I'm looking forward to spending the rest of my life showing you just how much."

Tenderly, he caught and held her lips beneath his. It was a soft kiss meant to seal her words between them. He felt as if his heart would explode with happiness. Did anyone deserve to feel this happy? He thought not as he wrapped her tightly against him. Chuckling a little, he told her, "Well, maybe as of today, we'll start a new family dynasty. A blend of Cunningham and Donovan blood."

The thought of having Jim's baby made her feel fulfilled as never before. Rachel laughed a little. "You can't have a feud this way, can you?"

"No," he answered, sighing. So much worry and strain sloughed off him in that moment as he moved his large hand across her rounded abdomen. Rachel had wide hips and he knew she'd carry a baby easily within her. Their children. The thought brought him a sense of serenity he'd never known before this moment.

As Jim looked down at Rachel, he cupped her cheek and whispered, "I'll love you forever, princess. You and as many children as we bring into the world because of the love we hold for one another."

* * * * *

A career Air Force officer, **Merline Lovelace** served at bases all over the world. When she hung up her uniform for the last time, she decided to try her hand at storytelling. Since then, more than twelve million copies of her books have been published in over thirty countries. Check her website at merlinelovelace.com or friend Merline on Facebook for news and information about her latest releases.

Visit the Author Profile page
at Harlequin.com for more titles.

TEXAS MISSION

Merline Lovelace

For my own handsome hero, and all the days and nights
we spent under Texas skies during our assignments
in Fort Worth and San Antonio.
Thanks for the memories, my darling.

Chapter 1

A shrill buzz cut through the air-conditioned silence, haunting the small farmhouse just outside Mission Creek, Texas. Like a deer speared by truck headlights, Haley Mercado froze. Her glance sliced to the FBI agent who'd acted as her controller for the past year.

Across the living room Sean Collins met her desperate look. They'd been waiting for this call, she and Sean. So had the small army of agents guarding the safe house where the FBI had stashed Haley until they captured Frank Del Brio.

Frank Del Brio. The smooth, handsome head of the Texas mob who'd once shoved a square-cut, three-carat diamond on Haley's finger and announced that she was going to marry him. The ruthless thug who'd forced her to flee her home in South Texas and to assume another identity abroad. The vicious killer whose horrific acts had brought Haley out of hiding a year ago and sent her undercover, determined to assist the FBI in bringing Del Brio down.

Frank Del Brio, who'd kidnapped the child she'd placed in safekeeping while she worked undercover, the child who only a few nights ago had been spared in a wild shoot-out that had left her father in ICU and Haley under close protection at this secluded farmhouse.

The phone shrilled again, sending a jolt of desperate hope into her chest. They've got him! Please, God! Please let this call be from the FBI command center, advising that they've cornered Frank and rescued her baby! Her heart in her throat, she wiped her palms down the front of her jeans and kept her gaze locked on Sean as he reached for the cordless phone.

"Collins here."

When the FBI operative's face tightened, Haley's hope shattered into a thousand knife-edged shards.

"How the hell did you get this number?"

It was Frank, she thought on a wave of sickening certainty. It could only be Frank.

Collins confirmed it in the next breath. "No way I'm putting her on the phone, Del Brio. You can damned well talk to me."

The mobster's response sent a tide of angry red surging into the FBI agent's cheeks. His eyes blazing fire, Sean snarled back.

"Listen to me, you two-bit piece of slime. You hurt that baby and there won't a patch of dirt anywhere on this earth big enough for you to dig a hole and crawl into."

Haley flew across the living room. "Let me talk to him."

"I'm warning you, Del Brio—"

"Let me talk to him!"

The agent relinquished the instrument reluctantly, signaling for Haley to string out the conversation as long as she could. She understood. The communications technicians hooked into the line would need a few moments to trace the call. She understood, too, that the events of the past year were rapidly spiraling to a terrifying conclusion.

"Frank! Frank, are you there?"

"Hello, Daisy."

The deep, rich baritone made her skin crawl.

"You fooled me with that brassy hair and nose job, babe, but I have to admit I like the new look."

Haley didn't bother to comment on the fact that he'd penetrated the cover she'd been using for the past year. The long months she'd spent as Daisy Parker didn't matter anymore. All that mattered was her baby. Only her baby.

"Don't hurt her, Frank. Please, don't hurt her."

She hated to beg, hated hearing the abject pleading in her voice, almost as much as she hated Del Brio for the pain he'd caused her and her family.

"What do you want?" she whispered. "What do I have to do to get Lena back?"

"Two million just might do the trick. In unmarked, nonsequential bills. Nothing bigger than a hundred. I'll let you know where and when to deliver it."

His voice dropped to a low caress. Soft and husky, it scraped across Haley's raw nerves like a rusty nail.

"I'd better not see one cop or one fed, particularly your pal Collins or that bastard Justin Wainwright."

Haley's heart squeezed with pain. They'd come so close, so very close. Mission Creek's sheriff and the FBI had almost—almost—captured Del Brio three nights ago. He'd made his escape, gunning down her father in the process. Taking her baby with him.

"If I even smell their stink when you deliver the ransom," Frank snarled, "you'll never see your brat again. You understand me?"

"Yes."

"Good. Talk to you soon, babe."

"Wait!" Her frantic shout bounced off the walls. "Don't hang up! Tell me how she's—"

The hum of the disconnected line thundered in Haley's ear. She wanted to scream, to shriek and batter the receiver against the phone. But she'd spent the past year living a dangerous lie. A year undercover, risking her life every day to ferret out the details of the mob that had operated out of Mission Creek. If nothing else, those torturous months had taught her to subdue every natural impulse. To smile when she shook inside with fear. To hide her anguish as she watched another couple love and cherish the baby she'd been forced to give up temporarily for the child's own safety.

All those months had left their mark on Haley. Instead of shrieking or hurling the cordless phone at the wall, she merely handed it to Sean and listened in stony silence while he barked at the communications techs working the trace.

"Did you pinpoint the location?"

She knew. Even before she saw his mouth twist into a disgusted grimace, she knew. Frank was too smart to trip himself up with a simple phone call.

"Okay. Thanks."

His jaw tight, Sean punched the off button. Frustration gave a sharp edge to his broad New York accent when he confirmed what she already suspected.

"Del Brio used some kind of electronic scrambler. We couldn't confirm his location."

She nodded. That was all she could manage. From the day Lena was kidnapped, Haley had carried both fear and dread around inside her like a stone. It crushed in on her now, so massive and heavy she could hardly breathe.

"He'll kill her."

"Listen to me, Daisy—"

The special agent caught himself. He'd insisted they use her alias of Daisy Parker in every communication and every conversation for the past year. Although that cover was now blown, Sean hadn't quite made the transition back to her real name.

"Listen to me, Haley. Del Brio can't kill Lena. Not until he gets what he wants. He knows we'll demand proof she's still alive before we play his game."

The iron control she'd exercised for more than a year slipped and came close to shattering at that moment. "It's not a game!" she snapped furiously. "This is my child's life we're talking about!"

"Dammit, I know that."

Months of unrelenting tension sizzled and spit between them. With a little push Haley could almost have hated Sean Collins, too.

"I'm sorry," he said finally, shagging a hand through his thick, reddish hair. "You know I'll do whatever it takes to get Lena back. I want Del Brio as much as you do."

"No," she countered swiftly, her throat raw. "You couldn't. It wasn't your mother Frank murdered, Sean. Your father he tried to destroy. Your trusted friend and advisor he blew away."

She closed her eyes, aching for her mother. Grieving for the white-haired Texas judge who'd helped her arrange her escape and acted as her lifeline all those years she stayed in hiding. Hurting, too, for the father who now lay in ICU, battling for every breath.

Frank Del Brio had wreaked such havoc on her life. Haley knew he wouldn't hesitate to take the next fatal step. She wrapped her arms around her middle and squeezed tight, wishing with every ounce of her being she could hold in her terror for her child and keep it from spilling into reality.

Eyes closed, she pictured Lena the last time she'd seen her. The one-year-old was such a happy, bubbly child. All smiles and gurgles and bright blue eyes. With her mother's pointed chin and her father's black curly hair.

Her father. Oh, God! Her father.

Luke Callaghan.

Swallowing the moan that tried to escape, Haley dug her hands into her sides. She had to tell Luke. Had to confirm what the DNA tests had already substantiated. He was Lena's father. When she admitted that, she'd have to confess, too, that the blond waitress he knew as Daisy Parker was Lena's mother.

She cringed at the thought of having to explain to Luke the tangled web of lies and deceit she'd woven to protect herself and Lena, but every instinct told her he was now her only hope. Frank had warned her not to bring the feds when she delivered the ransom. He hadn't said anything about the baby's father.

Her mind worked feverishly. Del Brio was ruthless and totally without conscience. He also exercised an extensive network of contacts. He'd known how to reach Haley here, in this supposedly secure haven. He'd probably get word within minutes if she left it and went to Lena's father. He wouldn't worry, though. If there was a chink in Del Brio's armor, it was his arrogance. He wouldn't doubt his ability to handle the combination of a terrified mother and a blind father.

But could Haley handle it? After all this time, could she face the man who'd fathered her child? The man she'd loved as long as she could remember?

She could.

She had to!

Spinning, she bolted for the front door. Sean followed hard on her heels.

"Where are you going?"

"To find Luke Callaghan."

"No way! You're not setting foot outside this safe house."

"Safe?" Whirling, she leapt to the attack. "What's safe about it? Frank knows where I am. He got through your command center's elaborate electronic screens with one call. If he wanted to, he could probably order one of his goons to launch a shoulder-held missile from a mile away and put it through that window right now."

The fact that they both knew she was right didn't lessen Sean's bulldog stance. "We've made it this far together, Dai—Haley. Don't give up on me now."

"I'm not giving up. I've just decided to play the game by Frank's ground rules." Icy resolve coated every word. "He wants two million dollars. As you pointed out, he's not likely to hurt me or my child until I deliver it. And I do intend to deliver it. With Luke Callaghan."

"Christ! Callaghan's a good man. A war hero, no less. But he can't see a red flag waved two inches in front of his face."

A new ache pierced Haley's heart, adding another layer to the hurt and guilt and fear she'd carried for so long. Seeing the pain on her face, Sean backpedaled gruffly.

"Look, I'll admit Callaghan has moved mountains to help us find Lena. Once DNA tests indicated that he was her father, he let us tap his phones. He offered to provide the ransom, when and if it was demanded. He even volunteered the theory that he was the source the kidnappers intended to milk right from the start. With all his millions, it was certainly a distinct possibility."

More than a possibility. Since Lena had been taken just days before Luke returned to Mission Creek, everyone on the task force initially suspected his vast wealth had sparked the kidnapping.

"Callaghan also worked his own net," the FBI agent conceded with a touch of grudging admiration. "He has more contacts than any six men I know. And not just in the government. He and those three buddies of his scoured more dives, bribed more drunks and coerced more lowlifes into spilling their guts than our entire task force. But he can't—"

"No buts," Haley interjected swiftly, fiercely. "Luke Callaghan is Lena's father. I can't let him stand idly on the sidelines now while Frank Del Brio barters her for blood money."

Reaching for the door, she yanked it open. Sean's big, beefy hand smacked hard against the wood panel.

"Don't try to stop me," Haley hissed. "Don't even think about trying to stop me. I've done everything you asked me to, Sean. All these months I risked my life to provide the information you wanted. I will not risk my child's."

"All right!" Conceding defeat, the FBI operative nodded. "Hang loose a minute. I'll have my people track Callaghan down for you."

Haley drove away from the farmhouse a few moments later, trailed by a dusty white van and armed with the 9 mm Glock that Sean had instructed one of his agents to hand over.

She knew how to fire the handgun. She'd grown up in this patch of South Texas, on a sprawling acreage just outside Mission Creek. Indulged by her parents and spoiled shamefully by her older brother, Ricky, she'd spent most of her after-school hours in voice lessons, dance classes and giggling with her girlfriends as they checked out the hunks at the pool of the luxurious Lone Star Country Club. Ricky had taken her out to ping tin cans off fence poles often enough for Haley to know one end of a gun from another, though.

Grimly, she locked her hands around the steering wheel and drove through the night. A million stars winked in the inky sky. The moon hung low, dazzling in its silver glow. Haley didn't even spare it a glance.

As promised, Sean had pinpointed Luke Callaghan's present location. He was with one of his buddies. At the Saddlebag. The same watering hole where Haley had bumped into him two years ago, with such earth-shattering consequences.

The irony of seeking Luke out at the Saddlebag ate into her soul. He hadn't recognized her that hot July night two years ago. The London plastic surgeon who'd altered Haley's face had more than earned his five thousand pounds. Luke wouldn't recognize her tonight, either. Not just because he'd lost his sight, but because she'd all but crawled into the skin of the fictional Daisy Parker. No one—until Frank—had penetrated her cover.

Although…

Lately, Luke had been asking questions about the blond waitress with the thick-as-road-tar Texas twang. He'd even cornered her once at the Lone Star Country Club. He'd brushed his mouth across hers, as if testing his memory. He'd tested Haley's nerves, as well. She'd shied away, refusing to admit she knew him.

Now she'd not only admit that she knew him and that she'd had his baby, but she'd grovel at his feet if necessary to gain his help in reclaiming their child.

Her mouth had settled into a determined line when she wheeled into the Saddlebag's jam-packed parking lot some twenty minutes later and nosed her car into the narrow space between two pickups. The white van parked some yards away. At this point Haley couldn't say whether the FBI's watchful vigilance reassured her or added to the stress that crawled across her shoulder blades like a Texas scorpion.

Her throat tight, she climbed out of the car. The Saddlebag hadn't changed much in two years. The same wooden sign creaked in the breeze above the door. The same dim spotlights cast arcs of light against its gray, weathered siding. The same motel units were strung out behind the bar like plump, feathered hens roosting for the night. With a stab of acute pain, Haley wrenched her gaze from the largest of the ten or so units and headed for the bar.

When she pushed through the front door, the country-western music pouring through the wall-mounted speakers competed with the remembered clack of pool balls. Haley stood beside an arch formed by branding irons, hidden in its shadows. Narrowing her eyes, she peered through the blue haze. Establishments in this part of South Texas didn't run to separate smoking sections.

Her gaze skimmed the handful of customers at the long curved bar that wrapped clear around to the back of the lounge. She recognized several patrons. She'd waited on them at the country club. Ignoring the sudden, hopeful gleam in one man's eye and the welcoming wave of another, she turned her attention to the half dozen tables at the rear of the bar.

With a sudden thump of her heart, she spotted two men nursing dew-streaked long-necks at one of the tables. Her glance skimmed past Tyler Murdoch to lock on Luke. His back was to her, but Haley couldn't mistake the curly black hair cut military short under his summer straw Stetson or the athletic shoulders stretching the seams of his blue denim shirt. Every inch of Luke Callaghan's powerful, muscular body was imprinted on her memory.

She'd been in love with him for as long as she could remember. The orphaned son of wealthy parents, Luke had grown up on the Callaghan's lavish estate just north of Mission Creek, cared for by a devoted housekeeper and an absentee uncle not above dipping into his nephew's trust fund to maintain his free-wheeling lifestyle. Luke and Haley's brother had been friends since grade school, then roomed together at V.M.I.—Virginia Military Institute—where Luke and Ricky and three other classmates from the local area had formed their own special clique. The Fabulous Five, Haley had secretly labeled them. A band of brothers so tight and close it seemed that nothing could ever shake their friendship.

Ricky Mercado, the brother she adored.

Flynt Carson, scion of one of the old cattle king families that had settled this corner of South Texas.

Spence Harrison, brown-haired, brown-eyed and all male.

Tyler Murdoch, rugged, rough-edged, with an uncanny flair for anything and everything mechanical.

And Luke. Laughing, blue-eyed Luke Callaghan.

Haley had developed severe crushes on each of her brother's pals at one time or another, but Luke had stolen her heart. She was so young when she'd first tumbled into love with him, just growing into the seductive curves and smoldering Italian looks she'd inherited from her mother. A typical teenage girl, she'd alternated between outrageously blatant attempts to attract Luke's attention and tongue-tied shyness when she did.

He'd been kind to her, she remembered on a wave of stinging regret for those golden days of her girlhood. Teasing and big-brotherly and kind. If he'd recognized the signs of adolescent fixation, he never let on.

During her college years she'd seen Luke less frequently, but each time she did, she'd fallen a little more in love with him. He and Ricky and the others had joined the marines by then. They made only brief trips home for the holidays or lightning-quick visits en route to some mission or another. To Haley's chagrin, Luke didn't spend enough time at home to notice that Ricky's sister was now all grown up.

If he hadn't noticed, however, Frank Del Brio certainly had.

Shuddering, Haley recalled how the handsome older man had started hitting on her soon after her graduation from the University of Texas. It shamed her now to admit that his attentions had flattered her at first. Dark-haired, dark-eyed, and six-two of solid muscle, Frank could charm the knickers off a nun if he wanted to. Only after Haley had come to understand how deeply Del Brio was involved in her uncle Carmine's more dangerous undertakings did she try to break things off.

He'd given her a first taste of his temper then, and of his ruthlessness. Her father was in the family business, too, Frank had reminded Haley with a smile. Not as deep as his brother, Carmine, certainly, but deep enough to make him a target for the feds or for rival mob members if the right hints were dropped in the wrong ears. The threat was still hanging heavy on her mind when Frank slid a diamond ring onto her finger.

Then Ricky and Luke and their friends had volunteered for a highly classified, dangerous mission during the Gulf War. To this day Haley knew only vague details of that mission. Her brother never talked about it. Nor did any of the other four. All she knew was that they'd been dropped behind enemy lines, destroyed a biological weapons manufacturing plant, were captured and spent agonizing months as POWs until their commander, Phillip Westin, mounted a daring rescue raid.

The Fabulous Five came home to a hero's welcome. Haley would never forget the parade held in their honor one blazing June morning. Or their wild, lakeside celebration that night.

That was the night Haley Mercado died.

Chapter 2

More than a decade earlier

"Guys! Hey, guys!"

Waving wildly, Haley shouted to the occupants of the powerful speedboat cutting across Lake Maria.

"Luke! Ricky! Over here, darn it!"

With a disgusted huff that lifted the tendrils of her mink-brown hair, Haley gave it up as hopeless. The long shadows creeping across the lake had reached the dock. They couldn't see her, and she knew they couldn't hear her above the engine's roar.

Retreating to the sleek little two-seater sports car she'd parked at the head of the pier, she groped for the headlight switch. It took several bright flashes, but she finally caught the boaters' attention. The man at the wheel waved, leaned right and brought the craft into a sharp turn.

Haley drifted back down to the dock to await its arrival. Her brother, Ricky, and his four buddies had been water-skiing all afternoon, slicing through the water with reckless abandon. She could certainly understand their craving to feel the sun and the wind on their skin.

They'd more than earned these hours on the lake, considering the morning they'd just put in. From nine o'clock on, the returning POWs had been on display. After all, folks around here considered them genuine Texas heroes, not to mention poster ads for the United States Marine Corps. Spit-shined, square-shouldered, and heart-stoppingly handsome in their uniforms, they'd ridden in the parade organized in their honor. Then, of course, they'd had to sit under the hot sun, steaming in their high-collared dress blues, while local dignitaries gave long-winded speeches about South Texas's own. They'd even signed autographs for the kids who'd swarmed the platform after the speeches.

The minute the crowds had dispersed, however, they'd shed their decorum along with their uniforms and headed for the lake. They'd been here for a good five hours, tossing down beer and celebrating their hard-won freedom. The sun was now a flaming ball hanging low above the hills surrounding Lake Maria. If they didn't come in and dry off soon, they'd be navigating in the dark. More to the point, they'd miss the lavish barbecue Isadora and Johnny Mercado were throwing at their lakeside cottage to welcome Ricky and his friends home.

Leaning her hips against a piling, Haley peered across the rippling water at the approaching boat. Her heart contracted painfully as she made out the features of the man at the wheel. Luke Callaghan stood wide-legged and strong, his bare chest glistening in the slanting rays of the sun. Leather-tough Tyler Murdoch sat beside him. Although she couldn't make out the figures in the back of the boat, she knew their faces as well as her own. Too-serious Flynt Carson. Intense, intent Spence Harrison. And Ricky, Haley's adored older brother.

Thank God they'd all made it back safely, she thought on a wave of bone-deep relief. With their return, at least one of the worries that had kept her sleepless and hollow-eyed these past weeks had been allayed. The other...

The other she'd take care of tonight.

Her stomach clenching, Haley glanced down at the square-cut diamond on her left hand. The enormity of what she planned to do just a few hours from now started nausea churning in her stomach.

Damn Frank Del Brio!

The speedboat's throaty roar brought her head up. Squinting, she watched as Luke brought the powerful machine skimming toward the dock. With consummate skill, he throttled back mere yards from the pier, reversed thrust on the dual engines and floated the craft up to the pilings. The man sprawled beside Luke grinned up at her as she caught their line.

"Hey, sweet thing."

"Hey, Tyler."

The former all-conference wide receiver skimmed an appreciative glance from her shoulders, left bare by the red-checked halter top tied just below her full breasts, to the long legs showing beneath her red linen shorts.

"You're looking good tonight."

"Thanks."

Luke appeared to share his opinion. Haley's skin

prickled as his gaze made a slow pass from her neck to her knees. But when he addressed her, his voice held the same carelessly affectionate tone he always used with his best buddy's little sister.

"Want to go for a spin?"

"I wish I could," she said with real longing. The water looked so dark and green and cool, and Luke so sleek and powerful in his wet swimming trunks. Wrenching her gaze from his broad chest and flat belly, Haley searched the back of the boat for her brother.

"Where's Ricky?"

"We dropped him off at the marina about fifteen minutes ago. He said he had to pick up Melissa and take her to the party your folks are throwing for us."

"Well, shoot!"

"Is that a problem?"

"No, not really. Melissa called the house a half hour ago, asking where he was. Like a good sister, I drove all the way around the lake to fetch him. Now I'll have to drive all the way back."

She glanced across the wide expanse of water. The lights the Mercados had strung in the backyard of their lakeside cottage in preparation for the barbecue winked like lightning bugs in the gathering dusk. Those pin-pricks of light punched a fist-size hole in Haley's heart.

Isadora Mercado had thrown herself into arranging this party. It looked to be one of the biggest events of the year. A joyous celebration. A gathering of all Ricky's and Luke's friends beneath a star-filled Texas sky.

Only Isadora's daughter—and Judge Carl Bridges—knew it would be the last night Haley Mercado would spend with her family. The last hours she'd share with her friends.

The last moments she'd have with Luke.

Her right hand closed over her left with bruising force. The edges of the diamond gouged into the undersides of her fingers. Frank Del Brio was to blame—for everything.

"We were just planning to head across the lake to the party ourselves," Luke said, cutting into her chaotic thoughts. "Why don't you come with us? It'll save you the long drive."

"No, I… I can't."

Haley would go out on these dark waters soon enough. When she did, she wouldn't come back in.

"Sure you can," Spence Harrison countered from his seat behind Luke's. "Haul your butt back here, Tyler, and make room for the lady."

She shook her head. "I need my car."

Her sporty little vehicle represented an integral element of the plan she and Judge Bridges had worked out. Haley would slip away from the party once it was in full swing. Drive to a secluded cove on this very lake. Leave the coverup to her bathing suit on the front seat. Go for a late-night swim. Disappear forever.

"You can retrieve the car tomorrow," sandy-haired Flynt Carson put in. "Better climb in, kid, or you'll miss the festivities."

Haley's glance darted to Luke. The urge to spend just a few more minutes with him pulled at her like talons dug deep into her heart. She'd never see him again after tonight. Never know if the lazy glances he'd sent her way in the past year or so might have developed into something deeper, something that had nothing to do with the brotherly affection he always showed her.

Misinterpreting the reason for her hesitation, Luke

cocked a brow. "Are you thinking we've downed too much beer to get you safely across the lake? Don't worry about the open cans littering the back of the boat. We're big boys. We knew we were getting close to our limit. To avoid temptation, we emptied the last couple of six packs over the side right after we dropped Ricky off. You're safe with us, Haley."

Oh, God. If only that were true!

"Here." Smiling, Luke held up his hand. "I'll help you in."

The fierce desire to slip her hand into his sliced through Haley. Frantically her mind raced to revise her carefully laid plans. She'd leave her car here and borrow one of her parents' when it was time to sneak away from the party. Then, she could take this last boat ride with Ricky's friends and steal another few moments with Luke.

Her hand eased into his. His grip was strong and sure and wet from the spray as he helped her into the boat. Once she'd found her footing, he held her fingers up to the light. Turning her hand from one side to the other, he studied her ring. The multifaceted diamond caught the last rays of the sun. Brightly colored sparks leapt from her hand.

Luke had seen the ring before, of course. Haley had been wearing it like a brand since the day he and Ricky and the others had returned home. This was the first time he'd examined it up close, however.

"That's some rock," he commented with a grin.

"Yes." Her response was flat and lacking any emotion. "It is."

"Funny," he murmured, searching her face, "I never saw you and Frank Del Brio as a match."

"Funny," Haley got out in a strangled voice, "neither did I."

What a fool she'd been! What a naive, idiotic fool! She'd been so convinced she could turn aside Frank's increasingly ardent demands. So sure he would understand when she told him she just didn't feel the same passion he seemed to feel for her.

He'd make her feel it, Frank had insisted. Make her love him. All she had to do was give him a chance. And remember how much he knew about her father's involvement with the fringes of the mob.

Haley had agreed to the engagement in a desperate attempt to buy time. Now that time was about to run out. With her supposed wedding day rapidly approaching, she'd realized that the only way she could save her father—and save herself—was to disappear. Permanently.

Which she intended to do tonight.

But first she'd spend these few last moments with Luke, she decided fiercely.

"Want to take the wheel?" he offered.

"Of this behemoth?" She forced a smile. "I don't know if I've got the strength to muscle her all the way across the lake."

"No sweat. I'll act as your backup."

Positioning Haley at the wheel, he stationed himself behind her and worked the throttles. Slowly the high-powered speedboat backed away from the dock. Once it was clear, Haley brought its nose around. Luke's deep drawl sounded just above her ear.

"Ready?"

His warm breath sent shivers rippling along her bare shoulders. "Ready."

"Okay, let's open her up."

He shoved the throttles forward. With the snarl of an oversize jungle cat, the engine revved. The speedboat shot straight ahead. The hull lifted half out of the water, came down with a sharp crack, then rocketed across the surface.

The forward thrust knocked Haley against Luke. Legs spread wide, he grabbed the edge of the windshield to steady himself and to give her added support. With the wheel close against her front and Luke hard against her back, there wasn't room for Haley to pull away, even if she wanted to.

Spray flew into her face. The wind whipped her hair around like hissing snakes until Luke laughed and caught the flying strands. Holding them in his fist, he rested his hand on her shoulder. Haley forced herself to relax and to lean against him. Keeping the nose of the boat aimed at the lights winking on the far shore, she fought a sliver of pure pain.

How many times had she fantasized about Luke holding her like this? How many nights had she fallen asleep aching for the feel of his warm, hard flesh against hers? How often had she wished he would lock his arms around her and make her forget the rest of the world?

Now, at this minute, she'd come as close to realizing her dream as she ever would. Closing her eyes, she tried to burn the imprint of his body into her memory. Her senses recorded the clean, lake-washed scent of his skin. The way her head fit perfectly into the muscled curve of his shoulder. The bulge of hard masculinity nudging her behind.

"Haley! Watch out for that submerged log!"

Her eyes flew open, locked for a second or two on the glowing lights, then dropped to the water's surface. Shocked by the sight of a thick weathered branch on the lake dead ahead, she threw the boat into a turn. The right gunwale went down, slicing deep into the dark water. The left rose high into the air. The high-powered speedboat raced on with water sloshing into its deck well and five startled occupants all scrambling for a handhold.

Shoving her aside, Luke dived for the wheel. The movement destroyed Haley's already shaky balance. She made a frantic grab for the windshield, the seat, anything to anchor her, but her flailing, spray-slick hands found nothing but empty air. With a little cry, she tumbled over the side.

"Haley!"

Luke's shout was the last sound she heard before she sank into the water. She plunged downward, her movements jerky and uncoordinated until she conquered her momentary panic. She'd spent hours as a toddler dog-paddling in this lake. Many more as a youngster jet-ski-ing and water-skiing across its vast surface. The lake was her friend.

Her escape.

Tucking her legs, she righted herself and shot toward the surface. Her ascent was as smooth as her descent had been wild and tumultuous. For the first second or two, anyway.

She was still four or five feet below the surface when something scraped along her neck and jerked her to a halt. Fright almost stripped the last of her air from her lungs. Thrashing, twisting, she fought a long tentacle of the submerged tree she'd swerved to avoid. The tip of the branch had slipped right under the neck strap of her halter. Her body's buoyancy and her own frantic movements kept the damned thing securely lodged.

Her chest burning, Haley tore at the knot tied just under her breasts. Air bubbles were escaping her aching lungs by the time the knot finally gave. Abandoning the scrap of fabric, she scissor-kicked frantically. She burst through the surface a second later. Gasping, choking, she dragged in huge gulps of air.

When she gathered her strength enough to make a quick spin, what she saw almost sucked the air right back out of her lungs.

"Dear God!"

She felt as though she'd been under water for hours, but it must have been only a few seconds. Not long enough for Luke to regain control of the speedboat, which now tipped even more precariously to one side. Water flew up in white sheets as it cut a crazy swath toward the flickering lights.

"Luke! Tyler!" Treading water, Haley screamed a desperate warning. "Flynt, she's going to flip. Get the heck out of there, guys!"

They were too far away now to hear her shout. Or too busy throwing their weight against the upraised side. The maneuver might have worked on a sailboat tacking into the wind. On a speedboat with one of its dual engines still churning at full power, it had little effect.

As Haley squinted through the darkening shadows, horrified, the fiberglass hull raised even higher. A second later the entire boat went over and hit with a crack that rifled across the lake like gunfire. Her heart stayed lodged firmly in her throat until she saw dark shapes bob to the surface.

One. Two. Three.

Where was the fourth? Oh, God, where was the fourth!

She kicked, launching into a desperate stroke, but knew she'd never cover the distance that now yawned between her and the men thrown from the speedboat to do any good. They were closer to the far shore than they were to her. The people running down to the pier of her parents' lakeside cabin would reach the capsized boat long before she could.

Still, she swam doggedly, desperately, until a fourth dark shape broke the surface. Half choking, half sobbing with relief, Haley slowed her stroke until she was again treading water.

They couldn't see her, she realized, when she shoved her wet hair out of her eyes. The last, dying rays of the sun illuminated the far shore, but shadows were deeper out here. Darker. None of the figures on the far shore could spot her from that distance.

But they'd come looking for her. As soon as they reached Luke and the others and learned Haley had been in the boat, too, they'd come in search of her. Her father. Her brother.

Frank Del Brio.

The heat generated by Haley's frenetic swim evaporated. Ice crystals seemed to form in her veins. Her arms grew as heavy as the gray granite boulders lining the shore, her heart even heavier.

She'd intended to disappear tonight. Not in such a dramatic manner, perhaps, but... Well, a drowning was a drowning.

She swallowed. Hard. With little finning movements with her hands, she brought her body around. The closest spit of land was a hundred or so yards away. Several miles from the secluded cove where she'd planned to park her car to go for her last swim, but within walking distance of the judge's isolated fishing cabin.

Judge Carl Bridges. The one man she could trust. The lawyer who'd been both longtime friend to her family and calm advisor to an increasingly desperate Haley. With his cloak of client-attorney privilege, the judge knew how deeply Johnny Mercado had become entangled in his brother Carmine's deadly web. He also knew that Frank Del Brio's threats were anything but idle. He suspected the smooth, handsome thug of complicity in several vicious killings. He understood Haley's wrenching decision to protect her father in the only way she could—by removing herself completely from the equation. If she was gone, Frank would have no reason to threaten her father.

During the past weeks the judge had obtained a forged passport and purchased airline tickets that would send Haley crisscrossing three continents and, hopefully, cover her tracks from even the most determined scrutiny. Everything was ready. Tonight was the night. And, with this bizarre boating accident, she'd never have a better opportunity to make her death look real.

Her heart splintering, Haley threw a last look over her shoulder. In a ragged whisper she said goodbye to her home and to her family.

"I love you, Mom," she whispered. "You and Daddy both. Keep safe, and keep Ricky safe."

Dragging off Frank's engagement ring, she threw it as far as she could. Then she slipped beneath the cool, dark waters once more.

Chapter 3

Half-naked and totally exhausted, Haley dragged herself out of the lake. She didn't look back. She didn't dare.

Twenty minutes later she stumbled down the path to a small, ramshackle fishing cabin tucked among a stand of scrub pine. No lights showed at the shuttered windows. The judge hadn't yet arrived at the agreed-upon rendezvous site. But he would. Soon, she guessed.

Once inside the back door Carl Bridges always kept unlocked, she grabbed a blue plaid flannel shirt from the hooks on the wall and hunched on one of the sturdy chairs drawn up to the scarred plank table.

The immensity of what she'd just done—and what she was about to do—almost overwhelmed her. Shaking from head to toe, she wrapped her arms around her middle and rocked back and forth. Lake water dripped from her hair and ran down her legs to puddle on the scrubbed pine floor.

She done it. She'd completed the first phase of her plan. Not the way she and the judge had envisioned it, precisely, but the speedboat accident would certainly make things more realistic. Now she just had to find the courage to take the next step. Could she really put her parents through the agony of believing she'd drowned? Really leave Texas and start a new life, away from everything and everyone she knew?

Away from Frank?

With a little moan, Haley dug her fingers into her sides. She had no choice. Frank would destroy her father. He was that determined. And that vicious.

She'd find a way to let her parents know she was okay, she swore. Later, when she was sure it was safe.

The thought gave her the strength to make it through the wait for Judge Bridges. As an old and trusted friend of the family, he'd been invited to celebrate the boys' homecoming. He would have been one of the crowd gathered under the flickering lights. One of the witnesses to the accident out on the lake. When Luke and the others made it known Haley had been a passenger in the boat, Carl would guess that she'd altered the schedule.

Sure enough, tires crunched on the dirt-and-gravel road leading to the cabin less than a half hour later. Haley was a bundle of raw nerves, but her rapidly developing self-preservation instinct kept her out of sight as she peered through the bedroom window. She almost wept with relief when Judge Bridges slammed the car door. His prematurely white hair shining like a beacon in the darkness that now blanketed the earth, he rushed to the cabin.

"Haley? Haley, are you here?"

"Yes!" She ran in from the other room. "Yes, I'm here."

"Thank God!"

His lined face was a study in worry and relief. Opening his arms, he crushed her against his chest. Haley clung to him with everything in her. He was her last link with her family. The last link between the woman she was and the stranger she would soon become.

Finally his hold loosened. He eased her away a few inches. "I thought… We all thought…"

His Adam's apple bobbed up and down. Behind his old-fashioned black-rimmed glasses, his watery blue eyes glistened. Blinking furiously, he glared at her with a combination of anger and admiration.

"Why the dickens did you flip over Luke's speedboat? That was a dangerous stunt and not part of our plan."

"I didn't flip it! Well, I guess I did, but not on purpose. I swerved to avoid a submerged log and lost control."

"Well, it sure adds a grim authenticity to our plan. They're searching the whole lake for you, missy."

"Oh, Judge!" Wracked with guilt, Haley almost abandoned the scheme right then and there. "My parents must be frantic. Maybe I should go home. Maybe I should just marry Frank."

Her tortured doubts acted like a spur on the judge. The steely resolve that had sustained him through fifteen years at the bar and ten on the bench stiffened his spine.

"No, Haley, you're doing the right thing. You've got to get away. Your parents did everything they could to give you and Ricky a different life. If you go back now, you'll nullify all their years of sacrifice and worry."

She knew he was right. Carl Bridges had been both friend and advisor to Johnny and Isadora Mercado for decades. If Haley had at times suspected the hint of sadness in the judge's eyes when they rested on Isadora went beyond friendship, beyond regret, she never let on. Only after she'd turned to him to help her escape Frank Del Brio had she learned how much of a role he'd played in both her and her brother's life.

Carl Bridges hadn't been able to keep his old friend Johnny from sliding into his brother Carmine's web, but he'd added his voice to Isadora's when she'd pleaded with Johnny to send Ricky off to a military school to keep him away from Carmine's thugs. The judge had also encouraged Haley to go up to Austin to attend his alma mater, the University of Texas, to keep her from discovering her father's growing entanglement with the Texas mob.

The ploy had worked. Until Haley spent two summers working in her father's office, she'd remained oblivious of the shady operations Carmine Mercado had dragged his brother into. Even after curiosity had led her to dig deeper into the family business than her job as a receptionist warranted, she'd pretended ignorance. She loved her father too much to confront him with the startling bits of information she'd picked up. She bled a bit inside whenever Johnny Mercado tried to bluster and disguise what he'd become from his family, but she kept his secrets tucked in a deep, dark corner of her heart. Now she'd take those secrets to the grave with her.

With a ragged sigh, she buried her doubts in the same watery grave. "You're right. I'm just…nervous now that it's really happening."

"We'll have to move fast," the judge warned. "I said I was going to drive around the lake and search for you. We'd better get you away before someone else decides to do the same. Stay here. I'll get the suitcase from the trunk."

He was back before Haley could once more start to question what she was doing again. Mere moments later she'd changed into the outfit she'd bought and stashed with the judge in preparation for this night. The baggy tan slacks and loose-fitting top completely disguised her generous curves. Tucking her still-damp, shoulder-length hair up under a pixie-cut wig, she changed her brown eyes to a smoky green with tinted contacts. There wasn't much she could do about the little bump in her nose she'd inherited from her mother until she made a visit to a plastic surgeon, but the oversize glasses she slipped on would detract attention from it.

The judge was pacing the front room when she emerged. Running a critical eye over her, he nodded. "I hardly recognize you. Ready to go?"

She swallowed the bitter taste of guilt and regret. "Yes."

"Okay. Let's get you on your way."

Taking her elbow, he hustled her out to his car. "Your temporary ID, credit cards and passport are in the dash. I'll send new ones when...if you decide to go ahead with cosmetic surgery."

Gulping, Haley retrieved the documents and fingered the embossed passport. She could only guess the favors the crusty jurist had been forced to call in to manufacture her temporary identity.

"I'm sorry I pulled you into this mess, Judge."

"I've made plenty of mistakes in my life, missy. I don't count helping Isadora's daughter as one of them."

"I don't know how I'll ever repay you."

"I don't expect you to. Now duck down and stay out of sight until I get you to the rental I parked down the road earlier this afternoon. It's only a few miles."

The wily judge had thought of everything, even obtaining a nondescript sedan from a rental agency. Judge Bridges had made sure there was no way the car could be traced to him, or to the woman who'd park it at the San Antonio airport later tonight.

The drive to the hidden vehicle seemed to take forever, yet was all too brief. Haley crouched low in the seat, trying desperately to blank her mind to the frantic search she knew was taking place out on the lake. She'd made the wrenching decision to leave. For her father's sake, she had to follow through with it.

"Here we are."

Slowing, the judge pulled off onto a narrow track. Branches scraped against the sides of his car as it bumped down the path. When the headlights picked up the gleam of metal, he shoved the gearshift into park but left the engine running.

The hot Texas night wrapped around them as they made their way to the waiting Ford. Digging the keys out of his pocket, Carl passed them to Haley.

"You'll need some cash," he said gruffly. "Here's two thousand for immediate expenses. I'll wire more when you get settled."

"Judge, I—"

Her throat closed, tears burned behind her eyelids. This was it, the moment she'd both dreaded and planned for so meticulously. Her last seconds as Haley Mercado.

No, not as Haley Mercado. Haley was already dead. Lost beneath the dark waters of Lake Maria.

"You'd better get going," the judge said gruffly, his own voice thick. "It's a good stretch of road to San Antonio, and you have a plane to catch."

She couldn't get a single sound past the ache in her throat. Awkwardly, Carl patted her shoulder.

"Don't worry. I'll look after Isadora and Ricky. And I'll do what I can to extricate your father from the mess he's gotten himself into over the years. I can still pull a few strings 'round these parts."

Maybe then she could come home again. Clinging to that hope, Haley threw her arms around his neck and hugged him.

"I hope so, Judge. God, I hope so! Keep me posted, okay?"

"You know I will. Now scoot, girl, before we both start bawling like new-weaned calves."

She gave him another fierce hug, then slid into the sedan and waited while he backed his own car down the track. Its headlights stabbed into Haley's eyes. Almost blinded, she turned onto the paved road. She idled the car for a moment, waiting for the black spots to fade, then slowly accelerated. A few moments later a turn in the road took her away from Lake Maria.

In the weeks that followed, Carl Bridges was Haley's only contact with Texas and the life she'd left behind.

The judge's assurances that her family was working through their shock and grief sustained her through long days and lonely nights in strange cities. After a circuitous journey across several continents to cover her tracks, she found refuge in the comfy flat Carl had leased for her in London. There she found funds waiting to cover her expenses, including the cosmetic surgeon who altered Haley's features.

Under the surgeon's knife, her nose lost the little bump she'd inherited from her mother, and her slanting, doelike eyes became rounded. She considered breast reduction and possibly liposuction to diminish her lush curves, but by then stress had carved off so many pounds that she carried a far more slender, if still subtly rounded, silhouette. Dying her hair a glowing honey-blond, she adopted a sleek, upswept style that gave her an unexpectedly sophisticated look.

With her degree in graphic arts, it didn't take her long to land a terrific job. She'd just begun to feel comfortable in her new skin when a call from Carl shattered her shaky sense of security. It came mere weeks after her supposed death. She could tell from his terse greeting that he was upset.

"What's the matter?" she asked, her pulse kicking into overdrive. "Are my parents okay? Ricky's not hurt, is he?"

"No, no one's hurt." His voice took on an odd note. "No one we know, anyway."

"Tell me, Judge. What's happened?"

"They found your body."

"What!"

"Some fishermen out on Lake Maria hooked on to a corpse. It's badly decomposed, but it matches your height and physical characteristics with uncanny exactness."

"Frank!" she breathed. "Frank must have planted it."

"That's what I'm thinking, too."

According to Carl, Del Brio had gone beserk when divers found his fiancée's halter top still tangled in the branches of the submerged tree. In a bitterly ironic twist, he'd insisted the local authorities arrest Luke and the others for taking Haley out on the lake and operating a high-powered speedboat while under the influence. Tests had confirmed a high level of alcohol in the men's blood, and now the four marines had been charged with reckless endangerment.

"All hell's broken loose 'round here," Carl related. "Your father wouldn't let Isadora view the corpse, but he and Ricky went down to the morgue. They both near about fell apart. Now even Ricky's out for blood. He's turned against Luke, blames him for taking you out in the boat when he was drunk."

"Luke wasn't drunk! I don't care what the tests showed. He was completely in control of himself that night."

"He's going to have to prove that in court. I don't know what kind of hold your uncle Carmine and Frank Del Brio have over the county D.A., but the idiot's upped the charges against Luke and the three others to manslaughter. They've been put on administrative leave from the marines and are being held in the county jail without bail until their trial."

"Oh, no!" Shattered by the unforeseen consequences of her deception, Haley searched desperately for a way to clear the four men. "What about DNA tests? They'd prove the corpse isn't me."

"They would if we had a sample of your DNA to use for a comparison. Your mother's kept your room just as you left it, but she's had it thoroughly cleaned. We couldn't find so much as a hair caught in a comb or an old toothbrush to take a sample from."

How like her mother. Isadora Mercado wouldn't

allow a single mote of dust to settle on her precious daughter's belongings.

"I'll catch the next plane home, Judge."

"Now hold on a minute, missy."

"I won't let Luke and the others take the blame for my death!"

"Those boys aren't going to take the blame. I know more about the law than any six attorneys in this state, including that pea-brained D.A. I'll step off the bench to represent them and I'll get them off," he promised with utter confidence. "I'm only telling you about the fuss because I know you have the *Mission Creek Clarion* sent to a fake name at a post office box. I didn't want you to see the headlines and have a spasm."

"I'm pretty close to a spasm now!"

"Look, if it'll make you feel any better, go down to a newspaper kiosk tomorrow morning and buy a paper from Berlin or Hong Kong or anyplace but London. Take a picture of yourself holding up the paper and overnight it to me along with those before-and-after photos the plastic surgeon took of you. If worse comes to worst, I'll produce proof that you're still alive. I won't tell anyone where you are, though. You'll still be safe."

"I will, but will you? If Frank finds out you helped me escape, he'll kill you."

The judge huffed. "I'm an ornery Texan, missy, and tough as shoe leather. What's more, I've got a few tricks up my sleeve Frank Del Brio never thought of. You just send those pictures and don't worry about Luke and the boys."

The sensational trial dragged on for months.

Haley followed its progress in the *Mission Creek*

Clarion. The local paper remained sympathetic to the war heroes, but the Corpus Christi and Dallas dailies played up every scandal from the defendants' past.

Old feuds were resurrected, including the long-standing battle between Flynt Carson's great-grandfather and his former ranching partner, J. P. Wainwright. Tyler Murdoch's youthful brushes with the law after his mother abandoned him made for juicy copy. Spence Harrison's pre-law degree came into play as he assisted Carl Bridges in his own defense.

The tabloids may have had a field day with Flynt and Tyler and Spence, but they went for Luke's jugular. They seemed determined to paint him as rich and shamelessly indulged by the absentee uncle who'd acted as his guardian. Several papers ran disgusting, tell-all interviews with women Luke dated both before and after he'd joined the marines. Instead of a healthy young bachelor with normal appetites, he came across as an oversexed playboy who'd plied his best friend's sister with beer and coaxed her out on the lake so he and his buddies could take turns with her.

Despite the sensationalism, or maybe because of it, Judge Bridges made good on his promise to Haley. He got the four men acquitted.

The trial left its mark on all four defendants, though. They soon separated from the marines. Flynt took over management of the vast Carson ranching interests. Infuriated by the spurious charges brought against him, Spence went on to law school, spent his time in the trenches as a prosecutor, then campaigned for and won the D.A.'s job. Tyler disappeared into some shadowy, quasimilitary organization. And Luke seemed determined to live up to the reputation as a playboy he'd gained during the trial.

Haley's heart pinched every time she read another story about the jet-setting millionaire. Invariably, he was photographed with some toothpick-thin supermodel or overendowed starlet hanging all over him. Once, she read that he was in London, attending the opening of a new musical he'd backed. She'd been tempted, so very tempted, to pay the outrageous sum the scalpers were asking for the sold-out performance to search the audience for a glimpse of Luke. But she didn't. She'd wreaked enough havoc on his life. She refused to take even the remotest chance that she might cause more.

That fierce resolve kept her in London for almost a decade.

Waves of homesickness attacked often during those years, especially at night. Determined to immerse herself in her new identity, Haley refused to give in to the despair that seeped into her heart whenever she thought of her family and friends.

Gradually the cosmopolitan city took her to its generous bosom. She grew to love the pigeons and the parks and the bright lights of Piccadilly Circus. She even acclimated to the cold, foggy winters. Slowly she began to feel safe in her new identity. Carefully she built a small, intimate circle of friends.

She'd just returned from dinner with those friends when another call from Carl Bridges plunged her back into danger...and into Luke Callaghan's arms.

The call came on a muggy July evening. The phone was jangling in that distinctive European way when Haley unlocked the front door.

"Your mother's been beaten," the judge informed her with the closest thing to panic she'd ever heard from him. "Brutally beaten. The doctors…"

His voice wavered, cracked.

"The doctors aren't sure she's going to make it."

Haley caught a flight home that same night.

Chapter 4

The desperate need to reach her mother's bedside dominated Haley's every thought during the long flight from London to JFK, then on to Dallas and, finally, Corpus Christi. Exhausted but coiled tight as new barbed wire, she stepped off the jet to the rippling palms and ninety-nine percent humidity of the Texas Gulf. Too tense to even notice the sweltering heat, she rushed through the airport to the rental car desk.

Years of living under an assumed identity had honed her self-preservation instinct to a fine edge. Her altered features should give her anonymity, but just to be sure, she made a brief stop at a costume shop before leaving Corpus Christi. Improvising hastily, she explained that she'd been invited to a party that night, thrown by officers from the nearby naval air station. She left the shop with a nun's habit and wimple tucked under her arm. The convent of the Sisters of Good Hope was located just a few miles north of Mission Creek. Since the sisters made frequent visits to area hospitals, Haley would hide under their mantle until she determined just what the heck had happened to her mother.

The moist air of the coast followed her out of the city as she headed west on Highway 44. Soon the marshy flatlands of the coastal plains gave way to rolling hills cut by dry arroyos and dotted with mesquite, cacti and creosote. With the wind whipping her hair, Haley breathed in the hot, dusty air for almost an hour. At Freer, she turned left onto Highway 16 and headed home.

Home.

Her chest squeezed tighter with each familiar landmark. As much as she'd grown to love London's lights and glitter and sophisticated aura, Texas was home. In her heart, it would always be home.

She pulled off the road some miles north of Mission Creek to exchange her slacks and sleeveless turquoise silk sweater for the dove-gray habit. The long-sleeved dress raised an immediate sweat in the hundred-degree heat. Haley had to struggle with the wimple and short, shoulder-length veil, but finally got them right. The little makeup she'd had on when she'd answered Carl's call had long since worn off. Inability to sleep during the long flight had added a hint of grayness to her olive-hued skin. Satisfied that she more than looked the part, Haley slid back into the rental car and turned the air-conditioning up full-blast.

She kept her head averted when she passed Lake Maria. The memory of that awful night almost a decade ago still seared her soul. Mission Creek's historic downtown called her hungry gaze, however. The old granite courthouse looked exactly the same. So did the bank, founded in 1869 and still serving the local community. She flicked quick glances at Jocelyne's fancy French restaurant and the Tex-Mex favorite, Coyote Harry's. Her taste buds tingled at the remembered fire of Harry's Sunday special—huevos rancheros topped with mounds of French fries, all drenched in his award-winning chili. As hungry as she was, she had no thought of stopping. Her one goal, her one driving need, was to get to the Mission Creek hospital.

Luckily she arrived post-afternoon visiting hours and pre-supper. The staff was busy getting ready to feed the patients, and the visitors had all departed. Haley took the elevator to the second floor and picked the most harried candy-striper to ask directions.

"Excuse me."

The aide flicked her a quick glance. "Can I help you, Sister?"

"Yes, please. Which is Isadora Mercado's room?"

"Three-eighteen. Around the corner, at the end of the hall."

"Thank you."

Tucking her hands inside her loose sleeves in imitation of the nuns who'd taught her during her Catholic grade-school days, Haley glided around the corner. Halfway down a long corridor that smelled strongly of pine-scented antiseptic, she stumbled to a halt.

A heavyset man lolled in a chair at the far end of the hall, his nose buried in the paper. Haley guessed instantly he was one of the mob's goons. He had the disgruntled air of a man who'd rather be out shaking down pimps and two-bit dealers than spending empty hours in a hard, straight-backed chair.

What was he doing here? Why did Isadora need a guard? Swallowing a sudden lump in her throat, Haley lifted her chin and glided past the man. He gave her a curious glance and went back to his paper.

The door to Room 318 whispered open, then whooshed shut behind her. For a moment she thought she'd stepped into a hothouse. Glorious arrangements of gladioli, long-stemmed roses, and irises occupied every horizontal surface and filled the air with a heavy scent. Gaily colored balloons bobbed above the baskets. The room was such a riot of color that it took a moment for her to focus on the petite, slender woman hooked up to the bank of monitors beside the bed.

Despite Carl Bridges's warning that Isadora Mercado had been brutally beaten, the sight of one side of her mother's bruised, battered face had Haley reeling in shock.

"Oh, my God! What did they do to you?"

She couldn't hold back the soft, broken cry. In her horror, she forgot to color her voice with the light British accent she'd deliberately cultivated over the years. For that brief, paralyzing moment, she was Haley Mercado, ripped apart by anguish for her mother.

With agonizing slowness, Isadora's head turned. Bandages covered part of her face. What was exposed showed mottled bruises. Both eyes were swollen shut, but evidently the beating hadn't affected her hearing. Swiping her tongue along dry, cracked lips, she croaked out an agonized whisper.

"Haley? Is…is that you?"

Tears streamed down Haley's cheeks. She couldn't

move, couldn't speak. She hadn't planned beyond this moment, hadn't formed a coherent strategy beyond just seeing her mother.

"Please," Isadora begged brokenly. "Please don't play this cruel game. Are you... Are you my daughter?"

Haley couldn't deny her mother's need, any more than she could deny her own. Sinking into the chair beside the hospital bed, she groped past the IV lines for her mother's hand.

"Yes, Mom. It's me."

A fierce joy lit Isadora's battered face. "I knew it! I knew all along you weren't dead."

Her fingers gripped Haley's convulsively. Tears squeezed through the swollen lids. Her throat worked, forcing out each hoarse, joyful word.

"Johnny kept insisting we had to accept the brutal truth. Even Ricky gave up and took out his grief on Luke and the others. But I never stopped believing you'd come home, Haley. Not for one minute!"

"Oh, Mom, I'm so sorry. So very, very sorry."

Overcome with guilt, Haley dropped her forehead onto their joined hands. For a moment the only sounds that filled the room were the soft beep of the IV pump and Isadora's quiet sobs.

As if seeking assurance, her mother reached across the bed with her other hand and patted her daughter's cheeks, her chin, her nose.

"What's happened to you? Your face, your bones. You feel so thin. So different."

"I've lost weight. And I had surgery, Mom. Just around the cheeks and eyes. And here. Feel my nose."

Her fingers trembling, Haley guided her mother's

hand down the smooth, elegant slope the cosmetic surgeon had crafted.

"Our little bump is gone," Haley said, smiling through her tears. "I miss it. Almost as much as I've missed you and Daddy and Ricky."

"Oh, Haley!" Her bruised face contorting, Isadora gripped her daughter's hand with both of hers. "What happened that night, out on the lake? Where did you go? Where have you been all this time?"

She answered the easiest question first. "I've been in London."

"Why didn't you let us know you were all right?"

The anguish in her mother's voice cut her to the quick.

"I couldn't, Mom. I had to let you and Frank believe I was dead."

"Frank? Frank Del Brio is the reason you disappeared?"

"Yes."

"But you accepted his ring. You were engaged. I never understood why, but I thought…we all thought you must have seen something in the man the rest of us didn't."

"I did. His utter ruthlessness."

She debated how much to tell her mother. She wasn't sure whether Isadora knew about her husband's involvement with the mob. Her parents had never talked finances or business affairs in front of their children. Haley herself would never have known about the shady side of the family business if curiosity hadn't made her dig deep during those two summers she'd worked in the offices of the Mercado Brothers Paving and Contracting.

As it turned out, Isadora was all too aware of her husband's involvement in his brother's schemes. Her fingers gripped Haley's brutally as she pinpointed the reason for her daughter's flight with uncanny accuracy.

"Frank threatened to expose your father, didn't he?"

Still, Haley hedged. She'd given up her family and the only home she'd ever known to protect her dad. It went hard against the grain to admit the truth, even now.

"Tell me, Haley."

"Yes, he did."

"I knew it had to be something like that. You wouldn't just disappear without good reason. Thank God you got away from that bastard. At least you're safe. Frank can't beat you to bring your father into line."

Haley reeled in shock for the second time in less than ten minutes. "Frank did this to you?"

"Oh, it was made to look like a mall parking lot mugging, but Frank was behind it. He wanted to let your father know he couldn't disobey orders from the family anymore."

No wonder one of Frank's goons sat outside the door. He was there to make sure Isadora Mercado didn't tell her story to the police. Resolve hardened inside Haley. Cold. Unwavering. Lethal.

"I'll see he pays for this. Whatever it takes, I'll see that he pays."

"Frank, or your father?"

The bitterness in her mother's voice shocked Haley into silence.

"Your father dragged us into this mess," Isadora said, baring her soul to her daughter for the first time. "You. Me. Ricky. All of us. I've been telling him for longer than I can remember that anyone who swims with barracudas will eventually get bloodied. Your father's in deep now, Haley. Too deep for you or Judge Bridges or anyone else to save him." Pain that had nothing to do with her bruises crossed her face. "So is Ricky."

"Oh, no! Ricky's working with Uncle Carmine?"

"I think so. He won't talk to me. He won't talk to anyone. He's turned so hard and distant since he broke off his friendship with Luke and Tyler and the others."

"This is all my fault. I should never have tried to get away by faking my death. I'll come home, Mom. I'll make things right."

"No!" Isadora's voice rose to a frightened croak. Clutching her daughter's fingers in agitation, she protested vehemently. "No, you can't come home. I can't bear it if Carmine and Frank sink their claws into you like they have Johnny and Ricky. Please, Haley. Please go back to London. Today. Tonight. Let me know at least one of my family is safe and happy."

Haley tried to calm her.

"I'll be careful, Mom. But I need to try to straighten out the mess my disappearance caused."

"You can't. Don't you understand, it's too late for you to save your father. Too late for Ricky. Go back to London. Promise me you'll go back to London."

In her heart Haley knew her mother was right. If she came home now, Frank would wreak a diabolic revenge for her attempt to escape him. Not just on Haley, but on her family. She was caught in a trap of her own making.

"All right," she promised, her throat aching. "I'll go back to London."

"Today?"

"Tomorrow. Today I'm going to spend as much time with you as I can."

* * *

Mother and daughter said goodbye at nine-thirty that evening, with whispered promises to meet in Paris in the fall. It broke Haley's heart to leave Mission Creek without seeing her father or Ricky, but her mother had pleaded with her not to reveal herself to either. They were too close to Frank Del Brio and might let something slip.

She walked out of the hospital intending to make the drive back to Corpus Christi and catch a flight out in the morning, but the fact that she hadn't eaten since her dinner with friends back in London suddenly caught up with her. Hunger piled on top of her accumulated tension and jet lag to make her suddenly dizzy.

Food. She needed food before she tackled the drive back to Corpus. And something icy cold to drink. Coyote Harry's would be closed. So would the Mission Creek Café and pricey Jocelyne's. She didn't dare drive out to the Lone Star Country Club. She'd spent too many happy hours at the plush resort, counted too many of its patrons as her friends. After the pain of parting with her mother, she didn't need another reminder of all she'd given up when she'd left her home.

It would have to be the Saddlebag. The roadside bar was dark and smoky, but served the juiciest burgers this side of the Brazos. And since this was Sunday night, the place wouldn't be as crowded as it was on other nights. With any luck, she wouldn't bump into anyone who'd known Haley Mercado.

She could hardly walk into a bar dressed as a nun, though. The disguise had allowed her to blend in at the hospital, but would make her stand out like a beacon in the Saddlebag. She'd have to trust in the cosmetic surgeon's skills and the new persona she'd perfected during her years in London.

With a quick look around to make sure the hospital parking lot was deserted, she pulled on her slacks and turquoise silk top and dragged off the wimple and hot, scratchy habit. Gulping in relief, she tucked a few loose honey-blond strands into the clip that held her hair up and added a touch of gloss to lips she'd chewed almost raw with worry.

Despite Haley's confidence in the person she'd become, every nerve in her body tingled when she pulled up at the weathered Saddlebag. The parking lot was nearly empty, thank goodness. So were the parking spaces of the ten or so motel units behind the saloon.

As she walked into the bar, she had to keep reminding herself that she was a different person now. Physically and emotionally. She hardly recognized herself when she looked in the mirror these days. Still, she half expected one of the patrons to shout her name and come charging around the long, curved bar to accost her.

No one shouted anything. Nor did Haley spot anyone she knew among the few patrons. The two women present gave her a curious once-over before turning back to their companions. The cowboys knocking balls around the pool table at the back of bar displayed considerably more interest in the newcomer, but Haley nipped it in the bud by simply ignoring them. Skirting the dance floor with a lone couple barely moving to a Trisha Yearwood ballad, she claimed a table in a dim corner.

"I'll have a cheeseburger," she told the waiter who appeared at her table a few moments later. "Medium well. And a lager. Draft."

"Lager, huh?" He cocked his head, studying her beneath the brim of his battered black Resistol. "You're not from around these parts, are you?"

Only then did Haley realize one of the British idioms she'd cultivated so deliberately over the years had slipped out.

"No, I'm not."

"Didn't think so. I'll bring your beer, uh, lager, right over to you."

"Thanks."

It wasn't the waiter who delivered the foaming mug some moments later, however. It was a tall, broad-shouldered cowboy with a silver belt buckle the size of a dinner plate and laughing blue eyes.

"This one's on me, beautiful."

Haley's heart stopped. Literally. She felt it thump, then contract, then simply die. She sat frozen, every nerve turning to ice as she stared at the strong, tanned face above the open collar of a crisp white shirt.

Her utter lack of response might have daunted a lesser man. Not this one. His mouth curving into a half grin, he deposited two mugs on the table.

"I figured if I brought one for each of us, I might just get lucky and be invited to join you."

She couldn't speak. She didn't dare. She prayed he'd take the hint and go away. Instead he seemed to regard her silence as a personal challenge. Not waiting for an invitation, he claimed the chair opposite hers.

"The waiter said you're not from around here. But when you first walked in, I could have sworn I knew you."

Her pulse kicked in with a painful surge. Panic raced along her iced-over nerves as his gaze lingered on her eyes, her nose, her carefully sculpted cheekbones.

"Have we met somewhere?" he probed, sprawling loose-limbed and comfortable in his chair. "Dallas, maybe? New York?"

She had to answer. She couldn't sit mute any longer. But it took everything she had to infuse her voice with polite disinterest.

"If we've met, I don't seem to recall it."

His grin widened at the deliberate put-down.

"Guess I'll have to see what I can do to make a more lasting impression this time."

Blue eyes gleaming, he tipped two fingers to the brim of his summer straw Stetson. "The name's Luke. Luke Callaghan."

Chapter 5

The blond stranger had drawn Luke across the bar like the scent of doe drew a stag. Not only was she gorgeous, but she'd appeared at the Saddlebag at just the right moment.

Luke had piled up almost three weeks of idle time since wrapping up a particularly nerve-bending covert operation deep inside a breakaway Russian republic. He was already bored with the free-wheeling playboy lifestyle he adopted between jobs for the shadowy government agency that had recruited him after he'd separated from the marines. He needed a distraction, and this delicious blonde certainly constituted that.

She'd hooked his interest the moment she walked into the Saddlebag. From a distance, she was stunning. Up close, she thoroughly intrigued him. Take the way she stared at him. Those huge brown eyes seemed to look right through him. Then there was the little hesitation before she returned his greeting. Her aristocratic nose quivered, and he could have sworn her hands trembled before she buried them in her lap.

If he made her nervous, she recovered quickly enough. Inclining her head in a regal nod, she acknowledged his introduction.

"How do you do, Mr. Callaghan?"

Luke had traveled extensively, both in the marines and in the dangerous operations that now took him to all parts of the globe. He placed her soft, lilting accent without difficulty. She was British. From London, probably, but she spoke with an odd inflection that he couldn't quite pin down.

"I answer better to Luke," he replied, waiting for her to reciprocate and offer her name. When she didn't, the decidedly male interest she'd piqued when she'd walked into the Saddlebag took on an added dimension. Now she stirred not only his masculinity. She challenged the rather unique skills he'd acquired over the past few years.

Only a handful of people knew about those skills. Or that Luke Callaghan now worked for an organization so secret its name would never appear on any governmental organizational chart. Luke hadn't told anyone in Mission Creek about being recruited by OP-12, even his four best buddies.

Three best buddies, he corrected with an inner grimace.

The thought of Ricky Mercado, who'd once been closer than any brother, itched like a raw scab that refused to heal. Luke missed Ricky's friendship. He missed the good times they'd had, both at V.M.I. and in the Marine Corps. For that matter, he missed the corps. The old cliché was true. Once a marine, always a marine.

Unless you caused the death of an innocent young woman.

Then you had no business wearing the uniform of a United States Marine. No business holding yourself up as an example for your men to follow. Judge Bridges might have gotten his four defendants off, but Luke accepted full responsibility for the tragic accident. He should never have encouraged Haley to take the wheel. The speedboat was too big for an unskilled driver, its engines too powerful.

Despite the judge's warning to keep his mouth shut, Luke had freely admitted his criminal negligence during the trial. To this day he carried the guilt for that accident like a burr lodged just under his skin. He always would. It tugged at him now as he studied the stranger's face. She didn't look anything like Haley Mercado. Her face was thinner, the features were more defined. Yet for a moment there, when she'd first walked into the bar, Luke's pulse had hitched.

He tucked the memory of the young, vibrant Haley into the corner of his heart where she'd always remain.

"Are you here in the States on business or pleasure?"

Her glance wavered, dropped to the beer she'd yet to taste. His went to the hands she wrapped around the frosted mug. No wedding ring, he noted. No rings of any kind. Short, oval-shaped nails polished the natural-looking shade women called French white for reasons Luke had never understood.

"Personal business," she said after a moment, meeting his gaze again. "But I'm just passing through Texas."

Well, well. Stretching out his long legs, Luke set out to seduce the woman across the table. It was a game he played, the same game all men played when they spotted a beautiful, unattached female. As often as not, he struck out. Occasionally he got lucky. In either case, he enjoyed the preliminary mating rituals that presaged getting to know a woman. Particularly a woman as delectable as this one.

"Too bad you can't spend more time 'round these parts."

"Why?"

"If you can get past the heat and the dust, this corner of Texas isn't a bad place to sit and doterize awhile."

The lazy drawl took some of the stiffness out of her spine. She sat back in her chair and rewarded him with the faintest glimmer of a smile.

"'Doterize'?"

"It's a local expression," he said with a grin that admitted he'd just made up the word, "for forgetting all your problems and pretty much doing nothing."

"I see."

She took a sip of her beer, leaving Luke more intrigued than ever. This cool, self-contained beauty certainly didn't suffer from an excess of volubility. Or curiosity. Most folks who'd just met someone for the first time would be launching a few discreet probes by this time. Either she wasn't interested or she was content to let Luke set the pace, which he was more than willing to do.

"So how do you occupy your time when you're not passing through Texas?"

She took her time before replying. Luke formed the distinct impression she was weighing what she'd tell him right down to the gram.

"I'm a graphic designer," she said finally.

"What do you design?"

Again she hesitated. The arrival of a platter of greasy fries and a cheeseburger provided an obvious excuse for her not to answer. With a murmur of thanks to the waiter, she squared the plate in front of her and arranged her face in a polite expression of dismissal.

"If you'll excuse me, Mr. Callaghan, I'm—"

"Luke."

"If you'll excuse me, Luke, I'm rather hungry."

No way was she going to shake loose of him that easy.

"Matter of fact," he replied, sniffing appreciatively, "so am I. Hey, Charlie!" He pointed to the burger slopping over the sides of her platter. "Bring another one of those, would you? Rare. And two more beers."

This was crazy! Absolutely insane! Behind Haley's polite mask, her thoughts spiraled perilously close to hysteria. She couldn't believe she was sitting across a table from Luke Callaghan, engaging in the seductive, sensual game played the world over by men and women who meet in bars.

She knew it was a game. She also knew that Luke was far more adept at it than she was. If the stories she'd read about him in the tabloids held even a photon of truth, the handsome, jet-setting millionaire had racked up more wins in this particular arena than any rock star or overmuscled, overpaid jock.

Common sense and the self-preservation skills Haley had honed these past years told her to push away from the table. Now. This very moment. Walk out of the smoky lounge. Walk away from Luke.

Maybe if the visit to her mother hadn't left her so raw

and bleeding, she might have done just that. Or if she'd ever been able to exercise any common sense around Luke Callaghan. All the man had to do was smile at her in that careless way of his and she melted like the tangy cheddar dribbling over the sides of her burger.

She'd stay for another half hour, Haley swore silently. Just long enough to finish her meal. She wouldn't satisfy the curiosity that gleamed in his blue eyes. She couldn't. But she'd store up every minute of this unexpected interlude to take back to London with her.

She stuck to that plan through their burgers and beers. Luke downed his in man-size swallows. Haley took considerably smaller bites of the cheeseburger and nursed her second beer sparingly. She was fiddling with the mug, knowing it was time for her to leave, when another ballad drifted above the muted conversation and clack of pool balls. Martina McBride this time. One of her new hits that was just making its way across the Atlantic. A smooth, mellow song about an old love and missed chances.

Her gaze lifted to Luke's. An old love. Missed chances. A new life that had yet to bring her the private passion she'd once felt for this man. It was still there, she acknowledged. Buried deep under the layers she'd pulled over herself these past years, but still there. It would always be there.

"McBride's good," Luke commented, meeting her gaze. "Too good to pass up. Care to take a turn around the floor?"

A polite refusal formed on her lips. Luke saw it coming. In a preemptive move, he pushed back his chair, rounded the table and held out his hand. Memories of the disaster that had followed the last time she'd slipped her hand into his kept Haley in her seat.

"One turn." Undeterred by her obvious reluctance, he smiled. The tanned skin beside his eyes crinkled. "It'll help settle those fries."

Two seconds passed. Five.

Slowly, Haley entwined her fingers with his.

As she let him lead her to the dance floor, her doubts and insecurities fell away. One touch, and she knew this dance would lead to another. One feel of his body against hers, and she gave up fighting the hunger he stirred in her. Strangely she no longer felt the least hesitation. She wasn't a frightened girl any longer, torn between her desire for one man and the desperate need to escape another. She was a woman, with a woman's needs and a woman's cravings.

Tomorrow she'd honor her promise to her mother and return to London. Tonight she'd create an indelible memory to take with her.

Luke felt the change the instant he took her in his arms. Without knowing how or why, he understood she'd altered the rules of the game. She didn't put up so much as a token resistance when he wrapped an arm around her waist and pulled her against him. Thigh to thigh, they moved to the music.

Lord, she felt good. As if she'd been molded to fit to him. His chin grazed her temple, right where curly strands feathered her forehead. Her high, full breasts were positioned to cause the maximum disruption to his rational thought processes.

A corner of his mind warned that he knew next to nothing about this mysterious stranger. Not even her name. Yet her reticence didn't set off any silent alarms. Not the kind that would have raised the hairs on the back of his neck and made him check the snubnose .38 he usually carried in an ankle holster, anyway. Shutting down that busy, intensely curious corner of his mind, he gave himself up to the pleasure of her body moving against his.

When the song ended, Luke didn't release her. She tipped her head back. Her brown eyes regarded him steadily. It wasn't a question he saw in their gold-flecked depths, but an invitation. Only too happy to oblige, he bent his head and brushed her lips with his.

If she hadn't already aroused him both mentally and physically, the taste of her would have done the trick. In a heartbeat he went from hard to aching.

His arm tightened around her waist. He considered inviting her out to his place, but she might bolt if he turned her loose long enough to make the twenty-minute drive. He was trying to figure out how best to get her out of the bar and into the closest bed when she answered the question he hadn't asked.

"Yes."

"Yes what?"

"Yes, I'll go to one of the rooms out back with you."

Whoa! Now this was getting lucky and then some! Disguising his astonishment behind a swift, slashing grin, Luke steered her back to the table. While she collected her clutch purse, he made a quick detour and tossed a fifty down on the bar.

"The key to the presidential suite, Charlie. And hurry."

"The presidential suite, huh?"

Grinning, the combination bartender/motel clerk slid a key across the smooth-grained oak. The unofficial designation of the largest unit was a joke among the several generations of cowboys who'd occupied it for varying lengths of times over the years, Luke and his friends included. From past experience, however, he knew it was clean, comfortable and recently renovated. He wouldn't take any woman there if it wasn't, much less this enigmatic, thoroughly arousing stranger.

As they crossed the parking lot, Luke half expected her to change her mind and call a halt to things. That she didn't surprised and aroused him all over again. By the time they reached the largest unit, he was walking with a hitch in his step.

He couldn't remember wanting a woman as much as he wanted this one. Maybe it was the secrets she held to herself. Or how she flicked her tongue along her lower lip in obvious nervousness. Yet she didn't so much as blink when he curled his hands around her upper arms and pulled her to him. He couldn't quite believe it when he heard himself offer her a last chance to back out.

"You sure about this, sweetheart? Not that I want to see you walk away, you understand. I'd just hate for you to wake up with regrets come morning."

She made a small, choking sound. Sliding her palms up his shirtfront, she gave him a half smile. "Oh, I'll wake up with plenty of regrets. But not about this. I'll never regret this."

Luke would have had to be a hell of a lot more—or less!—of a man to hold back at that point. Swooping down, he captured her lip with his.

Her mouth opened under his. Warm. Willing. So incredibly erotic that the ache in his groin speared up, into his belly, and down, right to his boots. He'd had his share of women—more than his share, Tyler and Flynt and Spence often groused. He'd also developed one or two sophisticated techniques for finessing a woman out of her clothes over the years.

There wasn't anything sophisticated about the need that rose up now and kicked him square in the gut. Taking his cue from the way her fingers dug into his shoulders, he widened his stance, dragged her hard against him and drank his fill.

Or tried to.

The more he took, the more she gave, until Luke couldn't tell whose need kept them locked together, their bodies straining. All he knew was that he wanted this woman with a fire that burned clear through him. With a low growl, he fumbled the clip from the back of her head, thrust his fingers through the thick silk of her hair and anchored her head for his kiss.

All too soon, the mating of their mouths and tongues wasn't enough. For either of them. Bending, he scooped her up. They landed on the bed in a tangle of arms and legs and wild, searching hands. Shedding their clothes completely took more time and restraint than either of them possessed at that moment. Luke did manage to get her slacks and bikini pants down to her knees and her sweater off one arm. Gasping, she writhed under the skillful play of his hands and tongue and teeth on her breast.

He was full and heavy and pushing hard against his zipper when she went to work on his shirt buttons with frantic fingers. Suddenly she frowned. Panting and dewed with a fine sheen of perspiration, she fingered the raw, puckered scar in his left shoulder.

"What is this?"

"Just a scratch," he replied, swooping down to nip at her throat.

"Some scratch." She wiggled to one side and tried to get another angle on the wound. "Is that from a bullet?"

The last thing Luke cared about right now was the souvenir he'd brought home from the breakaway Russian republic.

"I dodged when I should have ducked," he admitted, raking his teeth lightly along the underside of her jaw.

"But what...? When...?"

He cut off the the questions he couldn't answer with a hard, hungry kiss. At the same time he hooked an ankle over hers and spread her legs. His hand slid down her belly.

Haley almost came apart when Luke slipped a finger inside her. He wasn't her first. She'd dated a good deal in college and indulged in a brief fling with a stockbroker in Dallas.

No man had ever claimed her heart, though. That had always belonged to Luke. And none had ever stirred such wild, white-hot sensations with his mere touch.

"Luke!" Gasping, she arched under his hand. The slow, deliberate strokes had her primed and poised on the edge. "I can't hold back much longer."

"Good," he growled, replacing his hand with the tip of his shaft. "Neither can I."

They made love most of the night. The first time was hard and fast and sweaty. The second, slower and sweeter, with Luke plying a cool washcloth over her body in ways she was sure were illegal in most South Texas counties.

The third was just before dawn, when he roused her

from an exhausted doze and rolled her over, sleepy-eyed and protesting. She didn't protest for long.

The fourth came with the sun. She kept her eyes open this time, memorizing the curve of his shoulder. The short, wiry hair at the nape of his neck. The muscular slope of his back and buttocks.

When they finished, she barely had the strength to drag the spread over her sweat-sheened body and to aim a quick glance at the clock radio on the nightstand. It was late. Past eight. She'd have to hustle to get the car back to Corpus Christi and catch a flight to Dallas that would connect with the London direct.

"You want first dibs on the shower?"

"What?" Blinking, she dragged her gaze back to Luke.

"The shower. Do you want to hit it before I do?"

"It's all yours."

"There is another option, of course." Hooking a finger in the spread, he tugged it down an inch or two and dropped a kiss on her breast. "We could conserve water and soap each other down. I've still got a few washcloth tricks up my sleeve."

Haley summoned a smile. "Any more of your tricks and I won't be able to walk for a week. Better save them for next time."

He looked up then. His blue eyes narrowed. Behind the teasing gleam, they were keen and sharp. Too sharp.

"Will there be a next time?"

"Who knows?" Haley tossed back lightly.

She was gone when Luke came out of the shower.

He'd figured she would be. He hadn't missed the worried glance she'd aimed at the clock radio. Or the strained edginess to her smile.

He'd find her. He had the resources of a high-tech, covert agency at his disposal. When he did, he might just unlock a few of the mysterious stranger's secrets. That was his intent, anyway, until he drove home, logged onto his laptop and found a blinking light indicating a secure transmission from OP-12.

An hour later he climbed into the private, twin-engine jet he kept fueled and ready at the Mission Ridge airport and set a course for an isolated airstrip high in the Andes.

When he returned after six exhausting weeks, the beautiful stranger's trail had gone stone cold.

Chapter 6

Isadora Mercado died of heart failure three days after Haley returned to London. A devastated Carl Bridges delivered the news.

"She died peacefully," the judge related hoarsely. "In her sleep."

Shattered, Haley gave a small, animal moan and slumped against the wall behind her. His voice raw with his own pain, the judge tried to ease hers.

"I visited your mama the day she went. She was happier than I'd ever seen her. Knowing you were alive, that you were safe from Frank… It made all the difference to her, missy. Thank God you got to be with her when you did."

Still Haley couldn't speak. Her knees folded. She slid down the wall to the floor. Blindly she stared at the windows opposite her. A hard rain hit the panes, crying the tears that burned behind Haley's lids.

"Your father's made all the arrangements. She's going to be buried at St. Mary's, Haley. Beside you."

"Oh, Judge!"

"I know what you're thinking. You're thinking you should come home and be with your father and Ricky during their time of grief. Well, you can't. Your mother died with joy in her heart because she knew you were safe. You'll desecrate her memory if you put yourself right back in Frank's clutches."

Blinded by the tears that stung her eyes, Haley stared sightlessly at the window. She kept visualizing her mother's face as she'd last seen it, so bruised and battered.

"Mother told me she was convinced Frank was behind her beating. She was bitter at Daddy for still trying to straddle the fence. Playing Mr. Nice Guy even though his hands were dirty."

"He's always done that," Carl said in disgust.

"The trauma of that beating probably contributed to Mom's heart attack." Her fingers gripping the phone, Haley swore vengeance with a fervor that would have done her uncle Carmine proud. "Frank's going to pay for that beating. Someday he's going to pay!"

A month went by. Six weeks. London steamed in the July heat. August rolled in on waves of choking exhaust fumes. Services practically shut down as shopkeepers and government workers all took their annual holiday and jammed subways, trains and motorways.

Haley drifted through the jostling crowds. She took the tube to work, came home, avoided her friends. She felt as though she was living in a small, dark cocoon woven from grief, regret and bitter, corrosive anger. She couldn't seem to break the shell, couldn't find the energy to try. The heat drained her. Thoughts of her home and family haunted her.

All that saved her from complete despair was the memory of her stolen hours with Isadora.

And with Luke. The night Haley had spent in his arms would remain etched in her heart forever. She didn't realize how deeply until the first week in September, when the reason for her continuing lethargy finally sank in.

She was pregnant.

It took two trips to the pharmacy and three home-pregnancy kits before she could bring herself to accept the possibility. A visit to a women's clinic converted probability into fact.

She was pregnant.

Haley walked out of the clinic into bright September sunshine. Dazed, she made her way to the small park a few blocks from her flat. Pigeons fluttered and cooed from the statue of some forgotten general on his rearing charger. Leaves rustled in the oaks fringing the park. Bit by bit, the hard shell around Haley's heart cracked and fell away.

She was pregnant!

With a joyous whoop that earned her curious stares from passersby, she hugged her middle. She wouldn't be alone anymore. She wasn't cut off from her family any longer. She hadn't left Luke Callaghan behind forever.

She'd have his baby. Their baby. A new life to fill the void of her old. For the first time since Frank Del Brio had shoved that diamond on her finger, Haley's spirits soared high and free.

In her joy and eagerness, she welcomed the minor inconveniences and major physical changes that came with pregnancy. She also reestablished contacts with the small circle of friends she'd begun to make in London.

The days and weeks sped by. She spent hours converting the spare bedroom in her flat to a nursery. More hours with one of her married co-workers, shopping for the astonishing number of items a newborn evidently required. October brought gray skies. November, icy drizzle. December blew in cold and snowy, but Haley hardly noticed the weather. Happy and by now well-rounded, she thrilled at every twinge or kick that gave evidence of the life growing inside her.

January brought the first small indications that the nest she'd built for herself and her child might not be as safe and cozy as she thought. She let herself into her building, her cheeks rosy and her breath steaming from the cold, and noticed what looked like scratches around her mailbox lock. Frowning, she ran her gloved fingers over the faint marks. When she inquired of the doorman, however, he shrugged.

"Can't say how those scratches got there. Might a been workmen. We had a crew working in the lobby a few days ago. I'll check on it for you."

"Thanks."

When the doorman's inquiries returned no information about the marks, Haley shrugged them off, until a week later when she retrieved her mail and could have sworn that one of her letters had been opened. It was only a form letter, reminding her of her next dental appointment, but the joyous cloud she'd been floating on for months began to dissipate.

The hang-ups and wrong numbers began in late February, just weeks before her projected delivery date. The first two or three annoyed her. By the fourth or fifth, she had begun to feel distinctly nervous.

She didn't dare go to the police. She'd entered the country on a false passport, was living with forged identity papers. Nor could she contact her one rock. Carl Bridges didn't answer either his phone or the e-mails an increasingly worried Haley fired off. He'd told her he had some business to attend to and might be incommunicado for a while. But why did it have to be now? Just when she needed him.

In March, worry sent her into labor a week early, but she delivered a healthy, beautiful baby girl. She had her father's silky black curls and, Haley saw with a sob, his eyes. They were the color of a summer Texas sky. She named her Lena, after her mother's mother, Helena.

The next day she brought her baby home to the nursery she'd decorated so lovingly and prayed she'd be safe there.

Eight weeks later the taxi carrying Haley and Lena to the baby's two-month checkup took a wrong turn.

"This isn't the way," she informed the turbaned Sikh driver. "You should have turned right on Hyde Street, not left."

The driver stared straight ahead and whizzed down a broad street lined with leafless chestnut trees. Frowning, Haley leaned forward to rap on the Plexiglas partition separating the front seat from the back.

"Excuse me. You're heading in the wrong direction."

The driver didn't so much as blink.

Haley stared at the back of his head, ice forming in her veins. "Stop here," she ordered. "Let us out."

In reply, he flicked a switch. All four door locks clicked down.

Panic raced through Haley, swift and all-consuming. She wasn't afraid for herself, but for her baby. Dear God, her baby!

Snatching Lena from the carryall, she cradled the newborn against her chest. A dozen frantic schemes jumped into her mind. She'd roll the windows down at the next traffic stop. Scream for help. Pass Lena out the window to a pedestrian. Tell him or her to run like hell.

She never got the opportunity to implement any of her wild schemes. Mere moments later the cab swerved onto a side street. Halfway down the block, a blue painted garage door rumbled up. The cab slowed, swerved again and rattled into the garage. The blue door dropped down with a clank.

After the bright sunshine outside, the gloom of the windowless garage was impenetrable. Haley clutched Lena to her shoulder, almost frantic with fear for her child. Suddenly dazzling white light flooded the garage. She couldn't see a thing, but she could hear.

The door locks clicked.

The driver climbed out and opened the rear passenger door.

Footsteps sounded on concrete.

Blinking furiously to clear her vision, Haley made out two figures approaching the cab. One she didn't recognize. The other had her gasping.

"Judge!"

Giddy with relief, she started to scramble out of the cab. The jurist's haggard expression halted her. He looked defeated, utterly, completely defeated. His shoulders slumped. His white hair lay lank and disordered, as though he hadn't combed it in days. Behind his black-framed glasses, his faded blue eyes held pain.

Belatedly, it occurred to Haley that Frank might have had the judge kidnapped. Maybe he'd been tortured. Or fed drugs. Forced to disclose his role in the supposed death of Haley Mercado. She shrank back against the seat, Lena clutched to her shoulder.

"It's okay, Haley." Desolation wreathed the judge's face as he coaxed her from the vehicle. "Please. Come out. We have to talk to you."

She emerged slowly, warily. Her glance darted to the man beside Carl. Short and stocky, with hair a bright shade of copper, he wore a nondescript gray suit and a bulldog expression.

Behind him, three others moved out of the gloom, watching her with dark, intent eyes.

"Who are these people?" she asked the judge, her heart pumping hard and fast.

"This is Sean Collins. He's a special agent from the New York office of the FBI."

Oh, no! All Haley could think of at that moment was that the FBI had busted Carl for procuring her fake passport and identity papers. Depositing the sleeping Lena in the carryall still resting on the back seat, she whirled and launched into a passionate defense.

"Judge Bridges isn't the one to blame for any wrong-doing. He was acting as my agent when he obtained that forged passport. I'm the one responsible. I had to get out of Texas, out of the States."

"We're not here to talk to you about a forged passport," the agent identified as Sean Collins replied.

"Then why are you here?"

"Because we have reason to believe your mother didn't die of natural causes."

Shocked and confused, Haley turned to the judge. "What's he talking about? You told me Mom had a heart attack."

"She did," Collins answered for him. "But based on evidence only recently uncovered, we obtained a court order to have her body exhumed. The medical examiner performed an autopsy and discovered traces of potassium chloride in her body. We think someone slipped the drug into her IV and deliberately caused her heart to fail."

"Frank," Haley whispered hoarsely. "Frank must have done it to keep her from talking."

"Actually," Collins explained, "our guess is that Del Brio killed her because she wouldn't talk. Word is, he was hot to know the identity of the nun who visited her right before her death. He's been asking a lot of questions about the Sisters of Good Hope. Questions that led us to theorize Isadora's daughter might still be alive."

Pain splintered through Haley, cutting into her heart like a thousand needle-pointed shards. Her face now as haggard as the judge's, she stared at the agent through a haze of despair.

"I killed her. My visit. That disguise. I killed my mother."

"No, you didn't!" Snapping out of his near stupor, Carl grasped her arm. "You listen to me, missy. Your visit filled your mama with profound peace. Knowing you'd escaped made up for what she'd had to endure all these years."

"But—"

"No buts!" he said fiercely. "Isadora and I talked for

years about taking you kids and leaving Mission Creek. She never forgave Johnny for dragging all of you into the morass with him. But he was her husband, and you and Ricky needed your father and—"

"And she was a devout Catholic," Haley finished for him. "She didn't believe in divorce."

Nodding, he let out a ragged sigh. "God knows, I tried my damnedest to talk her into one. I loved her, Haley. I've loved her for as long as I can remember."

"I know, Judge."

She sank back against the taxi fender, her thoughts whirling. Shock and pain gradually sharpened into fear. If Frank Del Brio had grown so suspicious that he was trying to track the nun who'd visited Isadora, he could be closing in on her. That would explain the scratches on her mailbox and sudden spate of hang-ups.

Nausea rolled around in Haley's stomach. As sickening as it was, she had to face the truth. She couldn't run far enough to escape Frank Del Brio. As long as she lived—as long as he lived—she'd never be safe.

Nor would Lena.

Agent Collins apparently agreed. "We're only a few steps ahead of Del Brio, Miss Mercado. We're just lucky that we were able to convince Judge Bridges to tell us what he knew of Isadora Mercado's mysterious visitor. He brought us to you because he now realizes the life you've so carefully constructed for yourself in London is about to come tumbling down around your ears. We need to get you and your baby away from here and to provide you both with protection."

"In exchange for what?" Haley asked, wary of strangers bearing gifts.

"We'll talk about that later."

"No, we'll talk about it now. I want to know exactly what you want from me, Mr. Collins."

Palming his thick reddish hair, the agent chose his words carefully. "The FBI has been building a case against your uncle Carmine for years. After his health had begun to fail and Frank Del Brio moved up to number two in your uncle's organization, we've shifted a lot of our attention and our assets to him. We thought we had him nailed awhile back on extortion and racketeering charges, but the bastard eliminated both of our key witnesses."

"So how do I make up for the loss of those witnesses?"

His hazel eyes drilled into hers. "We need someone inside, Miss Mercado. Someone who understands the power structure. Someone who wants to take down Frank Del Brio as much as we do."

The enormity of what he was asking of her left Haley speechless. Collins used her stunned silence to press home his point.

"You worked at Mercado Brothers Paving and Contracting for two summers, Miss Mercado. You know the family business. Enough of it to understand what looks right and what doesn't, anyway. We're hoping you can help us ferret out times, dates, drop-off points, contacts. Anything that will tie Del Brio to the smuggling and racketeering operations we know he runs."

Haley cleared her throat. "Let me make sure I understand you," she said carefully. "You want me to infiltrate the mob. Spy on Frank Del Brio. Gather evidence against him. And by the way, gather evidence against my father and possibly my brother, as well."

"We're prepared to offer you a deal. Immunity for your father and brother in exchange for the detailed information we need to indict Del Brio. We'll also place your baby with a family who'll love and protect her while you're undercover."

"No!" she said fiercely. "No deal! I'm not giving up my baby. She's only two months old."

"I understand how you feel," Collins replied gravely. "I know you'd do anything to protect her. Anything."

"You bastard! You're deliberately playing on my fears for my baby to gain my cooperation."

"Maybe. But you've got plenty to fear, Miss Mercado."

She hated him in that moment. He was only voicing the brutal truth she'd already admitted to herself, yet Haley wasn't prepared to hear it said out loud. Nor was she prepared to give up her baby, even temporarily.

"I have to think. I need some space. And some time."

"I'm afraid time is the one thing you don't have much of, Miss Mercado. We'll give you what we can, though. We've already booked a room for you in a hotel under an assumed name. We'll take you there."

Another assumed name, Haley thought on a wave of near hysteria. Another carefully constructed identity. More background details to memorize. More lies to dish out. She'd already told so many she wasn't really sure who she was anymore.

True to his word, Agent Collins gave Haley space to think. Time ran out all too swiftly, however.

Collins showed up at her hotel room the very next afternoon. Judge Bridges was there, still worn, still haggard. The judge took one look at the agent's face and moved to stand behind the sofa where Haley sat cuddling Lena.

"What's wrong?" she asked, already afraid of the answer.

"Someone broke into your flat last night, Miss Mercado. Scotland Yard managed to lift some good prints. Evidently the perp was one of Del Brio's henchmen. If we're going to get you out of London and into a new identity, we'll have to move quickly."

This was the way it would always be, Haley thought with an ache in her chest. Constantly running. Always looking over her shoulder. Worrying every time she dropped her daughter off at day care or nursery school. Unless and until the threat to Lena was removed.

Closing her eyes, she kissed her baby's black, downy curls. She had no choice. She had to help Collins destroy Frank Del Brio and dismantle the operation her uncle had built. But she was damned if she'd place her baby with strangers.

There was only one person she'd trust with Lena. One man who possessed both the power and the resources to protect her. Only one other person with a parent's responsibility.

"All right," she told Agent Collins. "I'll go back to Texas with you. I'll work undercover. But I won't place Lena in the care of strangers. I want her to go to her father."

"That can be arranged."

The judge eyed her curiously. He'd respected Haley's privacy when she'd declined to identify Lena's father and said merely that she intended to raise her child on her own. Now she she had no choice when he voiced the question she saw on his face.

"Who is the father, Haley?"

"Luke. Luke Callaghan."

Chapter 7

Ten days later Haley stared intently into a lighted makeup mirror. She and a small army of FBI agents had been holed up in a motel in Clearwater Springs, twenty miles east of Mission Creek, for more than a week now, perfecting her cover and orchestrating her transition to her new identity.

The transition was now complete. Another stranger stared back at her from the lighted mirror. Frowning, she forked her fingers through what she could only call her mane, now permed and dyed a lighter blond.

"Fluff it up more than that," the female agent observing her directed. "We're going for real Texas-style big hair here."

"I was born and lived most of my life in Texas," Haley said with a wry smile. "I never wore my hair this big."

"You do now," the FBI specialist replied, returning her assortment of combs and brushes to a gray steel case. "Don't forget, the intent is to exaggerate, exaggerate, exaggerate. Draw the eye from those features we didn't have time to alter to those we did. Now pouf those curls out another inch or so."

Grimacing, Haley complied, then studied the result in the mirror. She had to admit the makeup artist knew her business. The slender Londoner who'd lived in Haley Mercado's skin for so many years had disappeared. In her place stood Daisy Parker.

A loose tumble of butterscotch curls framed her face. Botoxin injections had added a ripe, sensual fullness to her lips. Her eyebrows were now thicker, darker. Purple shadow and the liberal application of mascara and liner gave her eyes a sultry air. A short black skirt and a blouse unbuttoned to display a hint of cleavage completed the transition. The look stopped short of barroom cheap, but definitely came down on the other side of refined.

It would do, she thought grimly. It would have to do.

Besides, the only person she really had to fool was Luke Callaghan. The cosmetic surgery she'd undergone in London had altered her enough that she'd be a stranger to everyone except him. Hopefully, he wouldn't match this gum-snapper with the sophisticate who'd flamed in his arms.

An impatient rap rattled the bedroom door. "Are you finished in there? It's almost six-thirty."

"We're finished," the agent called. Closing her steel case, she gave Haley a warm smile. "Good luck, Miss Mercado. Sorry. I mean, Miss Parker."

The two women emerged into a small sitting room still curtained against the night. Dawn was beginning to break, though. Faint fingers of pink showed at the edges of the blinds. This was it. The first day of her new life as Daisy Parker.

Taking in a deep breath, she faced the team of FBI operatives who'd assembled to craft and train this new entity. Communications technicians. Documentation specialists. Evidence-gathering experts. The language coach who'd spent hours coaxing Haley to grossly exaggerate her native Texas drawl and smother the faint British lilt she'd so carefully cultivated.

Planting his hands on his hips, their team leader ran a critical eye over his creation. "Good," Sean Collins murmured in approval. "Very good. You'll fit right in with the other waitresses at the Lone Star Country Club."

"If I get the job."

"You'll get it. Don't forget, Daisy Parker has waited tables at some of the best clubs and restaurants in Dallas and Fort Worth. If the manager checks your references, he'll get nothing but glowing reports from your former employers. Just don't drop too many trays your first day or two."

"I'll try not to."

The bald-headed language coach wagged an admonishing finger. "Tut, tut! Let's have that again, shall we?"

With a sardonic glance in his direction, Haley laid it on with a trowel. "Ah'll surely to goodness try not to drop anythang, cowboy."

"Excellent," the coach beamed. "Excellent."

Special Agent Collins checked his watch. "All right, folks. This is it. Operation Lone Star is officially under way. You ready, Judge?"

All eyes turned to Carl Bridges. He glanced down at

the baby tucked into the combination baby carrier/car seat by his side and nodded. "I'm ready."

"Wait!"

Haley rushed across the room. She'd kissed and cuddled Lena for hours last night. The good-natured baby had cooed happily, waving her fat, dimpled fists and blowing bubbles from her rosebud mouth until she'd dropped into sleep. This morning Haley had barely gotten her diapered, changed and fed before the FBI makeup artist arrived with her box of magic tricks.

Now that the moment of separation had arrived, Haley had to hold Lena again, had to kiss her soft curls and breathe in her powdery scent one last time. Collins had warned Haley that this undercover operation could take months. The thought of missing all those weeks of her baby's development drove a stake right through her heart.

Folding back the baby's fluffy pink blanket, she tucked the well-fed, sleepy child against her. Doubts about the elaborate scheme Carl Bridges had worked out to deliver Lena to her father without revealing the identity of her mother had her throwing an anxious look at the judge.

"You're sure Luke will be at the country club this morning?"

Understanding her reluctance to part with her baby, Carl Bridges nodded and went over the same ground they'd already covered half a dozen times.

"Luke, Flynt Carson, Tyler Murdoch and Spence Harrison have a standing six-fifteen tee time every Sunday morning. Depending on how crowded the course is, they generally finish the first nine holes around eight."

"Yes, but—"

"I called Luke last night on the pretext of wanting to invite him to lunch at the club. He suggested brunch instead, after he and the others finish their round. He'll be there, Haley."

"Daisy," Collins corrected from across the room. "We all have to start thinking of her as Daisy."

"Daisy," the judge echoed. "Don't worry, missy. I won't put Lena on the ninth tee box until I see Luke and the others holing out on number eight."

"You're sure they won't be able to see you?"

"I'll be in the groundskeeper's shed. It's separated from the tee box by a thick hedge. I found a spot where I can slip Lena's carrier through the hedge, watch the guys approach, then skedaddle."

"What about the note? Do you think we got the wording right?"

Patiently, he quoted from memory the phrases the entire FBI team had helped draft and redraft.

Luke—
I'm your baby girl. My name is Lena. Please take good care of me until my mommy can come back for me.

Nuzzling her baby's downy curls, Haley fought a wave of fierce, last-minute doubts. "I hope we're doing the right thing!"

"I hope we are, too," Sean Collins muttered.

He'd argued against leaving Lena with Luke, who lived right there in Mission Creek. He'd wanted to place her with a couple in Nebraska so Haley wouldn't catch glimpses of her child and become distracted. "Out of sight, out of mind" was his strategy.

She'd pointed out that she'd worry far more about Lena if she couldn't see her occasionally and know she was being well cared for. Collins had caved finally, with the caveat that the note indicate that Lena's mother had departed the area. The last thing he wanted was for folks to connect the baby found on the ninth tee with the new waitress at the Lone Star Country Club.

"It's getting late," the judge warned. "I'd better take her, Haley."

"Daisy!" Collins snapped. "Haley Mercado is dead. From now on we all think and talk Daisy Parker, even in our sleep!"

"Duly noted," the judge retorted, a half a breath away from cutting the FBI agent down to size. "Here, let me have her, Daisy."

Haley swore she wouldn't cry. She hadn't cried since the day her mother died. She didn't have any tears left to shed. But her throat felt as though she'd swallowed a bucket of broken glass when she dropped a feather-light kiss on her daughter's crown and passed her to Carl.

She couldn't know that was the last time she'd hold her child for more than twelve terrifying months.

Chapter 8

Present day

Now, over a year later, Haley stood in the shadows of the Saddlebag's noisy bar and wondered how it all could have gone so wrong.

She'd done exactly what Sean Collins had asked. She'd spent more than a year undercover. She'd gathered more than enough evidence for the FBI to take down Frank Del Brio and destroy his network. She'd dodged and sidestepped and somehow managed to keep from tangling herself in the web of lies she'd lived with daily.

In that time her uncle Carmine had died. Carl Bridges had been murdered. And Frank had managed to strip away Daisy Parker's layers one by one. The bastard had not only escaped the net the FBI had tried to throw over him, he'd kidnapped her baby.

Now her cover was blown. Operation Lone Star was

falling apart. And Luke Callaghan had yet to hold his child in his arms.

That wasn't entirely her fault, Haley reminded herself with an ache just under her ribs. Carl Bridges had placed Lena right where the four Sunday morning golfers would find her. Who could have anticipated that water from the sprinkler-wet hedge would drip onto the note and obliterate the father's name? Or that Luke wouldn't show that morning, of all mornings?

He'd been gone for months. Long, agonizing months, while Haley watched from a distance as Flynt and Josie Carson cared for Lena. Endless, torturous months, when she lived every hour of every day on the edge. And then, when Luke finally returned to Mission Creek, he was blind in both eyes.

Her heart aching, Haley stared across the smoke-filled bar at the man she'd been in love with for as long as she could remember. His back was to her, but she recognized the short, curly black hair showing under his straw Stetson. Recognized, too, the strong column of his neck and the athletic shoulders under the denim shirt. She should. She'd run her hands and mouth over those strong, muscled shoulders repeatedly the night they'd created their child. The child she'd do anything—anything!—to get back safely.

Dragging in a ragged breath, she threaded a path through the tables. The man sitting opposite Luke saw her first. Tyler Murdoch's brown eyes narrowed as he tracked her approach. He lounged in a comfortable slouch, his chair tilted back against the scarred paneling. The lazy sprawl didn't fool Haley. Nor did she fail to note how he kept his back to the wall. Evidently his recent marriage to a fiery Spanish interpreter hadn't dulled the mercenary's razor-edged instincts.

"Looks like we've got company, buddy. It's Daisy Parker, the waitress from the country club."

She caught Murdoch's murmur. Caught, too, the way Luke's head cocked to one side. Just an inch. Maybe two. Like a cougar listening to the rustle of the dry Texas grass. Or a stallion scenting danger on the wind.

Her heart hammering, Haley stopped beside his chair. The stress of the past months showed on his face. Beneath the rim of his hat, she could just make out the trace of white scars from the shrapnel that had blinded him. Could see, as well, the deep grooves bracketing his mouth.

Despite the scars, despite the strain carved into his face, Luke Callaghan was still the most elemental male Haley had ever encountered. His startlingly blue eyes might not register anything except darkness now, but they stared straight ahead with disconcerting directness. And his mouth. Lord, his mouth! Haley could almost feel it on hers again as she drew her tongue nervously across her lower lip. Shedding her poured-on Texas twang like last year's winter coat, she murmured a soft, urgent request.

"I need to talk to you, Luke. Privately. Please!"

Luke recognized her voice.

He'd always heard that people who'd lost their sight honed their other senses to a razor's edge. If so, these past six months had proved him the exception to the general rule. Neither his sense of smell nor his tactile abilities had sharpened to any appreciable degree since the explosion deep in the jungles of Central America that had left him totally blind, until this last week when he'd begun to see dark shadows. He wouldn't have said that his hearing had improved all that much, either, but this woman's voice was burned into his memory.

He'd heard it before right here at the Saddlebag. Two years ago. She'd spoken with more of British lilt then. Not with Daisy Parker's thick, down-on-the-border accent, nor the subtle one he heard now. The suspicions about the waitress Luke had been harboring for some weeks now hardened into certainty.

"I want to talk to you, too," he ground out in a tone so low and dangerous she took an involuntary step back.

He heard the small shuffle. The sudden, nervous movement had him shoving back his chair. Following the sound, he reached out. His hand closed around her upper arm, but not before his knuckles made contact with a full, lush breast.

His entire body went taut at the touch. Memories of that night two years ago knifed into him. She'd welcomed him so eagerly that night, so generously. As though she'd been waiting for him all her life. When he'd come out of the shower the next morning, though, she'd disappeared.

Luke had made a few inquiries about her. After the mission that had taken him high into the Andes, he'd exercised some of his special contacts within the government in an attempt to locate the gorgeous blonde. He'd finally concluded the lady had had her reasons for slipping away with the dawn. Only recently had he begun to connect the beautiful stranger with the waitress who'd started work at the Lone Star Country Club right about the time his buddies discovered a baby on the ninth tee.

His baby. The child he'd never seen. The child who'd been kidnapped right before his return to Mission Creek. The child, he was now certain, this cold-hearted witch had callously abandoned.

"We'll talk outside," he growled.

Behind him, Tyler called a quiet question. "Need me to come along, buddy?"

"No. This is between Daisy and me."

The brutal grip on her arm told Haley this confrontation was going to be even tougher than she'd anticipated. Luke held her manacled, as though he didn't trust her not to bolt. He also, she noted in the small corner of her mind that wasn't numb with fear for her child, threaded his way through the tables with an assurance that gave no hint of his impaired sight. He let her guide him, following her lead with a sure tread, but to a casual observer they must have looked like any couple slipping away from the noisy bar to one of the motel units out back.

Deliberately, Haley blanked her mind to the night when they, too, had done just that. This wasn't about her and Luke, or about that night. This was about Lena. Only about Lena.

After the air-conditioned smoke of the bar, the humid June night wrapped around them like a sponge. Haley didn't mind the heat or the humidity or the dust that swirled on the night air. After all those years living in London's damp, misty climate, she and Lena had come home to wide-open skies and the blazing Texas sun. She could only pray that they'd never have to leave again.

"My car's parked near the back of the lot," she told Luke.

"Lead the way."

The beat-up sedan the Bureau had supplied her with when she'd first gone undercover looked like a small, stray dog amid the herd of muscled SUVs and pick-ups. The white van that had followed her from the safe house was still parked a few rows from the rust-spotted sedan. Haley didn't see the agents who'd driven it, but suspected they weren't far away. After all, she was the FBI's best hope—their only hope!—for luring Frank Del Brio out of hiding.

She reached for the handle of the passenger door, thinking Luke would slide into the seat so they could talk inside the vehicle, but he used his grip on her arm to swing her around. The sedan's roof was to her back. A large and obviously angry Luke crowded close at her front. Too close.

Planting his hands against the car, he caged her. The brim of his Stetson shadowed his face, but she couldn't miss the muscle that ticked in the side of his jaw as he fought for control.

"You're her, aren't you?"

"Her?" she murmured, stalling for time while she tried to figure out where to begin her tangled explanations.

The question seemed to add to the anger that radiated from Luke in waves. The muscle at the side of his jaw jumped again.

"Don't mess with me, lady."

Haley had known him all her life. She'd also spent the most passionate night of her life in his arms. Yet this was a Luke Callaghan she'd never seen. Hard. Cold. Dangerous. He might have thoroughly intimidated her if she hadn't lived with fear so long that she'd learned to tip her chin and stare it straight in the eye.

"You're the woman I hooked up with here at the Saddlebag two years ago." It wasn't a question this time, but a flat statement. "You weren't passing yourself off as Daisy Parker then, but it was you."

"Yes, it was."

His breath hissed out. For a moment, maybe two, that night hovered between them. Haley ached to reach up, to touch his cheek. To beg him to fold her into his arms again and to let her lose herself in his heat and strength. Suspecting what was to come, she kept her fists clenched tightly at her sides.

"We made more than love that night, didn't we? We made a baby."

"Yes," she whispered again.

"So you brought our daughter back to Mission Creek. Thought you'd cash in on her, big time."

"Cash in on her?" Shocked, she gaped up at him. "What in God's name are you talking about?"

He leaned closer, crowding her against the car. "I'm guessing you came back intending to initiate a nice fat paternity suit. But her millionaire father was gone. Out of the country. Unreachable. So you dumped the kid on the golf course at the country club, where some other rich sucker was sure to find her, and walked away."

"No! That's not how it happened!"

"That's exactly how it happened. Flynt Carson told me he and Tyler and the others found the baby in a carrier, with only a blurred note that gave her name. Christ, how could you abandon your own child like that?"

"I didn't abandon her! You don't understand—"

"You're right, I don't." Scorn laced every word. "I don't understand how any mother could leave her child in the care of total strangers. But I'm getting the picture now. I'm also beginning to understand why Lena was supposedly 'kidnapped' from Flynt Carson's ranch."

"Supposedly?" Her voice spiraled to a near screech. "There's no 'supposedly' about it!"

"Come on, sweetheart. You don't have to playact anymore. You dumped the kid because no one knew where I was and you got desperate. You could have waited until I came back to Mission Creek to establish paternity. The DNA results would have made that a breeze. But you hit on a better scheme, didn't you? Instead of child support spread out over a number of years, you decided on a nice, fat ransom paid all up front. You won't get it," he warned in a voice so cold it could have cut glass. "You won't get a cent from me that way."

"Oh, God!" Stunned, she tried to wrap her mind around his accusations. "You think I arranged to have my own child kidnapped so I could extort money from you?"

His lip curled. "Prove me wrong, Daisy. Tell me you didn't come to the Saddlebag tonight to deliver a ransom demand."

"Luke, listen to me. You've got this all backward."

"How much?" he snarled. "Tell me, dammit! What's the asking price for a baby these days?"

"All right! They want two million!"

"Two million, huh?"

Luke would have paid ten. An hour ago he would have cashed in every stock and bond he owned to buy the safe return of his child.

He didn't understand this urgent need to hold this daughter he'd never seen. He wanted a family, sure. Someday. He'd spent most of his childhood in boarding schools under the loose guardianship of his uncle, but

Stew had shown far more interest in the leggy show-girls he wined and dined in Vegas than in his nephew.

The military had become Luke's substitute family. First at V.M.I., then in the marines. Although he'd shed his uniform after being charged with contributing to Haley Mercado's death, the tight bonds forged during his years in the service had provided all the kith and kin he'd needed. Until he'd learned he had a daughter.

Tyler Murdoch had delivered the news. Deep in a steamy jungle, right after the explosion that had sent shards of shrapnel slicing into Luke's face.

The knowledge that he'd fathered a child had sustained Luke throughout the painful operations that followed. He'd come home to Mission Creek blind but determined to do right by his daughter. Determined, too, to find the woman who'd abandoned her. He'd pictured her frightened. Desperate. Unable to care for her baby and driven to the extreme of leaving her on a golf course. He could have forgiven her that.

What Luke couldn't forgive was that the baby had been kidnapped just days before his return to Mission Creek. The timing was too close to write off as mere coincidence. More to the point, the evidence he'd so painstakingly gathered over the past months implicated this waitress in Lena's disappearance.

Disgust bit into him, so deep and bitter he could taste it. He still didn't know who she really was or where she'd sprung from, but he was sure of one thing. When they recovered Lena—which they would—there was no way in hell Luke would leave his daughter with this sorry excuse for a mother.

Bringing his face down to within inches of hers, he stripped matters to their core. "Let's get one thing absolutely straight between us, lady. You're not getting one cent from me, let alone two million. But you are going to take me to wherever you've stashed our baby. We'll sort matters out from there."

Haley snapped. After all she'd been through, after all the stress and false identities and lies she'd been forced to live, Luke Callaghan had the nerve, the unmitigated, unfettered, unqualified gall, to accuse her of using her own baby in a scheme to extort money from him! With a surge of fury, she shoved at his chest and opened enough space between them to spit out her rage.

"Listen and listen good, cowboy! You're dead wrong on every count but one. The man who snatched our child has demanded a ransom, but I didn't come here intending to shake you down for the two million. I don't want your money, Callaghan!"

"Is that right?"

"That's right, dammit!"

He looked anything but convinced. "Then what do you want?"

"Your help. You're the one man I can take with me when I go after my baby."

"Right." Skepticism cut deep into his voice. "Because you've suddenly decided to admit I'm her father?"

"No, you jackass. Because you're blind."

He reared back, jerking away as if she'd hauled off and open-handed him. He recovered almost immediately, though. She'd give him that. Whatever else Luke had lost in the jungles of Central America, he could still spring to the attack with lethal agility.

"Why don't you run that by me one more time?" he suggested with biting derision. "I'm having a little trouble understanding exactly how my impaired vision plays in this situation."

"I'll tell you exactly how it plays. I just got a call from the kidnapper. He told me to get together two million in unmarked, nonsequential bills. He said he'd contact me later with instructions on when and where to deliver it. At the same time, he swore… He warned…"

She choked. Swallowing hard, she forced out the words that sliced at her throat like shards of glass.

"He warned that I'd never see Lena alive again if there was a police officer or a federal agent anywhere within a hundred miles when I make the delivery. That's why I'm asking—why I'm begging you to go with me. He'd suspect anyone else, think I was trying to set him up, but he wouldn't… That is, he couldn't…"

"He wouldn't worry about a blind man."

She bit her lip, hating to throw his disability in his face but determined to use whatever weapon she could.

"Look, all I need is for you to distract Frank, to divert his attention for a few seconds. I'll take it from there."

"Frank?" His black brows came together. "Are you talking about Frank Del Brio?"

"Yes. We suspected it all along. After the shootout the other night, we were certain. But until he called a little while ago, we didn't know what he wanted for her."

Luke reached for her again, his hands fumbling until they locked around her upper arms. He pulled her up, as if to feel and not just hear what she had to say.

"Who's 'we'?" he demanded fiercely. "Who the hell are you, Daisy? And what's your connection to the Texas mob?"

She hesitated, trying to decide which bomb to drop

first, searching for a way to lay bare the secrets she'd buried deep inside her for so long.

Suddenly the slamming of car doors ricocheted through the night, followed by the thud of running footsteps. The sound triggered an instant response in Luke. Shoving Haley behind him, he spun to meet the threat he could hear but not see. Pinned against the car, she wiggled frantically until she made out the shadowy figures rushing toward them with weapons drawn.

"Move away from her!" the lead runner shouted.

She felt Luke tense, sensed him readying to spring.

"It's okay!" Grabbing the sleeve of his blue denim shirt, she held him back. "They're FBI!"

"What?"

The two agents fanned out to either side, weapons held high, no doubt remembering Sean Collins's terse instructions to keep his star witness safe at all costs.

"Move away from her, Callaghan. Slow and easy. Keep those hands right where we can see them."

Luke complied. He took a step to the side, his hands held at waist level.

Breathing out a sigh of relief, Haley shoved her hair out of her eyes and eased out from behind the protective shield of his body. The lead agent kept Luke covered while he speared her with a quick glance.

"You okay, Miss Mercado?"

The man beside her went still. Absolutely still.

"Mercado?" he echoed softly. Dangerously. "Did he just call you Miss Mercado?"

Chapter 9

Haley swallowed a curse. She'd imagined a hundred different scenarios in which she finally revealed her real identity to Luke. None of those scenarios had been played out in a parking lot, with guns drawn.

Nor had she expected this sudden, Arctic silence. Disbelief, yes. Anger, of course. The kind of deep, visceral anger a man once accused of causing Haley Mercado's death was entitled to feel. She suspected that would come, though, and soon.

Delaying the inevitable, she answered the agent's question first. "Mr. Callaghan wasn't threatening me. We were just talking."

"Didn't look much like talking from where we sat," he returned. "You sure you're okay?"

"Yes."

He eyed Luke speculatively. "Want us to hang loose while you finish your chat, Miss Mercado?"

"No. Please, just leave us alone."

"All right. If you say so. But we're close if you need us."

They retreated to the van, shutting the doors behind them. Stillness settled over the parking lot once more. The hot, dusty quiet plucked at Haley's raw nerves like a hag with boney fingers. Bracing her shoulders, she turned to Luke.

He might have been carved from the granite dug out of the hills of north Texas. He stood rigid, unmoving, his eyes narrowed to slits. As if he could actually see her. As if he was trying to strip away the layers of lies and deceit with which she'd cloaked herself.

"I wanted to tell you the truth, Luke. You and the others. I couldn't."

He didn't answer. The silence stretched tight and thin. He broke it with a savage command.

"Get in the car."

"What?"

His jaw worked. "Get in the car. You've got some serious explaining to do, Miss Mercado. I've got a few things to say to you, too, but I'll be damned if I'll say them in a parking lot with the FBI and God knows who else listening in."

The white van followed them all the way to Luke's sprawling estate on Lake Maria.

Since the Callaghans had made their millions in oil and the stock market, the property Luke had inherited didn't run to thousands of acres like the cattle ranches owned by the Carsons and Wainwrights, Mission Creek's two most prominent families. The house sat on five hundred acres of prime real estate, though, bounded by the lake to the east and low, rolling hills to the west.

Haley pulled up at massive wrought-iron gates, which slid open at a click of the thin, quarter-size remote dangling from the key ring Luke dug out of his pocket. When she drove through, the gates slid shut again.

"Stop here for a moment," Luke snapped.

Aiming the remote at some invisible target, he clicked out a code. Haley neither saw nor heard any evidence of the security system he was obviously reactivating, but she guessed it would be elaborate given his long and frequent absences from Mission Creek.

While her rust-spotted sedan idled just inside the gates, the FBI van rolled to a halt outside. Its headlights blazed in her rearview mirror. She half expected the driver to lean on the horn and demand entrance, but he must have radioed the FBI command center for instructions. A moment later the van backed up and parked beside the stone gatepost.

Seeing the FBI settling in on the other side of the gate raised an odd, prickly sensation on Haley's skin. She'd worked with them for more than a year, passing information, receiving coded instructions. Now Sean Collins's team was on the other side of the fence, literally, and she was on her own.

No, not on her own. She was with Luke.

The prickly sensation intensified, raising goose bumps all up and down her arms.

"It's set," the man beside her said tersely. "Just follow the drive. The house is about a mile up."

"I know."

Her soft reply didn't go down well. Like Haley, Luke

had to be remembering the little sister who'd tagged along when Ricky had come to shoot pool or to check out the lasted foal sired by the Callaghan championship stud. The same little sister Luke had believed dead all these years.

"That's right," he bit out. "You do."

He stared straight ahead into his own private darkness while Haley negotiated the drive. The tires swooshed on the tarmac. A smooth, manicured lawn rolled down to the lake. A shiver rippled along her spine as she glanced off to the left. She couldn't see the water in the darkness, but she knew it was there.

She had so much to explain, so much to account for. Dreading the ordeal ahead, she brought the car to a stop under a tall portico supported by white columns on either side. A massive wrought-iron coach lamp hung suspended by chains, illuminating the wide front steps and double doors framed by additional lamps. Easing out from behind the wheel, Haley rounded the front of the car to take Luke's arm.

"I've learned to count the steps," he informed her, shaking loose of her hold. "I manage in my own home."

"Sorry."

"Just walk ahead of me."

He wasn't just counting his steps, she realized a moment later. He was listening to the echo of her footfalls, first on the drive, then on the stairs, and pacing himself accordingly. Once he'd gained the wide porch, he moved with confidence.

Skimming his left hand down the door, he found the key slot and inserted a narrow plastic card with his right. The card unlocked the door and activated the lights inside. Brushing past him into the soaring, two-story foyer, Haley waited while he reinserted the card, this time into a wall unit that contained several rows of infrared discs and a palm-size screen.

"That's a pretty elaborate security system," she murmured.

"Tyler designed it to my specifications. The sensors emit silent pulses instead of sound." His mouth twisted. "The sequencing of those pulses allows even a person who can't see to pinpoint the location of an intruder without letting him know he's being tracked."

Like a panther stalking its prey in the night.

With a little shiver, Haley followed him into the living room just off the hall. The cavernous room faced east, with a long wall of windows to let in the morning light. The windows were shuttered now, and the only illumination came from a desk lamp that flickered on at their approach. The inch-thick Persian area rugs that used to cover the oak floorboards had been removed, she saw. Probably so Luke wouldn't trip over them. The floor plants were gone, too, no doubt for the same reason.

The man-size sorrel-leather sofas and chairs were still there, though, arranged in comfortable groupings facing the massive stone fireplace that dominated the room. So was the rack of the Texas longhorns mounted above the mantel. A good twelve feet long, the horns speared to sharp tips.

Haley's glance drifted to the exquisitely woven Mexican blanket draped across the back of one sofa. The colorful throw was a treasured gift, she knew, from the couple who'd acted more like surrogate parents to Luke than his own, irresponsible uncle.

"I hope we didn't disturb Mr. and Mrs. Chavez, coming in so late like this."

"They moved out of the main house into the guest cottage three years ago," Luke informed her in a clipped tone. "They needed space for their grandkids to romp and tear around when they come to visit."

With four bedrooms, a wraparound porch, and a breathtaking view of the lake, the guest cottage was larger than most family homes. The Chavezes' lively brood would certainly have room to romp. The rest of the staff, Haley remembered, lived off the grounds. So it was just her and Luke, all alone in this two-story mansion.

As if reading her thoughts, he tossed his hat onto one of the chairs, hitched his hips against a high sofa back and folded his arms. "All right, Haley. No one's going to interrupt us now. You've got a few things to explain. Why don't you start with your miraculous resurrection from the dead?"

She ran her tongue over dry lips. She'd held her secrets for so long, guarded every word, measured every lie, that she had to drag the truth from deep inside her.

"I'll have to begin before my resurrection."

"Begin wherever the hell you want," he said with brutal callousness. "Just get on with it."

Haley shoved her hands into the front pockets of her jeans. It shamed her to admit she'd run away. Shamed her even more to admit the reasons why.

"I don't know how much you knew about my family's business," she began.

"I'd heard rumors," Luke said acidly.

More than rumors. Hell, he couldn't have formed

such a close friendship with Ricky and not suspected the source of the Mercado family income.

"Then you have some idea of the kinds of things my uncle Carmine was involved in. He and Frank Del Brio."

"Oh, I've got a good idea what your fiancé was involved in."

Stung by the derision in his voice, Haley fired back. "I didn't get engaged to him by choice, you know."

"No, I don't know. If you didn't want to marry Del Brio, why the hell did you wear his ring?"

"Because Frank knew every detail of my father's involvement in Uncle Carmine's operations. He threatened to leak what he knew if I didn't marry him."

"I only met your uncle a couple of times," Luke scoffed, "but I can't see Carmine Mercado allowing anyone to set up his brother and force his niece into marriage against her will."

"Can't you? Maybe that's because you're an outsider. You don't understand the family. My uncle wanted me to marry Frank. Carmine trusted him. More than he trusted my father by that time. So I went along with the engagement. I had to. But I began plotting my escape the same day."

"Right. Your escape." His jaw hardened. The disdain in his voice took on the cutting edge of disgust. "You don't have to tell me about your escape. I was there, remember? So were Tyler and Spence and Flynt."

His fury flared white-hot. Leaping across the room, it singed Haley from head to toe.

"Do you know how many frantic hours we spent searching for you? Do you have any idea of the guilt we've all carried since that night?"

"Yes, I—"

"No, lady, you don't. You can't. Any more than you can imagine how it feels to stand trial for the wrongful death of your best friend's sister."

"I didn't mean for you to take the blame! Any of you! I intended to slip away during the barbecue that night. I'd planned to leave my sandals and coverup by the shore so people would think I'd gone swimming and drowned. But when I went out in the speedboat with you and we almost hit that tree, I—I took advantage of the situation."

"You sure did. Just out of curiosity, whose decomposed body did they pull out of the lake?"

"I don't know. I'm guessing Frank arranged to have that body dropped in the lake to solidify the case against you. He would have wanted you and the others to pay for his fiancée's supposed death."

Luke gave a short, bitter laugh. "That's understating the case considerably. Del Brio did everything but bribe the jury. Hell, for all I know, he probably did that, too."

"Carl said he tried."

"Carl? Carl Bridges?"

"Yes."

"Let me get this straight. You were in communication with my attorney?"

"Yes."

"During the trial?"

"Before, during and after," she admitted. "The judge helped me slip out of the country. He arranged for a fake passport and got me set up in London. He was also the one who told me about the trial. I know you won't believe me, Luke, but I wouldn't have let you or the others take the blame. I was ready to jump a plane and come home as soon as I heard charges had been filed against you."

"Sure you were."

"The judge talked me out of it. He swore he'd get you off. I sent proof that I was still alive, just in case, but he never had to use it."

"So why did you come back?" he demanded. "That night, two years ago, when I bumped into you at the Saddlebag, why did you come out of hiding then?"

"I came back to see my mother. She was in the hospital. She'd been badly beaten. It was made to look like a mall mugging, but it was a warning to my father to tow the line."

That pulled Luke up short. With a low, savage oath, he pictured the woman who'd always treated him with the loving warmth she showed her own son.

"I'd heard Isadora was hospitalized, but after the trial things got so bad between me and your family that I didn't want to upset her with a visit. She died soon after that, didn't she?"

"Yes, she did."

She couldn't have feigned the raw pain in her reply. A good chunk of Luke's anger melted as the enormity of what she was telling him sank in.

"I need a drink," he muttered. "How about you? I keep some cognac here in the bar, but I could brew coffee or—"

"Cognac's fine."

Measuring his steps, he crossed to the built-in bar and felt for the Waterford decanter glinting in the soft light. The heavy crystal stopper chinked as he removed it and nudged brandy snifters under the decanter's lip.

After pouring healthy portions for both of them, he carried the snifters back across the room and held one out.

When Haley reached for it, her fingers brushed his. The heat was still there, Luke discovered with a jolt. The same glowing spark they'd fanned into flames two years ago.

Retreating, he moved to the sofa. Haley followed his lead. Luke heard the soft whoosh of the leather cushions as she settled in a chair on the far side of the marble slab that served as a coffee table.

"So you came home to visit your mother," he said, picking up where they'd left off. "After which you stopped in at the Saddlebag for a drink and we ended up in bed."

"Yes."

He heard the wince in her voice at his phrasing, followed by a blunt honesty that surprised him.

"Just for the record, I don't regret that night, Luke. I could never regret it. It gave me Lena."

The anger he'd tried to bank came back, swift and fierce. "Funny. For a moment there, you sounded as though you almost regret abandoning our child."

"I didn't abandon her!"

The fragile crystal sang out as Haley snapped it down onto the coffee table.

"I couldn't keep Lena with me while I was undercover."

That caught Luke's attention. In the past hour he'd come up with a dozen different reasons in his mind for Haley to be posing as a waitress at the Lone Star Country Club. The possibility that she might be acting as a federal agent wasn't one of them.

"I've been working with the FBI for over a year now," she revealed, "helping them build a case against Frank."

Well, that explained the guys who'd jumped them in the parking lot. Frowning, Luke tried to sort through the details of her incredible story.

"I don't understand. You engineered your own death. You lived in London for years under an assumed identity. You'd just had a baby. Why did you suddenly decide to go to work for the feds?"

"The FBI said they had evidence my mother didn't die of natural causes. Someone injected potassium chloride into her IV."

Luke shot upright, splashing cognac onto his hand. "The hell you say!"

"The FBI thinks she was killed because she wouldn't disclose the identity of the stranger who…who visited her in the hospital."

The small, anguished quaver wasn't lost on Luke. He stored it away to think about later, when he had time to sort through his thoughts. Right now it was all he could do to absorb the tale she went on to tell of tampered mail and phone hang-ups.

"I realized I'd never be safe as long as Del Brio was free," she finished. "More to the point, I knew Lena would never be safe. That's why I decided to cooperate with the FBI. First, though, I had to make sure Lena was cared for while I was undercover."

"So you left her on the golf course?" he asked incredulously. "That's your idea of ensuring she was cared for?"

"She was left where her father would find her. Only you were gone that particular Sunday." Her tone took on an edge of sharp accusation. "You stayed gone for months. Dammit, where were you when your daughter needed you?"

Not particularly happy at being put on the defensive all of a sudden, Luke fired back. "One, I didn't know I had a daughter. Two, I didn't know she needed me. Three—Oh, hell. Three doesn't matter. All that matters now is Lena."

Haley could have wept with relief. After all the hurt and anger and guilt, they agreed on the only point that mattered. Her hands clutched tight, she waited while Luke downed the rest of his cognac with a distinct lack of respect for its age.

"All right," he said grimly. "The past is past. Let's cut to tonight. I want to know exactly how Del Brio contacted you. Exactly what he said, word for word. Any background noises or sounds you might have picked up. Any significant nuances in his voice."

An hour later Haley was limp with exhaustion. She hadn't slept more than a few hours since the shoot-out three nights ago. Frantic fear for Lena and worry over her father had wrung her inside out. Luke's relentless grilling sapped the small reserve she had left.

"That's it," she said hoarsely after she'd repeated every detail for the fourth time. "That's how Frank left it. He'll let me know when and where to deliver the ransom."

"We have to assume he'll know how to reach you. He tracked you to the FBI safe house. He'll track you here. I'll contact Sheriff Wainwright and..."

"No!"

Haley's sharp protest earned her a swift frown.

"Frank said not to let Justin or the FBI in on the

ransom delivery," she reiterated. "That's why I came to you, Luke. I can't... I won't risk Lena's life in another shoot-out."

He conceded with a curt nod.

"All right. But we'll need help to pull this off. I'll get Spence and Tyler over to rig some electronics on the phone lines. Flynt can go to the bank for me tomorrow and retrieve the two million. In the meantime..."

"In the meantime?"

"You'd better get some rest. You sound as if you're about to drop."

"I'm okay."

"You can't help your daughter if you're too exhausted to think straight," he said with brutal candor. "Stretch out on the couch here if you don't want to go upstairs, but for God's sake get some sleep."

She couldn't have climbed that wide, curving staircase if she'd wanted to.

"All right. I'll take the couch. Do you mind if I use the phone first to call the hospital? I want to check on my father."

"Of course I don't mind," he said, then added gruffly, "he was holding his own when I called ICU this afternoon."

"You checked on my dad?"

"Your parents were good to me, Haley. After you died—disappeared—I couldn't bridge the gap that opened between us, but I still cared about them. Go ahead, make your call. I'll wait in the den and make mine when you're finished."

He was almost out of the room before Haley worked up the courage to call to him.

"Luke."

He half turned, angling his head in that careful, listening way. "Yes?"

"Thank you."

"For what?"

"For listening. For putting the past behind you. Most of all, for helping me with Lena."

His face hardened. "She's my daughter. Whatever I can do for her, I will. We'll work out the arrangements for her future when we get her back."

As he made his careful way down the hall, Haley felt the blood drain from her face. Good Lord! Did Luke intend to battle her for custody? Could he use the fact that she'd had to place her baby in safekeeping against her? Would she wrest Lena away from Frank only to lose her to her father? The prospect tightened the band of fear around her heart.

She couldn't handle another crisis right now, Haley decided bleakly. She'd just check on her father, then curl into a tight ball here on the sofa, close her eyes and picture her baby's happy face.

Chapter 10

Luke stood in the den he'd converted to a clean, utilitarian office and tried to rein in his chaotic thoughts. He still couldn't quite believe the woman down the hall was Haley Mercado. Sweet, curvaceous Haley Mercado.

He'd known her since grade school, for crissake! He'd watched her transition from coltish girl to precocious teen. By the time he and Ricky and the others returned from the Gulf War, Haley had blossomed into full, sensual womanhood. Luke might have seriously reconsidered his self-imposed hands-off policy at that point, but muscle-bound Frank Del Brio had beat him to the punch. He'd claimed Haley as his and, assuming any of the incredible story she'd just strung out was true, had driven her to incredibly desperate measures to escape him.

Was the story she'd just fed him true?

Despite his anger, his instincts said yes. He'd spent

enough time with Ricky to sense how closely Johnny Mercado flirted with danger. Luke could well believe he'd gotten himself in so deep that Del Brio had plenty to coerce Haley with. Looking back, he could almost—almost!—understand her crazy reasoning for deciding to disappear.

Damn! For more than a decade she'd pretended to be dead, only to then risk everything by going undercover for the FBI. His first call would be to the Bureau, he decided grimly. He'd sure as hell get verification before he—

A small sound cut into his whirling thoughts. Every one of his senses went on instant alert. He stood still, listening intently.

The muffled noise came from the living room. Trailing his fingers along the wall, Luke moved silently down the hall.

She was crying. Quietly. Agonizingly. From the sound of it, she'd buried her face in cushions, but nothing could completely drown the wrenching sobs.

Luke stood just beyond the arch, his jaw working. This woman had played him for a world-class fool. Repeatedly. First by letting him and his friends take the fall for her death. Then by pretending she was a stranger that night at the Saddlebag. Not to mention failing to inform him about the small matter of their child. Luke sure as hell wasn't going to let her twist him inside out again.

Gritting his teeth, he started back for the office. He took two steps. Three. Stopped.

The utter desolation in those muffled sobs ripped at him. Swearing viciously, he swung around again. A moment later he gathered her into his arms.

Startled, she tried to jerk away. "Wh-what are you doing?"

"Damned if I know."

Holding her loosely, he eased them onto the sofa. The leather whooshed under his weight, the cushions tilting so that Haley rolled against him. Gulping, she tried to halt the wrenching sobs.

"I'm sorry. I didn't mean to—I don't—"

"Shhh." Cupping the back of her head, he cradled her face in the hollow of his shoulder. "It's okay."

"No, it's not." Blinking furiously, Haley dragged in a hiccuping breath. "I feel like an idiot. I never cry."

Not since her mother's death, anyway. She'd shed all the tears she had in her then. Tonight, though, her emotions were stripped to the bone.

"We'll get her back," Luke said gruffly, zeroing in on the cause of her distress with pinpoint accuracy.

She wanted desperately to believe him, but the brutal reality of the situation made a mockery of hope. "You don't know Del Brio like I do. He'll stop at nothing to get what he wants. Nothing!"

"Del Brio doesn't know me, either. Whatever it takes, we'll get Lena back."

The flat certainty in his voice tilted her head back. Blinking away the teary residue clinging to her lashes, she studied the face so close to hers. Luke stared straight ahead, his blue eyes unblinking but fierce. Stubble shadowed his cheeks and chin and made the white scars on his temple stand out in stark relief.

The evidence of his pain distracted her momentarily from her all-consuming fear for her baby. Oh, God, what had really happened in that jungle in Central America? How much had Luke suffered? Her fingers trembling, she lifted a hand to trace the spidery scars.

Luke sensed the movement and abruptly brought his

head around to meet it. In the process, his lips grazed her palm.

They both went still, each waiting for the other to pull away. His mouth was hot and damp under her palm. Her skin burned where he touched it. Seconds ticked by with agonizing slowness, each one seeming to take months and then years with it, until Haley was at the Saddlebag again, aching for this man with all the passion she'd kept bottled up inside her for so long.

No, not this man. She hadn't really known the Luke Callaghan she'd given herself to that night, any more than he'd known her. With all their secrets, they were strangers then. They were strangers now.

It took everything Luke had to pull away. He didn't trust this woman, and sure as hell couldn't trust the desire that knotted his belly and almost made him forget who she was. Still, he couldn't bring himself to release her. Not yet. Not while her tears still dampened his neck and tension held her in a tight coil.

"You've got to let it go and get some rest, Haley."

"I wish I could," she murmured, her breath a ragged sigh against his neck.

"Blank your mind for a few moments. Just wipe away every thought."

"I can't."

"Yes, you can," he countered, recalling the technique that had saved his sanity during his weeks as a POW. "Don't think. Don't feel. Don't paint any pictures in your mind. Just imagine a blank canvas. A big, white, empty space."

She tried too hard. Her lashes feathering his neck, she scrunched her eyes shut. He felt her tension and frustration as she searched for the emptiness.

"Relax, Haley." He lowered his voice to a slow, hypnotic murmur and began to stroke her hair. "Just relax. Wrap yourself in a haze. A soft, gray haze."

"Like a London fog."

"Like a London fog, only warmer. It covers everything. Smooths all the jagged edges. Dulls the sharpest fears. Feel how soft it is? How warm it is?"

She gave a little grunt, wanting to be convinced but not quite there yet. Luke continued the unhurried stroke, smoothing her hair, calming her with his touch the way he'd calm a skittish colt.

"Let the haze surround you. Drift through you. There's nothing there. Nothing but a cloud of cotton."

Silence dropped over them. Moments went by. Slowly, so slowly, she slipped into that half state between worry and mindlessness. Luke felt her muscles slacken, then a little jerk as she resisted dropping into sleep.

"It's okay, Haley. Let yourself go. You're warm and safe and secure."

He murmured the words without thinking. Not until she gave a little moan and curled against him did he realize how desperately she must have craved both security and safety all these years.

With a silent curse, Luke set out to lull her back to sleep. Planting his boots on the polished marble coffee table, he eased down until his head hit the sofa back and did his damndest to ignore the press of full, rounded breasts against his chest.

Haley drifted awake to the scent of fresh-brewed coffee. She let the aroma tease her groggy senses for long moments before prying her eyes open. They felt dry and scratchy, the way eyes always did after a bout of tears.

After all the years and months of hiding her every thought and emotion, she couldn't believe she'd dissolved into such a pitiful bundle of incoherence last night. Or that she'd fallen asleep in Luke's arms.

At a loss to explain either his actions or her own, she tossed back the blanket and swung her stockinged feet to the floor. A quick glance at the cheap watch she'd worn in her Daisy Parker persona showed it was just past 5:00 a.m.

Panic darted through her at the thought that she might have slept through another call from Del Brio, but logic quickly squelched the thought. Either the buzz of the phone or Luke himself would have awakened her.

Pushing off the couch, she listened intently. She didn't hear any sounds. She assumed Luke was in the kitchen brewing the coffee. Before she faced him again, she needed to splash some cold water on her face.

Her stockinged feet made no sound as she mounted the curving oak staircase to the second floor. Open doors gave her glimpses into the rooms on both sides of the hall. Like the downstairs rooms, they were decorated with an eclectic mix of priceless antiques, comfortable furnishings and the best of Texas. One guest bedroom sported a canopy bed. Another, a huge four-poster that had to have come across Texas in a covered wagon.

Avoiding the master bedroom suite at the end of the hall, she made liberal use of the amenities in the well-stocked guest bathroom. Fifteen minutes later she headed back downstairs, face scrubbed, teeth clean and her bottle-blond hair tangle-free.

As she'd guessed, Luke was in the kitchen. It was a warm, welcoming place, one she remembered well. A beautiful old wrought-iron gate was suspended from chains above the center island, displaying an assortment of antique cast-iron frying pans, speckled tin cookware and a dented, ten-gallon coffeepot that had to have seen duty on the cattle trails. The cabinets were distressed cypress, reminding Haley of the trees that lined the creeks in this part of the country. Their glass fronts displayed an assortment of brightly colored crockery. A rectangular table of the same weathered cypress was set in an alcove surrounded on three sides by shuttered windows.

Luke sat at the table, with a cell phone close at hand and a laptop computer in front of him. Haley couldn't tell whether he'd slept at all or not, but he'd obviously showered. His cheeks and chin were smooth, and his black hair glistened. He'd changed into a crisp white cotton shirt with the sleeves rolled halfway up and a freshly laundered pair of jeans.

She made a futile attempt to smooth the wrinkles from her slept-in tank top before she remembered Luke couldn't see it. As soft as it was, the swish of her hands brushing down her front alerted him to her presence.

"Haley?" he asked sharply.

"I'm sorry. I didn't mean to sneak up on you. I'm in my socks."

"I heard the water running upstairs and figured you'd be down soon."

Neither one of them mentioned the fact that she'd fallen asleep in Luke's arms last night. He seemed as willing to dance around the topic as Haley was.

"The coffee's fresh, if you want some," he told her. "Mrs. Chavez won't be over to fix breakfast for another couple of hours, but she always leaves the fridge full if you need something to tide you over until then."

At the mention of breakfast Haley's stomach sat up and took notice. She'd been so sick with worry over Lena and her father these past few days, the mere thought of food had made her nauseated. Her few hours sleep seemed to have restored her appetite, however. Taking advantage of Luke's invitation, she helped herself to coffee and downed several gulps while she surveyed the contents of the stainless-steel, commercial-grade fridge.

"Good grief! There are enough covered dishes in here to feed everyone in Mission Creek."

"Yeah, I know," he drawled. "Teresa is firmly convinced that all I need to regain twenty-twenty vision is rest and plenty of good, healthy food."

Haley shot him a quick look. "Any chance she's right?"

"Who knows?" He rolled his shoulders under the white cotton shirt. "The docs don't have any other advice to offer at this point."

"Has there been any improvement at all since you came home?"

He hesitated, obviously unwilling to offer false hope to anyone, himself included.

"I'm seeing some shadows, mostly in contrast, They seem to be getting a little less dark and dense. Probably just wishful thinking on my part. See anything that looks good in the fridge?"

Following his deliberate change of subject, she dragged her glance back to the neatly stacked containers. Each lid was labeled, she saw, marked with a thick plastic strip with raised letters so Luke could run his fingers over it and identify the contents.

"How does cinnamon toast and Mexican lasagna sound?"

"Pretty good."

While the spicy tortilla, cheese and beef casserole heated in the microwave, Haley slathered thick slices of Texas toast with butter, sprinkled on cinnamon and popped them in the toaster oven. Her stomach rumbling in earnest now, she took the coffee carafe to the table to refresh Luke's cup as well as her own.

She felt awkward, as though they were strangers. Two people whose pasts had crossed and now shared only a single link to the future. Firmly suppressing the panic that fluttered just under her skin each time she though of Lena, she eyed the computer and its array of peripherals spread out in front of Luke.

"What's all this?"

"I've been making lists of what we need to do to get ready for Del Brio's call."

It was Haley's turn to hesitate. She had little experience with physical disabilities and didn't want to harp on Luke's, but curiosity compelled her to ask how he could read what was on the computer screen.

"Obviously, I don't. The computer is specially rigged with raised-letter keys and voice recognition software for data input. It also produces both visual and audio output."

He tapped a key. A digitized voice filled the kitchen.

"Spence to retrieve ransom from bank. Two million. Unmarked, nonsequential bills. Flynt to attach microdots and scan bills into computer. Tyler to rig explosive in briefcase handle. Obtain spectrascope for—"

"Wait a minute!" Haley exclaimed. "What explosives?"

"—the SIG Sauer. Load high-velocity bullets. Test scope with—"

"Luke, turn that thing off!"

A quick click of a key cut off the electronic recitation. Shaken, Haley gripped her coffee cup with both hands. "What the heck is all this? Why are you making lists that include explosives and high-velocity bullets?"

"You don't think I intend to just hand the ransom to Del Brio and let him walk away, do you?"

"Yes! No!"

A frown gathered between his brows. "Which is it? What exactly did you have in mind, Haley?"

"Well, I haven't worked out the exact details yet. I thought maybe you could distract Frank while I got the drop on him."

"Right."

The sarcastic drawl raised her hackles.

"Look, I came to you to help me retrieve my baby. Our baby. I didn't expect you to mount a full-scale military offensive that might get her blown up, for God's sake!"

Luke started to reply, but cut off whatever he intended to say. His head cocked.

"Something's burning."

"Damn! The toast."

By the time Haley had scraped the black edges off the cinnamon bread and plunked it down on the table, she'd recovered a measure of her poise.

"We need to talk about this," she said with deliberate calm. "I appreciate that you feel the need to take an active role in Lena's recovery, but I won't let you endanger her."

"You won't, huh?"

Thrusting out his long legs, he sprawled back in his chair and fixed his gaze on her face. Although she knew he couldn't see her, Haley felt the full force of that penetrating stare.

"Seems to me you forfeited your rights to dictate what I can and can't do for my child when you abandoned her."

The warm, welcoming kitchen abruptly lost its glow.

"I'll repeat myself just one more time," Haley said, gritting her teeth. "I did not abandon her. I had to place Lena in safekeeping while I went undercover for the FBI. I thought you understood."

With a grimace of self-disgust, he nodded. "I do. I'm sorry. You didn't deserve that."

No, she didn't. Silence stretched out between them, broken by the sudden ping of the microwave. Luke pushed his chair back at the same time Haley rose.

"I'll get it," she muttered, still ruffled by the hostilities that had erupted so unexpectedly between them. Retrieving the casserole from the microwave, she let it steam on the stovetop while she located dishes, napkins and silverware.

"I'm left-handed," Luke said when she carried two well-filled plates to the table. "If you position the dish with the food at nine o'clock, I can eat without making too much of a mess."

"Right. Nine o'clock. Careful, it's hot."

The clipped reply told Luke she'd yet to forgive him for the attack a few minutes ago. Disgusted with himself for delivering such a swift counterpunch to what he'd interpreted as a lack of confidence in his ability to handle Frank Del Brio, he waited until she'd seated herself to make amends.

"You were right, Haley. I shouldn't be making lists or plans without consulting you. Nor should you be working up some wild scheme of your own. We're in this together, with a single goal. We need to work together as a team."

"Yes, we do."

Her relief was palpable. Luke felt it clear across the table.

"I called Flynt and Spence and Tyler last night," he told her. "They should be here within an hour or so. Before they arrive, I'll fill you in on what I think we can and should do, and you can give me what you know of the way Del Brio operates."

"That might take a while," she warned. "I've been gathering information on Frank and his cohorts for a year now."

"Then let's get to it."

Chapter 11

Haley soon discovered that Luke's idea of teamwork and hers differed considerably. He was used to being in charge and making things happen. She'd learned to live by her wits and to operate alone. As a result, they spent an hour at the kitchen table alternately sharing information, brainstorming possible scenarios for the ransom delivery and arguing about the best way to handle Frank Del Brio. They were still at it when Mrs. Chavez arrived.

Startled to find her employer sharing breakfast with a stranger, the housekeeper's curiosity gave way to openmouthed disbelief when Luke introduced her as the long-dead Haley Mercado.

"No, it cannot be!" She gaped at Haley, then emphatically shook her graying head. "You're joking with me, Luke."

"It's true. I just found out myself last night."

"But Haley Mercado drowned," the housekeeper exclaimed. "Right here in our lake." She turned a fierce frown on the intruder in her kitchen. "They found her body."

"I don't know who that poor woman was, but I'm very much alive."

Unconvinced, Teresa Chavez folded her arms and scowled. "You do not look at all like Haley Mercado."

"I had cosmetic surgery. Around the eyes and nose, mostly."

The housekeeper searched her face again, more intently this time. Haley saw disbelief give way to doubt, then to anger. Her scowl deepening, Teresa glared at Haley.

"My Luke and his friends stood trial. They almost went to prison because of you."

"Yes, I know."

"Haley wanted to come home during the trial," Luke said, surprising her by coming to her defense. "Judge Bridges assured her he'd get us off."

"Ah, Judge Bridges." The anger went out of the older woman's face. "So sad about the judge. And about your mother," she added, her glance shifting once again to Haley. "It broke Isadora's heart when she thought she lost you."

"It broke my heart to let her think she had. I'm just glad I got to see her before she died."

The warmhearted housekeeper clucked in distress. "There has been so much death around Mission Creek of late. So much sadness. And now that little child is missing, the one my Luke says is his. Ayyyy, if I should ever meet the woman who walked off and left such a sweet little baby on the golf course, she would hear a thing or two from me, I can tell you that."

Wincing, Haley prepared once again to shoulder the blame for the scheme the judge had assured her was infallible.

"Haley is the baby's mother," Luke said calmly.

Teresa's jaw dropped. "How can that be?"

He gave an expurgated version of their meeting two years ago and Haley's subsequent return after Lena's birth. Clucking her tongue again, the goggle-eyed housekeeper tried to take it all in. She was still trying when the intercom buzzed. Shaking her head, she went to the wall unit and pressed the speaker button.

"It's Spence, Teresa. Luke wants to see me. Let me in, will you?"

"Yes, yes. We are in the kitchen. Come around to the side door."

Haley used the few moments it took for Spence Harrison to pull his high-powered SUV up to the kitchen entrance to brace herself for another confrontation. She didn't know how much Luke had told the hard-edged former prosecutor, but she suspected he'd greet Haley Mercado's return from the dead with something less than wild enthusiasm.

Sure enough, the look Spence sent her when he entered the kitchen could have sliced through tempered steel. Hooking his thumbs in his belt, he ran a hard eye over the waitress who'd served him and his new wife at the country club.

Haley returned his narrow-eyed scrutiny. Marriage agreed with him, she thought. Spence had always been intense and, from what she'd heard through Carl Bridges during her years abroad, had made a hell of a prosecutor. Since his marriage to a single mom with a school-aged son, though, he'd given up the D.A.'s job to become a private law consultant and to spend more time with his new family. The change showed in his face. The lines were softer, the angles less sharp.

"I hear you've had a rough time of it," he said finally.

Haley had no answer for that.

"Luke explained why you disappeared the way you did. He also said you're Lena's mother." A rough sympathy glinted in his brown eyes. "We'll get her back."

She could have kissed him for putting aside the past and concentrating only on the urgent present.

"Thank you."

To her relief, at least one of the two men who arrived a few moments later appeared ready to do the same. Tyler Murdoch tossed a small leather satchel onto the table and gave her a slow once-over, much as he had when she'd approached his table at the Saddlebag last night. The taciturn, one-time mercenary made no reference to her supposed drowning, however, and said only that he was there to help.

Flynt Carson seemed to have the toughest time accepting Haley's resurrection. Not because he, along with the three others, had been charged with her death. But because the ruggedly handsome rancher had taken Lena into his home and into his heart.

In her cover as Daisy Parker, Haley had ached inside every time Flynt and his wife, Josie, brought Lena into the country club and showed her off with such love and pride. She'd also seen that they were as shattered as Haley herself when the baby was kidnapped from their ranch four months ago. She fully expected Flynt to lay into her now for setting him and Josie up for that kind of pain. The regret she saw in his piercing blue eyes surprised her.

"You could have trusted us, Haley. Luke and I and the others would have helped you, both when you needed to escape Mission Creek and when you came back."

"I know I could trust you." A lump lodged in her throat. "You were Ricky's closest friends. I had crushes on each one of you at various times. I just couldn't let you—any of you—put your lives at risk."

The brutal reality behind the statement silenced Flynt. Haley had nothing more to say, either. Shoving her hands into her jeans' pockets, she glanced from one man to the other.

How many times had she seen them standing shoulder to shoulder like this? How many times had she heard their shouts of laughter echoing through the Mercado house?

Luke. Spence. Tyler. Flynt.

And Ricky. If only Ricky were here! The Fabulous Five would be together again, guilt and blame forgotten, the past erased.

Maybe soon, she thought wearily. Now that she'd confessed the truth, maybe the five men could mend the broken links of their friendship. Maybe these four could pull Ricky from the pit he'd fallen into after Haley's supposed death. Clinging to that thin hope, she joined the group at the table. Teresa Chavez bustled around, serving coffee and the remains of her spicy stacked tortilla lasagna to the three hungry males before heading for the front of the house to make her morning rounds.

"Just to recap," Luke said, "Frank Del Brio contacted Haley at an FBI safe house a little past nine last night and demanded two million dollars for Lena's safe return."

"Did the FBI get a trace on the call?" Tyler asked quickly.

"No."

"Well, hell! What the heck kind of equipment are they using, anyway?"

"I don't know."

"What kind of proof did he offer?" Flynt put in. "How do we know Del Brio actually has Lena?"

"We don't, at this point. That's one of the conditions we'll stipulate. He'll have to deliver visual, real-time evidence that she's alive and unhurt before we deliver the two million."

"Aren't you going to negotiate?" Spence asked, frowning. "I hate to see scum like Del Brio make off with a cool two million."

"Del Brio knows I'm good for it," Luke replied. "He won't settle for less and I don't want to waste time with lengthy negotiations. I want to get the money ready so Haley and I can deliver it to the specified point at the specified time."

"Haley and you?"

Three pairs of eyes switched to the woman at the table. Tyler asked the question that showed clearly in each face. "Del Brio agreed to that?"

"No. He told me to make sure there were no cops or anyone who even faintly smells of FBI within fifty miles of the scene or I'd never—" Her voice hitched. "Or I'd never see Lena again. It was my idea to ask Luke for help."

"She figured Del Brio wouldn't consider me much of a threat," he explained wryly. "She also suggested I could provide some sort of distraction while she takes Del Brio down."

Haley braced herself, expecting Luke's three friends to become indignant on his behalf. To her surprise, they gave her plan serious consideration.

"She has a point there," Tyler mused, tapping his blunt-tipped fingers on the weathered wood of the table. "The little contact I've had with Frank over the years was enough to convince me that he's an arrogant bully. He wouldn't consider you a threat, Luke."

"If you play it right," Spence added slowly, "you might just get within range."

"That's what I'm counting on."

Luke's feral smile raised the small hairs on the back of Haley's neck. His three friends wore similar expressions. They'd closed ranks, she saw. Their shared training and military experience, not to mention the hardships they endured as POWs, had sent their minds racing along parallel tracks. Luke called on that experience now.

"Think you can fix me up, Tyler?"

"I've got a few tricks in my electronic grab bag that might just surprise ole Frank."

"Like what?" Haley asked. Her earlier argument with Luke had made her distinctly nervous. This one was adding to her uneasiness by the minute.

The mercenary shifted in his seat, obviously reluctant to lay out the tools of his trade. She leaned forward to make sure she had his full attention, as well as that of the other men at the table.

"Luke and I have already had this discussion, Tyler. We've agreed that we'll operate as a team. I don't want any surprises when we go to deliver the ransom. No wild pyrotechnics going off when I least expect them or explosive devices that might endanger my child."

Tyler still needed confirmation from their unspoken leader before he'd agree. "Luke?"

"Haley's right. She'll be out there on point with me when we deliver the ransom. She has to know who and what is backing her up."

"True," his friend conceded with a shrug. "Okay, here's what I'm thinking. We could outfit you with a miniaturized phased-array scanner. The army's testing one up at Fort Hood right now. It's the size of an ordinary wristwatch, but the damned thing sends out high-intensity radar waves, identifies objects that fit certain parameters and returns a perfect signature."

"So Luke won't need sight to track Del Brio's every move," Spence put in for Haley's benefit. "The scanner will do it for him."

Tyler continued to outline his plan. "I can also rig a special infrared laser scope that will lock on to a target and follow it. What weapons are you planning to take with you, Luke?"

"A SIG Sauer 9 mm. Maybe an ankle-holstered .38 Special, as well."

Haley listened in a growing daze. They'd already moved so far beyond her original, half-formed plan using Luke as a distraction that she could scarcely keep up.

"What about explosives? I know where there's a stash of high-impact, zero-centered grenades."

"No explosives," Luke said swiftly. "At least not until Haley and Lena are well away from the scene. At which point," he added, "there won't be enough left of Frank Del Brio to blow up."

Tyler nodded. "Good enough. I'll chopper up to Fort Hood as soon as we finish here and get working on this stuff."

Nodding, Luke pushed a slip of paper across the table in Spence Harrison's general direction.

"Spence, I need you to retrieve the money for me. I e-mailed Hoyt Bennington last night and told him to expect you. Here's the authorization to withdraw the two million from my cash reserve account. Del Brio specified nonsequential bills, no larger than hundreds. Hoyt promised to have it banded and ready when you get there."

"I'm on it."

"Flynt?"

"Right here, buddy."

"I don't plan to let Del Brio walk away with the ransom, but just in case, we'll have to tag the bills."

"He insisted they had to be unmarked," Haley interjected.

"What Del Brio wants and what he gets are two different sacks of beans," Flynt drawled. "Don't worry. Tyler has a supply of some very interesting chemical agents. They can't be picked up by X-ray machines, light scanners or explosive-sniffing dogs. We'll treat the bills and, as backup, I'll also scan their serial numbers so we can send an alert through the Federal Reserve computers. If Del Brio walks with the cash, he won't walk far."

"I don't know how much time we have," Luke warned the assembled team. "Del Brio could contact Haley at any time with instructions for delivery. We'll counter with a demand for proof of life, which should buy us at least a few hours, but we'll have to hustle."

Chairs scraped the floor as the three friends rose.

"Not to worry," Tyler assured him. "We're off on our assigned tasks. We'll let you know if we run into any glitches. And just so Del Brio doesn't intercept our communications, we'd better use these."

Unzipping the leather satchel he'd tossed onto the table earlier, he passed out what looked to Haley like ordinary cell phones.

"They operate off a secure satellite and send scrambled signals," he explained. "The V.R.S.—Voice Recognition System—built into each phone restricts transmissions to only the person whose speech pattern the scrambler recognizes. Punch in 0-1-0-6 and say 'Mary had a little lamb' to activate the V.R.S."

Spence snorted. "'Mary had a little lamb'?"

"Hey, when Luke called late last night, Marisa and I were, uh, otherwise engaged. A nursery rhyme was the best I could come up with at the time."

"Considering that you and Marisa have been married for all of three weeks," Spence retorted, "I'm surprised he could get you out of bed at all."

"It took some doing," Luke drawled.

"What can I say?" the mercenary replied with a goofy grin. "I've finally been broken to the bit."

"From what Marisa's told me," Spence retorted, "you're a long way from being broken to the bit. But if anyone can do it, she can."

Silently, Haley agreed. She'd only crossed paths with Tyler's fiery, fiercely independent new wife a couple of times. The brief encounters had made a definite impression.

"I still can't believe all three of you went down in flames so quickly, one right after another." Shaking his head, Luke snapped closed the laptop's lid. "Single women all over the world are probably weeping as we speak."

The good-natured jab elicited a quick response from Flynt.

"You'll understand when you give up your free-wheeling bachelor ways," he predicted with the utter confidence of a man who, against all odds, had been given a second chance at love. His blue eyes flickered in Haley's direction before returning to his friend. "And in case you've forgotten, you've got a daughter to help raise now."

Haley stiffened. She wasn't prepared to discuss Luke's role in Lena's future. They'd work out the necessary arrangements if—when!—they got Lena back.

Luke evidently shared her reluctance to discuss the matter in front of his friends. Charging them to keep him posted on their progress during the next few hours, he sent them off on their various assignments.

With their exit, the intense energy levels that had swirled around the kitchen for the past hour seemed to drop a good ten or twenty amps. Suddenly Haley felt as drained. Pushing out of her chair, she started clearing the table of the plates and coffee mugs.

"You don't have to do that," Luke informed her. "Teresa has a helper who comes in. She'll take care of the dishes."

"I need to keep busy."

"Suit yourself." Tucking the laptop under his arm, he left her to her self-appointed task. "I'll be in the den."

Trailing his right hand along the marble countertop, he made his way out of the kitchen and down the hall. His footsteps echoed on the polished parquet floorboards. Belatedly, Haley realized the Persian runner that used to add such a glow of jewel-like colors to the hall was gone. Rolled up and stored away like the ones in the living room, she guessed, so Luke wouldn't trip over it.

Thinking how both their worlds had changed so dramatically, Haley collected the dirty dishes. A few minutes later she tucked the last of them into the dishwasher, wiped her hands on a handy towel and followed Luke to the den.

He was standing at the front windows, his hands shoved into his back pockets, staring through the sparkling panes as though he could actually see the glorious Texas morning now spreading its gold across the surface of the lake.

"What do we do now?" she asked.

"We wait."

Chapter 12

"Why doesn't he call?"

Clutching a dew-streaked iced-tea glass in a tight fist, Haley checked her watch. It was almost noon. Three and a half hours since Luke had sent his friends off on their appointed tasks. Fifteen since Frank Del Brio's call last night. She'd just about worn a rut in the den's hardwood floor with her pacing.

"He wants to keep you on edge," Luke stated calmly, following the sound of her voice.

"Well, he's doing a damned good job of it."

She'd been a bundle of nerves all morning. A call to the hospital assured her her father was holding his own. That had helped steady her, for a little while anyway. But the slow, dragging hours had piled tension on top of fear on top of frustration.

"He'll try to up the pucker factor until you won't stop

to think when he does call, you'll just jump. Don't play into his hands, Haley. Sit down. Force yourself to relax."

"I can't make myself visualize a soft gray haze right now," she muttered, too tense to attempt the relaxation technique that had worked so well last night. "I don't want to think about anything except Lena."

"So visualize her. Better yet, help me visualize her. Tell me about her."

The ploy worked. Haley's emotions shifted instantly from gnawing worry about her daughter to the remembered joy of cuddling her small, warm body. With a sigh, she dropped down in the overstuffed leather chair next to Luke's.

"She's so beautiful. Honestly! This isn't just a proud mother speaking. She's got fat little apple cheeks and the happiest gurgle. And she was born with the most incredible head of hair. Thick and black, like yours. The nurses tied a pink bow in it the day we left the hospital."

Swirling the ice in her watered-down tea, Haley savored the memory. What could have been such a wrenching experience for a single woman had in fact been the most momentous event of her life.

"She has your eyes, too. At least she did the last time I saw her," she added with a hitch in her voice. "That was four months ago. Four months! She was just coming up on her first birthday."

"Is that the magic point?" Luke asked, dragging her back from the brink again with his deliberate calm. "One year? After that, a baby's eye color doesn't change?"

"Not if the books I read are right. Supposedly the pigment cells in the irises accumulate and the eye color matures by the time the baby's a year old."

"So she's got my hair and eyes. What did she inherit from you?"

"My stubbornness," Haley replied without hesitation. "For such a tiny bit of fluff, she's got a temper she doesn't mind showing every so often. She has my skin tone, too, compliments of her Italian heritage. Her nose is still just a button, thank goodness. I'm hoping she doesn't develop the little bump in the bridge my mother passed on to me. I didn't miss that when the cosmetic surgeon gave me a new nose."

"The surgeon did a good job. I remember thinking you looked familiar when you first walked into the Saddlebag that night. I couldn't place you, but there was something. Your walk maybe, or the way you held yourself. But I knew I'd never seen your face before. I would have remembered it. What do you look like now?"

With a start, Haley remembered he'd never seen her in her Daisy Parker persona. He'd left the country just before she began her stint as a waitress at the country club. When he returned, he'd lost his sight.

"I have the same face I did that night at the Saddlebag. I just use a lot more makeup."

Or she had, until the shoot-out three nights ago that left her father in ICU and Haley buttoned up in the FBI's safe house. She'd hardly eaten or slept since, let alone bothered with makeup.

"When I first went undercover, I had injections to make my lips fuller. I've lost weight these past months, too. Except for my hair, which is a lighter blond now, I'm pretty close to the woman I was two years ago."

She hesitated, then placed her glass on a coaster and slipped out of her chair to sit on her heels beside his. Reaching for his left hand, she guided it to her cheek.

"Do you recognize that woman, Luke?"

The roughened pads of his fingers moved across her cheek to her nose. With a small frown of concentration, he followed the smooth slope down and up again before tracing the line of her brows. Leaning forward, he brought his right hand up to join the left. His palms cupped her cheeks. His thumbs moved over her lips in slow exploration.

Haley's breath caught. His touch was light and gentle, but her skin prickled with each slow stroke. He was so close to her now, his elbows resting on his knees, his face mere inches from her own as he rediscovered the woman whose mouth and body he'd claimed repeatedly the night they'd conceived their child.

At the memory of those stolen hours Haley felt her womb clench in a spasm of pure sexual need. She hadn't been with another man since that night with Luke, hadn't felt the least desire for someone else's touch.

She closed her eyes, determined to level the playing field with Luke. With each quiver of her nostrils she took in the faint, lime-scented tang of his aftershave. With each brush of his thumbs along her lips she tasted herself on his skin. She heard his breathing quicken, roughen. Felt his hands slide to her nape.

Sensation after sensation crashed through her. Her belly clenched again, lower, harder. Liquid heat poured into her veins. Two years of pent-up emotion burst through the dike. She could scarcely breathe. Part of it, she knew, was sheer relief that he'd put the past behind them and agreed to help her get Lena back. Another part—deeper, more visceral—was the want she'd carried with her for as long as she could remember. The want that had led her to take his hand that night at the Saddlebag. Hunger arced through her. Fierce. Unrelenting.

He pulled her closer, communicating his own need in a way that drew an instinctive response. Rising up on her knees, she looped her arms around his neck and brought her mouth to his.

After the first startled instant, he got into the kiss. His mouth slanted over hers, as hard and hungry as Haley's was warm and willing.

She was breathless when she finally sank back on her heels. Eyes wide open now, she stared up at his face and tried to rein in her wildly galloping thoughts. Luke got his under control before she did.

"Yep," he said with a wry halfsmile. "You're most definitely the woman you were two years ago. And more, Haley. One helluva lot more."

She had no idea how to respond to that. Thankfully she didn't have to. The intercom buzzed at that moment, ripping through the sensual haze enveloping her. Startled, she twisted around, lost her balance and ended up in a heap on the floor beside Luke's chair.

The intercom buzzed again, three short, impatient jabs, before he got to it.

"It's Spence, Luke. Flynt's with me. We've got the cash and a high-speed scanner. Open the gates."

Haley hadn't stopped to consider how many hundred-dollar bills it would take to meet Del Brio's ransom demand. Her eyes widened as Spence opened a well-worn leather case and dumped its contents onto the kitchen table.

"There you are," the former D.A. announced. "Twenty

thousand hundred-dollar bills, banded in bundles of ten thousand dollars each."

"Twenty thousand bills!" Haley gasped. Four faces swung in her direction. "Sorry," she murmured. "I didn't do the math. Tell me what to do."

"Your job is to unband a bundle and fan out the bills so I can run this optical scanning wand over the serial numbers. Flynt will man the laptop and make sure the data enters correctly. Then you pass the bills to Luke and he'll mark a corner of each with this stuff Tyler left us."

The "stuff" came in an unmarked, quart-size plastic container. It gave off a light, almost fruity odor when Spence unscrewed the lid and carefully filled a tube-like marker with a pinpoint sponge tip.

"I don't understand," Haley said. "If we're scanning in the serial numbers, why is it necessary to mark the bills, as well?"

"Federal Reserve banks have the personnel and the resources to conduct periodic screens of serial numbers," Spence explained. "They can help authorities track dispersal patterns across the country over an extended period of time. For quicker results, we're treating the bills with a chemical that reacts instantly when exposed to the kind of fluorescent lights used in department and grocery stores."

The lawyer's mouth curved in a wicked grin. "If you think that stuff smells distinctive now, you should take a whiff of it once it's been exposed to fluorescent lighting."

"Del Brio may pass one or two of the bills," Luke said with grim satisfaction. "That's all he'll pass. Okay, folks, let's get to it."

It was slow work. Physical, too. Haley had kept in shape the past twelve months hauling heavy trays and working ten- to twelve-hour shifts, but her back soon sent out warning signals each time she bent over to fan the bills.

Teresa Chavez came in a half hour after they got started. When she saw her kitchen table carpeted in hundred-dollar bills, her eyes bugged out. She didn't have to be told what they were doing, though. Luke had already informed her of the ransom demand.

"How can I help?" the housekeeper asked.

"We've got a good routine going," Luke replied, "but we're sure working up an appetite. You could rustle us up some lunch."

With a start, Haley realized her breakfast of cinnamon toast and Mexican lasagna had long since worn off. With the same enthusiasm as the men she fell on the coleslaw, thick-slabbed ham sandwiches and baked beans Teresa produced. After tucking the hearty meal under their belts, they went back to work with renewed energy.

They'd marked almost a fourth of the bundles when the phone rang. Everyone at the table froze. Their eyes cut instantly to flickering red light on the cordless house phone.

Luke rapped out two swift commands. "Flynt, get on the extension in my office. Teresa, let it ring twice more before you answer it."

The rancher sprang out of his chair. The housekeeper gulped and moved toward the cordless phone.

"Damn," Spence muttered as the phone shrilled a second time. "We should have had Tyler rig a tracking device on your house phones."

"Haley and I talked about that," Luke replied grimly. "Del Brio's too smart to stay on the line long enough to work a trace. He proved that last night. I've hooked up a recorder, though. I'll get—"

He broke off at the third ring. Cocking his head, he listened intently as Teresa punched the talk button on the cordless phone.

"Callaghan residence." Her dark eyes shifted to Haley. "Yes, she's here."

Sick certainty curled in Haley's stomach. It was Frank. It could only be Frank.

"Who may I say's calling?"

The reply sent red rushing into the housekeeper's cheeks. Her lips folded into a thin line, she marched across the room and held out the phone.

"This *malhechor* says he's your fiancé."

Haley jammed the phone to her ear with a white-knuckled fist. "Is Lena all right? Is she there with you?"

Frank's chuckle floated over the line. "She's here, babe. Right beside me."

"How do I know you're not lying?"

"What, you want me to pinch her or something to make her squeal?"

"No!" The idea of Frank bruising her baby's delicate skin made her frantic. "No, please! Don't hurt her!"

With a smothered oath, Luke reached across the table and pried the phone out of her hand. "This is Callaghan, Del Brio."

"Well, well. So she came to you for the money, did she?"

"You know damned well she did or you wouldn't have called here."

"Don't get smart with me, Callaghan. I'm the one

holding all the cards in this hand." Sloughing off his false geniality like a snake shedding its skin, Del Brio switched gears. "Rumor is you're the brat's father. That true?"

"Yes."

"Have you and Haley been getting it on all this time? Were you doing her when she was wearing my ring?"

There was more than anger behind the questions. There was an overlay of sick, twisted jealousy. Luke made a mental note of both before replying.

"If I was, she wouldn't have been wearing your ring. You couldn't keep her then, and you're sure as hell not going to have another chance at her."

"What, you think you're gonna get between us, you blind, useless cripple? I don't think so. I've seen the way your friends lead you around like a puppy on a leash. Haley needs a real man."

"Like you?"

"Yeah, like me. She's mine, Callaghan. You hear me? You might have slipped past me once when I wasn't looking, but I'm telling you now, I'm going to—"

"You're going to what, Del Brio?"

As if realizing how much of himself he'd exposed, he abruptly switched topics. "You got the two million?"

"I've got it, but you won't see a penny until we have proof Lena's alive and well."

"Proof? You want proof? All right, I'll give you proof. I'll send you one of the brat's fingers."

"Cut the crap, Del Brio. You're a businessman. You wouldn't pay for damaged goods and neither will I. Send proof, then we'll talk."

With a click of a button, Luke cut the connection.

Absolute silence followed. Spence frowned in intense

concentration. Teresa Chavez stared at her employer. Haley sat in stunned shock.

She cleared her throat. Slowly. Painfully. Even then, all she could manage was a hoarse croak. "Damaged goods? Were you talking about Lena?"

Luke smothered a curse. He could hear the near panic she was fighting to control. For a second or two he considered glossing over Del Brio's threat. Just as swiftly he discarded the idea. He and Haley were in this together. A team. Besides, she'd probably insist on listening to the tape of the call.

"Del Brio wasn't happy when I said he wouldn't get his money until we received proof Lena was still alive. He said he'd send one of her fingers."

Haley gave a small, strangled sound. Teresa's was louder and sharper.

"Ayyyy!" Her face contorting, the housekeeper made the sign of the cross three times in rapid succession. "That poor little baby!"

"He was bluffing."

"How do you know that?" Fury broke through Haley's incipient panic. "How can you know that?"

"I know."

"That's not good enough, damn you! If Frank harms my daughter, I'll never forgive you."

"She's my daughter, too," Luke fired back, gripped by the savage need to hunt Del Brio down and skin him alive. "Do you think I'd deliberately goad someone into mutilating my child?"

"How do I know what you'd do? We've spent exactly one night together in over a decade!"

"Two, if you count last night."

"Well, I don't! I mean, last night wasn't—We

didn't—Oh, hell!" The air escaped from her lungs like a deflating balloon. "Do you really think Lena will be all right?"

"Yes, I do. I also think we can expect Frank to deliver something within the next few hours. You guys get back to work while I make a quick call."

Luke joined Flynt in the den he'd converted to a modern, functional office. Fitted with flat workspaces and ample storage cabinets, it contained an array of computer and electronic wizardry that would have made Bill Gates drool. The gadget attached to the phone was the one that had caught Flynt's attention.

"What's this small flat disc?"

"It's a scrambler. Ordinarily it would be buried within the instrument itself, but I'm testing a new system for some folks in Washington."

"I though you were finished with that business."

"I am, pretty much."

"After getting blown all to hell and back, you should damned well cut the tie completely."

"You never cut the tie completely."

Not with OP-12, anyway. Even a blind operative had his uses. Particularly one with Luke's years of experience.

Flynt grumbled under his breath, clearly not happy. He and Spence still hadn't quite forgiven Luke for never once clueing them in about his years with OP-12. Tyler came closer to understanding. He'd left the marines to freelance, assuming a sort of quasi-official status with the covert military agency he worked for. Still, even Tyler had been stunned when he'd learned his playboy pal Luke Callaghan had spearheaded an ultrasecret, multinational thrust deep in the Mezcayan jungle to rescue their old commander, Colonel Phillip Westin.

After the rescue attempt went bad and Luke lost his sight, Tyler had stepped in—but not before ripping a strip a mile wide off his friend for keeping his three buddies in the dark all these years.

Well, those years lay behind Luke now. His only contribution to OP-12 these days was to test equipment and, when requested, to offer operational advice. He hadn't lost his clout in the organization, though. After verification of his identity by code and by voice recognition, he was put right through to the acoustics branch.

"I need a full analysis run on the call just received at this number," he told the branch chief.

"You got it," the woman at the other end of the line replied.

"I want it quick."

"How quick?" she asked warily.

"Like yesterday."

The cheerful mother of three with double Ph.D.s in mechanical and audio engineering laughed. "So what else is new? I'll get back to you within an hour."

The branch chief had been with OP-12 almost as long as Luke had. From past experience, he knew she was as good as her word.

That task done, he ran a hand along the work surface until he located the recorder hooked up to the phone. Frowning, he ejected the CD Rewritable disc and hefted it in the palm of his hand. The conversation burned onto it was already etched into his mind.

"Did you catch that bit about Haley still belonging to Del Brio?" he asked Flynt.

"Yeah, I did. I also noticed that he still refers to himself as her fiancé." The rancher let a couple of seconds tick by. "Are you thinking maybe ole Frank is more interested in getting his hands on Haley Mercado than on the ransom?"

"That's exactly what I'm thinking."

Chapter 13

Spence agreed with Flynt and Luke's assessment. So did Tyler when he returned from his trip to Fort Hood a half hour later and listened to the recorded call. His face thoughtful, he strolled back into the kitchen, which had become their unofficial command center, and addressed the small group.

"Well, this certainly alters our approach. Sounds like we need to plan for a possible snatch and run, not just a recovery operation."

His glance drifted to Haley. She sat at the table working her bundles of hundreds, but the call from Frank had shaken her so much that she couldn't regain the smooth rhythm she'd established previously.

Was Luke right? Was Frank more interested in getting his hands on her than on the ransom? The possibility made her physically ill, but she'd give herself to Del Brio in a heartbeat in exchange for Lena's safety.

"Actually, a snatch and run makes things simpler," Tyler mused. "I was worried Del Brio would send someone else to pick up the ransom. From the drift of that call, I'm betting he'll insist Haley deliver the ransom to him personally."

"In which case," Luke put in, his face granite-hard, "he'll have to use the baby as enticement to make sure she shows."

"Exactly." Tyler's brown eyes locked on Haley. "You were right. Looks like you're going to be out there on point, after all. Sure you're up to it?"

"I've been 'out there' for over a year," she reminded him. "I'm up to it."

Admiration flickered across his tanned face. "Yeah, I guess you are."

Luke didn't miss the subtle change in the tenor of the conversation. Nor the way his friends were now responding to Haley. Like him, they'd greeted the news of her return to the realm of the living with stunned disbelief, confusion and a healthy jolt of anger. Luke wasn't the only one who'd carried a load of guilt around all these years.

And like Luke, the three men had swiftly worked past their anger. They now understood the reason for her desperate flight. They were beginning to understand, too, the incredible courage it took for her to return to Mission Creek to go undercover as Daisy Parker.

She had that in spades, Luke admitted silently. Courage, smarts and a sensuality that acted on him like a cattle prod every time he got within touching distance of her. He'd just about lost it earlier this afternoon in the den. One kiss, and he'd been ready to stretch her out on the floor. Hell, just thinking about the feel of her mouth under his had him itching to tell his buddies to hit the road.

"How did you make out up at Fort Hood?" he asked Tyler, forcing himself to concentrate on the matter at hand.

"Like a kid in a candy shop! Man, you wouldn't believe the toys those guys are playing with up there. I sure as hell wouldn't want to get on the bad side of the United States military these days."

"I don't think anyone else does, either," Flynt put in. "Our guys have sure kicked ass recently."

"Particularly the Fourteenth Marines," Spence added with savage satisfaction.

For a moment the four friends shared a tight, fierce loyalty to their former unit. Only those who'd experienced combat could understand the almost indestructible bond it forged between comrades-in-arms.

Almost indestructible. The fact that one of their group was missing still gnawed at Luke. Where the hell was Ricky? He had to know by now Frank suspected his sister was still alive. Had to guess Del Brio had kidnapped her baby to lure her out of hiding. Had he been secretly involved in the shoot-out three nights ago, when Del Brio slipped through the FBI net? Was he, too, on the run?

Tyler broke into his troubled thoughts. "You and I should go down to the lake, buddy. We need to test this little hummer. Make sure it works as advertised."

"Right." Turning toward the woman whose scent and warmth now acted like a beacon in the shadows, Luke offered what reassurance he could. "I'll take the phone with me. If Del Brio calls, let me handle him. He knows he can use your worry for Lena to twist you into knots."

"Do you think we'll hear from him soon?"

The best he could do was a shrug. "As he said, he's holding most of the cards right now. We'll hear from him when he's ready."

The next contact from Frank didn't come until ten-fifteen that night.

Spence, Flynt and Tyler had left some hours earlier. They'd offered to stay, but the bills were marked, the serial numbers scanned, and Luke had been thoroughly checked out on the wristwatch-size phased-array radar that gave him a startlingly accurate return signature.

He'd also received the promised return call from OP-12. Acoustics had run every analysis in the book, but could provide only limited information. The call was made at a pay phone located within a half mile of a major highway. Semis had roared by in the distance. The acoustics wizards had also detected the sound of a tractor, which narrowed the area some, given that this was primarily range country.

Luke contacted the FBI and passed the information to Sean Collins, along with a scathing rebuke for not reading him on Daisy Parker's identity. Doggedly un-apologetic, Collins agreed with Luke's insistence that they share all information from here on out.

"Sheriff Wainwright's here with me," the agent informed Luke. "He's offered the entire resources of his department to help."

"Tell Justin I appreciate the offer," Luke said sincerely. He hated having to cut out the man who'd risked his life, alongside his wife, in the abortive attempt to rescue Lena. But Del Brio had been adamant. So had Haley. This was their operation now, hers and Luke's.

Haley listened to the exchange in silence and re-sumed the pacing she'd begun earlier this afternoon. Luke finally convinced her to go upstairs and indulge in a long, hot soak.

Twenty minutes later the computer in his office pinged, announcing the arrival of an e-mail.

Counting his steps in the way that had become sec-ond nature to him now, Luke navigated the short dis-tance to his office. A quick click with the mouse took him to his e-mail program. Another click activated the speech component. An instant later Del Brio's voice leapt out at him.

"You wanted proof, Callaghan. Here it is."

A series of soft pings indicated that the computer was downloading an image. Eyes narrowed, Luke strained every nerve in his body in an effort to make out the pic-ture on the screen. All he could distinguish was a hazy blur of dark on light.

Swearing viciously, he sat staring at the screen. He'd never regretted the loss of his vision more than he did at this moment. He couldn't see his own child. Didn't know whether she was laughing or crying or lying in a pool of blood.

His spine locked, shoulders roped with tension, he waited for Haley to come downstairs. He heard her flip-flopping down the hall some fifteen minutes later.

"I raided your closet for some slippers and one of your shirts. I hope you don't mind."

Consumed with the need to know what was on the screen, Luke barely registered the faint combination of starched cotton and lemony shampoo that came into the office with her.

"I didn't hear the phone ring."

"Del Brio chose another communication medium this time. I've been waiting for you to look at this."

Slippers flopping, she rushed forward and bent over his shoulder. Luke could feel her body tremble where it contacted his, and the kink in his gut took another vicious twist. He hated not being able to prepare Haley for what she might see on the screen.

"Dear God, that's Lena!"

She'd never know how much it took to keep his voice level and calm. "How does she look?"

"Happy. Oh, Luke, she looks happy." Giddy with relief, she drummed a fist on his shoulder. "She's clutching a fluffy stuffed rabbit and she's laughing at the camera."

Some of the tension holding Luke in a rigid brace seeped out of his spine. He relaxed, leaning back in his chair. The slight movement brought the back of his head in direct contact with the warm, soft swell of Haley's breasts. With a vicious effort, he blanked his mind to the sensations that raced through him.

"Describe the background details. What do you see in the image besides Lena?"

"She's sitting on the floor in front of a TV. It looks like there's some kind of a news show on. CNN's 'Headline News,' I think. Yes, it's 'Headline News.' I can see the banner at the bottom of the screen."

"Does it show a time and date?"

"Yes. Today's date. The time is…"

She leaned closer to the screen. Luke felt himself begin to sweat.

"The time is seven thirty-six. Only a little over three hours ago!"

"Computer images are easy to doctor," he cautioned,

hating to douse the joy and relief in her voice. "I doubt if this one was, since Frank knows we'll check it out. Still, it won't hurt to have a few experts take a look at it."

"No, it won't. Just print me a copy, will you?"

While his high-tech laser color printer whirred, Luke composed a brief message to a nameless, faceless entity in a building outside McLean, Virginia, and hit the send key. Next, he tapped out a quick e-mail to Special Agent Sean Collins at the FBI command center. Extracting the printed copy of the photo, he swung his chair around. She chose the same moment to lean across him and reach for the photo herself.

Luke's shoulder caught her square in her ribs. Off balance, she stumbled sideways and would have fallen if Luke hadn't grabbed for her. One hand contacted starched cotton. The other, bare skin. With an adroit maneuver he managed to convert her fall into an awkward tumble that brought her into his lap. She landed with a little plop and a shaky laugh.

"Good catch, Callaghan. Thanks."

"You're welcome."

He fully intended to remove his hand from her bare thigh. In a minute. Curling his palm around the smooth flesh, he held her balanced on his knees.

"Sorry about the body block. I didn't hurt you, did I?"

"No, you didn't."

Luke half expected her to wiggle off his lap. She had to feel the heat she was raising in him. Hell, his hand burned like a brand where it wrapped around the silk of her inner thigh. Drawn by the fire, he slid his palm up another inch or so.

She made a queer little breathy sound, louder than a sigh, softer than a gasp. "Luke?"

His hand stilled. "Yes?"

"About that kiss in the living room this afternoon…"

"What about it?"

"I didn't plan it."

"I know. I wasn't planning on this one, either."

He managed to find her lips with only minimal bumping of chins and noses. Her head tipped back to improve the contact, bunching her still-wet hair against his shoulder. Luke registered the dampness through his shirt for a moment or two before her mouth opened under his. With a grunt of sheer male satisfaction, he shifted her higher on his lap.

The small movement tipped Haley's soaring emotions over the edge. She was ecstatic at seeing evidence her baby was happy. Overwhelmed by all Luke was doing to help rescue Lena. If she hadn't ached for him before, the feelings he roused in her now would have done the trick.

Joy swiftly became hunger. Relief crashed into need. Want left her mindless of the oversize shirt falling off her shoulders. Her mouth turned greedy, her hands even more so as she slid her palms over his chest and shoulders.

Luke's greed matched hers. She could feel him straining against her, under her. Taking full advantage of the now widely gaping shirt, he found her breast. The calloused pads of his palm raised shivery sensations against her skin. Within moments his busy fingers had brought her nipple to an aching peak.

"I've carried a picture of you in my head since that night at the Saddlebag," he muttered, hitching her up another few inches. "I remember your mouth soft and swollen from my kisses. Your nipples dusky red and stiff."

"You'd better hang on to that mental image," she said on a shaky laugh. "I've aged a bit since then. I've also had a baby. I have the stretch marks to prove it."

"Do you? Where? Here?"

His hand slid down, charting a path past the starched folds of the shirt. Haley's stomach quivered at the exploratory touch. She wasn't wearing panties. She'd washed out the pair she'd had on when she'd rushed out to find Luke. They were upstairs, draped over the shower rod in the guest bathroom alongside her bra.

Luke obviously approved of the omission. After only a stroke or two, he abandoned his search for stretch marks and found the heat between her legs. The heel of his hand exerted an exquisite pressure on her mound, while his thrusting fingers nearly carried her to climax. Embarrassed, Haley clenched her legs and tried frantically to stem the tidal wave of sensations.

"Luke, wait! It's been two years!"

She hadn't intended to provide that particular item of information. It just slipped out, along with every bit of breath in her lungs as he deliberately, wickedly increased the pressure.

"Are you saying you're too out of practice?" he asked, nipping at her neck.

"No. I'm saying I'm too ready."

Laughter puffed against her throat. "Oh, sweetheart, that's the last thing you should tell a man when you want him to stop."

"Who said I want you to stop?"

Wriggling like a stranded fish, Haley twisted around

and straddled his thighs. They were face-to-face now. Breath-to-breath.

"What I want," she informed him, yanking at his belt buckle, "is to feel you inside me."

His breath snagged. His belly hollowed. With a growl he shoved aside her fumbling hands and freed himself from his jeans. She was wet when he lifted her hips, and ready, so ready, when he entered her in a smooth, sure thrust.

They made wild, greedy love in his office before moving to Luke's king-size bed for a slower, more deliberate joining. He positioned the phone on the nightstand within easy reach in case Frank called, then took Haley to magical places, where she almost—almost—forgot Del Brio altogether.

Limp and totally sated, she nestled her head on Luke's shoulder and let her sleepy gaze roam his bedroom. As the rest of the house, it was furnished with an eye to masculine comfort blended with family antiques and Texas treasures. Stressed leather covered three walls above the waist-high paneling. Bookshelves took up the fourth, with a Remington bronze occupying the place of honor in a specially lighted central niche. An iron bootjack sat beside an oversize arm chair and served a necessary purpose.

It was a man's room, she thought, yet one a woman could feel cherished in. All it needed was a few feminine touches. Sweet-scented potpourri instead of cigars in the humidor on the bedside table, maybe. Her clothes hanging opposite Luke's in that cavernous walk-in closet.

With a frown she brought her thoughts to a jerky halt.

She was getting ahead of herself here. Way ahead of herself. She shut down that treacherous line of thought, only to discover Luke was doing some thinking of his own.

"Haley?"

"Mmm?"

"All those years in London you never found anyone to hold you and keep you safe?"

"I wasn't looking."

"Why not?"

"At first I was too nervous. I kept pretty much to myself until I got comfortable in my new identity. Even then I allowed myself only a small circle of friends."

"There wasn't anyone special?"

Only you.

Not ready to admit how often Luke Callaghan had figured in her private dreams all those years, Haley merely shrugged. He wasn't ready to let the matter drop, though. Stroking her hair, he continued his probe.

"Why did you go with me that night at the Saddle-bag?"

"Seeing my mother so bruised and battered shook me, Luke. Badly. I'd never felt more alone than I did that night. Or more lonely."

"So you went with me out of loneliness?"

"Yes. Partly."

"Only partly?"

Slipping out from under his hand, she raised up on one elbow. "What do you want me to say? That I needed a man?"

"Well, I was hoping for something more specific. Like maybe you needed me."

"Okay, maybe I did. Does that make a difference?"

"Yeah, it does."

"Why?"

"Because I'm beginning to think the feeling was mutual. It's hard to put into words, but after you drowned— After you left," he amended hastily, "I kept a part of myself hidden, too."

"From what I read in the tabloids," Haley said dryly, "you didn't exactly lack for companionship."

"I didn't. But I never felt the need I felt that night at the Saddlebag."

"Are you saying you were lonely, too? That's what brought you over to my table that night?"

"Partly," he said, echoing her earlier reply.

She struggled to adjust her mental image of the man Luke Callaghan had been with one who'd lived with as many secrets as Haley had herself. She wasn't quite there when his mouth curved in a wicked grin.

"The other part," he confessed, dragging her down for a kiss, "was pure lust."

Chapter 14

The next morning Haley lingered in the guest bathroom long after she'd showered and blow-dried her hair. Luke had given her first crack at the master bath, but she'd opted for the one down the hall she'd already more or less claimed as her own. She needed some space—and some privacy—to sort through her confusion.

Funny what a difference a few hours could make.

Last night she'd tumbled into Luke's arms without a thought for the complications or the consequences that might follow. Just as she'd done two years ago. This morning she was having second, third, and fourth doubts. Just as she'd done two years ago.

"Talk about your slow learners," she muttered, plucking a few blond strands from her comb and tossing them in the wicker wastebasket.

How could she make such a fool of herself twice with the same man? Thank goodness she'd stopped short of telling him the real reason she'd gone with him that night at the Saddlebag. She could just imagine his re-action if she'd admitted that she'd loved him for as long as she could remember.

He, on the other hand, had been right up front with her. He'd been feeling a touch of loneliness two years ago. And a whole lot of lust. Love hadn't figured into things that night. Nor did it come into play now.

On his side of the equation, anyway.

Time Haley accepted that basic fact and hauled her butt downstairs. She had more pressing concerns to worry about, chief among them her daughter. Plunking the comb down on the marble vanity, she followed the scent of fresh-brewed coffee to the kitchen.

Luke stood at the center island, a coffee mug in hand. Glancing up, he zeroed in on her with such pinpoint ac-curacy that Haley forgot he couldn't actually see her. Self-consciously, she tugged at the hem of the pale blue shirt she'd borrowed from him. Even with the sleeves rolled up, she swam in the cloud-soft cotton.

"I should make a run to my apartment," she said by way of greeting. "If Frank doesn't call soon with in-structions on when and where to deliver the ransom, I'll deplete your entire wardrobe."

"It's safer for you here. Make a list of the items you need and I'll have someone pick them up for you."

The clipped response lifted Haley's brows. From the sound of it, she wasn't the only one experiencing a few morning-after doubts.

"All right. Have you had breakfast?"

"Just coffee. I'm not hungry. Help yourself to what-ever you want."

"Just coffee will do for me, too."

She joined him at the island, filled another mug and took a cautious sip.

"We need to talk about last night, Haley."

The sip turned into a gulp. Hastily she downed the too hot brew. "Yes, I guess we do."

"I don't usually make that kind of mistake."

His words burned worse than the scalding coffee. Carefully she placed her mug on the granite counter. "You consider last night a mistake?"

"Hell, yes. Don't you?"

"I'm beginning to."

Grimacing at her strained reply, he shook his head. "You can't blame me any more than I blame myself. If I'd acted as irresponsibly in the field as I did last night, I would have come home in a box."

He slid his hand along the counter and found hers. His grip was warm and, she supposed, intended to be reassuring.

"I'm sorry, Haley. I know worry over Lena has kept you on a constant roller coaster ride. I felt your burst of relief after seeing her picture last night and knowing she was happy and well cared for." The disgust came back into his face. "I can't believe I took advantage of your emotional vulnerability that way."

"You think that's why I fell all over you? Out of relief?"

"Didn't you?"

"Okay, maybe some. But there were other emotions involved. Like that lust we talked about. I wanted you, Luke."

"I wanted you, too. So bad, I hurt with it." He squeezed her hand. "But this is one of those intense situations where things get distorted easily."

"I seem to be a little slow this morning. What exactly have we distorted?"

"Nothing, yet. I'm just saying the potential is there. Look, Haley, you know I'll do whatever it takes to get Lena back safely. Once that's accomplished, I don't want you to feel obligated in any way or think you're tied to a…" His mouth twisted down at one side. "How did Del Brio put it? To a blind, useless cripple."

The irony took Haley's breath away. Here she'd been writhing inside, worrying Luke had sensed that her feelings for him went far deeper than want, thinking he was warning her off.

Evidently he was, but for an entirely different reason than the one she'd postulated. She hadn't considered, hadn't remotely imagined, that his impaired vision might be a factor.

"Is that what this is all about?" she asked incredulously. "Your sight, or lack of it?"

"It has to be considered."

"You idiot! Of course it does. But not in any discussion about last night or how we might or might not feel after we get our baby back."

His black brows slashed down. The look on his face wavered between surprise and a scowl. Obviously, Luke Callaghan wasn't used to being contradicted. Too wound up to soothe his ruffled feelings, Haley tugged her hand free of his.

"You're right about one thing, though. In a situation like this, things can easily become distorted. Why don't we drop the whole topic of last night? For now, anyway."

After his little noble speech he could hardly refuse. His scowl lingered, however, as they downed the rest of their coffee.

* * *

It was still there, feathering around the edges of his mouth, when Mrs. Chavez bustled into the kitchen just before eight, followed in short order by Spence Harrison, Flynt Carson, Tyler Murdoch and their wives. In the space of mere minutes, the atmosphere in the kitchen went from intense to chaotic.

"Sorry, buddy." Ruefully, Flynt explained the sudden invasion. "When I got home last night, Josie guessed something was up. I told her about the call from Del Brio. She told Ellen, who in turn relayed the news to Marisa."

"Yes," the statuesque Marisa Rodriguez Murdoch said with a toss of her glorious, blue-black hair, "and we are not happy, Josie and Ellen and I, that our men are such fools they did not tell us sooner so we could come and help."

Wisely, the three fools in question kept their mouths shut and let Luke take full blame.

"Sorry. That was my doing. I asked them to keep this operation as close-hold as possible."

"If you think we women couldn't assist," the fiery Spanish interpreter snapped, "then you, too, are a fool."

"Funny," Luke drawled. "That seems to be the general consensus this morning."

Brushing past her husband, slender, vivacious Josie Lavender Carson crossed the kitchen. She'd met Haley only in her cover as a waitress at the Lone Star Country Club and was still obviously astounded at her real identity.

"I couldn't believe it when Flynt told me you're Ricky Mercado's sister. And Lena's mother."

Haley stiffened, expecting reproach from the nanny

Flynt had hired to care for the baby he and the others had found on the golf course, but Josie's emerald-green eyes held only sympathy.

"It must have killed you all those months to see me holding and cuddling your child."

"It did," Haley confessed. "The only thing that kept me from snatching her out of your arms was knowing she was loved and well cared for."

"Now that I have a baby of my own," the new mother said gently, "I appreciate the courage it took for you to do what you did."

Ellen Wagner Harrison seconded Josie's opinion. She'd lost a husband to cancer and raised a son on her own. Until Spence turned up, dazed and bleeding from a car accident, she'd been fighting her own battle with loneliness and near desperation over finances. Her one joy—her only joy—during those dark years was her son. The thought of giving him up, even for his own safekeeping, left her aching for this woman she'd met only once or twice in the past year.

With the quiet competence that characterized her, she deposited an overnight bag on the granite counter. "Spence said you've been holed up here with Luke for going on two days now. I thought you might need a few things. I remembered that we're about the same size."

"Bless you! As you can see, I've been raiding Luke's closet. I just told him a few minutes ago that I'd have to retrieve some things from my apartment if something doesn't happen soon."

"Del Brio hasn't made contact?" Tyler asked sharply. "Hell, I was sure he would have delivered proof that Lena's okay by now."

"He did. He e-mailed a photo of her last night, right after you left."

"Where is it?"

"In my office."

"Hang loose, I'll get it."

Tyler was back a few moments later, carrying not just the printed photo but the innocuous-looking device he'd strapped onto Luke's wrist yesterday.

"I found the picture. I also found this on the floor, under your desk."

"And 'this' is?"

"Sorry. The radar transmitter I brought back yesterday from Fort Hood. Did the strap come loose?"

"No," Luke replied with a carefully neutral expression. "I took it off."

Haley's face flamed. She remembered exactly when he'd unstrapped the small watchlike device. Right after its stem had left a sizable scratch on the inside of her right thigh. She'd gathered up the clothes they'd scattered all over the office floor, but had obviously missed the scanner.

Her cheeks hot, she caught Spence's speculative glance. Thankfully the color photo of Lena diverted the keen-eyed former prosecutor's attention. The picture was passed from hand to hand, with the women expressing excitement and relief. The men were more restrained. Flynt and Tyler left it to the lawyer to voice their collective doubts.

"The courts don't accept computer-generated images as evidence for a reason," Spence reminded Luke. "Are you satisfied this one's for real?"

"I e-mailed the photo to some folks in McLean. They say it's genuine."

An almost palpable sense of relief spread through the kitchen.

"All right," Tyler said briskly. "We've cleared the first major hurdle. Now we can concentrate on ransom delivery scenarios. We're pretty well agreed Del Brio's going to insist Haley deliver it in person," he told the women. "We also suspect he wants her as much or more than he wants the cash. Luke as much as told Del Brio he won't get his hands on either his money or his woman."

Incredulous, Marisa swung to the man at her side. "And you thought this would make matters easier, Luke?"

"I wasn't trying to make things easier. I was trying to throw Del Brio off balance."

"Which you did," Flynt said dryly. "You surely did."

"We'll make sure you knock him more off balance when he comes to collect the money," Tyler put in gleefully. "Ladies, if you want to help, one of you could put on a pot of coffee while—"

"Careful, my dear husband," Marisa cooed. "If you plan to sleep in our bed tonight, you'll consider carefully what you were about to say."

Blinking, the leather-tough mercenary made a quick recovery. "What I was about to say, my dear wife, is that one of you ladies could put on a fresh pot while I get more mugs down from the cupboard."

Making no effort to hide her grin, Ellen volunteered for coffee duty. Soon the scent of rich Colombian blend percolated through the kitchen, and all four couples gathered at the weathered cypress table to strategize possible ransom delivery scenarios.

Three couples, Haley corrected silently as she swept a quick glance around the assembled group. Taciturn

Flynt and vivacious Josie so obviously belonged to-gether. As did Spence and his quiet, competent Ellen. Tyler and Marisa struck so many sparks off each other they generated a heat all their own.

She and Luke were the odd ones out. Their tangled pasts had brought everyone else to this place and this time, yet theirs was also the most nebulous relationship. It consisted of one part passion, two parts worry for their daughter, with a large dash of uncertainty thrown in to spice things up even more. Frank wasn't the only one Luke had thrown off balance.

Haley might have decided to put all discussion about last night on ice, but Luke soon discovered his buddies were less reticent. Spence waited only until the four men had walked down to the lake for more practice with the wrist-radar to fall into his prosecuting-attorney mode.

"So what's with you and Haley?"

"Besides a mutual concern for our child? Nothing you need to know about."

"Bull! There was so much electricity between the two of you when we arrived, the air had turned blue. Then there's the matter of that little toy strapped to your wrist. Haley colored up like a Christmas tree when Tyler asked how it got under your desk."

"Come on, Luke," Tyler put in. "Give. How did it get under there?"

"None of your damned business."

Flynt spoke up for the first time. "That's where you're wrong, buddy. It is our business. We're in this all the way with you. And we need to know you won't do something stupid when and if Del Brio makes a grab for Haley."

"Such as?"

"Such as offering yourself as a target in order to get a clean shot at him."

"I'll do whatever it takes to bring him down," Luke said softly, savagely. "Neither Haley nor Lena will be safe until he's out of the picture. Now one of you walk out fifty yards or so and let me get a read on you."

Yesterday afternoon's practice session had provided Luke a general feel for the variations in vibrations the radar returned when it encountered an object. This time he kept all three friends outside in the blazing sun until he was satisfied he could differentiate between their individual radar signatures. As Tyler had reported, the radar was so precise and the vibrations so fine-tuned, Luke should be able to track Del Brio with no difficulty...once he got him away from Lena and Haley.

"You should be okay if only Del Brio shows," Tyler muttered, dragging his forearm across his forehead. "If he brings more than one or two others with him, things could get dicey. Sure you don't want one of us to go along with you?"

"I can't risk it."

Flynt clapped a hand on his shoulder. "We won't be more than a radio call away. I've got my chopper fueled and ready. Once we know the target area, Justin will mobilize his Air Ops Branch. The C.O.'s lined up military air out of Corpus Christi. The FBI's ready to roll. One signal from you, and we're on Del Brio like dirt on a dog."

"The C.O.? You read Colonel Westin in on this?"

"I did. He's flying in this afternoon. Should be here anytime now."

Luke's pulse kicked up a few notches. Once their old

commanding officer arrived on the scene, they'd come close to constituting a team again. The only one missing was Ricky Mercado.

"Anyone seen or heard from Ricky since his father was hit?" Luke asked.

"No," Spence replied. "He dropped completely out of sight. My guess is he's either cut his losses and run or he's hunting Del Brio himself."

"There's a third option we have to consider," Luke reminded them. "According to Haley, Frank doesn't trust the son any more than the father. He might have taken Ricky out."

For Haley's sake, he hoped he was wrong. As strong as she was, even Haley might break under the strain of losing another member of her family.

The need to protect her blazed fierce and hot. She'd suffered enough. Endured enough. Luke was damned if he'd let anyone hurt her again.

"Move back down to the lake, Spence. I want more practice with this radar unit."

Haley had thought the waiting was bad before. The twenty-four hours following Frank's e-mail left both her nerves and her patience as thin and as brittle as new ice.

The presence of Luke's friends helped. Some. The men refused to display anything but calm confidence. Their wives were warm and supportive. Gradually, Haley got to know the women and they, in turn, came to understand the stress she'd lived with for so many years.

Phillip Westin's arrival late that afternoon provided a welcome distraction. Tall, lean and leather-tough, the marine colonel reminded Haley instantly of a middle-aged Clint Eastwood. She couldn't help but notice how his former troops squared their shoulders, sucked in their stomachs and peppered their conversation with "Yes, sir" and "No, sir" whenever they addressed him.

After demanding to know how the heck this bunch of "jar heads" had wound up with such smart, beautiful women, Westin got right down to business. For the rest of the day and a good part of the next, the entire group gathered around the kitchen table, reviewing possible scenarios, postulating potential actions, dissecting every conceivable response.

Frank finally sent the ransom delivery instructions that hot Wednesday evening. They came in the form of another e-mail, short and to the point.

Farm Road 1306.
8.6 miles past intersection with Highway 48.
7 p.m.
Tonight.

"Hell," Tyler muttered, peering over Luke's shoulder. "That's less than an hour from now. You and Haley will have to make tracks to reach the designated rendezvous by seven."

"We'll reach it," Luke vowed. "You guys just take care of the satellite coverage of the area and get the aircraft in the air."

"Will do, buddy." He squeezed his friend's shoulder. "Good luck."

Her heart pounding, Haley accepted a round of fierce hugs from both the men and the women. She couldn't speak, could barely breathe as the team sprang into action like a well-oiled military machine.

Chapter 15

Luke's years with OP-12 had taught him that there was only one absolute certainty when it came to field operations.

If something could go wrong, it would.

There was no way to plan for every contingency. No way to account for every variable. Yet he tried to cover as many as possible with Haley during the long, tense drive to the designated site.

"There'll still be some daylight left when we get there. That's good for Frank, not as good for us."

"I know."

"Del Brio may have checkpoints set up. If so, one of his men will pat you down for weapons."

"I know."

Haley stared straight ahead, her palms clammy on the steering wheel of Luke's pickup. The big, heavy truck was dusty, utilitarian and fitted with sheets of steel inside the door panels. Tyler and Flynt had rigged the shields themselves.

"If there's any exchange of fire while we're in the vehicle, you hit the deck. Got that, Haley? You go down and stay down."

She dragged her tongue over dry lips. "I've got it."

"Once we're on the scene, we'll both exit the vehicle. Odds are Frank will instruct you to walk toward him with the briefcase, but you don't take a step until you see Lena. Once we've established her exact position and are sure she's not in the line of fire, you go forward. At an angle."

"I know."

"Whatever happens, don't get between me and Del Brio."

Biting on her lower lip, Haley forced down a rush of hot, bitter nausea. She understood how important it was to maintain a clear field for Luke's radar scanner to pinpoint Frank's position. She also understood that the same clear field gave Frank an unobstructed shot at Luke.

She'd already decided she wouldn't let Frank take that shot. He'd destroyed her family, murdered her mother, almost killed her father. God only knew where her brother was now. She wouldn't, couldn't, let Del Brio destroy Luke, too.

That resolve deepened with every mile they traveled along Farm Road 1306. Sensing how tightly strung she was, Luke had her read the odometer out loud, marking each mile from the turnoff, then every tenth of a mile along the two-lane dirt road.

"Eight point one," she read, wrenching her gaze from the road that cut straight as an arrow through range land dotted with creosote and mesquite.

"Eight point two."

"What time is it?"

"Seven. We're late."

"Just keep going. Tell me what you see."

"Nothing. No cattle. No horses. No houses. Just miles of barbed-wire fence on both sides of the road. Whoever owns this patch of south Texas hasn't put the land to use."

"That's no doubt why Frank chose it. What's the odometer reading?"

"Eight point four."

"Look down the road. See anything?"

"No!" Her stomach roiling, she slowed the truck and read off the last two increments. "Eight point five. Eight point six."

She stood on the brakes. The pickup fishtailed to a stop in the middle of the road.

"There's no one here!"

"Look around. Any hills or trees they could be parked behind, watching our approach?"

Her nerves screaming, she scanned the flat terrain. "No. Nothing bigger than an anthill. All I can see is scrub and—Oh, my God!"

Frantic, she scrabbled for the door handle. Luke wrapped an iron fist around her arm and yanked her down in her seat.

"Talk to me! Tell me what you see."

"There's something caught on the upper strand of the fence just to my left. At first glance, I thought it was a dead animal, but I think... Oh, Luke, I'm sure! It's the stuffed rabbit Lena was holding in the picture Frank e-mailed. And there's a note pinned to it!"

She made another lunge for the door. Once again he hauled her back. "It could be a booby trap."

Instantly sobered, Haley gave him her full attention.

"We'll get out of the truck on my side," he told her. "We take one step at a time. Only one. You'll have to be my eyes."

"Tell me what to look for."

"Depressions in the dirt. Trip wires. A light beam. A pile of grass. Broken creosote branches."

By the time they got within five feet of the stuffed toy, the sleeveless cotton blouse Ellen had brought Haley was damp with sweat. She shook so hard she could barely read the note. "It says to turn right at the next intersection, go twenty-two miles north, head west on 329 to an abandoned farmhouse. We've got thirty minutes to get there."

Luke pushed out a long breath and reached for the cell phone in his shirt pocket. One click activated the Voice Recognition System and brought his team up on the net.

"Look like Frank is going to send us chasing across half of Texas." Swiftly, he repeated the instructions Haley had just read. "Get a satellite lock on the abandoned farmhouse. We're on the way there now."

Snapping the phone shut, he took Haley's elbow. She should have been the one steering him back to the truck, but he gave her as much or more support than she gave him.

They found another note at the farmhouse, this one directing them to a phone booth at a gas station halfway to San Angelo. Dusk crept across the rolling hills as the pickup sped across Texas. Early stars glowed bright in the lavender sky. Haley didn't spare the sky more than a glance. She kept her eyes on the road ahead and the accelerator hard against the floorboard.

They reached the gas station a good ten minutes ahead of the specified time. Leaving the keys in the ignition, she climbed out and waited for Luke to come around to join her.

"Can you see the booth?"

"Yes."

"Describe it to me."

"It's an open cubicle, with graffiti scrawled all over it. There's no note stuck to it. No note anywhere."

"Go stand on the other side of the truck."

"Why?"

"I want to see if the phone's working."

"You think Frank might have rigged it with explosives?"

"No, I don't. I think he's going to call in a few minutes with more instructions. Just to be safe, though, I want to check out the phone before it rings. Tell me when you're behind the truck."

Haley didn't move. "No, Luke."

"No what?"

"I won't let you take any more risks." Sick with fear for both him and her baby, she fought to keep her voice level. "I shouldn't have come running to you the way I did. I panicked and didn't think things through. I'm the one Frank contacted. I'm the one he wants revenge on. He won't hurt Lena or you if he has me."

"Yeah, well, what Frank wants and what he gets are—"

"Listen to me, Luke. I'm telling you there's been a change in tactics. If Frank is planning a snatch and run, as you and Tyler and the others seem to think, I intend to let him know right up front that I'll go with him voluntarily. My only condition is that he leaves Lena with you."

She expected him to get all macho and blast her with a dozen different arguments. Instead, he folded his arms and let the summer night swirl hot and dusty around them.

"Just out of curiosity, when did you decide on this change in tactics?"

"A while ago."

"When, Haley?"

"Look, it's been building inside me for the past couple days, okay? The guilt. The fear. The worry that I've dragged you into the same pit my family got dragged into. I can't do it, Luke. I can't let Frank destroy you, too."

"It's been building inside me, too," he said quietly. "The guilt because I wasn't there when you and Lena needed me. The fear that I can't protect either of you. The worry that I might lose you again."

Trailing his knuckles along her cheek until he found her nape, he pulled her forward.

"I'm breaking all the rules here, Haley. This isn't the time or the place for this. But yesterday morning, when it didn't seem to matter to you that I might never fully regain my sight, it made me think... Made me realize... Oh, hell, I'm not any good at this."

Haley's pulse tripped. For a moment the dust-streaked glass of the phone booth blurred. The stars faded. The night sky became a backdrop. Her entire being focused on the man standing in front of her.

"Any good at what?"

"Telling a woman that I love her."

When she didn't answer, a small, wry smile played at one corner of his mouth.

"Like I said, I'm breaking all the rules here. The last thing I should do is add to your stress. I don't expect you to feel the same. Nor do I expect you to think about this right now. I just want you to understand why I can't step aside and let you do this alone."

She stood silent for so long, Luke figured she'd taken him at his word and decided not to think about anything but Lena.

"You're right," she said at last. "This isn't the time or the place for this, but we might not get another. I love you, too, Luke. I've loved you since I was old enough to figure out what Barbie and Ken were up to when they closed the door to her Dream House. You don't have any idea how many times I padded my bras to get you to notice me. Or how many nights I went to bed almost screaming with frustration when you didn't."

"I noticed, sweetheart. Believe me, I noticed. But you were Ricky's sister and I…"

"I know. You wouldn't cross the line. I did, though. Too many times. I ached for you so much I had to steal one more hour with you that awful night on the lake. I was the one who suggested we go out back at the Saddlebag. I was thrilled when I found out I was pregnant. Knowing my baby would have some of you in her made her doubly precious to me."

Luke was humbled. Completely humbled. Cupping her cheeks, he bent to express his feelings in the surest, most direct way he knew. The phone jangled before he could do more than graze her lips.

Cursing, he thrust Haley away. "Get around to the other side of the truck."

"Luke, wait!"

Ignoring her cry, he followed the sound and wrapped his fist around the receiver. "Tell me when you're in position."

The phone shrilled again.

"Move, Haley. If it rings too many times, he'll get suspicious."

He heard her take one step, then hesitate. Another jangle cut through the night.

"Move!"

She stomped around to the far side of the pickup, and Luke snatched up the receiver.

Luke made the last leg of their journey blind. Literally and figuratively. The road Del Brio directed them to was another two-lane dirt track, with no streetlights to provide enough contrast for Luke to see so much as a shadow. And this time they hadn't been given any instructions about how far to go. They could keep going, Del Brio had sneered, until they were stopped.

The first clue that they were approaching the rendezvous point came via secure radio/phone net.

"The military LanSat network picked up three stationary vehicles," Colonel Westin reported crisply. "They're in a triangular vector approximately five miles north, six west, and five-point-four south-southeast of your present position."

"Roger that."

"Given your heading and the condition of the road, we estimate you'll make contact with the vehicle to the west of you in about ten minutes."

"Ten minutes. Got it."

"We'll be just over the horizon. Good hunting, Luke."

"Thanks, Colonel."

Snapping the lid down on the phone, he tucked it in his shirt pocket and activated the miniaturized scanner on his left wrist. The titanium case vibrated violently as the radar wave it sent out bounced off the dash. His nerves dancing in response, Luke raised his arm and aimed the scanner at the windshield. The vibrations died instantly.

Satisfied that there was nothing out there for the radar to pick up, he reached into his boot and slid the snubnose .38 from its ankle holster. Staring into the darkness, he released the cylinder, ran his thumb around the six chambered rounds and closed the weapon with a small snick. He would have preferred the SIG Sauer 9 mm Tyler had fitted with a special scope. After testing several different ways to conceal it, however, he'd opted for the smaller Smith & Wesson.

"We should make contact within the next few minutes."

Her response was quick and gritty. "I'm ready."

"We're a team, remember? We're in this together. I want you to promise you won't deliberately place yourself in the line of fire."

"Luke, I—"

"I can't risk a shot unless I know you and the baby are clear," he said fiercely. "Don't give him any more advantage than he already has. Promise me, Haley."

"All right, all right! I promise."

That pledge thundered in Haley's mind when she topped a small rise a few moments later and drove smack into a blaze of light. With a smothered oath, she stomped on the brakes.

Luke was right there beside her, calm but urgent. "What do you see?"

"There's a vehicle parked smack in the middle of the road approximately twenty yards ahead. Its high beams are on. The damned things almost blinded me."

"Just maneuver the bastard in front of those lights," Luke said on a note of triumph, "and I won't need any high-tech scanners to get him in my sights."

His utter confidence gave Haley a badly needed shot in the arm. Maybe, just maybe, they might pull this off. She was shaking when she reached behind her for the ransom money, but not completely mindless with terror.

"Remember the drill," Luke cautioned as she tugged on the door handle. "We get out together. You stay left. I stay right. Don't take one step until Del Brio produces Lena."

"I've got it."

"Here we go."

Shouldering open the heavy, reinforced door, Haley emerged into the hot Texas night. She heard the passenger door slam shut, but couldn't see a thing in the glare of the headlights. The thought flashed into her head that she and Luke had reversed roles. The blazing lights blinded her, but would provide just the contrast he needed to make out Frank's silhouette. Assuming they could get Del Brio to step in front of his car, that was.

"Frank?" Holding up her arm to shield her eyes, she squinted at the other vehicle. "Frank, are you there?"

His chuckle floated to her through the night. "I'm here, babe."

The sound of his voice twisted Haley into knots.

"I see you brought the money," he called. "Callaghan, too. Keep your hands where I can see 'em, both of you."

His laugh twisted into a sneer. "Not that I need to worry about you, do I, Callaghan? I ought to blow a hole in you right now, you useless son of a bitch, and put you out of your misery."

Afraid he'd do just that, Haley rushed into an explanation. "Luke came along because of Lena. He provided the money for her ransom. He just wants to make sure she's okay."

"That right, rich boy? You just want to check on your brat? Well, I guess I can let you have a look." Snickering at his cruel joke, he raised his voice. "Bring her out, Erica."

A healthy chunk of Haley's hate for Frank Del Brio took an instant detour into fury.

Erica. He could only mean Erica Clawson.

Haley had worked with the short, carrot-topped waitress for more than a year. Although she hadn't gotten close to anyone except Ginger Walton, the one friend she'd made as Daisy Parker, she'd fretted when Erica gushed about her new boyfriend, yet came to work with bruises and, once, a black eye.

She tried to coax the younger woman into talking to a counselor, but didn't want to get too close, reveal too much of herself. Then Lena had been kidnapped from Flynt's ranch, and Erica Clawson dropped instantly from Haley's list of worries.

Dammit all to hell! Why hadn't she seen beyond the waitress's appearance? Why hadn't she connected Erica's mysterious, ready-fisted boyfriend with Frank Del Brio? The FBI hadn't made the connection, either, but that didn't lessen Haley's biting self-disgust.

"You want to see your kid, Callaghan?" Frank's laughter rolled through the night again. "Here she is."

A lump the size of a Texas armadillo lodged in Haley's throat as a tall, muscled figure moved into the spear of lights. She didn't have to fake her quaver of fear when she called out to Del Brio.

"We can't see anything from here. You're just a dark blur."

"Come take a look. Bring the money."

She took one step, heard Luke's hiss and stopped. "No. I'm not delivering the money until I know Lena's all right. Bring her halfway, Frank, then step back."

"Aw, babe. It's breakin' my heart you don't trust me."

The words came out playfully enough, but Del Brio's real feelings broke through as he picked up the carrier and sauntered forward.

"Just like it broke my heart you didn't trust me all those years ago when we were engaged. I would've taken care of you, Haley. I would have covered for your father. Why did you run? Why did you leave me thinking you were dead?"

She could feel his anger. It swept across the blaze of lights in palpable waves. She could feel the hurt, as well. In his own sick way, he'd loved her. Her flesh crawled when he made it plain he still did.

"I've been wondering what you did with your ring," he called.

"I lost it in the lake, Frank." No way she was going to tip him over the edge by admitting she'd thrown it as far away as she could. Not when she was this close to Lena.

"Never mind. I'll buy you another one. Bigger. Flashier. This time we'll do it right, Haley. When I put it on your finger, you won't want to take it off."

"Frank!"

Erica Clawson's shriek split the night.

"What's this crap about putting a ring on that bitch's finger? You promised to marry me!"

Erica charged out of the darkness and was met with a lash of scorn.

"Don't be stupid. Why would I marry a slut like you? You spread your legs for me, you'll spread 'em for anyone in pants."

"Me? You're calling me a slut?" Her outrage piled on top of anguish. "What about Princess Daisy here? She's the one who spread her legs. You're holding the evidence of that in your hand."

"Haley made a mistake," Frank snarled. "You, you're nothing but a tramp."

"Tramp! I'll show you tramp!"

Her hands curled into claws, Erica launched herself at Frank. He whirled to meet her, one arm swinging the baby carrier in a wide arc, the other aiming a dark shape that could only be a gun at Erica's heart.

Haley didn't stop to think. Didn't give a single consideration as to whether she was putting herself between Frank and Luke. She hurtled forward at the same instant Del Brio fired.

Knocking the carrier out of his hand, Haley came down on top of the hard plastic. With a small, stunned cry, Erica came down on top of her. Frantically, Haley stooped over the carrier, shielding it with her body.

She heard more shots. Two. Three.

A hoarse shout.

Someone called her name.

Drenched in Erica's blood, hunched like a crab over her baby, her ears ringing from the shock waves of Frank's pistol fired at close range, she prayed that someone was Luke.

It wasn't.

It was her brother.

She recognized his voice finally, after his frantic hands pulled Erica's lifeless body away and the reverberations in her ear died enough for her to hear.

"Haley! Dear God, Haley, are you hurt?"

Dazed, she abandoned her protective crouch and raised up on her knees. Her stomach lurched when she spotted Frank Del Brio lying facedown only a few yards from Erica's lifeless body. It took another dive when she looked into the face of the man standing over her.

"Ricky?"

"Yeah, it's me." Hunkering beside her, he gathered her into his arms. "I thought I'd lost you. I thought I'd lost both you and Lena."

Lena! Dear God, Lena!

Only then did a series of indignant squalls pierce the clanging in Haley's ears. Shoving out of her brother's arms, she righted the overturned carrier.

Her face brick-red, Lena waved her fists in the air and let everyone in south Texas know that she was very unhappy. Haley's eyes brimmed with tears as she fumbled with the straps, pulled her baby from the carrier and dropped a kiss on her curls. Lena tight in her arms, Haley swung to face her brother.

"Ricky, where's Luke?"

The frantic question no sooner tumbled out than Luke himself answered.

"I'm right here."

He stepped out of the darkness into the arc thrown by the headlights. With a small cry, Haley rushed to him. The acrid stench of gunpowder clung to his shirt. She had no idea whether he'd fired the shots that brought

Frank down, and didn't care. The only thing that mattered was that he was safe. He and Lena.

The baby's squalls didn't lessen in either volume or intensity as Haley held out the bundle of flailing arms and legs.

"Meet your daughter, Mr. Callaghan."

Epilogue

It was a perfect day for a wedding, Texas-style.

The summer sun floated in a cloudless sky. Heat rose in shimmering waves from the manicured fairways of the Lone Star Country Club. The assembled guests weren't worried about patches of unsightly sweat staining their pastel tea gowns and dove-gray morning coats, however. Giant fans discreetly positioned behind hedges blew cool, refreshing mists.

Most of Mission Creek, including the influential Carsons and Wainwrights, had gathered under the bright sun. Old feuds forgotten, the long-divided families intermingled in row after row of white-skirted chairs. Colonel Phillip Westin sat in the front row, stiff-backed and square-jawed in his dress blues, his medals gleaming in the sun. Next to the colonel sat Teresa Chavez, who picked her husband's pocket for a dry handkerchief to replace the one she'd already soaked.

"It's so beautiful," she murmured, dabbing her eyes. "All these roses."

It seemed as though every hothouse in south Texas had been raided. Garlands of yellow roses were draped between the rows. White netting entwined with thousands of the same fragrant blossoms festooned the patio where the reception would be held. Hundreds more climbed the arch that had been hastily constructed over the tee box of hole number nine.

Five men stood under the arch. Tall. Tanned. Shoulder to shoulder. At their feet, squarely in the center of the raised platform, was a baby carrier. A toddler with a lacy elastic headband holding back her black curls waved her arms and legs and blew happy bubbles into the air.

Hooking a hand in his white tie, one of Lena's honorary uncles glanced around the elegant scene and grinned. "I still can't believe your woman decided to make things official here on the golf course, Callaghan."

"Believe it, Murdoch."

"We heard you had to sign a promise in blood that you'd show this time," Spence drawled.

"I would've used a pen," Luke tossed back, "but Lena had just tried out her new back teeth on my finger. The ink ran a little red."

"Well, I think holding the ceremony out here makes perfect sense," Flynt murmured. "This is where it all began."

Not quite, Luke thought. It began years ago, with a gawky teenager who blossomed into a lush, beautiful woman and a hardheaded Texan who put friendship ahead of his growing hunger.

Luke didn't turn his head or try to focus the blurred

images that were becoming a little sharper each day. He knew his best man stood beside him, as he'd stood beside him so many times in the past.

Luke and Ricky had recovered a lot of ground since the night they took down Frank Del Brio. According to the coroner, it was anyone's guess whether Del Brio died from the bullet through his heart or through his brain.

Neither Luke nor Ricky particularly cared. Del Brio was out of the picture. Haley and Lena were safe. The FBI had come through with their promise of immunity for Ricky and Johnny Mercado. The band of brothers stood together again.

All was right with the world, Luke decided. But he didn't have any idea how right until a rustle of movement swept through the guests. Luke heard a few excited murmurs. A moment later the organist hit a loud chord and Mendelssohn's glorious "Wedding March" pumped into the air.

"Here we go." Ricky's murmur reached him over the swelling notes. "You ready, pal?"

"Just keep that ring handy."

A swish of skirts announced the arrival of Haley's maid of honor. Ginger Walton Turner had wanted Daisy Parker to perform the same service at her wedding a few months ago. Haley hadn't dared risk the exposure then. Today the two friends could both bask in their happiness.

Three bridesmaids followed Ginger along the petal-strewn carpet to the tee box. Ellen Harrison, Josie Carson and Marisa Murdoch took their places beside Ginger.

Suddenly the organist put all she had into the equivalent of a drumroll. The notes rose higher, louder, startling a cry from Lena. Five men bent toward the infant. With a sheepish grin, four stepped back.

Luke straightened a moment later. With his daughter nestled in the crook of his arm, he stood tall and waited for Haley. She came down the aisle slowly, matching her pace to her father's. Only days out of the hospital, Johnny Mercado still moved cautiously, but both father and daughter were serenely oblivious of the gasps of astonishment that rose when they appeared.

"She's wearing red!" Luke heard someone exclaim.

Not any red. Hot, chili-pepper red. Red gown. Red shoes. Red roses wreathed in her hair. She'd worn it for Luke, so he could see the haze of bright color silhouetted against the white chairs and miles of netting. So he could see his bride.

He hadn't thought that he could love her any more than he already did, but his heart swelled at that glorious blaze. His heart swelling, he stepped down to take her hand from her father's.

"Couldn't you leave that child in her carrier for a half hour?" she asked, laughing.

"Nope." Hitching Lena up higher, he escorted his women back to the platform. "Any more than I can leave her behind when we take off on our honeymoon."

"Which begs the question," Haley murmured as the music swelled to a final crescendo, "where are we going?"

"You pick it. The Caribbean. Hawaii. Europe."

"I'd like to go back to London. We left in such a hurry, I never said goodbye to my friends."

The music died. The minister stepped forward. Luke cut him off before he got out more than "Dearly Beloved."

"Hang on a minute, will you, padre?"

Startled, the minister looked to the best man, who shook his head. The guests exchanged equally confused glances as Luke smiled down at the pale, blurred oval of Haley's face.

"We can go anywhere you want, my darling, whenever you want, as long as we come home once in a while."

More astonished gasps rose from the guests as the bride threw her arms around her not-quite-yet husband's neck.

"I am home. For good this time. It's you and Texas, Luke. Now and forever."

"That's all I wanted to hear, sweetheart."

He bent toward her, provoking an amused observation from the minister. "The kiss usually comes after the vows, you know."

"Not this time, padre."

Glorying in the love that radiated from the woman in red, Luke wrapped his free arm around her waist. As he pulled Haley up against him, Lena laughed in delight and patted him on the cheek.

* * * * *

The silence on the car ride to the public hearing at the Chicago
Board of Education building on Madison Street was jaw-dropping.
Mingus maneuvered his car through traffic, his expression smug
as he stole occasional glances in her direction. Joanna stared out
the passenger-side window, still lost in the heat of Mingus's touch.
That kiss had left her shaking, her knees quivering and her heart
racing. She couldn't not think about it if she wanted to.

His kiss had been everything she'd imagined and more. It
was summer rain in a blue sky, fudge cake with scoops of praline
ice cream, balloons floating against a backdrop of clouds, small
puppies, bubbles in a spa bath and fireworks over Lake Michigan.
It had left her completely satiated and famished for more. Closing
her eyes and kissing him back had been as natural as breathing.
And there was no denying that she had kissed him back. She hadn't
been able to speak since, no words coming that would explain the
wealth of emotion flowing like a tidal wave through her spirit.

They paused at a red light. Mingus checked his mirrors and
the flow of traffic as he waited for his turn to proceed through

the intersection. Joanna suddenly reached out her hand for his, entwining his fingers between her own.

"I'm still mad at you," Joanna said.

"I know. I'm still mad at myself. I just felt like I was failing you. You need results and I'm not coming up with anything concrete. I want to fix this and suddenly I didn't know if I could. I felt like I was being outwitted. Like someone's playing this game better than I am, but it's not a game. They're playing with your life, and I don't plan to let them beat either one of us."

"From day one you believed me. Most didn't and, to be honest, I don't know that anyone else does. But not once have you looked at me like I'm lying or I'm crazy. This afternoon, you yelling at me felt like doubt, and I couldn't handle you doubting me. It broke my heart."

Mingus squeezed her fingers, still stalled at the light, a line of cars beginning to pull in behind him. "I don't doubt you, baby. But we need to figure this out and, frankly, we're running out of time."

The honking of a car horn yanked his attention back to the road. He pulled into the intersection and turned left. Minutes later he slid into a parking spot and shut down the car engine. Joanna was still staring out the window.

"Are you okay?" he asked.

Joanna nodded and gave him her sweetest smile. "Yeah. I was just thinking that I really like it when you call me 'baby.'"

Don't miss
Tempted by the Badge *by Deborah Fletcher Mello,*
available March 2019 wherever
Harlequin® *Romantic Suspense books*
and ebooks are sold.

www.Harlequin.com

HRSEXP0219

Looking for more satisfying love stories
with community and family at their core?

Check out **Harlequin® Special Edition**
and **Love Inspired®** books!

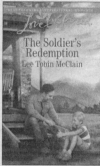

New books available every month!

CONNECT WITH US AT:

Facebook.com/groups/HarlequinConnection

 Facebook.com/HarlequinBooks

 Twitter.com/HarlequinBooks

 Instagram.com/HarlequinBooks

 Pinterest.com/HarlequinBooks

ReaderService.com

**ROMANCE WHEN
YOU NEED IT**

HFGENRE2018

SPECIAL EXCERPT FROM

H HARLEQUIN®

INTRIGUE

*Looking for his long-lost father reunites cowboy
Dexter Hawk with the only woman he's ever loved.
But can he protect Melissa Gentry when a killer
makes her his next target?*

Read on for a sneak peek at Hostage at Hawk's Landing
from USA TODAY bestselling author Rita Herron.

He knew she was shaken, but he wasn't ready to let her out of his
sight. "Melissa, you could have been hurt tonight." Killed, but
he couldn't allow himself to voice that awful thought aloud. "I'll
see that you get home safely, so don't argue."

Melissa rubbed a hand over her eyes. She was obviously so
exhausted she simply nodded and slipped from his SUV. Just as
he thought, the beat-up minivan belonged to her.

She jammed her key in the ignition, the engine taking three
tries to sputter to life.

Anger that she sacrificed so much for others mingled with
worry that she might have died doing just that.

She deserved so much better. To have diamonds and pearls.
At least a car that didn't look as if it had been rolled twice.

He glanced back at the shelter before he pulled from the
parking lot. Melissa was no doubt worried about the men she'd
had to move tonight. But worry for her raged through him.

He knew good and damn well that many of the men who
ended up in shelters had simply fallen on hard times and needed a
hand. But others…the drug addicts, mentally ill and criminals…

He didn't like the fact that Melissa put herself in danger by
trying to help them. Tonight's incident proved the facility wasn't
secure.

The thought of losing her bothered him more than he wanted
to admit as he followed her through the streets of Austin. His gut
tightened when she veered into an area consisting of transitional
homes. A couple had been remodeled, but most looked as if they

were teardowns. The street was not in the best part of town, either, and was known for shady activities, including drug rings and gangs.

Her house was a tiny bungalow with a sagging little porch and paint-chipped shutters, and sat next to a rotting shanty, where two guys in hoodies hovered by the side porch, heads bent in hushed conversation as if they might be in the middle of a drug deal.

He gritted his teeth as he parked and walked up the graveled path to the front porch. She paused, her key in hand. A handcrafted wreath said Welcome Home, which for some reason twisted his gut even more.

Melissa had never had a real home, while he'd grown up on the ranch with family and brothers and open land.

She offered him a small smile. "Thanks for following me, Dex."

"I'll go in and check the house," he said, itching to make sure that at least her windows and doors were secure. From his vantage point now, it looked as if a stiff wind would blow the house down.

She shook her head. "That's not necessary, but I appreciate it." She ran a shaky hand through her hair. "I'm exhausted. I'm going to bed."

She opened the door and ducked inside without another word and without looking back. An image of her crawling into bed in that lonely old house taunted him.

He wanted to join her. Hold her. Make sure she was all right tonight.

But that would be risky for him.

Still, he couldn't shake the feeling that she was in danger as he walked back to his SUV.

Don't miss
Hostage at Hawk's Landing *by Rita Herron,*
available March 2019 wherever
Harlequin® Intrigue books and ebooks are sold.

www.Harlequin.com

Love Harlequin romance?

DISCOVER.

Be the first to find out about promotions, news and exclusive content!

Facebook.com/HarlequinBooks

Twitter.com/HarlequinBooks

Instagram.com/HarlequinBooks

Pinterest.com/HarlequinBooks

ReaderService.com

EXPLORE.

Sign up for the Harlequin e-newsletter and download a free book from any series at **TryHarlequin.com.**

CONNECT.

Join our Harlequin community to share your thoughts and connect with other romance readers!
Facebook.com/groups/HarlequinConnection

HARLEQUIN®

ROMANCE WHEN
YOU NEED IT